Hello!

Thank you for picking up *The Best Man!*

One of the things I wanted to do with this book was to describe a place that would feel like home and also like a vacation, a place you could see as clearly as if you were there.

The Finger Lakes region of New York is one of the most beautiful places I've ever been. The lakes are long and narrow, and very deep, giving them an ethereal, dark blue color. The hills are golden with grapevines, and the autumn foliage is beyond compare. The hills are populated with vineyards and Mennonite farms; it's not at all uncommon to be waiting at a stoplight next to a horse and buggy. Manningsport is based on Hammondsport, and a prettier town I've never seen. Glens and waterfalls are plentiful; the sound of rushing water is never far away, and the sense of community and pride the Finger Lakes residents have for their home is palpable.

I also wanted to write a story where the hero and heroine had a lot of reasons to stay apart...but you know how it is. Love has a way of sneaking up on people. Faith and Levi are a case of opposites attract, but they may have more in common than they might think. Both characters love their families and communities, and both have to get out of their own way to get that happily ever after.

Hope you like the book! Drop me a line—I always love hearing from you.

Kristan

www.kristanhiggins.com

KRISTAN HIGGINS

the best man

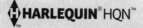

Recycling programs
for this product may
not exist in your area.

ISBN-13: 978-0-373-77792-1

THE BEST MAN

Printed in U.S.A.

www.Harlequin.com

Thanks so much to my wonderful and wise agent, Maria Carvainis, and to Martha Guzman, Chelsea Gilmore and Elizabeth Copps for all their support and help. Thanks also to the incredible team at Harlequin, especially my editors, Keyren Gerlach and Tara Parsons, as well as the many others at Harlequin for their faith and enthusiasm for every dang book I've written. Thanks to Kim Castillo of Author's Best Friend for being truly that, and to the lovely and insightful Sarah Burningham of Little Bird Publicity.

I could not have written this book without the generosity of the warm, down-to-earth people of the Finger Lakes wine industry. I owe a great deal to Sayre Fulkerson, owner of Fulkerson Winery, who gave up half a day to show me around his beautiful fields and woods. John Izard, vice president of operations at Fulkerson, answered many, many questions, and I am very grateful to him, as well. Thanks to Kitty Oliver and Dave Herman at Heron Hill Vineyards and to Glenora Vineyards for such wonderful hospitality. Morgen McLaughlin at Finger Lakes Wine Country arranged my introduction to the area, and I'm happy to say it was love at first sight. Kimberly Price at Corning Finger Lakes was wonderfully helpful, too.

Thanks to Paul Buckthal, M.D., who answered my questions about epilepsy, and to Brad Wilkinson, M.D., whose name I left out of the last book (sorry, Brad!). Thanks also to Sergeant Ryan Sincerbox of the Hammondsport Police Department, who was so helpful, to Staff Sergeant Ryan Parmelee, United States Army, and the very nice information officer at the Army recruiting office in Horseheads, New York. When I asked if he'd like an acknowledgment in the book, he only laughed and said, "Thank the U.S. Army instead." And so I do, not just as an author, but as a grateful citizen, as well.

For their friendship, input and the many, many laughs we've shared, thanks to Huntley Fitzpatrick, Shaunee Cole, Karen Pinco, Kelly Morse and Jennifer Iszkiewicz. My brother Mike, owner of Litchfield Hills Wine Market, advised on all things grape (any mistakes are all mine). As ever, thanks to my sister Hilary, my dear mom, and my sister-in-law and greatest friend, Jackie Decker.

To my beautiful children and heroic husband—there really are no words to express my love for you, but I expect you know that you three are my whole world.

And you, dear and wonderful readers...thank you. Thank you for spending a few hours of your lives with my books. I can't tell you what an honor that is.

the
best
man

This book is dedicated to Rose Morris-Boucher, my very first friend in the world of writing, and my friend still. Thank you for everything, Rosebud!

PROLOGUE

On a beautiful day in June, in front of literally half the town, wearing a wedding dress that made her look like Cinderella and holding a bouquet of perfect pink roses, Faith Elizabeth Holland was left at the altar.

We sure didn't see that one coming.

There we all were, sitting in Trinity Lutheran, smiling, dressed up, not a seat to be had, people standing three deep in the back of the church. The bridesmaids were dressed in pink, and Faith's niece, just thirteen years old, looked as pretty as could be. The best man wore his dress blues, and Faith's brother was an usher. It was beautiful!

The wedding day of these two kids—Faith and Jeremy, together since high school—was set to be one of the happiest days our town had seen in years. After all, the Hollands were a founding family here, salt of the earth types. They had more land than anyone in the Finger Lakes wine country, acres and acres of vineyard and forest, all the way down to Keuka—the Crooked Lake, as we call it. The Lyons, well, they were from California, but we liked them, anyway. They were more the money type. Nice folks. Their land abutted the Hollands', so the kids were next-door neighbors. How sweet was that? And Jeremy, oh, he was a doll! He could've gone pro in the NFL. No, really, he was that good. But instead, he moved back as soon as he became a doctor. He wanted to practice right here in town, settle down with that sweet Faith and raise a family.

The kids met so romantically, in a medical sort of way—Faith, then a senior in high school, had an epileptic seizure. Jeremy, who'd just transferred in, elbowed his way to her side, picked her up in his brawny football-hero arms, which, come to think of it, you're not supposed to do, but his intentions were noble, and what a picture it made, the tall and dark Jeremy carrying Faith through the halls. He brought her to the nurse's office, where he remained by her side until her dad came to get her. It was, the story went, love at first sight.

They went to the prom together, Faith with her dark red hair curled around her shoulders, her skin creamy against the midnight blue of her dress. Jeremy was *so* handsome, six-foot-three inches of sculpted football-god physique, his black hair and dark eyes making him look like a Romanian count.

He went to Boston College and played football there; Faith went to school at Virginia Tech to study landscape design, and the distance alone, as well as their age…well, no one expected them to stay together. We could all see Jeremy with a model or even a young Hollywood starlet, given his family's money and his athletic ability and those good looks. Faith was cute in that girl-next-door way, but you know how those things go. The girl gets left behind, the boy moves on. We'd have understood.

But no, we were wrong. His parents would complain about the enormous cell phone bills, the vast number of texts Jeremy had sent Faith, almost like Ted and Elaine were bragging—*See how devoted our son is? How constant? How in love with his girlfriend?*

When home on break, Faith and Jeremy would walk

through town hand in hand, always smiling. He might pick a flower from the lush window boxes in front of the bakery and tuck it behind her ear. They were often seen on the town beach, his head in her lap, or out on the lake in his parents' Chris-Craft boat, Jeremy standing behind Faith as she steered, his muscular arms around her, and didn't they look like a tourism ad! It seemed as if Faith had hit pay dirt, and good for her for nabbing someone like Jeremy—we all had a soft spot for her, the poor little girl Mel Stoakes pulled out of that awful wreck. Laura Boothby liked to brag about how much Jeremy spent on Faith's flowers for the anniversary of their first date, for her birthday, for Valentine's Day and sometimes "just because." There were those of us who thought it was a little much, out here in the country of Mennonite farms and Yankee reserve, but the Lyon family was from Napa Valley, so there you go.

Sometimes you'd see Faith and a few girlfriends at O'Rourke's, and one or two of them might vent about their neglectful, immature boyfriends who cheated or lied, who broke up via text or a status change on Facebook. And if Faith said something sympathetic, those girls might say, "You have *no* idea what we're talking about, Faith! You have *Jeremy*," almost as if it was an accusation. The mere mention of his name would bring a dreamy smile to her face, a softness to her eyes. Faith would occasionally tell people she'd always wanted a man as good as her father, and it sure as heck seemed as if she'd found one. Even though he was young, Jeremy was a wonderful doctor, and every woman in town seemed to come down with something or another the first few months after he set up his practice. He took time to listen, always had a smile, remembered what you said last time.

Three months after he finished his residency, on a beautiful September day when the hills burned red and gold and the lake shimmered with silver, Jeremy got down on one knee and presented Faith with a three-carat diamond engagement ring. We heard all about it, oh, sure, and the planning began. Faith's two sisters would be bridesmaids, that pretty Colleen O'Rourke the maid of honor. Jeremy's best man would be the Cooper boy if he could come home from Afghanistan, and wouldn't that be nice, to see a decorated war hero standing up there next to his old football buddy? It would be so romantic, so lovely…truly, it made us all smile, just thinking about it.

So imagine our surprise, then, when the two kids were standing right there on the altar of Trinity Lutheran, and Jeremy Lyon came out of the closet.

CHAPTER ONE

Three and a half years later

FAITH HOLLAND PUT DOWN her binoculars, picked up her clipboard and checked off a box on her list. *Lives alone.* Clint had said he did, and the background check showed only his name on the rental agreement, but a person couldn't be too careful. She took a pull of Red Bull and tapped her fingers against the steering wheel of her roommate's car.

Once upon a time, a scenario like this would've seemed ridiculous. But given her romantic history, a little footwork was simply smart. Footwork saved time, embarrassment, anger and heartbreak. Say, for example, the man was gay, which had happened not just with Jeremy, but with Rafael Santos and Fred Beeker, as well. To his credit, Rafe hadn't known Faith thought they were *dating;* he'd thought they were just hanging out. Later that month, determined to keep trying, Faith had rather awkwardly hit on Fred, who lived down the street from her and Liza, only to have him recoil in horror and gently explain that he liked boys, too. (Incidentally, she'd fixed him up with Rafael, and the two had been together ever since, so at least there was a happily ever after for someone.)

Gay wasn't the only problem. Brandon, whom she'd met at a party, had seemed so promising, right until their second date, when his phone rang. "Gotta take this, it's my dealer," he'd said blithely. When Faith had asked for clarification—he couldn't mean *drug* dealer, could he?—he'd replied sure, what did she think he meant? He'd seemed confused when Faith left in a huff.

The binocs were old school, yes. But had she used binoculars with Rafe, she would've seen his gorgeous silk window treatments and six-foot framed poster of Barbra Streisand. Had she staked out Brandon, she might've seen him meeting unsavory people in cars after they'd flashed their headlights.

She'd attempted to date two other guys since moving to San Francisco. One didn't believe in bathing—again, something she might've learned by stalking. The other guy stood her up.

Hence the stakeout.

Faith sighed and rubbed her eyes. If this didn't work out, Clint would be her last foray for a while, because she really was getting worn out here. Late nights, the eye strain associated with binocular use, a stomachache from too much caffeine... It was tiring.

But Clint might be worth it. Straight, employed, no history of arrest, no DUIs, that rarest of species in S.F. Maybe this would make a cute story at their wedding. She could almost imagine Clint saying, "Little did I know that at that very minute, Faith was parked in front of my house, chugging Red Bull and bending the law...."

She'd met Clint on the job—she'd been hired to design a small public park in the Presidio; Clint owned a landscaping company. They'd worked together just fine; he was on time, and his people were fast and meticulous. Also, Clint had taken a shine to Blue, Faith's Golden retriever, and what's more appealing than a guy who gets down on his knees and lets your dog lick his face? Blue seemed to like him (but then again, Blue tended to like any living creature, the type of dog who'd leg-hump a serial killer). The park had been dedicated two weeks ago, and right after the ceremony, Clint had asked her out. She'd said yes, then gone home and begun her work. Good old Google showed no mention of a wife (or husband). There was a record of a marriage between a Clinton Bundt of Owens, Nebraska, but that was ten years ago, and her Clint Bundt a) seemed too young to have been married for ten years; and b) was from Se-attle. His Facebook page was for work only. While he did mention some social things ("Went to Oma's on 19th Street; great latkes!"), there was no mention of a spouse in any of the posts of the past six months.

On Date Number One, Faith had made arrangements for Fred and Rafael to check him out, since gaydar was clearly not one of her skills. She and Clint met for drinks on a Tuesday evening, and the guys had shown up at the bar, done the shark-bump test on Clint, then gone to a table. Straight, Rafael texted, and Fred backed him up with Hetero.

On Date Number Two (lunch/Friday afternoon), Clint had proven to be charming and interested as she told him about her family, being the youngest of four, Goggy and Pops, her grandparents, how much she missed her dad. Clint, in turn, had told her about an ex-fiancée; she'd kept her own story to herself.

On Date Number Three (dinner/Wednesday, in the "make him wait to measure his interest level" philoso-phy), Clint had met her at a cute little bar near the pier and once again passed every criteria: held her chair, complimented her without too much detail (*That's a pretty dress,* she'd found, set off no warning bells, unlike *Is that Badgley Mischka, OMG, I love those two!*). He'd stroked the back of her hand and kept sneaking peeks at her boobage, so it was all good. When Clint had asked if he could drive her home, which of course was code for sex, she'd put him off.

Clint's eyes had narrowed, as if accepting her challenge. "I'll call you. Are you free this weekend?"

Another test passed. *Available on weekends.* Faith had felt a flutter; she hadn't been on a fourth date since she was eighteen years old. "I think I'm free on Friday," she'd murmured.

They stood on the sidewalk, waiting for a cab as tourists streamed into souvenir shops to buy sweatshirts, having been tricked into thinking that late August in San Francisco meant summer. Clint leaned in and kissed her, and Faith let him. It had been a good kiss. Very competent. There was potential in that kiss, she thought. Then a taxi emerged from the gloom of the famed fog, and Clint waved it over.

And so, in preparation of the fourth date—which would possibly be *the* date, when she finally slept with someone other than Jeremy—here she was, parked in front of his apartment, binoculars trained on his windows. Looked as if he was watching the ball game.

Time to call her sister.

"He passes," Faith said by way of greeting.

"You have a problem, hon," said Pru. "Open your heart and all that crap. Jeremy was eons ago."

"This has nothing to do with Jeremy," Faith said, ignoring the answering snort. "I'm a little worried about his name, though. Clint Bundt. It's abrupt. Clint Eastwood, sure, that works. But on anyone else, I don't know. Clint and Faith. Faith and Clint. Faith Bundt." It was much less pleasing than, oh, let's say, *Faith and*

Jeremy or *Jeremy and Faith*. Not that she was hung up on the past or anything.

"Sounds okay to me," Pru said.

"Yeah, well, you're Prudence Vanderbeek."

"And?" Pru said amiably, chewing in Faith's ear.

"Clint and Faith Bundt. It's just…off."

"Okay, then break up with him. Or take him to court and force him to change his name. Listen, I gotta go. It's bedtime for us farm folk."

"Okay. Give the kids a hug for me," Faith said. "Tell Abby I'll send her that link to the shoes she asked about. And tell Ned he's still my little bunny, even if he is technically an adult."

"Ned!" her sister bellowed. "Faith says you're still her little bunny."

"Yay," came her nephew's voice.

"Gotta go, kid," said Pru. "Hey, you coming home for harvest?"

"I think so. I don't have another installation for a while." While Faith made a decent living as a landscape designer, most of her work was done on the computer. Her presence was only required for the last part of a job. Plus, grape harvest at Blue Heron was well worth a visit home.

"Great!" Pru said. "Listen, ease up on the guy, have fun, talk soon, love you."

"Love you, too."

Faith took another pull of Red Bull. Pru had a point. Her oldest sibling had been happily married for twenty-three years, after all. And who else was going to give her romantic advice? To Honor, her other sister, if you weren't calling from the hospital, you were wasting her time. Jack was their brother and thus useless on these matters. And Dad…well, Dad was still in mourning for Mom, who'd been gone for nineteen years.

The wash of guilt was all too familiar.

"We can do this," Faith told herself, changing the mental subject. "We can fall in love again."

Certainly a better option than having Jeremy Lyon be her first and only love.

She caught a glimpse of her face in the rearview mirror, that hint of bewilderment and sorrow she always felt when she thought of Jeremy.

"Damn you, Levi," she whispered. "You just couldn't keep your mouth shut, could you?"

TWO NIGHTS LATER, Faith was starting to think that Clint Bundt was indeed worth the ten minutes she'd taken to shave her legs and the six it'd taken to wrestle herself into the microfiber Slim-Nation undergarment she'd bought on QVC last month. (Hope. It sprung eternal.) Clint had picked an upscale Thai place with a koi pond in the entryway, red silk wall hangings making the room glow with flattering light. They sat in a U-shaped booth, very cozily, Faith thought. It was so romantic. Also, the food was *really* good, not to mention the lovely Russian River chardonnay.

Clint's eyes kept dropping to her cleavage. "I'm sorry," he said, "but you look good enough to eat." He grinned like a naughty boy, and Faith's girl parts gave a mighty tingle. "I have to tell you," he went on, "the very first second I saw you, I felt like I was hit on the side of the head with a two-by-four."

"Really? That's so sweet," Faith said, taking a sip of her wine. So far as she could recall, she'd been dressed in filthy jeans, work boots and soaked to the skin. She'd been moving some plants around in the rain, trying to

ease the mind of the city councilman who was concerned over the park's water runoff (which, please, had
been nonexistent; she was a certified landscape architect, thank you very much).

"I wasn't sure I was capable of speech," Clint now
said. "I probably made a fool out of myself." He gave
her a sheepish look as if acknowledging he'd been quite
the love-struck suitor.

And to think she hadn't even noticed that he'd been…
well…*dazzled* by her. That's how it went, right? Love
came when you weren't looking, except in the case of
the millions who'd found mates on Match.com, but,
hey. It sounded good.

The server came and whisked away their dinner
plates, setting down coffee, cream and sugar. "Did
you see anything you liked on the dessert menu?" he
asked, smiling at them. Because really, they *were* an
adorable couple.

"How about the mango crème brûlée?" Clint said.
"I don't know if I'll survive watching you eat it, but
what a way to go."

Hello! Tingling at a 6.8 on the Richter scale. "The
crème brulee sounds great," Faith said, and the waiter
sped away.

Clint slid a little closer, putting his arm around
Faith's shoulders. "You look amazing in that dress," he
murmured, trailing a finger down the neckline. "What
are the odds of me getting you out of it later on?" He
dropped a kiss on the side of her neck.

Oh, melt! Another kiss. "The odds are getting better," she breathed.

"I really like you, Faith," he whispered, nuzzling her
ear, causing her entire side to electrify.

"I like you, too," she said and looked into his pretty

brown eyes. His finger slid lower, and she could feel her skin heating up, getting blotchy, no doubt, the curse of the redhead. What the heck. She turned her face and kissed him on the lips, a soft, sweet, lingering kiss.

"Sorry to interrupt, lovebirds," said the waiter. "Don't mind me." He set the dessert on the table with a knowing smile.

"This!"

The bark made all three of them jump. Clint's elbow hit her glass, the wine spilling onto the tablecloth.

"Oh, shit," Clint said, shoving away from her.

"Don't worry about it," Faith said. "I do stuff like that all the time."

Clint wasn't looking at the wine.

A woman stood in front of their booth, a beautiful little boy dangling from her hands as she held him out in front of her. "*This* is what he's ignoring because of you, whore!"

Faith looked behind her to see the whore, but the only thing there was the wall. She looked back at the woman, who was about her age and very pretty—blond hair and fury-flushed cheeks. "Are you…are you talking to me?" she asked.

"Yes, I'm talking to you, whore! *This* is what he's missing when he's wining and dining *you.* Our son! Our baby!" She jiggled the toddler to demonstrate.

"Hey, no shaking the kid," Faith said.

"Don't speak to me, whore!"

"Mommy, put down!" the toddler commanded. The woman obeyed, jamming her hands on her (thin) hips. The waiter caught Faith's eye and grimaced. He was probably gay, and thus her ally.

Faith closed her mouth. "But I didn't… Clint, you're not married, are you?"

Clint was holding up his hands, surrender-style. "Baby, don't be mad," he said to the woman. "She's just someone I work with—"

"Oh, my God, you *are* married!" Faith blurted. "Where are you from? Are you from Nebraska?"

"Yes, we are, whore!"

"Clint!" Faith yelped. "You bas—" She remembered the kid, who looked at her solemnly, then scooped up a fingerful of crème brûlée and stuck it in his mouth.

"I'm so sorry," Faith said to Mrs. Clint Bundt (well, at least Faith wouldn't be saddled with that name). The kid spit out the dessert and reached for the sugar packets. "I didn't know—"

"Oh, shut up, whore. How dare you seduce my husband! How dare you!"

"I'm not sedu—doing anything to anyone, okay?" Faith said, more than a little horrified that this conversation was taking place in front of a toddler (who looked like a baby Hobbit, he was so dang cute, licking sugar from the packet).

"You're a slut, whore."

"Actually," Faith said tightly, "your *husband* was the one who…" Again, the kid. "Ask the waiter. Right?" Yes, yes, get some confirmation from the friendly waiter.

"Um…who's paying tonight?" he asked. So much for the love she inspired in the gays.

"It was a business dinner," Clint interrupted. "She came onto me, and I didn't expect it, I didn't know what to do. Come on, let's go home, babe."

"And by home, I'm guessing you don't mean your bachelor pad in Noe Valley, right?" Faith bit out.

Clint ignored her. "Hi, Finn, how's it going, bud?" He tousled his child's hair, then stood up and gave her a sorrowful, dignified look. "I'm sorry, Faith," he said somberly. "I'm a happily married man, and I have a beautiful family. I'm afraid we won't be able to work together anymore."

"Not a problem," she said tightly.

"Take that, whore," said Clint's wife. "That's what you get, trying to break up my family!" She put her hands on her hips and twisted out her leg, the Angelina Jolie Hip Displacement look.

"Hi, whore," the little boy said, ripping open another sugar packet.

"Hi," she said. He really was cute.

"Don't speak to my child!" Mrs. Bundt said. "I don't want your filthy whore mouth speaking to my son."

"Hypocrite," she muttered.

Clint scooped up the boy, who'd managed to snag a few more sugar packets.

"If I ever see you near my husband, whore, you'll be sorry," Mrs. Bundt hissed.

"I'm not a whore, okay?" Faith snapped.

"Yes, you are," said his wife, giving her the finger. Then the Bundts turned their backs to her and walked away from the table.

"I'm not!" Faith called. "I haven't slept with anyone in three years, okay? I'm not a whore!" The little boy waved cheerily from over his father's shoulder, and Faith gave a small wave in return.

The Bundts were gone. Faith grabbed her water glass and chugged, then rested the glass against her hot cheek. Her heart was pounding so hard she felt sick.

"Three years?" said one of the diners.

The waiter gave her the check. "I'll take that whenever you're ready," he said. Great. On top of all that, she had to pay for dinner, too.

"Your tip would've been a lot bigger if you'd backed me up," she told him, digging in her purse for her wallet.

"You really do look great in that dress," he said.

"Too late."

When she'd paid the bill (and really, Clint, thanks for ordering a seventy-five dollar bottle of wine), she went out into the damp, cold San Francisco air and started walking. It wasn't far to her apartment, even in heels. The streets of San Francisco were nothing compared to the steep hills of home. Consider it her cardio. Pissed-Off Woman Workout. The Stomp of the Righteous and Rejected. It was noisy down here at the wharf, the seagulls crying, music blaring out from every bar and restaurant, a dozen different languages bouncing around her.

Back home, the only sound would be the late-season crickets and the call of the owl family who lived in an old maple at the edge of the cemetery. The air would be sweet with the smell of grapes, tinged with wood smoke, because already, the nights would be cooling down. From her old bedroom window, she'd be able to see all the way to Keuka. She'd spent her childhood playing in woods and fields, breathing the clean air of western New York, swimming in glacier-formed lakes. Her love of the outdoors was the main reason she'd become a landscape architect—the chance to woo people from their increasingly interior lives and enjoy nature a little bit more.

Maybe it was time to start thinking seriously about moving back. That had always been the plan, anyway. Live in Manningsport, raise a family, be close to her sibs and father.

Clint Bundt. Married with a kid. *Such* a hemorrhoid. Well. Soon she'd be home with her dog. Liza probably was out with her guy, the Wonderful Mike, so Faith could watch *Real Housewives* and eat some Ben & Jerry's.

Why was it so hard to find the right guy? Faith didn't think she was too picky; she just wanted someone who wasn't gay, married, unkind, amoral or too short. Someone who'd look at her…well, the way Jeremy had. His dark, liquid eyes would tell her she was the best thing that ever happened to him, always a smile in their depths. Never once had she doubted that he loved her completely.

Her phone rang, and she fished it out of her purse. *Honor.* "Hey," she said, feeling the faint pang of alarm she always felt when her sister called. "How are you?"

"Have you talked to Dad recently?" her sister said.

"Um…yeah. We talk almost every day."

"Then I suppose you've heard about Lorena."

Faith twisted to avoid a cute guy in a Derek Jeter T-shirt. "I'm a Yankees fan, too," she told him with a smile. He frowned and took the hand of an irritable-looking woman next to him. *Message received, buddy, and jeesh. Only trying to be friendly.* "Who's Lorena?" she asked her sister.

Honor sighed. "Faith, you might want to get home before Dad gets married."

CHAPTER TWO

LEVI COOPER, CHIEF OF POLICE of the Manningsport Police Department, all two and a half of them, tried to give people a break. He did. Even the tourists with the lead feet, Red Sox stickers and complete disregard for speed limits. He parked the cruiser in plain sight, the radar gun clearly visible. *Hi there, welcome to Manningsport, you're going way too fast and here I am, about to pull you over, so slow down, pal.* The town depended on visitors, and September was prime tourism season; the leaves were starting to turn, buses had been rolling in and out of town all week, and every vineyard in the area had some special event going on.

But the law was the law.

Plus, he'd just let Colleen O'Rourke off with a stern lecture and a warning while she tried to look remorseful.

So another speeder just wasn't going to be tolerated today. This one, for example. Seventeen miles an hour over the limit, more than enough. Also, an out-of-towner; he could see the rental plates from here. The car was a painfully bright yellow Honda Civic, currently clocking in at forty-two miles per hour in a twenty-five-mile-an-hour zone. What if Carol Robinson and her merry band of geriatric power-walkers were out? What if the Nebbins kid was riding his bike? There hadn't been a fatal crash in Manningsport since he'd been chief, and Levi planned on keeping it that way.

The yellow car sailed past him, not even a tap on the brakes. The driver wore a baseball cap and big sunglasses. Female. With a sigh, Levi put on the lights, gave the siren a blip and pulled onto the road. She didn't notice. He hit the siren again, and the driver seemed to realize that, yes, he was talking to her, and pulled over.

Grabbing his ticket pad, Levi got out of the cruiser. Wrote down the license plate number, then went over to the driver's side, where the window was lowering. "Welcome to Manningsport," he said, not smiling.

Shit.

It was Faith Holland. A giant Golden retriever shoved its head out of the window and barked once, wagging happily.

"Levi," she said, as if they'd seen each other last week at O'Rourke's.

"Holland. You visiting?"

"Wow. That's amazing. How did you guess?"

He looked at her, not amused, and let a few beats pass. It worked; her cheeks flushed, and she looked away. "So. Forty-two in a twenty-five-mile-an-hour zone," he said.

"I thought it was thirty-five," she said.

"We dropped it last year."

The dog whined, so Levi petted him, making the dog try to crawl over Faith's head.

"Blue, get back," Faith ordered.

Blue. Right. Same dog as from a few years ago.

"Levi, how about a warning? I have a, um, a family emergency, so if you could drop the cop act, that'd be super." She gave him a tight smile, almost meeting his eyes, and pushed her hair behind one ear.

"What's the emergency?" he said.

"My grandfather is…uh…he's not feeling well. Goggy's concerned."

"Should you lie about stuff like that?" he asked. Levi was well acquainted with the elder Hollands, as they made up about ten percent of his work week. And if Mr. Holland really was under the weather, he'd bet Mrs. Holland would be picking out his funeral clothes and planning a cruise.

Faith sighed. "Look, Levi. I just took the red-eye from San Francisco. Can you give me a break? Sorry I was going too fast." She tapped her fingers on the steering wheel. "I'll take a warning. Can I go now?"

"License and registration, please."

"Still got that branch up your ass, I see."

"License and registration, and please exit the vehicle."

She mumbled something under her breath, then groped around in the glove compartment, her shirt coming out of her jeans to reveal a patch of creamy flesh. Looked like the fitness revolution had passed her by; then again, she'd always been a little ~~lush ripe~~ chunky, ever since he could remember. The dog took the opportunity to shove his head out again, and Levi scratched him behind the ear.

Faith slammed the glove box shut, shoved some papers in Levi's hand, got out of the car, nearly hitting him with the door. "Stay put, Blue." She didn't look at Levi.

He glanced at her license, then at her.

"Yes, it's a bad picture," she snapped. "Want a tissue sample?"

"I don't think that'll be necessary. This has expired, though. Another fine."

Her eyes narrowed, and she crossed her arms under her chest. Still had that amazing rack.

"How was Afghanistan?" she asked, looking over his shoulder.

"Really great. I'm thinking of getting a summer place there."

"You know what I wonder, Levi? Why are some people always such hemorrhoids? You ever wonder that?"

"I do. Are you aware that antagonizing an officer of the law is a felony?"

"Really. How fascinating. Can you get it in gear, please? I want to see my family."

He signed the paper and handed it to her. She wadded it up and tossed it in the car. "Am I free to go, Officer?"

"It's Chief now," he said.

"See someone about that branch." She got into the car and drove off. Not too fast, though not slowly, either.

Levi watched her go, releasing a breath. Up to Blue Heron Vineyard, the place her family had owned since America was a baby, to the big white house on the Hill, as her neighborhood was called.

He'd always known Faith Holland, the kind of girl who hugged her girlfriends six times a day in school, as if it'd been weeks since they'd seen each other, not two periods. She reminded him of a puppy trying to woo prospective owners at the pound... *Like me! Like me! I'm really nice!* Jessica, Levi's old neighbor from the trailer park and on-and-off high school girlfriend, had dubbed her Princess Super-Cute, always bouncing around in frilly outfits and pastel colors. Once Faith had started dating Jeremy...it was like eating a bowl of Lucky Charms topped with syrup, so sweet it made your teeth ache. He was surprised bluebirds hadn't fluttered around her head.

Funny, how she'd never noticed her boyfriend was gay.

Levi knew she'd been back over the years—Christmas and Thanksgiving, a weekend here and there, but her visits were short and sweet. She sure never stopped by the police station, though he was friendly with her family; sometimes her grandparents would ask him to stay for dinner after they'd summoned him to the house, and once in a while, he'd have a beer with her father or brother at O'Rourke's. But Faith would never think to drop by and say hello.

Yet once upon a time, when she'd cried herself dehydrated, she'd fallen asleep with her head in his lap.

Levi got back into his cruiser. Plenty of work to do. No point in dwelling on the past.

FAITH KNOCKED ON THE BACK door of her father's house and happily braced for impact. "I'm home!" she called.

"Faith! Oh, honey, finally!" cried Goggy, leading the stampede. "You're late! Didn't I tell you dinner was at noon?"

"Just got hung up a little," Faith said, not wanting to mention Levi Cooper, Ass Pain.

Abby, now sixteen and so pretty, wrapped herself around Faith, burbling out compliments: "I love your earrings, you smell so good, can I come live with you?" Pops kissed both her cheeks and told her she was his prettiest girl, and Faith breathed in the comforting scent of grapes and Bengay. Ned hugged her amiably, despite being twenty-one, and tolerated a hair muss, and Pru gave her a hard hug, as well.

Her mother's absence was still the most powerful thing in the room.

And finally there was Dad, who waited his turn for a

solo hug. His eyes were wet when he pulled back. "Hi, sweetpea," he said, and Faith's heart gave a tug.

"Missed you, Daddy."

"You look beautiful, sweetheart." He ran a purple-stained hand over her hair and smiled.

"Mrs. Johnson's not here?" Faith asked.

"It's her day off," Dad said.

"Oh, I know. I just haven't seen her since June."

"She doesn't approve of Grandpa's girlfriend," Abby whispered as she petted Blue.

"Hi, sis," Jack said, handing her a glass of wine.

"Hello, favorite sibling," she answered, taking a hearty slug.

"Don't drink it like it's Gatorade, sweetpea," her father chided. "We're winemakers, remember?"

"Sorry, Dad," Faith said. "Nice aroma of freshly cut grass, a rich, buttery texture, and I'm getting overtones of apricot with a hint of lemon. I love it."

"Good girl," he said. "Did you get any vanilla? Honor said vanilla."

"Definitely." Far be it for Faith to contradict Honor, who ran everything under the moon at Blue Heron Vineyards. "Where is Honor, by the way?"

"On that phone of hers," Goggy said darkly. She tended not to trust anything invented after 1957. "Get in the dining room before the food gets cold."

"I was serious when I asked to come live with you," Abby said. Prudence sighed and took a slug of her own wine. "Plus," Abby went on, "then I can establish residency in California and go to some awesome school out there at half price. See, Mom? Just saving you and Dad some money."

"And where's Carl, speaking of my favorite brother-in-law?" Faith asked.

"Hiding," Pru answered.

"Well, well, well! You must be Faith!" A woman's voice boomed as the downstairs bathroom door opened, the sound of a flushing toilet in the background.

Faith opened her mouth, then closed it. "Oh. I—I am. Lorena, I'm guessing?"

The woman Honor had warned about was a sight to behold indeed. Dull black hair, obviously dyed, makeup so thick you could carve in it and a squat body shown in horrifying detail through a clinging, leopard-print shirt.

The woman shoved a Sharpie pen in her cleavage where it stayed, quivering, like a syringe. "Just touching up my roots!" she announced. "Wanted to make a nice impression on the little princess! Hello there! Give us a hug!"

Faith's breath left her in a whoosh as Lorena wrapped her in a python grip. "Nice to meet you," she wheezed as Pru gave her a significant look.

"Can we please eat before my death?" Pops asked. "The old woman here wouldn't let me have my cheese. I'm starving."

"So, die already," Goggy answered. "No one's stopping you. I'll barely notice."

"Well, Phyllis Nebbins would notice. She got a new hip two months ago, Faithie. Looks like she's seventy-five again, out there with her grandson, always with a smile. Nice to see a happy woman."

Goggy slammed down a massive bowl of salt potatoes. "I'll be happy once you're dead."

"That's beautiful, Goggy," Ned said.

"You two are such hoots!" Lorena practically yelled. "I love it!"

Faith sat down, inhaling the scent of Goggy's ham, salt potatoes and home.

There were two houses on Blue Heron Vineyard: the Old House, where Goggy and Pops lived, a Colonial that had been updated twice since being built in 1781—once to install indoor plumbing, then again in 1932. Faith and her siblings grew up here, in the New House, a graceful if creaky old Federal built in 1873, where Dad lived with Honor and Mrs. Johnson, the housekeeper who'd been with them since Mom died.

And speaking of Honor… "Sorry, everyone," she said. She paused, gave Faith a brief kiss on the cheek. "You finally got here."

"Hi, Honor." She ignored the slight reprimand.

Pru and Jack were sixteen and eight years older than Faith respectively, and generally viewed their baby sister as adorable, if slightly incompetent (which Faith had never minded, as it got her out of a lot of chores back in the day). Honor, though… She was four years older; Faith had been a surprise. Maybe Honor had never forgiven Faith for stealing the title of baby of the family.

More likely, though, she'd never gotten over the fact that Faith had caused their mother's death.

Faith had epilepsy, first diagnosed when she was about five. Jack had filmed a seizure once (typical boy), and Faith had been horrified to see herself oblivious, her muscles jerking and clenching, eyes as vacant as a dead cow's. It was assumed that Constance Holland had been distracted by one such seizure and therefore hadn't seen the car that had smashed into them, killing Mom. Honor had never forgiven Faith…and Faith didn't blame her.

"Why are you just sitting there, Faith?" Goggy demanded. "Eat up, sweetheart. Who knows what you've been living on in California?" Her grandmother passed her a plate loaded with smoked ham, buttered salt potatoes, green beans with butter and lemon, and braised carrots (with butter). Faith imagined she gained a pound just by looking at it.

"So, Lorena, you and my dad are…?" Faith asked above the background noise of her grandparents bickering over how much salt Pops should put on his already heavily salted meal.

"Special friends, sweetheart, special, special friends," the woman said, adjusting her rather massive breasts. "Right, Johnny?"

"Oh, sure," he agreed amiably. "She was dying to meet you, Faith."

According to Honor, Lorena Creech had met Dad about a month earlier during a tour of Blue Heron. Everyone in the area knew John Holland had been devastated by his wife's death, had never wanted to date anyone, was happy among his children, grandchildren and grapes. Any attempts at a relationship had been gently rebuffed in the early days until it was accepted that John Holland Jr. would remain a widower the rest of his life.

Enter Lorena Creech, a transplant from Arizona, clearly a gold digger, and *not* a candidate for stepmother. All three local Holland kids had discussed this with Dad, but he'd just laughed and waved off their concern. And while Dad was many things, Faith thought, watching as Lorena held the silverware up to the light, he wasn't the most observant of men. No one had anything against Dad finding a nice woman to marry, but no one wanted Lorena to be sleeping upstairs in Mom's old bed, either.

"So how many acres have you got here?" Lorena asked, taking a huge bite of ham. Subtle.

"Quite a few," Honor said icily.

"Subdividable?"

"Absolutely not."

"Well, some of it is, Honor, honey," Dad said. "Over my dead body, of course. More green beans, Lorena?"

"This is nice," Lorena said. "The whole family together! My late husband was sterile, Faith. A groin injury when he was a boy. Tractor backed up, squished him in the soft parts, so we never could have kids, though, hell, we sure got it on!"

Goggy was staring at Lorena as if she was a snake in the toilet. Jack drained his wine.

"Good for you!" Pops said. "Have some more ham, sweetheart." He nudged the plate across the table toward Lorena, whose appetite was not restricted to the boudoir, it seemed.

"So, Faith," Jack said, "Dad says you'll be staying here for a while."

Faith nodded and wiped her mouth. "Yep. Finally gonna fix up the old barn up on Rose Ridge. I'll be here for about two months." The longest she'd been back since her wedding debacle, and not just to fix up the barn, either. Both the mission and the length of time gave her a pang of alarm.

"Yay!" Abby said.

"Yay," Ned echoed, winking at her.

"What are you doing with the old barn?" Pops asked. "Speak up, sweetie."

"I'll be turning it into a space for special events, Pops," she explained. "People would rent it out, and it'd bring in some extra income for the vineyard. Weddings, anniversary parties, stuff like that." She'd first come up with the idea when she was in graduate school—transform the old stone barn into something that blended into the landscape effortlessly, something modern and old at the same time.

"Oh! Weddings! I'd *love* to get married again," Lorena said, winking at Dad, who simply grinned.

"It sounds like too much work for you, sweetheart," Goggy said.

Faith smiled. "It's not. It's a great spot, and I've already got some plans drafted, so I'll show them to everyone and see what you think."

"And you can do that in two months?" Lorena asked around a potato.

"Sure," Faith said. "Barring unforeseen complications and all that." It would be her biggest project yet, and on home turf, too.

"So, what do you do again? Your father's told me, hell's bells, all he can do is talk about you kids, but I forget." Lorena smiled at her. One of her teeth was gold.

"I'm a landscape architect."

"You should see her work, Lorena," Dad said. "Amazing."

"Thanks, Daddy. I design gardens, parks, industrial open space, stuff like that."

"So you're a gardener?"

"Nope. I hire gardeners and landscapers, though. I come up with the design and make sure it's implemented the right way."

"The boss, in other words," Lorena said. "Good for you, babe! Hey, are those Hummel figurines real? Those get a pretty penny on eBay, you know."

"They were my mother's," Honor bit out.

"Uh-huh. A very pretty penny. How about some more of that ham, Ma?" she asked Goggy, holding out her plate.

Lorena...okay, she was kind of terrifying, there was

no getting around it. Faith had hoped that Honor was exaggerating.

A prickle of nervous energy sang through Faith's joints. Before she left San Francisco, she and her siblings had had a conference call. Dad was slightly clueless, it was agreed—he'd once been nicked by a car as he stood in the road, staring up at the sky to see if it might rain—but if he was ready to start dating, they could find him someone more suitable. Faith immediately volunteered for the job. She'd come home, work on transforming the old barn, and find Dad somebody great. Someone wonderful, someone who understood him and appreciated how loyal and hardworking and kind he was. Someone to take away the gaping hole Mom's death had left.

Finally, Faith would have a chance at redemption.

And while she was at it, she'd finally be able to do something for Blue Heron, too, the family business that employed everyone except her.

Dinner was dominated by Lorena's commentary, bickering between Ned and Abby, who really should be too old for that, as well as the occasional death threat between Goggy and Pops. Norman Rockwell meets Stephen King, Faith thought fondly.

"I'll do these dishes. Don't anyone move," Goggy said, a hint of tragedy creeping into her voice.

"Kids!" Pru barked, and Ned and Abby jolted into action and started clearing.

Honor poured herself an ounce of wine. "Faith, you'll be staying with Goggy and Pops, did Dad tell you?"

"What?" Faith asked, shooting Pops a quick smile to make up for the panic in her voice. Not that she didn't love her grandparents, but *living* with them?

"Pops is slowing down," Pru said in a whisper, as both grands were a bit hard of hearing.

"I'm not slowing down," Pops protested. "Who wants to arm wrestle? Jack, you up for it, son?"

"Not today, Pops."

"See?"

"You look good to me, Dad!" Lorena said. "Really good!"

"He's *not* your father," Goggy growled.

"You wouldn't mind Faith staying with you, would you?" Dad asked. "You know you've been getting a bit…"

"A bit what?" Goggy demanded.

"Homicidal?" Jack suggested.

Goggy glared at him, then looked more gently at Faith. "We would *love* for you to stay with us, sweetheart. But as a guest, not a babysitter." Another glare was distributed around the table before Goggy got up and went into the kitchen to instruct the kids.

"Pops, I wanted you to check out the merlot grapes," Dad said.

"Count me in!" Lorena barked cheerfully, and the three left the dining room.

With Abby and Ned in the kitchen, it was just the four Holland kids around the table. "I'm really staying with them?" she asked.

"It's for the best," Honor said. "I have a bunch of stuff in your room, anyway."

"So check this out," Pru said, adjusting the collar of her flannel shirt. "Carl suggested that I get a bikini wax the other day."

"Oh, God," Jack said.

"What? All of a sudden you're a prude? Who drove

you home from that strip club when you got drunk, huh?"

"That was seventeen years ago," he said.

"So big deal. Carl wants to 'spice things up.'" Pru made quote marks with her fingers. "The man is lucky he's getting *any,* that's what I think. What's your problem, Jack?" she called to Jack's back as he left.

"I don't want to hear about your sex life, either," Honor said. "And I'll return the favor and won't tell you about mine."

"Not that you have one," Pru said.

"You might be surprised," Honor returned.

"If I can't talk to you guys, who am I gonna tell? My kids? Dad? You're my sisters. You have to listen."

"You can tell us," Faith said. "So, no bikini wax, I take it?"

"Thanks, Faithie." Pru leaned back and crossed her arms across her chest. "So he says to me, why not give it a try? Like the Playboy models? So I say to him, 'First of all, Carl, if you have a *Playboy* in this house, you're a dead man walking. We have a teenage daughter, and I don't want her looking at fake boobs and slutty hair.'" She shifted in her chair. "A bikini wax! At my age! I have enough trouble with facial hair management."

"Speaking of terrifying older women," Faith said, ducking as Pru tried to swat her, "Lorena Creech. Yikes."

"She asked Jack to sit on her lap the other day," Pru said. "You should've seen his face."

Faith laughed, stopping as Honor cut her a cool look. "It's funny until Dad finds himself married to someone who's only after his money," Honor said.

"Dad has money?" Pru quipped. "This is news."

"And he wouldn't get married without it being some-one great," Faith added.

"Maybe not. But this is the first woman he's ever had as his 'special friend,' too. And why her, I have no idea." Honor adjusted her hair band. "She's asked Sharon Wiles about the price of building lots the other day, so, Faith, don't waste time, okay? I don't have the time to cruise dating websites. You do."

With that, she left, going back to her office, no doubt. All Honor did was work.

THAT NIGHT, AFTER FAITH had brought her stuff to the Old House and returned the rental car to Corning (Dad had said she could use Brown Betty, the aging Subaru wagon, while she was here), she climbed between the clean sheets in her grandparents' guest room and waited for sleep.

Mom wasn't the only one whose absence had been felt today. Faith still half expected to see Jeremy there, as well. He'd always loved her family dinners.

And at the moment, he was probably just down the road.

She'd been home seven times since her wedding day, and she hadn't seen him. Not once. Granted, she'd only been home for a few days at a time. She'd been into town, to the bar owned by her best friends, Colleen and Connor O'Rourke, but Jeremy hadn't shown up. He hadn't stopped by her family's house, though he did while she was away. People had gotten over the shock of his coming out, including her family (eventually). Jeremy had been a part of their lives, too, not to men-tion their doctor and next-door neighbor, though next door was a mile away.

But when she was home, he lay low.

For the first six weeks after their non-wedding, she and Jeremy had called each other every day, sometimes two or three times a day. Even with his stunning news, it was hard to believe they weren't together anymore. From the moment she'd seen him by her bedside in the nurse's office, for eight solid years, she'd loved him without one moment's doubt. They were supposed to be married, have kids, have a wonderful long life together, and the fact that all those future decades were just whisked away…it was hard to wrap her heart around it.

He tried to explain why he'd let things go so far. That was the hardest part. She'd loved him so much, they'd been best friends…and he never even tried to bring it up.

He loved her, he said it repeatedly, and Faith knew it was true. Every day, every conversation, he apologized, sometimes crying. He was so, so sorry for hurting her. So sorry for not telling her, for not accepting what he knew in his heart.

One night six weeks after their wedding day, after they'd talked to each other in gentle voices for an hour, Faith had finally told Jeremy what they both already knew: they needed to truly break up. No more emails, no more calls, no more texts.

"I understand," Jeremy had whispered.

"I'll always love you," Faith had said, her voice breaking.

"I'll always love you, too."

And then, after a long, long moment, Faith had pushed the button to end the call. Sat there on the edge of the bed, staring into space. The next day, she'd been offered a freelance job working with a well-known land-scape designer at a new marina, and her post-Jeremy life began. Her father had come out to visit three times that year—unheard of if you were a farmer—and Pru and the kids had come once. They all had called and written and texted.

Forcing yourself out of love…it seemed impossible. Sometimes, she'd forget—someone asked her if she wanted kids, and her answer was, "We definitely do," and then came the slap of remembering that there would be no beautiful, smiling, dark-haired kids running through the fields of the two vineyards.

And now, here in the Old House, it was impossible not to think of Jeremy. Memories of him were everywhere—he'd sat on the front porch, promising her father he'd take good care of her. He'd pushed Abby on the swing when she was little, took Ned for rides in his convertible, flirted with Pru and Honor, had beers with Jack. He'd helped her repaint this very room the same pale lilac it was now. They'd kissed right in that corner (lovely, chaste kisses, perhaps not what one would expect from one's twenty-six-year-old fiancé) until Goggy had walked in on them and told them there was no kissing in her house, she didn't *care* if they were engaged.

Faith had kept one photo of her and Jeremy, taken one weekend when they'd gone to the Outer Banks… the two of them in sweatshirts, hugging, the wind blowing her hair, Jeremy's big smile. Every day, she forced herself to look at it, and a small, cruel part of her brain would tell her to get over it.

She hadn't deserved him, anyway.

But for those eight years that they'd been together… it seemed that the universe had finally forgiven her for her dark secret, had presented Jeremy as a sign of absolution.

Seemed like the universe had the last laugh, and its

agent had been Levi Cooper. Levi, who'd always judged her and found her ridiculous.

Levi, who had known and never said a word.

CHAPTER THREE

LEVI COOPER MET JEREMY LYON just before senior year began. He never expected that they'd become friends. Economically, that wasn't how things worked.

Manningsport sat at the edge of Keuka Lake. The town green was ringed with picturesque businesses: antiques stores, a bridal shop, O'Rourke's Tavern, a little bookstore and Hugo's, the French restaurant where Jessica Dunn waited tables. Then there was the Hill, rising up and away from the village, the land of the rich kids whose parents were bankers and lawyers and doctors, or whose parents owned the vineyards themselves: the Kleins, the Smithingtons, the Hollands. Busloads of tourists would come in from April to October to see the beautiful lake and countryside, taste the wine and leave with a case or two.

Farther away from the lake were the pristine Mennonite farms, stretching on the hills, dotted with clusters of black-and-white cows, men in dark clothes driving iron-wheeled tractors, women with bonnets and long skirts selling cheese and jam at the farmers market on the weekends.

And then there were the other places, the long stretches of in-between. Levi lived at the base of the wrong side of the vineyards, where the shadow of the Hill made night fall a little earlier. His part of town had the dump, a grimy grocery store and a Laundromat where, legend had it, drugs were sold.

In elementary school, the well-meaning rich parents would invite the entire class to the birthday parties, and Levi would go, along with Jessica Dunn and Tiffy Ames. They'd remember their manners and thank the mom for inviting them, hand over the gift that had strained the weekly budget. As for reciprocal invitations, no. You didn't have the class over for your birthday when you lived in a trailer park. You might hang out in school when you were young, might meet up in the summer to jump off Meering Falls, but way too soon, the economic divide started to matter. The rich kids started talking about what clothes they wore or what kind of new car their folks drove and where they'd be going on vacation, and that time you went fishing off Henleys' dock didn't matter so much.

And so, Levi hung out with Jessica and Tiffy and Asswipe Jones, whose real name was Ashwick (the kid's mother had been addicted to some British television show and clearly had zero clue about kids and names). Levi and his half sister grew up in West's Trailer Park, in a cheap double-wide that leaked in two spots, no matter how many times he patched the roof. After his mom had Sarah when Levi was ten (and another man had moved out of the picture), it felt pretty cramped, but it was clean and happy. It wasn't horrible, not by a long shot, but it wasn't the Hill or the Village. Everyone understood the difference, and if you didn't, you were either ignorant of real life or from out of town.

On the first day of football practice a month before senior year started, Coach introduced a new student. Jeremy Lyon was "someone who's gonna teach you lazy-ass pussies how to play football," Coach said, and Jeremy went around and shook hands with every damn member of the team. "Hey, I'm Jeremy, how's it going? Nice to meet you. Jeremy Lyon, good to meet you, dude."

Gay was the first word that came to Levi's mind.

But no one else seemed to pick up on it—maybe because Jeremy could *play.* After an hour, it was obvious he was crazy good at football. He looked as if he'd been in the NFL for years—six-foot-three, rock-solid muscle and a frame that could withstand three linebackers trying to wrestle him to the ground. He could thread a needle with that football, could dodge and twist and slip into the end zone, using what Coach called "Notre Dame razzle-dazzle."

Levi's job as wide receiver was to get downfield as fast as possible and catch those beautiful passes. He was pretty good at football—which wasn't going to translate into a scholarship no matter how much his mom hoped it would—but Jeremy was great. After four hours, the team started to speculate that they might have their first winning season in nine years.

On Friday of that first week, Jeremy invited everyone to his place for pizza. And quite the place it was; it was all modern and shit, windows everywhere, the kitchen floor so shiny that Levi took off his shoes. The living room furniture was white and sleek, like a movie set. Jeremy's room had a king-size bed, a state-of-the-art Mac, a huge TV with a PlayStation and about fifty games. His parents introduced themselves as Ted and Elaine and made it seem like nothing could be more fun than having thirty-four high school boys over. The pizza was homemade (in the pizza oven, which was one of four ovens in the kitchen), and there were platters of massive sandwiches on that expensive bread with the Italian name. Every kind of pop—the fancy kind, not generic, like Levi's mom bought. They had a wine cellar and a special wine fridge and beers from every microbrewery around. When Asswipe Jones asked for a beer, Mrs. Lyon just ruffled his hair and said she didn't feel up for jail today, and Asswipe didn't seem to mind one bit.

Levi walked through the house, carefully holding his bottle of Virgil's root beer, and tried not to gape. Modern paintings and abstract sculptures, a fireplace that took up an entire wall, an outdoor fireplace on the deck, a fireplace in the rec room downstairs, where there was also a pool table, foosball, another huge TV and PlayStation and a fully stocked bar.

Then, abruptly, Jeremy was at his side. "Thanks for coming tonight, Levi."

"Yeah, sure," Levi said. "Nice place."

"Thanks. My parents went a little nuts, I think. Like, do we really need a statue of Zeus?" He grinned and rolled his eyes.

"Right," Levi said.

"Hey, you wanna hang out tomorrow? Maybe catch a movie or just stay here?"

Levi took a long drink of pop, then glanced at Jeremy. Yeah. Gay, he was almost sure. "Uh, listen, dude," he said. "I have a girlfriend." Well, he slept with Jessica once in a while, if that counted. But still. Message given: *I'm straight.*

"Cool. Well, you can both come if you don't have anything better to do." Jeremy paused. "I don't know anybody yet, that's all."

It was a patent request, and why him, Levi didn't know. Eventually, he supposed, Jeremy would be told by some other rich kid that the Coopers were white trash, give or take, that Levi didn't own a car and worked two after-school jobs. But for now, a chance to hang out here, in this place, get a little peek at how the other half lived… "Sure. Thanks. I'll see if she's free. Her name's Jessica."

"Cool. Seven o'clock? My mom's a great cook."

"Thank you, baby," his mom said, coming into the room with a tray of sandwiches. Seeing the two of them standing together, she froze. Her smile was suddenly just a stretch of the mouth.

"It's the truth, Mom." Jeremy put his arm around his petite mother and kissed her on the head, then snagged a sandwich. "She beats me if I say otherwise," he added to Levi.

Mrs. Lyon was looking at Levi, a small frown between her eyes. "What's your name again, dear?"

"Levi," Jeremy answered for him. "He's a wide receiver. We're gonna hang out tomorrow, if that's okay. His girlfriend's coming, too."

"Oh, you have a girlfriend!" The mom instantly relaxed. "How nice! Of course! Yes, yes, both of you should come over. It'd be lovely."

"She might have to work," Levi said. "I'll check. But thank you."

"Does your girlfriend have a friend?" Mrs. Lyon asked.

"There she goes, trying to find her future daughter-in-law," Jeremy said, smiling easily. There was a crash from upstairs, followed by a curse. "That sounds like soda on white upholstery to me. Told you not to buy that couch," he added.

"Oh, stop. It's not like you're a bunch of animals," his mom said.

"Hate to break it to you, but we pretty much are,"

Levi said. Jeremy's grin widened, and he went with his mom to clean up the mess, presumably.

So, yeah. Jeremy was gay. Or just…Californian. Or both.

Levi went back the next night, needing to hitchhike from his own house after his shift ended at the marina. He'd spent six hours cleaning boats in dry dock, which, while exhausting, allowed him to work shirtless and be ogled by Amber What's-Her-Name, who was here for the weekend. Jess didn't want to miss the Saturday night tips, so Levi went alone.

At Jeremy's, they ate with the parents (duck, if you could believe it), then did the typical guy things—ate some more, played Soldier of Fortune on the down-stairs PlayStation. When Jeremy asked where Levi was thinking of going to college, Levi hesitated, not want-ing to clue Jeremy in just yet that college was so far out of reach he wasn't even thinking of applying. "Not sure yet," he said.

"Me, neither," Jeremy answered easily, though Levi had heard he was being heavily recruited. "So. Tell me who the cute girls are at school. I'm hoping to have a girlfriend this year."

It was so awkward that Levi almost winced. Still, there was something about Jeremy, an innocence or something. "Did you have a girl back home?" he asked, testing him.

"Not really. No one special. You know." Jeremy looked away. "With football and classes and all, it's kind of hard to find the time."

Levi's experience had been completely different; girls propositioned him constantly. Unless you were a prepubescent freshman, some chick would throw herself at you, so long as you wore the uniform on Friday nights, no matter how bad the team had sucked.

When it got late, Levi said he'd walk back, even though it was seven miles down the Hill and around the Village to West's. But Jeremy insisted on driving him; he had a convertible, for God's sake, and the thing was, he didn't act like an asshole. "Great night for a drive, huh?" Jeremy said amiably, hopping into the car without opening the door. Levi followed suit, which was what people did if they had convertibles, he guessed.

Jeremy talked all the way to Route 15, telling Levi about life in Napa (pretty awesome), the reasons his parents wanted to relocate (his dad had gotten an ulcer, and they figured New York was more mellow when it came to wine-making), asking him questions about Coach and some of the teams they'd be facing.

"Right here. West's Trailer Park." He waited for Jeremy to realize he'd picked the wrong teammate to befriend.

"Gotcha. Which one?" Jeremy asked, turning into the drive.

"Last one on the left. Thanks for the ride, man. And thank your mom for dinner."

"No, it was great to have you. See you at practice."

Then he waved and executed a neat little turn and drove off, the sound of the motor humming quietly in the distance.

And so a friendship began. Over the next month, Jeremy frequently asked Levi over for dinner until one day, Levi's mother snapped, "Why don't you ask him here? Are you ashamed of us or something?" When Jeremy showed up, he had flowers for Levi's mother, told Sarah she was gorgeous and made no comment on the

water-stained ceiling, the jug wine in the fridge or the
fact that the four of them could barely fit in the kitchen.

"Is that tuna casserole?" he said as Levi's mother set
the Pyrex dish on the table. "Oh, man, that's my favorite! I haven't had this in ages. My mom is so stuck-up
about food. This, though. This is living." He grinned
like they'd just pulled off a bank heist and ate three
helpings while Mom cooed and sighed.

"That is a *very* nice boy," she announced after Jeremy had left, her tone slightly reverent.

"Yeah," Levi agreed.

"Does he have a girlfriend?"

"I think you're a little old for him." He grinned at
her, and she did blush.

"*I'll* be his girlfriend," Sarah said fervently.

"And you're a little young," Levi said, pulling her
hair. "Go brush your teeth, kid." His sister obeyed.

His mom ran a hand through her dyed blond hair,
revealing black roots. "Well. I just meant, a handsome
boy like that, all that charm and nice manners. Maybe
some will rub off on you."

"Thanks, Ma."

"I bet *he's* not the type to go running around with
slutty girls."

"No, he's definitely not." Levi raised an eyebrow at
his mom. She missed his point.

"What you see in that Jessica Dunn is beyond me."

"She puts out." His mom slapped his head, and Levi
ducked, grinning. "She's also got a great personality,"
he added. "Or something like that."

"You're horrible. Help me clean up. I bet your *friend*
helps *his* mother."

One day, after school had started up again, Levi
and Jeremy were heading into the cafeteria. The door

was blocked by someone just standing there—Princess Super-Cute, her red hair in a ponytail, always asking people to sign up to collect bottles or save the seals, her life's mission to make sure everyone on earth liked her. Now she was just standing there, oblivious to the throng of people who couldn't get in to eat lunch.

"Move it, Holland," Levi said.

She didn't answer. Ah, shit, she was doing that thing, plucking at her little ruffly shirt and looking confused. Levi took a step forward, but before he could catch her, she crumpled to the floor and started jerking.

"Oh, my God!" Jeremy blurted, flinging off his backpack to kneel at her side. "Hey, hey, are you all right?"

"She's got epilepsy," Levi said. He pulled off his sweatshirt to stick under her head. A small crowd was forming, Faith's occasional seizure always a hit. Twelve years of the same kids…you'd think people would get used to it. Each year, the nurse would come in to their classroom and give the epilepsy talk, like they all needed a reminder and Faith needed the embarrassment. It was the one time of year that he felt sorry for her. Well, then, and when her mom died.

Jeremy already had his arms around her. "You're not supposed to move her," Levi said, but Jeremy picked her up and was shouldering his way down the hall.

And that was that. The school talked about it for days; how Jeremy was like some kind of *knight* or something, how could Faith *not* fall for him, it was *so* romantic, didn't you kind of wish *you* had epilepsy or fainted once in a while? Levi's eyes actually got tired from rolling.

"I'm in love, my friend," Jeremy said a couple weeks later. "She's amazing."

"Yeah."

"Really. She's beautiful. Like an angel."

Levi gave him a look. "Sure."

Despite not having a father, Levi was what his boss called a man's man. Football since fourth grade, an aptitude with tools, his first girlfriend at twelve, first sex at fifteen. He'd stayed back the year his father left and was therefore older than his classmates, had started putting on muscle in seventh grade, could drive sophomore year of high school, and those things ensured him some respect. He'd always run with a pack of guys.

And guys did not talk about their girlfriends being beautiful like an angel. They talked about their tits, their asses, if and when they might put out. If a guy was really in love, he'd just shut up and occasionally punch the person (often Levi) who speculated on the tits and ass of the girl in question.

Levi was no expert, but he guessed that Jeremy might not know he was gay. Or if he did, he might not want to admit it. Jeremy was awfully careful in the locker room, which was odd for a kid who'd played football for a decade. Most of the guys didn't think about it, though some liked to strut around naked, in love with their own junk. There were, of course, the gay jokes, and Jeremy laughed cautiously, sometimes glancing at Levi to see if it was actually funny (it never was). Nope, Jeremy just kept his eyes down until he was dressed. When Big Frankie Pepitone got a tattoo on his shoulder, all the other guys admired it and made sure to give Frankie a slap on the newly inked and still angry-looking skin (because football players liked to hurt each other, after all), but Jeremy could barely drag his eyes up to the tatt. "Cool" was all he said, and Levi got the impression that maybe Jeremy was afraid of what his face would show if he did look at Big Frankie.

Whatever. Jeremy was a good guy, and Levi didn't really care if Faith Holland was his beard or the love of his life. It was his senior year; he figured he'd be enlisting, so he was going to have all the fun he could. And being around Jeremy *was* fun. The guy was funny, smart, laid-back and decent as anything. Levi and Jess, Jeremy and Faith hung out sometimes, catching a movie or going to the Lyons' house, because Faith had too many siblings, and why go to the trailer park when Jeremy's house was a fricking playland? But Jess didn't much like Faith (and did a deadly impression of her), so, often, it was just the three of them, Jeremy, Levi and Faith.

Faith Holland…she was a little hard to take, yeah. Kind of cutesy and bouncy and tiring. She was smitten with Jeremy and seemed to be auditioning for her role as his future wife, always fluttering her eyelashes and snuggling up close, and Jeremy didn't seem to mind. She'd kiss up to Mr. and Mrs. Lyon, leaping to clear dishes and whatnot, and it was clear the Lyons thought she was wonderful.

"Thank God he finally found someone," Levi overheard Mrs. Lyon say to her husband one night, just as he was about to thank them for having him over.

"About time," Mr. Lyon answered. "I wasn't sure it'd ever happen." They gave each other a look, then went back to watching CNN.

So maybe Levi wasn't the only one who thought Jeremy might play for the other team.

Senior year was the best year of Levi's life. Football season ended with Jeremy sending a thirty-nine yard pass into the end zone that Levi could've caught just by flexing his fingers, so perfect was Jeremy's aim. The Manningsport Mountain Lions were divisional champs, though they lost in the next round. Didn't matter. They'd had their best season in the history of the school, so it was hard to feel bad.

And Levi, who had no brother and no father and no uncles, had his first true friend, different from Asswipe and Tommy and Big Frankie. Jeremy was more mature in a lot of ways, someone who seemed to feel as comfortable at Levi's as he did in his parents' glamorous house, who laughed easily and didn't get wasted for fun, who never cared that kids from the Hill weren't supposed to hang out with kids from the trailer park.

He tried a little too hard with Faith—once in a while, he'd kiss her, and it practically made Levi wince, it was so awful. Jeremy did these old-fashioned, corny-ass things that no straight guy would've ever dreamed of doing—putting a flower in her hair, shit like that. And Faith, God, she ate it up. She'd sit on his lap and suggest they all sign up to do a road cleanup, or maybe Levi and Jess would want to join the school chorus and go to the old folks' home and sing. Levi would occasionally point out that there were drugs for her type of condition. Faith would laugh, a little uncertainly, and then he'd feel like he'd kicked a puppy, and Jeremy would say, "Dude, be nice. I love her," and Faith's tail would start wagging again.

One spring night, Faith left the boys at the Lyons' place—Ted and Elaine were away, and Levi suspected she was uncomfortable with the fact that he and Jeremy had appropriated two beers from the downstairs fridge, and God help her if she condoned such illegality. Levi watched her go from where they sat on the deck, her pretty hair gleaming in the sun, the Hollands' big dog running by her side. "You and Faith doing it?" he asked out of idle curiosity.

"No, no," Jeremy said. "We're…old-fashioned. You know. Might wait till we get married."

Levi choked on his beer. "Oh," he wheezed. Jeremy just shrugged, a smile still on his face at the thought of Princess Super-Cute.

Then, out of the blue, there came that week where Jeremy and Faith "took a break." Shocked the whole school. Jeremy was uncharacteristically glum and didn't want to talk about it. Finally, Levi imagined, Faith had snapped out of it and figured out that something was off where her boyfriend was concerned.

He had his own stuff to deal with—a Division III college in Pennsylvania suddenly offered him a decent scholarship (thanks to Jeremy making him look so good all season). Between their offer and what he had saved, all Levi needed was five grand, and they could make it work.

He didn't ask his mom; five grand was still way too much. He could've asked Jeremy or the Lyons, and they would've fallen over themselves handing it to him, but it didn't feel right. He didn't want to owe anyone.

And so, he asked his father. Figured Rob Cooper might owe him, instead. Tracked him down and found that the guy lived two towns over. Levi hadn't seen him in eleven years. Not one phone call, not one birth-day card, but the guy lived twenty miles away in a nice ranch house painted dark blue, a new-model car in the driveway.

Rob Cooper might've been a deadbeat dad, but he recognized Levi right away. Shook his hand, clapped him on the shoulder and brought him into the garage.

"So, um, I'll get right to it," Levi said. "I need five grand to go to college. I have a football scholarship, but it's only a partial." He paused. "I was hoping you might be able to help."

His father—shit, his father had the same green eyes that Levi had, same solid arms—his father nodded, and for one stupid second, Levi's heart leaped.

"Yeah, I'd like to help you, man. How old are you now? Eighteen?"

"Nineteen. I stayed back in third grade." *The year you left.*

"Right, right." His father nodded again. "Well, the thing is, I just got married. Fresh start and all that." He paused. "My wife's at work. Otherwise, I'd introduce you." No, he wouldn't. "Wish I could help you, son. I just don't have it."

There were a lot of things Levi wanted to say. Things about back child support coming to a lot more than five grand. Things about how Rob Cooper had surrendered the right to call him *son* eleven years ago. About how he'd stayed back in third grade because he'd spent fuck-ing *hours* after school every day, sitting on the stoop, waiting for that mustard-yellow El Camino to turn into West's Trailer Park because Levi knew, he *knew* his father wouldn't just go away forever.

But his mouth stayed shut, and shame burned in his stomach because he'd let himself hope.

"I played football, too, did you know that?" his father asked.

"No," Levi said.

"Wide receiver."

"Cool. Listen, I gotta go."

"Sure. Sorry again, Levi."

It was hearing his name said by that voice, a voice still so well remembered, that almost broke Levi. He walked down the driveway carefully, as if he'd forgotten how, and got into Asswipe's battered truck. Didn't look back at his father and drove straight to Geneva to enlist. He wouldn't let his father take any more away than he already had. Got a little drunk with his old pals that night, had to have Jess put him to bed, but otherwise, no harm done.

By the end of that week, Faith and Jeremy had gotten back together, anyway. Blip on the screen.

When graduation came around, Levi had passed the Army's tests and was looking at sixteen weeks of basic training come August. All of a sudden, home suddenly became…everything.

Summer took on a bittersweet quality. He found himself sitting by his sister's bed while she slept, hoping she'd do okay without him. Took her swimming, visited her Girl Scout troop and made all the little girls promise to send him notes and cookies. Brought his mom flowers one day, only to have her burst into tears.

The dense green hills and rows of grapevines, the sweet smell of the air were all abruptly precious. It was hard knowing things would never be the same, knowing that he would change and leave behind his old life, that this perfect last year would never be repeated.

The night before he had to head off to Fort Benning, Mr. and Mrs. Lyon threw him a party, told his mom that she'd raised a great man, and the three parents cried a little together. Jess broke up with him during the party, nothing big, just "Hey, there doesn't seem like a point in keeping this up, do you think?" Levi agreed that no, there really wasn't. She kissed him on the cheek, told him to be careful and said she'd write once in a while.

Jeremy picked him up the next morning. Levi kissed his mom goodbye, hugged Sarah tight and told them both to stop crying. Might've wiped his own eyes, too. Then Jeremy asked him if he wanted to drive the Beemer, and hells yeah, he did.

They were quiet all the way to Hornell, where the bus would take him to Penn Station, then to Fort Benning. Jeremy was heading for Boston College next week to start football practice, where he'd be backup QB to the senior starter. The gulf in their lives, the one that Jeremy never acknowledged, suddenly yawned between them. Jeremy would be a football god at a cushy school, possibly get tapped by the pros and, either way, would live a life of ease and privilege. Levi would serve his country in a war that most people didn't think was doing much good and hopefully not get killed.

Jeremy bought a couple of coffees and waited until the Greyhound pulled up in a cloud of exhaust and the driver got out for a smoke.

"Looks like this is it," Levi said, hefting his duffel bag onto his shoulder.

"Get a window seat," Jeremy advised, as if he was experienced in the world of bus travel.

"Will do. Take care, dude," Levi said, shaking his hand. "Thanks for everything."

It was a shitty little phrase conveying nothing. *Thanks for not caring where I lived, thanks for trying to get me noticed by recruiters, thanks for sending me that pass, thanks for your parents, thanks for picking me to be your friend.*

"Thank you, too." Then Jeremy hugged him hard and long, pounding him on the back, and when he let him go, Levi saw that his eyes were wet. "You're the best friend I've ever had," Jeremy said, his voice shaking.

"Right back at you, bud," Levi said. "Right back at you." A long minute passed, and for whatever reason, Levi thought maybe he should crack the door a little, now that he was leaving. "That wouldn't change, either," he added.

"What do you mean?" Jeremy asked.

If you came out. The words stayed stuck. Levi shrugged a little. "I just...I'll always be here for you, man. Whatever happens. And you know...you can tell me anything. Call me. Email. All that good shit."

"Thanks," Jeremy said. They hugged again, and Levi got on the bus.

He didn't go back to Manningsport for almost five years.

CHAPTER FOUR

"THANK YOU FOR TAKING me out," Faith said three days after she'd landed in town. "I'm not sure how my grandparents haven't killed each other yet. When I'm trying to fall asleep at night, I can still hear them in my head. 'You want mustard. You always have mustard. How can you make a sandwich without mustard? Take the mustard.' I could be on fire, and they'd still be fighting over the French's." She took a generous sip of her martini, one of the best things about Hugo's Restaurant. "I'm starting to think that moving in with them was a fast road to suicide."

Colleen O'Rourke grinned. "Oh, you Hollands. Such a cute family."

Colleen and she had been friends since second grade, when Faith had had a seizure and Colleen had faked one, jealous of the attention Faith got. Colleen had been much more vigorous, the tale went, and ended up bumping her head on a counter and needing four stitches, which had made her very happy indeed.

"So, aside from the grandparents, how is it, being back?" Colleen asked now.

"It's great," Faith said. "My dad took me out to dinner last night, and it was great. The Red Salamander. Those pizzas are to die for."

"I'd marry your father if you'd let me." Colleen raised an eyebrow. "I mean, if he's tolerating that horror show, think of how he'd feel about me and all this." She gestured to her face and torso, which, admittedly, were beautiful.

"Don't you even look at my dad," Faith warned. "And for the love of God, please help me find him somebody. We're worried that Lorena will take him for a drive and they'll end up married, and Dad won't quite notice because it's harvest time." She took another sip of her drink.

"I'll keep an eye out," Colleen said. "No one good enough leaps to mind at the moment."

That was the problem. Good enough for Dad meant sort of a Mother Teresa/Meryl Streep vibe. Rare, to say the least. She'd spent three hours on eCommitment/ SeniorLove last night and came up with only one possible candidate.

"And how's your project?" Colleen asked. "The thingie? The barn?"

"Well, I've been tramping around our land for the past two days, taking photos, doing land grade studies, water drainage tests. Get that look off your face. It's fascinating stuff."

"So this is a building for weddings and stuff?"

"Yep. But there are plenty of great places to get married or have a party around here, so the barn has to be special. That's what I'm calling it. The Barn at Blue Heron. Do you love it?"

"I do! Very classy." Colleen smiled. "So you're back, Faith! You're here! This is so great. I've missed having you around. You're staying for two months?"

"Give or take. I talked to Liza last night and get the impression that Wonderful Mike is living there."

"Don't let him kick you out. I love having a place in Frisco."

"San Francisco. Only the tourists call it Frisco."

"I stand corrected, you snob." She waved to the server—they'd gotten their drinks at the bar from Jessica Dunn, who'd barely said hello, but this guy was male, and as such, nearly fell over himself running to the table.

"Hi, Colleen," he said warmly. "Haven't seen you in a while. You look incredible." He ignored Faith completely and leaned against the table, his ass on Faith's bread plate. This was the problem with having a beautiful nymph for a friend. Men swarmed around Colleen like mosquitoes around a hemophiliac. "I get off in an hour," the waiter added.

"Great!" Colleen said, tossing her dark hair back so he could see her boobs a bit better. "Do I know you? You're very cute."

The waiter made a huffy noise and straightened up. Faith pushed the plate away with the blunt end of her knife. "You don't remember me?" the waiter asked. "Wow."

"Why? Did we have a baby together? Are we secretly married? Wait, didn't I give you a kidney?" Colleen smiled as she spoke, and Faith sensed the waiter softening.

"You're such a tramp," he said warmly.

"Don't hate me because I'm beautiful," Colleen said, batting her eyelashes. "Can we get another round?"

"I also need another bread plate," Faith said.

The waiter ignored her. "Greg. My name is Greg."

"Greg." Colleen said the word like she was tasting it. "Can we get another round, Greg? Time's a-wastin'. And at *my* bar, I wouldn't keep the customer waiting." O'Rourke's was indeed the place to be, home of the best wine list in town as well as seventeen different microbrews and fantabulous nachos to boot. They'd come to Hugo's because Colleen wouldn't be able to talk if she was at her own place.

Plus, Faith was sort of easing back into Manningsport. And hiding from Jeremy, let's be honest, who was a regular at O'Rourke's. Not only was Jeremy the town doctor, he also gave to every charity that came a-knocking, sponsored four Little League teams and owned a vineyard, employing about a dozen people. He was probably the most popular man in town, if not on Planet Earth.

"Another round it is," Greg said, touching the back of Colleen's hand. "On the house to make up for the delay." Because, yes, she was that beautiful, she could stab him in the eye with her fork, and he'd still want to take her home.

"You're a witch or something," Faith said as the waiter walked away. "I'm filled with admiration."

"I may have slept with him this summer. Images are coming back to me. A white shag rug, a crisp, dry Riesling, from Blue Heron, of course... Anyway, have you run into any old friends or enemies?"

"Jessica Dunn is shooting me the death stare as we speak," Faith said. "Is she still slutty?"

"Can't say that I know. Have you seen anyone else?"

"Theresa DeFilio. She's expecting again. Isn't that nice?"

"So nice. And what about anyone else?" Colleen asked, narrowing her pretty eyes. "Anyone male who used to be engaged to you whose name starts with, oh, I don't know...*J?*"

Faith sighed. "I emailed him, okay? Are you proud? We're getting together next week."

Colleen sighed. "Do you still talk to his parents?"

Faith nodded. "Yep. We had lunch down in Pacific Grove last month."

"You're a saint."

"That's true. But if someone calls me 'poor thing' one more time, I may go postal and kill everyone around me. Except children and dogs. And old people. And you. And Connor. Fine, I won't kill anyone. But it's driving me crazy."

"I know!" Colleen said happily. "I'm suddenly really popular, too. Even more popular, I should say. People come in and plunk themselves down and say, 'Coll, is she…' tragic pause '…*okay?*' And I say, 'Sure! Why? Oh, you mean because Dr. Perfect dumped her at the altar? Ancient history, friend! She barely remembers.'"

"Thank you!" Faith said. "I've been getting these looks every time I go out. Did you see how Hugo came out to talk to me? First time ever." She took a slug of her martini. "I've been coming here all my life, and the owner only just spoke to me today."

"Don't worry, hon," Colleen said. "The gossips will find something else to talk about. Someone's wife will cheat or someone will embezzle from the library board and they'll all think about something other than you and Jeremy."

"We can only hope," Faith said.

Greg brought them their drinks *and* some cute little egg rolls, smiling at Colleen and ignoring Faith, who swiped another bread plate from an empty table.

"Hey, speaking of the library," Faith said, "Julianne Kammer, remember her? Skinny, brown hair, very nice, threw up in seventh grade during the math test?"

"Yes, I remember. I'm not the one who's been living on the left coast, honey."

"Right," Faith said. "Well, she asked me to do a job

while I'm here in town. The little courtyard behind the children's wing. I'm gonna have a little maze, see. Kids love that stuff. And I said I'd do it for free. Because I'm so nice."

"And a little drunk, am I right? How is it that a Holland can't hold her liquor?"

"I'm a throwback to my Puritan ancestors." Hmm. Yes. She might be slurring a little.

"So is the time right for you to come back permanently? Frisco was never supposed to be your forever home."

"San Francisco."

"Right, right, please forgive me. Hold that thought, I have to hit the ladies' room." Colleen got up, leaving Faith alone.

Faith took another sip of her martini, despite her increasingly numb tongue, and glanced around. Hugo's had been a good choice; it was quieter here, designed more for the tourist industry than a year-round, townie kind of place. The view of the lake was gorgeous, the tablecloths were crisp and white, sprigs of orchids in little vases. A group was just being seated; they'd been at Blue Heron today. Faith had filled in at the gift shop and recognized the pink teddy bear sweatshirt on one woman. Otherwise, Hugo's held no one she recognized, other than Jessica Dunn, who was a big meanie.

Faith and Jeremy used to come here. They had a special table, right over there by the window, where they'd talk and hold hands and occasionally kiss. Sometimes Levi would come, too, to see Jessica Dunn (known as Jessica Does back in high school). It was always a little awkward when the four (or three) of them hung out. Jessica had never liked Faith…and neither had Levi, for that matter.

While Faith had wholeheartedly believed that every girl on earth should have a boyfriend exactly like Jeremy Lyon, an odd charge filled the air when Levi was around, and it only grew when Jessica joined them. Jeremy was much more attractive (Faith always thought of him as an exotic prince, with his swarthy skin and dark, dark eyes), but Levi had something Jeremy didn't. Heterosexuality, she would learn.

But back in high school, Levi just made her nervous. He'd look at Jessica with those sleepy green eyes, his straight, dark blond hair always slightly messy, and you just *knew* those two were doing it—unlike herself and Jeremy, who were much more, uh, virtuous.

Once, Faith had caught Levi and Jessica making out in Hugo's coatroom, and it had stopped her in her tracks, the lazy hunger in that kiss, slow and deep and unhurried. Levi had looked like a man years before the rest of the boys—thickly muscled arms and big hands that were the speculation of every female at Manningsport High. Then those hands had slid down Jess's back, pulling her hips close against his own in an unmistakably sexual move, his mouth never leaving Jessica's as he leaned into her.

Holy hormones.

Faith had whirled around and hightailed back to the table and her boyfriend, her perfect, loving, protective Jeremy. Her face had been hot, her hands shaking. Crikey, she'd hoped they hadn't seen her. That little display had been so…crass. Yes. Crass.

Back then, she'd thought the reason Jeremy never kissed her like that was because they truly loved each other. It was something more pure and special than simple lust, that…that *rutting* that Levi and Jessica surely did.

Right.

"I hate that bathroom," Colleen said, pulling Faith out of the bog of memories. "It's freezing, first of all, and those automatic toilets are dangerous, like they could suck down an entire child." She sat back down. "Hey, did you notice I'm wearing a push-up bra, Holland? For you. Connor always says women get more dressed up for each other than for men."

"It's true. I'm wearing a Microfiber Slim-Nation undergarment for you."

"Really? Just for me? No wonder you're my best friend."

"You're welcome. But you always wear a push-up bra."

"You have a point. But I'm wearing glittery eye shadow, see?" Colleen batted her long, black, completely natural and totally unfair lashes for Faith to admire.

Suddenly, the back of Faith's neck prickled. She felt it first, that reverberation in her stomach, then heard it.

Jeremy's voice.

Oh, God, he had the *best* voice, low and warm and always with a laugh behind it, as if he found everyone and everything utterly wonderful.

"The time has come," Colleen confirmed.

"No! No, no, no. I'm, I'm not ready. I hate this sweater." Faith swallowed. "Coll, what do I do? What do I do?"

"Um…go say hi?"

"I can't! I have to lose fifteen pounds! Plus, I'm not ready. I have to…prepare."

Colleen laughed. "Just bite the bullet! You look great."

"No. Really. Not yet." She risked a glance at *him*— broad shoulders, that beautiful black hair, and he was laughing now, oh, crap! All he had to do was turn forty-five degrees, and he'd see her.

"Bathroom," she said, and bolted.

She made it. No one else was in here, praise the Lord. Her heart was doing a fair impression of Secretariat at the Belmont, and there was a good possibility she was about to puke.

Faith caught a glimpse of her face in the mirror. She *definitely* wasn't ready. First of all, the fifteen pounds. And her hair was dopey today. Also, she'd maybe put on some glittery eye shadow and something sexier than a black wrap sweater that looked like something a Mennonite would wear to a funeral. Honestly, what had she been thinking when she bought it? It wasn't even low-cut.

No. She had to prepare, because if she was going to see He Who Left Her at the Altar, she was going to look amazing *and* have some remarks planned. Not have two martinis inside her, and look at this! A blob of egg roll on her boob, and Colleen had said *nothing!* Some friend.

Okay. She'd just call Colleen, ask her to pay the bill and then let her know when Jeremy wasn't looking, and she'd bolt to freedom.

Futtocks. She'd left her purse (and phone) at the table.

Well. She had to pee, anyway. Terror did that to her. Going into the stall, she unwound her sweater—the Microfiber Slim-Nation undergarment (try saying that five times fast) required that she practically strip naked to use the bathroom—and wrestled up her undergarment. The martinis, while relaxing and excellent, didn't help her in the grace and coordination department, let alone the slutty, high-heeled boots she'd donned for Colleen.

Men never had to deal with this, Faith thought. Men didn't hide in bathrooms and wrestle microfiber and pantyhose. Totally not fair. Men had it easy. Did men get bikini waxed and wear uncomfortable underwear? No, they did not. Faith would bet her life that a man had invented thongs. Men sucked.

As she yanked the Microfiber Slim-Nation undergarment back into position, she reached for her sweater—so complicated! She got one arm in, couldn't find the other one, groped, missed…and all of a sudden, heard the roar of the child-sucking toilet. There was a tug on her arm, and Faith staggered back, watching in horror as her sweater peeled off and disappeared halfway down the toilet, one black arm dangling out like a dead snake.

Colleen had been right. The toilet was on steroids.

"Well, this…bites," she announced, her voice echoing. Her sweater was in the *toilet* and obviously she wasn't going to wear it. She picked up the dry sleeve and gave a tentative tug. *Whoosh*—there was the damn sensor again, and just like that, the sweater was gone.

And Faith was alone in the bathroom in a red skirt, slutty boots, a black 36-D push-up bra and beige Microfiber Slim-Nation undergarment slip that stopped under her boobage, the only reason she could still fit into this outfit.

She was trapped. Wait, wait…she had a raincoat in Colleen's car; Coll had driven tonight, and it had looked like rain, but it *hadn't* rained, so she'd left it in the car. There. A plan. She'd just call Colleen, ask her to get the raincoat, bring it in, then they could flee like the wind. Also, she should stop drinking martinis.

She turned for her purse. Dang. Right, it was back at the table.

Faith chewed on her lip for a second, then glanced down and adjusted her right breast. Okay. Time to summon the cavalry.

She tiptoed to the door—why tiptoe, who knew?—and peeked out. To see the actual dining room, she was going to have to leave the bathroom, go down the hallway a few steps and take her chances. But she should be able to flag down Colleen, who, after all, might possibly remember that her oldest friend was in distress.

She opened the door. No one was in sight. One step out. Another step. She crossed her arms over her chest, then over her Microfiber Slim-Nation undergarment. Which did she want to hide more, the boobage, or the fat-squishing undergarment? The Microfiber Slim-Nation undergarment it was. Another step. She could see three empty tables, but the noise level had escalated. Another tour bus, most likely. One more step and, yes, she could see her purse. Faith leaned forward a little more, ready to hiss at her friend to come save her.

But no.

Colleen wasn't there. Where the heck—oh, great. She was at the bar, flirting with Greg, the waiter.

And here came a little old lady with a cane.

Without thinking, Faith scrambled back to the bathroom, the air cool on her bare shoulders, and leaped into the farthest stall from the door. God, this was *so* embarrassing! She stood there, waiting for the woman to take care of business. The seconds ticked past. It was getting chilly, too.

Finally! The toilet roared, the woman exited the stall, then washed her hands (thoroughly, Faith was pained to note). A paper towel. And another one. And one more. Then came the blessed sound of the door squeaking open and wheezing closed.

It dawned abruptly that Faith could've asked the woman to get Colleen. She dashed out of the stall, causing the toilet to flush again, but the woman was gone…

fast little thing, considering the cane and all. Faith tip-toed as fast as she could down the little hall, hoping to catch her. Nope. Speedy Gonzalez, Senior Edition, was nowhere to be seen. And still no Colleen.

Jeremy, however, was just sitting down at the table nearest the hallway.

Cursing silently, she whirled and dashed again before he could see her, back to the sanctuary of the bathroom.

You know what? It was time to go. There was no exit back here, but there *was* a window in the last stall. Faith could slip out; it couldn't be too high from the back of the restaurant. She'd jump down, get her damn raincoat out of Colleen's car, find a pay phone, if the one by the post office still worked, call Colleen and tell her to get her flirtatious ass out of Hugo's.

It was a good plan, Faith thought, as far as this type of *sans*-clothing nightmare went. She stood carefully on the toilet seat (it flushed yet again, the hungry beast). The window wasn't huge; she did a quick assessment of her boobage and the width of the window. Fairly close, but she could make it. She'd have to squeeze out, rather than climb. But, hey, why not? When was too much hu-miliation really too much? Microfiber Slim-Nation un-dergarments and sweater-eating toilets were still better than angry wives and adorable toddlers calling you a whore, right?

She stuck her head out the window. Five or six cars, including Colleen's, and no people. It would be so, so great if her dad just happened to be pulling up at this moment and could save her. But, no, just a dog near the Dumpster. Feral? Savage? Savage and feral? "Hey, cutie," she said, trying to evaluate its ferocity. It wagged. "Good puppy," she said. The dog wagged again. A yellow Lab. Not feral.

It was nearly dark, thankfully. Perfect. Time to be Spider-man.

Faith put the heels of her hands on the window ledge and gave a little jump, using her arms as leverage as she maneuvered out the window. Head clear, shoulders clear, boobs clear, stomach clear. Then her momentum stopped abruptly.

Ass not clear.

She wriggled again. Nothing.

The dog barked in delight, sensing some fun coming on.

"Shh," Faith said. "Quiet, sweetie." She gave a flop, rather than a wriggle, figuring force might win over torque, or vice versa. Ground her hips down and pushed up with her arms. Kicked her legs, which had nothing to push against. Twisted and pulled. Twisted and flopped. Heaved. Pushed. Grunted.

Nada. Nyet. Nuttin.

Okay, fine. She'd have to go back in and think of something else.

But apparently "in" was not an option, either. Faith was stuck like a cork in a bottle.

"Okay, shit," she said aloud. Her head was a little dizzy from the two martinis or the fact that her blood supply was being choked off by the window, or both.

Pushing with her arms, she sucked in her stomach, and tried with more gusto. At least the Microfiber Slim-Nation undergarment was slippery. Oh, goody, she got another inch. Glanced back at her butt. Almost there. Of course, if her butt did suddenly clear the window, she'd fall right on her head and break her neck. *Woman Who Didn't Know Fiancé Was Gay Falls to Her Death Wearing Microfiber Slim-Nation Undergarment.*

"Come on!" she said a bit more forcefully. The dog

barked again, then jumped up, its paws against the outside wall of Hugo's. "Help me, Lassie," Faith muttered. She wriggled some more to no avail.

Then the glare of headlights washed over her as a Manningsport police car pulled into the parking lot.

CHAPTER FIVE

As a cop, Levi Cooper saw his fair share of odd things. Victor Iskin had all his pets sent to the taxidermist after they died. Sometimes, he'd invite Levi in to visit, and Levi would sit there, surrounded by motionless cats, dogs and a couple of hamsters. Methalia Lewis liked to show him how fat she was getting by hoisting up her shirt and grabbing her stomach in both hands. But Methalia was eighty-two years old and laughed merrily while doing it, then would inevitably offer him some pie. Joey Kilpatrick kept his gallstones, six in all, in a little glass bowl on the kitchen table, and liked to recount just how horrified the surgeon had been at the state of his infected gallbladder.

But Faith Holland's head and scantily clad torso hanging out of a window...black bra, too...that was a sight. He turned off the lights and sat there a moment as she wriggled in the fading evening glow.

Guess he should get out of the car. Then again, that was a pretty great view.

He wasn't one to smile much, as he was often told by Emmaline, the administrative assistant he still regretted hiring. But this...yeah. He felt a smirk coming on. Getting out of the car, he walked over to the restaurant window, which was about ten feet off the ground. Good thing Faith wasn't a little wisp of a thing; she might've broken something falling if she hadn't been wedged in there.

"Is there a problem here, ma'am?" he asked.

"Nope. Just taking in the view," Faith said, not looking at him.

"Me, too." Yep. He was smirking. "Nice night, isn't it?"

"It is. It's beautiful."

He nodded. "What happened to your shirt?"

One of her arms suddenly flew across her gorgeous rack as if she was just aware that he was getting quite a show. "I, um…I had a wardrobe malfunction."

"I see." The arm blocking his view couldn't stay there long; she needed it to brace herself or risk flopping. He waited. She glared. A second later, her arm went back again, treating him to the stellar view once more. *Very* nice, all that plump, creamy bodaciousness encased in a low-cut bra. Not that he particularly liked Faith Holland, but he did like breasts, and it had been a while since he'd seen such an exemplary pair. "So, what happened?"

Her face grew red. "I flushed my sweater down the toilet."

"That happens to me all the time." This earned another glare. "So you decided to climb out the window?"

"Mmm-hmm."

"Where you are now stuck."

"Wow. Those analytical powers of yours are just stunning, Levi. No wonder you're a cop."

That comment just bought her a few more seconds in the window. "Well, if there's nothing you need, I'll be on my way. You have a nice night, ma'am."

He started to get back in the car.

"Levi! Don't go! And don't call me ma'am. I'm still a miss. Help me out here. Aren't you a public servant?"

"I am." He raised his eyebrows and waited.

"So? Give me a hand and stop being such a hemorrhoid."

"Should half-dressed people wedged in windows call an officer of the law names, do you think?"

She huffed. "Officer Cooper, would you please help me?"

"It's Chief Cooper, and, yes."

He got back in the cruiser and pulled it up so the bumper almost touched the building, threw the car in Park and got out again. "I really have to wonder how climbing out the window seemed like the best decision," he said, climbing on the hood of the cruiser. "Is Jeremy in there?"

"Just help me," she ground out.

He'd take that as a yes.

They were at eye level—well, in Faith's case, eye and torso level. It looked as if she'd been shot through the wall. She was stuck, all right. Short of smearing her with butter (*Don't go there,* he warned himself), there was no way he was going to be able to do this without touching her. Which was always tricky, if you were the chief of police. Sexual harassment and all that.

"Okay," he said. "I'll just…is it all right, Faith, if I hold on to your arms and pull you out?"

"Yes! Isn't it obvious? Were you planning to use the Force instead?"

He cocked an eyebrow. "I think you should be a little nicer, Holland," he said, "given that I could call the fire department right now. Gerard Chartier lives for this sort of thing. And isn't your nephew a volunteer?"

"I will castrate you if you call the fire department. You're bad enough. Just help me."

He took hold of her upper arms and immediately chastised himself. Her skin was freezing, as the night had gotten cool. "Count of three," he said, bracing a foot against the building. "One…two…three."

He pulled, and out she came, half falling against him, all soft and white and plump in the gloom. He took a step back as soon as humanly possible, ending contact, and jumped off the hood of the cruiser, then looked back up at her.

"What is that?" he asked, tilting his head. She was wearing some kind of weird, beige, shiny tank top or something that ended just below her bra.

"It's a slip. Stop looking and don't you dare say another word."

He offered his hand as she climbed off the cruiser—imagine writing up that report. *The half-naked woman then fell off my cruiser because I didn't want to touch her.* Her hand was cold, too. "Want my coat?" he asked, shrugging out of it.

Faith ignored him, going to Colleen O'Rourke's red MINI Cooper. She tried the door. It was locked; that was good, as there'd been a few car break-ins lately. She sighed heavily, then turned back to him. He held out his jacket. "Thank you," she said, pulling it on without looking at him. "Can I use your phone, please?"

"Sure." He handed it over and watched as she dialed.

At that moment, Colleen's face appeared in the bathroom window. "What the hell are you doing out here, Faith?" she asked, starting to laugh. "Did you actually climb out the window? Hey, Levi."

"Colleen."

"I really needed you five minutes ago," Faith said.

"Can you please get my purse so we can get the hell out of here? Pretty please?"

Colleen obeyed, and before too long, Faith handed him back his jacket and put on her own raincoat. They were gabbling away, laughing about the incident now. "See you soon, Chief," Colleen said with a smile.

He nodded. Faith waved but didn't quite meet his eyes.

Then they drove off, and though his shift was technically over, Levi walked over to the station. May as well finish some paperwork.

His jacket smelled like Faith Holland's perfume. Vanilla or something.

Something you'd eat for dessert.

CHAPTER SIX

WHEN FAITH AND JEREMY BROKE up three weeks before the senior prom, it sent ripples of shock through Manningsport High. Who would be prom king and queen, if not the golden couple? Had Jeremy found someone else? If so, who was the lucky girl?

When Jeremy glumly informed Levi that he and Faith were "taking a break," Levi asked if he wanted to talk about it and was relieved when Jeremy said no.

It was a strange time. All anyone could talk about was where they'd be in the fall. A couple kids were going to the community college, a couple would be going straight into the workforce, but most were headed away and talked endlessly about the need to buy supplies, clothes, a new computer.

As the only recruit in their high school class (though Tiffy Ames was going to the Air Force Academy, and George Shea was Navy ROTC), Levi didn't have the same issues. His father had cemented the impossibility of college, and the Army felt like a good fit. But in addition to the sense of pride he already felt about serving in the military, a melancholy was descending. He tried to spend a night or two watching TV with his mom each week, knowing she was more worried than she'd say. He took Sarah fishing and read *Harry Potter* to her, hoping in the back of his mind that if something happened, she'd remember him. She was only eight.

He was ready. He wanted to serve, figured he'd be good at it. He'd passed all his tests, and his recruiter thought he might make a good sniper, based on the psych profile and his innate skill with a gun. Whatever the case, chances were high that Levi would be on the fast track to Afghanistan.

So things like Faith and Jeremy's relationship status tended not to matter, aside from the fact that his buddy was glum.

Ted and Elaine Lyon had hired him for the spring. They made Jeremy do the same thing, though they didn't pay him; said he was heir to the land, even if he did spit in their eye and decide to become a doctor (this statement was usually followed with a slap on the back or a hug). This week, however, Jeremy and Elaine had gone to California to visit relatives, so Levi was on his own. "If you don't mind working solo," Ted said, "the merlot trellises need checking. You just tie up the vines so the grapes won't fall off or touch the ground. You've done that before, right?"

"Yes, sir. Jeremy and I did that last week in the Rieslings," Levi answered. It wasn't exactly brain surgery.

"Great! Thanks, son." The lady from the tasting room gave him a bag lunch and a big bottle of water, and Levi headed to the western edge of the vineyard, close to Blue Heron, where the land got pretty steep, not too far from the woods.

He worked from the top of the hill downward, one row at a time. The sun beat on his back, and he pulled off his T-shirt after fifteen minutes. It was hot for early May, and he was glad he wore shorts. Might hit the lake for a swim later on, no matter how cold the water was.

He'd been working a good hour and was already damp with sweat when he heard the rumble of a truck.

It was John Holland's red pickup, identifiable anywhere due to its age and general filth…always mud-splattered and crusty. It stopped, and an enormous Golden retriever bounded out, followed by Princess Super-Cute.

She wore cutoff shorts, a white sleeveless shirt, the tails tied under her breasts, and a blue bandanna on her head. Levi felt a generic stir of lust. *Nothing personal, Holland,* he thought. He'd been stealing looks at her chest since he was fourteen.

The dog ran over to him, tail wagging, and barked once, then collapsed, rolling on his back. "Hey, buddy," Levi said, rubbing the beast's stomach.

Faith shaded her eyes and looked at him. "Hi," she called tentatively. "What are you doing?"

"Tying up vines. You?"

She smiled. "Same thing." She held up an apron, then tied it on. "My sister's cracking the whip." She paused. "I guess Smiley likes you."

Smiley. Leave it to Faith Holland to have a dog named Smiley. Speaking of, the dog apparently had had enough of a scratch, because he leaped up and went romping through the vineyard rows, tail waving.

Faith, however, came to within two rows of where he was, and he braced himself for questions about Jeremy, or an explanation, or a discussion. Girls, he well knew, liked to talk about their feelings until they had nothing left to say, at which point they'd start repeating themselves.

Instead, she bent over and started doing exactly what he was. Except she was better at it. The apron held twist ties, and she didn't have to check each shoot the way he did. She was kind of a pro, actually.

And when she bent over, there was that mighty rack

on display. He didn't have a lot of use for Faith Holland, but, man, that was a nice pair.

She glanced up. Busted. "I thought you were more of the princess type," he said as explanation. "Run out of townies to do the grunt work?"

She just laughed. "If you're a Holland, you're a farmer," she said. "If you're a farmer, you work. You don't just gaze out over the fields and sip wine." She gave him a knowing look and twisted on another tie, her fingers fast and clever.

"Guess I was wrong."

"Guess you were."

She bent over again, and the lust felt much less generic. "So this is the property line, huh?" he asked.

"Yep. See that stone marker up there? That's what divides Blue Heron from Lyon's Den." She secured three vines while she was talking, reminding him to drag his eyes off her breasts and get back to work.

She moved steadily, bending, sometimes kneeling, holding a cluster of the dusky grapes in her hand from time to time, and somehow, out here in the field, everything she did looked unabashedly sexual. She was soft and round and sweaty now, her red hair in pigtails, basically any male's fantasy of a farm girl.

Jeremy's girlfriend, dude, his conscience chided.

Except they weren't together anymore.

"So how you doing, Holland?" he asked, surprising himself.

She glanced over at him, then stood up, taking the bandanna off her head and wiping her face, then retying it. Yep. Everything she did looked like she was on a *Penthouse* photo shoot. Except for the clothes. If she'd take off the clothes, things would be perfect.

Damn.

"I'm fine. Thanks for asking."

What did he ask? Oh, right. Jeremy. Maybe he'd finally come out of the closet. Or maybe she'd guessed.

"When do you leave for basic training?" Putting her hands on the small of her back, she stretched, her breasts straining against her shirt.

"Uh, July twentieth."

"Are you nervous?"

He started to say no and put forth some of the bravado expected. "A little," he heard himself say. "I've never really been away before."

"Me, neither."

"You're going to Virginia, right?"

"Virginia Tech. It seems like a great school, but now all I can think of is how far it is from here." She gave him a funny little smile, half sad, half embarrassed.

"You'll do great. Everybody likes you." Aw. Wasn't he being super-sweet?

"Not everybody," she said, twisting those little ties with amazing speed.

"No?"

"You don't."

Well, shit. "Why do you say that?" he asked.

She laughed. "It's pretty obvious, Levi," she said. "You think I'm spoiled and irritating and ditzy. Am I right?"

Right now, I think you're edible. But yeah, I think you should be able to tell the difference between a straight guy and a gay guy. "Pretty much."

"Well, you've always been a snob."

"Me?"

"Yeah," she said.

"You're the one with the big house on the Hill." He tied up a vine.

"Doesn't make me a snob." She flipped a braid over her shoulder.

"And I am?"

"Yeah." Her voice was matter-of-fact. "You never talked to me till this year, and even then, it's only because of Jeremy. And even then, only when you have to."

He didn't answer, just tied up another vine. "So everyone has to adore you, is that it?"

"No. But we've known each other since third grade. We were both in that special reading club that Mrs. Spritz had, remember? And I invited you to our Halloween party."

Oh, yeah. Pumpkin carving and apple bobbing and a haunted hay ride. That'd been a fun night, even if it had been weird, being in the famed Holland house. "Right."

"But I wasn't cool enough for you to talk to. And when my mother died, you were the only one in our class not to write me a note."

He felt his face flush. "Quite a memory you got there, Holland," he muttered, tying up a few more branches.

"Well, you always remember people who hurt your feelings."

Oh, the poor little drama queen. "So you wanted to come to the trailer park and play?"

"One time," she continued, "I sat next to you at lunch, not to be near you, just because it was the empty seat next to Colleen. And you got up and moved, like you couldn't stand to sit near me." She stood up and put her hands on her hips, and the lust stirred again, even as she was listing his sins. "So." Her voice was calm with just a little edge to it. "Who's the real snob here, Levi?"

Girls. Way too complicated. He missed Jess, who more or less used him for sex. At least she was direct.

He bent over and tied up another dangling vine, lifting up the grapes carefully. "You're not very smart in the ways of the world, are you, rich girl?" he asked.

"I wouldn't say that."

He gave her a look. "I would."

"Why?"

He remembered how she and her mother used to come down to West's Trailer Park once in a while with a bag of clothes for Jessica. Lady Bountiful and her little angel, visiting the poor. Sometime around fifth grade or so, he'd found Jess hiding in the little cave of scrub bushes they used as a fort, waiting for the Hollands to leave. She'd been crying. Even then, he understood. Being poor was one thing; having the people on the Hill decide you were their charity case was another. Levi's mom may have had to work two jobs, and money was always a worry, but they'd done okay. Scrappy, his mom liked to say.

But the Dunns had been truly poor. Food stamps and electricity turned off kind of poor. No way they could turn away a bag of nice clothes and coats. Small wonder Jess hated Faith.

His silence seemed to make Faith mad. She grabbed a vine with gusto, her movements sharp, rather than flowing now. "It's funny that you think we're rich. We're not. We're not even close."

"I grew up in a trailer, Faith. Your idea of rich and mine are pretty different."

"Which made it okay for you to hate me all these years."

"I don't hate you, for crying out loud."

"No. You just ignored me and made me feel like a lump, and God forbid we should ever be friends."

"You wanna be friends? Fine. We're friends. Let's play Barbies and go to the movies."

She rolled her eyes and bent down to tie another vine. "I never understood why Jeremy thinks you walk on water. I think you're a jackass."

"Now, see? I want to be friends, and you're calling me names."

"Jackass."

"Does this mean no tea party later on?"

She glared. He grinned.

And then she blushed, her cheeks growing pink, color staining her throat and chest. Her eyes fluttered down his bare torso. Then she jerked her gaze back to the vine and fumbled for a tie. Dropped it.

Well, well, well. Levi's smile grew.

"You're doing a crappy job," she said, glancing back at his row. "You need to use more ties, or the grapes will be too heavy, and you'll lose the fruit."

"Is that right," he murmured. Actually, his work had gotten spotty only since she'd arrived.

She came over to his row and demonstrated. "This one, see, it's off the ground for now, but when the grapes mature, they'll get too heavy. See?"

"Yep." She smelled like grapes and vanilla and dirt and sunshine and sweat. The stir of lust became a throb.

"Tie it up higher," she said, kneeling down to demonstrate. Faith Holland, on her knees in front of him. How could he not picture what he was picturing? "Just go back along what you've already done and make sure you got everything."

"Yes, ma'am," he said. Her shirt brushed his ribs as she stood up and went back to her row.

Keep your eyes to yourself. And get going. The Lyons are paying you. You can jerk off later.

The mental advice worked for an hour.

She was much faster and steadier than he was, he had to give her that. He looked at the sky, which was a perfect, endless blue, and decided it was time to eat.

"You want some lunch, rich girl?" he called. She was twenty yards or so ahead of him.

"I brought my own," she answered.

"Then do you want to eat with me? Now that we're BFFs?"

"Such a jackass."

"Is that a yes?" He lowered his chin and gave her a patient look, something that had always worked well with girls.

"Sure," she grumbled.

Hey, idiot, his brain chided. *She was dating your best friend a few days ago. What are you doing?*

But the facts were blurring fast. First of all, there was the whole Jeremy-shouldn't-be-dating-a-girl thing. Speaking of Jeremy, he wasn't even in the Empire State at the moment. Then there was the breakup, or whatever they wanted to call it.

And let's not forget the sight of a dewy and dirty Faith Holland in cutoff jeans and a shirt tied under her generous chest, and the fact that she was irritated with him, which Levi had learned generally meant a girl was interested.

She came over to him, taking out her braids and retying her hair in a ponytail. "There's a nice place about five minutes from here. By the falls. Do you know it?"

He shook his head, looking at her steadily. She had blue eyes. He never really noticed before. Freckles.

She swallowed.

Oh, yeah. Faith Holland was feeling some feelings.

"Come on, then," she said. They walked up to her

father's truck, the dog running ahead. Levi grabbed his shirt from where he'd dropped it and pulled it on.

John Holland's truck smelled pleasantly of old coffee and oil, just as dirty inside as the outside, the dashboard and seats covered in dried mud and dust. Smiley jumped, his feathery tail hitting Levi in the face. "Sit, pooch," he said, and the dog obeyed, his furry side pressed against Levi's arm. Seemed like the Hollands always had a Golden retriever or two. There was always one in their brochures.

"You guys breed these monsters?" he asked Faith as she started the truck and put it in gear. The fact that she could drive a made-in-America pickup truck with a standard transmission only increased her hot factor.

"We belong to the Golden Retriever Rescue League," she answered. Smiley licked her face as if thanking her.

"Just another act of mercy from the great Holland family," Levi said.

"Jeesh! Stop being such a pain or I'll push you out of the truck and eat your lunch."

The truck jolted and rocked over the grassy, rutted paths that ran between fields, causing Levi to practically crack his head on the roof of the truck (but also treating him to a great view of Faith's bouncing cleavage). After about five minutes, they stopped at the edge of a field that was being cleared…the Holland family owned a ton of land. Woods were thick on one side.

Faith grabbed a blanket from behind her seat and a thermal lunch box (Hello Kitty, could've called that one). The dog raced off into the woods, and she followed on the little path without waiting for Levi.

Birds called and fluttered in the branches. From somewhere not too far away came the rush and splash of a stream. Levi tried to imagine looking out and seeing land, acres and acres of field and forest, all the way down to the lake, and knowing it was yours, and had been in your family since America had been a baby. Levi's mother's family was from Manningsport, too, but there were people who'd been around, and then there were founding families.

Over to the left was the ruin of an old stone barn, the rocks covered in lichen. A sapling grew in the middle, the roof long gone.

"You coming?" Faith called from up ahead.

Thick mounds of moss blanketed the ground, and the leaves were so green the air seemed tinted with it. They passed a huge grove of birch trees, the white bark glowing, and the edges of hemlocks brushed Levi's cheek as he walked. He slapped a mosquito, and a chipmunk peeped and ran across the narrow path.

The sound of rushing water was louder now. Faith had spread out the blanket on a rock and sat down. Juicy as a ripe peach. An image of her under him, legs around him, practically made him stagger.

He really had to stop thinking this way.

They were at the edge of a deep gorge, a waterfall cascading into a round pool about twenty feet below them. He wished he had a camera so he could look at this picture when he was deployed, baking in the sun of Iraq or Afghanistan or wherever the Army would send him. He'd show it around. *This is where I'm from. I had lunch with a pretty girl right on this rock.*

"Nice," he said, sitting next to Faith.

"The pool's pretty deep," she said, pointing as she took a sandwich out of her lunch box. "Maybe twenty, thirty feet. Jack says it's bigger underwater. Like a bell. He used to jump off that rock there."

"Did you?"

She glanced at him and took a bite of her sandwich. "No. Too scary for me. Honor never did, either. Said we'd already—well. No reason to risk your life just for the sake of it, you know?"

"Sure."

They ate in silence, the dog coming up to beg for a scrap. Birds twittered, the waterfall roared. Beside him, Faith finished her sandwich and seemed content to just watch the water. The mist of the falls had coated her hair in tiny beads, making her look like a slightly pornographic woodland fairy.

"Well," Levi said, suddenly aware that he'd been staring at Faith for too long, all sorts of hot, red thoughts pulsating through him. "I'm going swimming. Which rock do I jump off?"

"Oh, Levi, don't," Faith said, jerking to attention. "My phone's back in the truck. What if you hit your head or something? A tourist got a concussion a couple years ago. My brother broke his arm when he was fifteen. It's not safe. Please don't."

It was kind of nice, her begging for his well-being. Then again, that pool was frickin' gorgeous. He shrugged. "I'll try not to break anything." He stripped off his shirt, well aware that he was a pretty fine specimen. Pink crept into her cheeks, and she shifted her gaze straight ahead. "You coming, Holland?" It sounded like a proposition.

It was.

"Absolutely not," she said, all prim and proper. "Don't do it. I have to get back to work, anyway. So do you, right? And really, jumping is dangerous."

"I'm going into the Army in two months, Faith. Jumping off that rock is probably less dangerous than an IED or suicide bomber." He winked at her, went to the rock and looked down. The water was green and clear, churning where the falls poured in. "Geronimo," he said, then pushed off.

He went in feet first, shooting down, the water swallowing him, cold and silky and utterly beautiful. Opening his eyes, he could see that Faith was right—the pool expanded underwater by about ten feet, the stone walls like a church. He'd always been a pretty good swimmer, was one of the first into the lake each spring. This, though...this was unbelievable, so smooth and deep and secret. He ran his hand over the stone, amazed and a little sorry that he'd never been here before.

The thought came to him that if he'd been Faith's friend, he might've seen this place years ago.

Then he kicked to the surface, and looked up to see Faith's worried face above him as she peered over the edge. "Come on in, Holland," he called, treading water. "Live a little."

"*Live* is the key word," she said. The dog's face appeared next to hers, looking much happier than she did.

"I'm still alive. Come on. I'll catch you."

"You won't catch me. I'm not a little kid, and it's a twenty foot drop."

"I'll be right here. Don't be scared."

Her expression changed. She wanted to, he could see that. "Rich girls," he called up, swimming over to where a thin outcropping of rock stuck out into the pool, like a natural diving board. He grabbed onto it, aware that it would make his very healthy muscles bunch. "So boring."

"I'm not rich," she said.

"Well, you *are* boring if you just sit there and watch when you could be down here, having fun with me," he said.

She hesitated. "I'm not wearing a bathing suit."

"So?" Oh, yeah, he was making progress. Faith in a wet, white shirt, her red hair streaming down her back… even the cold water wasn't keeping his body from appreciating that image. "Come on, Holland. Do it for me, a young soldier about to leave home to protect your freedom." He grinned up at her, and after a second, her expression changed from worry to something else.

"Fine. But if I die, you have to tell my father in person, okay? And you have to take care of Smiley, because he'll miss me. He sleeps on my bed."

"I promise your dog can sleep with me if you die. Now get in here."

She went to the edge of the rock, and even from his vantage point, he could see her bare toes clenching. Retied her shirt more firmly, hiked up her shorts. "Okay, Private Cooper. Here I come."

Then she jumped, her hair sailing out behind her, eyes screwed shut, fists clenched. She cut into the water about ten feet from him, then popped up almost immediately, her hair in her face, spluttering and coughing.

Levi swam over to her, and she grabbed onto his shoulders instinctively, clutching him hard, her breasts pushing against his bare chest. He put his arm around her waist and swam over to the outcropping, which she grabbed with one hand.

Her other arm stayed around his shoulders, and her legs kicked between his, treading water, her smooth thighs brushing his. She didn't need to hang on to him, but she did. Her heart thudded against his, fast and hard, and he realized she was scared. From the jump, maybe. And maybe she was scared of him…maybe that, too.

"I've got you," he whispered.

This would be it. A moment to take with him, the

feeling of her sweet, wet softness, her cheek against his, treading the clear, pure water as the waterfall gushed and the leaves rustled and sighed.

Faith pulled back a little, her eyelashes starry with water. He could kiss her. He could just lean in an inch or two, and their mouths would be touching, and he'd bet she'd taste so sweet. His hand slid up her ribs, so close to her breast that she sucked in a shaky breath, and lust, hot and heavy, flowed through his blood.

He kissed her as gently as he knew how, not wanting her to push away, wanting only this, just one kiss. Her lips were soft and cool and wet from the water, and he couldn't help himself, he licked her bottom lip, she tasted so good. When she opened her mouth, he wanted a lot more, suddenly starving for the taste of her, abruptly rock hard. He pulled her hips against him, letting her know, and her fingers dug into his shoulders, her tongue answering his, a soft little sound coming from her throat, and it was so, so good he couldn't think, he could just drown here, more than happy to have this be his last day on earth.

Then she broke away, pushing away from him and scrambling up onto the rocks

"I—I—I can't," she said over the rush of the water.

It felt empty without her against him. Empty and cold.

"See, um, Jeremy and I, I mean, we're… We're not really… It's a break. We're not officially… So I can't. I can't kiss anyone else."

"Whatever," he said idly. Except he was furious, all of a sudden. Not just with her, either. With stupid Jeremy, who'd probably never kissed her that way before, who had no idea how. With himself, for kissing his best friend's girl. But, yeah, mostly with her. If she didn't want to kiss him, maybe, just maybe, she shouldn't have been hanging on to him like a spider monkey. She'd *wanted* that kiss, and he'd given it to her, and now she was Polly Purebred again.

Ah, crap. He'd just kissed Jeremy's girlfriend.

"We should get back," she said, her voice tight and pinched. She turned her back to squeeze the water out of her shirt. She did the same to her hair. Her hands were shaking, he noted. She turned around, her shirt clinging to her. If she'd been braless, he might've had to kill himself. As it was, the cold water (and rejection) were doing wonders for his condition. "Levi, I hope you won't be…"

"Mad?"

She hesitated, then nodded.

"Don't worry about it," he said casually.

She bit her lip. "Um…I don't think I'll tell Jeremy about this. I mean, it would just hurt him. Right? So I won't say anything." The plea in her voice was clear— *And you won't either, right?*

He swam to the rocks and hoisted himself out of the water, watching as her eyes scanned him. *That's it, rich girl. Heterosexual male. Enjoy.* He walked over to her and stood very close. "You know, I always did think you were ditzy and spoiled and irritating," he said in a low voice. "But before today, I never thought you were a tease."

With that, he made his way back up to their adorable little picnic area. The dog woofed at his approach and again offered its belly, but this time, Levi ignored him. Instead, he grabbed his shirt and pulled it on, picked up his brown bag and headed back to work for the Lyons, walking through the Holland fields in the bright light and hot sun.

Faith, he noted, didn't return.

That weekend, Jeremy called him, his voice its usual bouncy tone. "How you doing, bud?" he asked. "Wanna hang out?"

"Sure," Levi said. Whatever guilt he'd felt about kissing Jeremy's girlfriend he'd managed to ball up and toss into the dirty laundry area of his conscience. Hell, he told himself, he'd have kissed just about any female under the circumstances. It had just been a bad case of...whatever. "How was California?" he asked.

"It was great," Jeremy said. "And I have some good news. Faith and I are back together."

"Not surprised," Levi said. Like she was gonna dump the golden boy. The star quarterback. The future doctor. The heir to the Lyons' vineyard.

Levi saw Faith at school, of course. Jeremy's angelic girlfriend, who couldn't tell the difference between a guy who wanted to bang her silly and a guy who didn't.

CHAPTER SEVEN

MOST OF THE CALLS Levi had to respond to were pretty mild, and he liked it that way.

This call, however, was one of the livelier calls they'd had this week. On Tuesday, he'd sat out with a radar gun after Carol Robinson had complained about the speed on her road at 2:40 when the high school kids got out of school. Yesterday, he talked to the third-grade class about why drugs were wrong. There'd been a call from Laura Boothby, because she couldn't reach a vase on a high shelf of her flower shop and didn't want to fall by using her stepstool, which her no-good son had promised to fix and hadn't, and would Levi please come over and get it for her? (He had. Figured it was better than finding Laura with a broken hip three days from now.) Last night around eleven, there'd been another call from Suzette Minor—third this month—who'd heard suspicious noises and wanted Levi to come check her house (especially her bedroom). He had, though not with the results she wanted. The whole red swishy nightgown thing, the "Officer, please help me/I'm frightened/My, but you're strong" didn't work on him. He'd been hired to protect and serve, and "serve" did not mean "service."

Most of the calls to the Manningsport Police had more to do with being a good neighbor than any true police work. It didn't hurt that he was a local and, being a decorated veteran, someone who'd become pretty much universally loved. History had a way of fogging over when you were given a medal or two… Ellis Mitchum seemed to have forgotten the time he'd told Levi that his precious Angela wasn't going to get knocked up by some trailer trash like Levi. Now, Ellis loved nothing more than buying him a beer and reminiscing about Vietnam. (Angela, for the record, had gone on to get knocked up by a kid from Corning their senior year.)

Nope, Levi was no longer trailer park trash; when the time had come to hire a cop to help out Chief Griggs, the town council, including old Mr. Holland, just about fell over themselves to accept his application. One year later, the chief retired, and Levi got that job, too. He now presided over Everett Field, his deputy, and Emmaline Neal, the administrative assistant with a penchant for analyzing him. It also meant that Levi earned ten grand more a year, and since his sister was in college, that was welcome.

But, as chief, he had to go on almost every call, too.

"Oh, Chief, please!" Nancy Knox wept. "He's going to kill my baby! Please help!"

"Okay, okay, let me take a look," he said. He crouched down and looked. No murders yet. Everyone looked very calm. Even a little sleepy. "Everett, go to the other side of the porch in case he makes a run for it."

"Yes, sir, Chief. You bet. Going to the other side of the porch right now, roger." Everett paused. "Uh, is that the south or the north side, sir?"

"Just go around the porch, Ev," Levi said, trying to curb his impatience. "Don't let him get away."

"Roger that, Chief. Going to the other side, won't let him get away." Levi heard the click as Everett snapped open his holster.

"Put your gun back!" Levi barked. "For God's sake, Everett. You're gonna hurt someone with that someday."

"Oh, my poor baby! Is she still alive?" Mrs. Knox said. "I can't look! I can't!"

Levi looked back under the porch, where a dog and a chicken were eyeing each other. "She's alive, Mrs. Knox. Don't worry. Come here, pooch. Come on, fella."

The dog wagged and grinned but didn't move. If Levi wasn't mistaken, that was Faith Holland's dog, judging by the size of his enormous head and neon-green plaid collar. The Knoxes lived about a mile down the Hill from the Hollands, and they kept chickens that made up about seven percent of Levi's calls…they were free range, which meant they often wandered onto the road and had once caused a kid to veer off into the ditch. People were always calling to complain.

The chicken seemed just fine—the dog seemed delighted with the bird, which cocked its head and made a funny, burring noise. The dog wagged and panted, covered in dirt.

"Come on, Blue," Levi said. "Come on, buddy."

The dog smiled again. He was a great-looking dog, and dumb as a box of hair. Not that the chicken was Stephen Hawking, mind you. It could've walked out from under the porch at any time.

"Please, Chief. Please save my little baby."

Levi sighed. The Knoxes needed to have kids or cats or monkeys or something. "Okay, I'll go under."

"That dog is vicious." Mrs. Knox wept.

"Want me to call for backup?" Everett asked.

"No, Ev," Levi said. "The dog's fine." Levi had to belly-crawl, using his elbows to pull himself along. His drill sergeant at basic had loved making them do this.

Four tours in Afghanistan, and Levi had never once had to crawl. But here it was, coming in handy.

His cell phone rang. All police calls to the station were transferred to his cell if he was out on a call. "Chief Cooper," he said.

"It's me," his sister said. "I'm home. I couldn't take it another second."

"You gotta be kidding me."

"Is it Baby! Is she dead?" Mrs. Knox shrilled.

"She's not dead," Levi called back.

"Where *are* you?" Sarah demanded.

"I'm working. Why are you home? School started three weeks ago, Sarah, and you've already been back six times."

"I'm homesick, okay? I'm sorry I'm such a pain in your ass, but I hate it there! I need a gap year."

"You're not having a gap year. You're in college, and you're going to finish. Now, I'm busy, so we'll talk when I get home."

"What are you doing?"

"I'm rescuing a chicken."

"I am totally tweeting that. My brother, the hero."

He hung up. Gap year, his ass. She'd go back to college; he'd drive her back tonight…okay, maybe tomorrow morning. And she'd stay in school, she'd do great, and she'd thank him later.

About five more feet of crawling through the dirt—which appeared to be fertilized by the Knox chickens, so, yes, this really was a chickenshit job at the moment—till he could reach the dog. But apparently, the chicken decided there was nothing to fear, because it plunked itself down right against Blue's chest. The dog seemed quite pleased about that, resting his chin on the chicken's back. "They're cuddling," he called.

"What?" Nancy shrieked. "Did you say killing?"

"Cuddling!" Levi shouted back.

"Chief!" Everett shouted. "Are you in danger? I have drawn my weapon! Do you need assistance?"

"Everett! Put that gun away!"

"Roger that, Chief."

Levi sighed. More days than not, he imagined that he would die at the hands of Officer Everett Field's general ineptitude. Alas, Everett was the only child of Marian Field, Manningsport's mayor, and basically had a job for life. He wasn't a bad kid, and he had a wicked case of hero worship where Levi was concerned, but he drew his weapon roughly six times a day.

"Blue, old buddy," he said, "I'm gonna relieve you of this bird, if you don't mind." Blue wagged again, and Levi took the sleeping chicken in his hands, then reverse-crawled out. He was filthy. His shift was almost over, at least. Not that he stopped working; there was always something else to do, which suited Levi just fine these days.

"Here you go," he said, handing Mrs. Knox her chicken. "Think about an enclosure, okay?"

"Oh, Chief, thank you so much!" she said, beaming at him. "You're wonderful! What about that dog, though? He's evil! He should be locked up!"

The dog whined from under the porch, probably missing his little buddy. "I'll speak to the owner," Levi said.

"That was a great save, Chief," Everett said, coming over as Levi brushed himself off as best he could. "You did an amazing job. Wow."

Levi stopped himself from rolling his eyes. "Thanks, Ev. Listen. You draw that gun again, and I'm taking it away from you."

"Roger that, Chief."

Levi bent down and looked at the dog, who looked quite morose. "Wanna go for a ride?"

The dog flew out from under the porch, then streaked over to the cruiser, dancing eagerly.

"Maybe you should've said that first," Everett pointed out. "Then you wouldn't have had to crawl under there. You got really dirty."

"Thanks for pointing that out. Why don't you close up the station tonight, Ev?"

Everett's face lit up. "Really?"

"Sure." Levi would go back and check it afterward, because Everett always forgot something. Besides, the police station was forty-five seconds from where he lived. Plus, he'd be on the town green, anyway, as there was yet another wine event today. Every weekend, there was something going on, and it was fine. Good for the town, good for job security.

But for now, a shower. He looked at the dog. It didn't feel right to bring a huge, filthy animal into Mr. and Mrs. Holland's house, where he'd heard Faith was staying. Dog-washing. Another thing to add to his job description.

Since his wife dumped him a year and a half ago, Levi lived in the Opera House apartment building. Sharon and Jim Wiles had both spent and made a fortune on converting the building into the only apartment complex in town. A month after Nina had casually informed him that married life wasn't for her after all and reenlisted, Levi's mother had been diagnosed with a fast and furious pancreatic cancer. She'd died six weeks later. Sarah, then almost finished with her junior year in high school, had moved in with him.

He'd done his big brother shtick, putting his arm

around her and letting her bawl, making her grilled cheese and tomato sandwiches, like Mom had done. He missed their mother, too, but he'd been away for eight years. One thing combat had taught him was that in order to handle some of the awful shit they'd dealt with, feelings had to have the cuffs slapped on them, so to speak. He'd shed a few tears at his mom's bedside, don't get him wrong, but when real memories crept in—the time she took him to Niagara Falls when he was in fifth grade and she was pregnant with Sarah, so they could have one last day of it being just the two of them…how she sobbed when he came home for good…well, Levi tried to think about something else.

He'd done his best to take care of his sister, to get her into a good school, fill out all those damn forms and buy her what she needed, then ship her off and have her do great and maybe become a doctor or something. She'd be the first person in their family to graduate from college and graduate she would, if it killed him.

Which it might.

"You reek," Baby Sister said as he came in, Blue on his heels. "And whose dog is that? Is it ours? Can we keep him?" She gave Levi a once-over. "Seriously. You should take a shower. A long shower. God, Levi! Nasty!"

He gave her a cool look (which never worked on her). "The dog isn't ours. I'm aware that I'm filthy. Why are you here?"

She heaved a great sigh. "I just…I don't like it."

"Why?" Sarah went to a beautiful college at the north end of Seneca Lake; the place had its own movie theater, a huge athletic center, flowers everywhere, nice dorms. Honestly, what could she complain about?

"I don't know. I feel like I missed out on how things

are supposed to work. Everyone has friends already, and it's like I can't break in. I skipped dinner yesterday because I didn't want to go to the dining hall all alone. I feel like a loser."

"Sarah," Levi said, kneeling next to her chair, "you're not a loser. Just go sit down next to someone and start talking."

"And this advice comes from your personal experience? Because last I looked, you have exactly one friend."

He didn't take the bait. "You're smart, you're pretty and you're fun. Except now. Now, you're not fun. You're also not supposed to be home. I thought we agreed after last time."

"Take a shower, dude. I'm serious."

"So am I. You can't make college work if you keep coming home every three days. You have to tough it out."

Her eyes filled with tears. "I'm tired of toughing it out. I toughed it out through Mom dying, I toughed it out senior year and I don't want to tough anything out anymore. I want to be…indulged."

Levi lifted an eyebrow. "You're going to be enlisted if you don't shape up. That college is hardly toughing it out, sis. Your dorm room is three times as big as—"

"Oh, God, not another story from the trials and tribulations of Army, okay?"

"The Army, Sarah. You don't call it 'army.' I was in *the* Army. Try to get it right."

"Whatever. Come on, Levi, don't be a hard-ass. It's Thursday. I have one class tomorrow afternoon. I can skip it."

"No, you can't. I'll drive you back tonight."

"Levi! I'm so homesick! Please let me sleep here!"

He ran a hand through his hair, then surveyed the cobwebs he'd picked up under the porch. "Fine. I'll bring you back tomorrow morning. Pull up your schedule so I can make sure you're not lying."

She smiled, the winner of this round. "Sure. But take a shower or I'm gonna puke."

He stood up. "Want to help me wash the dog?"

"No. But I appreciate the offer."

He moved to ruffle her hair, but she ducked. "Levi. Clean up."

He knew his sister loved him. She'd even changed her last name to Cooper when she was sixteen, to make sure everyone knew who she was, she'd said. But he still wanted to kill her sometimes.

He took the dog into the bathroom—his own bathroom, thank God for that—and turned on the shower. The dog bent his head in deep shame. "Yeah, don't give me that, chicken chaser. Who's idea was it to go under the porch?" He took out his phone and dialed from memory. "Hi, Mrs. Holland, it's Levi Cooper."

"Dear! How are you? Do you know how to get flying squirrels out of the attic? Faith doesn't want us to set traps, and I don't want her to watch her grandfather fall to his death, though to be honest, widowhood is looking better and better these days. By the way, that pipe that burst last winter? Do you remember the name of the plumber you recommended? Ever since Virgil Ames moved to Florida, I don't know what to do! And Florida! Who'd want to live there? All those bugs and lizards and alligators and tourists."

"Bobby Prete should be able to fix the pipe, Mrs. H.," he said. "Listen, I've got Faith's dog with me."

"Oh, yes, he ran off when Ned was watching him."

"Can I bring him up?"

"Just give him to Faith, dear. She's down on the green, anyway. Which reminds me, I've got to get ready. Lovely talking to you."

Levi took off his shirt and threw it in the tub, giving it a good rinse before putting it into the laundry bin. "Come on, dog," he said to Blue, who'd curled up in a tight ball and was pretending to sleep. "Time to face the music."

CHAPTER EIGHT

THERE WERE PROBABLY five hundred people crowded onto the green and the streets around it for the Seventeenth Annual Cork & Pork, which sounded disturbingly perverted but was in fact a pig roast and wine tasting. Five hundred people, Faith noted, and it seemed like at least half of them were dying to console her—still—over being jilted on her wedding day.

"You were the most beautiful bride," Mrs. Bancroft was saying. "Really. We were all so shocked. So shocked."

"Thanks."

"Have you seen him? Is he here?"

"I haven't seen him yet, Mrs. Bancroft. But we're getting together next week."

Mrs. Bancroft stared at her, shaking her head. "You poor, poor thing."

"Oops. There's my brother. Gotta run." She left Mrs. Bancroft and went over to the Blue Heron tables and looped her arm through Jack's. "You needed me desperately, dear brother?"

"No," he said, pouring a one-ounce taste for a woman whose T-shirt proclaimed her as Texan and Carrying. "In fact, I'm not sure we're even related. How many sisters do I have, anyway? You seem to be multiplying."

"Mrs. Bancroft is the eighth person to call me a poor thing and ask how hard it is to see Jeremy again."

"You are pretty pathetic," he agreed. "Your name again?"

"Why are so many people in my way?" asked Mrs. Johnson. The long-time Holland housekeeper managed somehow to convey terror in her beautiful, lilting Jamaican accent. "Shoo, children. If you don't leave soon, there will be body parts everywhere, and I washed *and* starched and ironed this tablecloth this morning. If you want to live, move, I say." She straightened out the bottles so they were perfectly aligned.

"It's a wine tasting, Mrs. J.," Jack said. "We can't move." He turned to the gun-toting Texan. "What did you think? Can I pour you something else?" he asked.

"I'll just have more of the white zin," she said.

"It's a rosé," Jack said. Faith imagined he was trying not to weep over the misnomer of his beloved wine. The lady drained it, smiled and wandered off.

"Jackie," Mrs. Johnson said, "did you eat this morning? I brought you a sandwich. I don't want you eating any of the slop they're serving here." This earned her a dirty look from Cathy Kennedy, who was staffing the sausage booth for Trinity Lutheran. Mrs. Johnson returned the look hotly, till Cathy Kennedy broke. Most people did.

Mrs. J. unwrapped the sandwich and put it in Jack's hand.

"Yes, little prince," Faith said. "Eat up. Maybe Mrs. J. will chew the food for you so you don't have to work so hard."

"Don't be so disgusting and unladylike, Faith, and here, Jackie. Eat."

"Where's *my* sandwich?" Pru asked, joining them.

"Did I not make you griddle cakes this very morning?" Mrs. J. asked.

"Oh, God. I hear Lorena," Jack said. "Pru, uh, come help me with something really important. Faith can handle the tasting."

"Get back here," Faith hissed. It was no good. Both siblings bolted, leaving her to staff the tasting table with their housekeeper, who clucked in disapproval. "Mrs. J., why can't you marry Dad and make us all happy?" Faith asked. Though she wasn't completely sure, Faith thought Mrs. Johnson was widowed. Then again, the woman didn't spill about her personal life. Ever.

"Don't get me started on your father's many flaws, the least of which is his recently terrible taste in women." Mrs. Johnson stared at Lorena, her face swelling with regal disgust. "Five o'clock in the afternoon and she, with a dress that exposes more than half of those tired breasts. Shameful, shameful."

"I'm working on a replacement," Faith murmured, unable to tear her eyes off Lorena, who wore a strapless tiger-print sundress several sizes too small. The bodice was smocked, the stitching stretched to the "we can't hold on much longer" point. Dad, on the other hand, was in his customary aging Blue Heron shirt, stained Blue Heron cap and stained jeans, yucking it up with Joe Whiting, another winemaker from farther up Keuka. Dad was probably unaware that Lorena (and everyone around them) assumed he was on a date.

"You'd better work fast, my dear," Mrs. Johnson said. "Your father, he is not the most observant of men."

"I know." If it wasn't related to grapes, Dad tended not to notice. So, yes, it was possible that, before he fully realized what was happening, Lorena could move in, change his will and sell off ten acres to a water park developer. But finding the perfect woman, that was a challenge. Dad worshipped the memory of St. Mom.

"Can I have a taste of the Gewürztraminer?" a man asked.

"Absolutely," Faith answered, snapping to attention. "This one got a 91 from *Wine Spectator,* and we're very proud of it. It's been aged for eighteen months, so it's just now starting to speak. The nose is lovely, don't you think? Passionfruit, pepper, a little honeysuckle, just a touch of pencil lead in the body, with a whisper of lychee in the finish."

Mrs. Johnson snorted, and Faith bit down on a smile. Yeah, yeah, she'd made that all up, not having tasted the wine yet. Faith wasn't even sure whether or not lychee was an actual fruit. Those descriptions got a little silly sometimes, but it almost seemed the more ridiculous the description, the better the sales. Still, Honor would kill her if she heard. She took wine descriptions very seriously.

"Oh, yeah," the man said. "Pencil lead. I love it!"

At that moment, her dog bounded over to her. "Hi, baby!" she said bending over to ruffle his wet fur. "Where've you been? Did Ned take you swimming?"

"My brother and your dog just took a shower together," came a voice. "Kinda pervy, if you ask me."

Faith looked up. "Sarah! I haven't seen you in a long time. How've you been?"

Faith had always envied Levi for having a little sister; he'd always been very protective of her, one of his few (only?) redeeming qualities. Sarah had the same green eyes as Levi, though hers weren't filled with dismissal. Yeah. That was it. Levi could dismiss a person in one glance. He was, in fact, doing it right now.

"Keep a better eye on your dog, Faith," he said, deigning to speak to her. "He was terrorizing the Knoxes' chickens."

Right. Like Blue would terrorize anything. "Branch," she said. *Ass,* she mouthed.

"Chief Cooper! You're a sight for sore eyes," Mrs. Johnson said, getting a kiss on the cheek from Levi. Weird, seeing him acting with social graces.

Faith turned back to Sarah. "You must be in college now, right?"

"Yeah, I just started at Hobart."

"Great! Do you like it?"

"I hate it, actually."

"Hey, Sarah," Ned said, coming over and slinging an arm around Faith. "Faith, I'm here to take over, because Honor says you don't know what you're doing."

"Hi, Ned." Sarah blushed. Ned *was* very cute.

"How's school?" he asked, and the two started talking about classes and clubs. They looked nice together, Sarah with her blond hair, Ned tall and dark. And while Ned was already out of college, that didn't really matter. He didn't have a girlfriend that Faith knew of, and she interrogated him frequently on the subject.

Levi was watching the two of them. No smile. He glanced at her, scowled, then resumed his staring. Faith suppressed a sigh. It wasn't like she was playing matchmaker; she was just standing there. Like a lump, now that she thought of it.

Dad came over and handed her a bottle of water. "Make sure you drink enough, sweetpea," he said, his kind blue eyes crinkling. "It's hot compared to what you're used to."

Alas, Lorena appeared at his side. "Finally!" Lorena boomed. "Something decent to drink around here! Blue Heron has the best wine ever! I haven't had anything but swill all day long!" She gave Dad an exaggerated wink, and Faith suppressed a cringe. The winemakers in the region were a very tight bunch; there was some quiet competition, of course, and everyone wanted to win a medal or snag a great review. But what was good for one vineyard tended to be good for them all, so Lorena's type of PR wasn't scoring any points.

"Hi there, Sarah," Dad said. "How are you, sweetheart?"

"Fine, thanks, Mr. Holland."

"Levi," Dad said, "you've seen Faith since she got back, haven't you?"

She was abruptly aware that Levi was standing very close to her, smelling like soap, his hair damp. What had Sarah said? He'd given Blue a bath?

He gave her a look that fell around an eight on the Boredom Scale, something she'd first invented sophomore year of high school, when she'd asked if he wanted to sign up to tutor with her in Corning. One was *Oh. It's you.* Ten was *You're invisible.* And today's look, the eight, was *Really? You're still here?*

"Yes, sir," he said to her father. "Gave her a speeding ticket the other day."

Irritating. Then again, he hadn't mentioned the fact that she'd been wedged in a bathroom window, either. Points for discretion.

Dad gave her a surprised look. "You, honey? You're usually so careful."

"I didn't realize they'd dropped the speed limit, that's all."

"Well, you let me pay for that," he said.

Goggy appeared from the crowd. "Faith, take a look at what your grandfather is wearing. He knows I hate that shirt. It's polyester! And it's from 1972."

"A classic," Pops said, though he was already sweating from the airless fabric.

"Levi," Goggy said, laying her hand on his forearm. His tanned, smooth, muscular forearm. Little golden hairs caught the light. Faith cleared her throat and looked at something else. "The squirrels in our attic. They make noise every night! Faith can hardly sleep." This earned her another disgusted look from Levi.

"Goggy, it's fine. I'll go up there with some Havahart traps."

"I'll take care of it," Levi said.

"Oh, thank you, sweetheart," Goggy said. "I don't want Faith to fall."

Pru returned to the Blue Heron table, Abby in tow, and cuffed Levi fondly on the shoulder. "Here he is. Viagra for women."

"Mom, please! We're in public!" Abby said.

"You said it, Pru!" Lorena answered. "Can I get an amen? Right, Faith?"

"Yeah, no, I'm not feeling it," she murmured.

"Sorry, Sarah, didn't see you there," Pru said. "Didn't mean to ogle your brother in front of you. And what can I say? He's cute. Levi, you're cute."

Abby rolled her eyes. "Sarah, want to go find something to do? Get away from these horrifying adults?"

"Sure," Sarah said. "See you later, big bro." She smooched Levi on the cheek, who took it manfully. Even smiled.

It was just a small smile, but it took Faith unawares. Granted, she'd seen him smile over the years. Plenty of steamy looks at Jessica… Honestly, he probably practiced those in the mirror. Otherwise, it was the Boredom Scale for her.

Except for that one day when he'd shocked the living daylights out of her and kissed her. Chances were, he'd smiled then. And yes, there'd been a steamy look or two. Something else, too. Something…protective.

Or not. He was looking at her now, the smile gone and that much more familiar bored look…a six…now a seven…getting close to an eight. He crinkled his brow at her as if to say, *What, Holland?*

"Johnny!" Lorena boomed. "What's a girl gotta do to get a meal around here? Buy me a sausage, what do you say? I love me some sausage! Right, Faith? Us girls love sausage!"

"I'd say she has some nerve, calling herself a girl," Mrs. Johnson muttered darkly.

"What would you like, Lorena?" Dad asked. "Faith? No? Mrs. Johnson, how about you? Can I buy you some of that kettle corn you like? Hmm? I'll take that silence as a yes." He winked, then walked away, Lorena and her mammoth breasts flopping along beside him.

"Think he even knows she's interested?" Ned asked.

"Your grandfather is too good-hearted," Mrs. Johnson said. "That woman."

The next customer at the wine tasting was a familiar face. "Hi, Mrs. McPhales!" Faith said, her throat tightening. "It's so nice to see you!" Mrs. McPhales had been Faith's Girl Scout leader one year, one of those die-hard types who actually made scouts earn the badges. Ned, who was on the Manningsport Volunteer Fire Department, said they went up to her house fairly often these days. Apparently she was heading down the sad road toward dementia…today, she was wearing her slippers instead of shoes. Faith came out from behind the table and kissed the old lady. "What can I get for you, Mrs. McPhales? Would you like some wine?"

"I'll take a coffee, I guess," the old lady said.

"Coming up, dear lady. Cream and sugar?" Mrs.

Johnson asked. She really was a peach once you got over her Darth Vader type of omnipotence. Mrs. McPhales nodded, then seemed to recognize Faith.

"Faith! How are you? Aren't you and that nice Jeremy getting married soon?"

"We're not," Faith said. "Sorry."

"Oh! That's right! He's a confirmed bachelor, from what I hear."

"I think so," Faith said.

"You poor thing. Chin up, Faith, dear. You're very brave."

Faith thought she heard a snort. Right. Levi was still here. Brian, Mrs. McPhales's son, came up and took his mom by the arm, smiling at Faith as he led her away.

At the moment, there was no one around except Levi. "Thanks for washing Blue," she said, attempting to be friendly. "That was really nice of you. And unnecessary, but thank you."

"Keep him leashed." A five on the scale. "I'll have to start fining you if he runs loose all the time."

Sigh. "It was one time, Levi."

"Make sure it's only one." He wasn't even looking at her; casting about instead for someone more interesting to talk with.

Faith felt her jaw clenching. "Heard you got divorced, Chief."

His eyes came back to her. An eight. "Yes."

"How long were you married?" Colleen had passed on the details, of course, but why not torture him?

He waited before answering, his green eyes filled with disdain. "Three months," he finally said.

"Really! Wow. What a short time."

"Yes, Holland," he said. "Three months is a short time."

"Bet you wish someone had stopped your wedding."
She smiled sweetly. "Seems only fair, since you're so
good at doing that for others."

Levi was crinkling his brow at her again. "When do
you go back to San Francisco?"

"We'll see."

"Really? No job?"

"I'm very successful, actually. And I'm doing two
projects here, one up at Blue Heron, another for the library, so I'll be around for at least six weeks. Isn't that
great?" He didn't answer. "There's Julianne Kammer
now. I should go and talk to her."

"When are you going to see Jeremy?" he asked.

"Gosh. Is it really any of your business? Oh, wait, I
forgot. You're Jeremy's guard dog." She *was* going to
see Jeremy; it wasn't her fault he was in Boston for a
conference.

Levi leaned in close, and she could smell his sham-
poo, feel the warmth from his cheek, and an odd tension
coiled in her stomach. "Grow up, Faith," he whispered.

The man. Was. Suchapainintheass.

Then she went to talk to Julianne about the library
courtyard and tried not to feel Levi's eyes on her back.

On his first tour, Levi found that war was all it promised to be, at times stupefyingly dull…days on end of
doing nothing more interesting or challenging than
cleaning your gun. Then you'd be coming back to camp
and a kid who'd taken food from you the day before
might throw a grenade at your Humvee. Once, a car
loaded with explosives detonated just outside camp,
killing three soldiers, including one who'd won fifty
bucks off Levi the night before.

But there were good things, too. Levi liked the struc-

ture, liked his fellow soldiers, liked the feeling that as
screwed up as war always was, maybe they were doing
something important. His unit was the 10th Mountain
from Fort Drum, and they were the guys who got shit
done. Sometimes it was best not to think about what
those things were, but he was a soldier, a link in the
chain of command, and he did his job. After his tour
ended, he signed up for another. Made sergeant, then
staff sergeant. Re-upped again and sent the bonus home
to his mom.

Then one day, while on patrol in some horrible little
town where people lived in shacks and everyone seemed
to stare at them with dead eyes, a bullet sang right past
his head, shattering rock. Another crack, and before
Levi could even turn around, Scotty Stokes, a private
who'd just joined their unit, crumpled to the ground.
Levi grabbed him by the back of his vest and dragged
him to shallow cover. They were cut off from the rest
of the patrol, and the kid was bleeding badly from the
leg, maybe an artery. Levi tourniqueted the kid's leg
as best he could. Returned fire, killing one of the gun-
men, then hefted the kid over his shoulder and made
a run for it, praying that neither of them would be hit.

They made it. The medic thought Scotty would lose
his leg, but some badass ortho with a great pair of hands
managed to save it. Scotty would set off metal detec-
tors for the rest of his life, but he'd walk on the legs
God gave him. And Levi got a Silver Star, though to
him, it seemed more like dumb luck than any real fore-
thought or skill. Lots of training, maybe. His mom and
Sarah were proud, though. The Lyons, too, acted as if
he'd saved the world. They had Mom and Sarah up for
dinner, and all four of them Skyped with him, and that
was pretty great.

From the time Levi had left on that Greyhound until he came back to Manningsport, Jeremy stayed in touch. Sent him emails all the time, Skyped once in a while, always smiling, always able to tell him something funny. Stuff about college, football, dorm life. Those little glimpses were almost hard to picture—Levi had never been to Boston, couldn't imagine playing in a stadium that huge. When Levi described the desert sand storms, Jeremy sent him really excellent ski goggles and six boxes of Visine. Elaine and Ted sent him candy and organic potato chips, and of course Mom and Sarah sent him stuff constantly. Sarah's report cards, Mom's long, worried letters.

Everyone emailed pictures, but Jeremy went a step further and had them developed. Levi tacked them up next to his bunk—a picture of Sarah at Christmas, since the Lyons had had them over for dinner; the dense clusters of grapes hanging from the vines in the fall; the hills covered in snow in December, the water of the lake black and deep.

Home.

And when a car came screaming up to your outpost or you braced for the IED to blow you into chunks, when bullets streaked through the night air, home was the only thing that kept your shit together. On the days when the temperature hit a hundred and thirty and his gun was so hot he had to wear gloves to hold it, when his water was the same temperature as McDonald's coffee and his mouth felt like leather from being so dry, those pictures were little pieces of paradise.

Faith's name, which had been mentioned fairly often at first, stopped appearing after Jeremy graduated and started med school (he'd turned down the NFL, for crying out loud). There was some mention of one of Jeremy's fellow medical students, a guy named Steve, and Levi wondered if maybe there was something there. Honestly, though he didn't give it much thought. If his friend had come out of the closet, Levi would hear about it when Jeremy wanted him to.

Finally, five years after he'd first gone to Afghanistan, Levi got a leave long enough to go back. He'd seen his mom and Sarah twice since shipping out, once on a long weekend in New York City, once when he surprised them with a trip to Disney World. But this time, he wanted to go home. He popped in on Sarah at school in one of those tear-soaked CNN moments, endured an impromptu assembly in which the principal told him how proud they were (despite having given him a record number of detentions not so long ago). His mom made his favorite dinner—meat loaf and mashed potatoes, then wept happily all the way through it.

And finally, Levi called Jeremy; it was October, and Jeremy was home for the weekend from Johns Hopkins. "Hey, bud, wanna grab a beer?" he asked, then grinned as his friend cussed him out for not giving him more notice.

A few hours later, Levi was slightly drunk from all the beers bought for him. Connor O'Rourke had done a round on the house, and everyone had toasted Levi. He'd been hugged by every woman in the place and practically leg-humped by Sheila Varkas (total freak, that one), was repeatedly thanked for his service, had his back pounded and his hand shaken and was told how proud the town was. It was…nice. It was great, actually. The kid from the trailer park turned American hero and all that.

And then, finally, he and Jeremy got to sit down and talk.

"So how are you really, buddy?" Jeremy asked, his eyes as kind as ever.

Levi watched a drop of condensation slip down the side of his bottle. "Doing okay," he answered, not looking up.

Jeremy was quiet for a minute. "Do you need anything?"

A good night's sleep. War had definitely taken that away. A brain bleach to get some of the more horrific images out of his head. "No," he said. "But thanks for all those packages and stuff. Especially the pictures."

Jeremy leaned forward. "Well, listen. I don't know what it's like, I'm just some dumb-ass med student studying bowel disease." Levi gave a half smile. "But if you ever need anything, or want to unload or whatever, I'm here. And I'll be here the whole time, and when you get back, too. Okay? You're my best friend. You know that."

Levi gave a nod, peeled a shard from the label. Maybe there would be a day when he told Jeremy some of the things he'd seen…and done. It wasn't today, though. He looked up at Jeremy and nodded again. "Thanks."

Jeremy sat back in the booth and smiled, that broad easy grin that Levi remembered from football huddles, when Jeremy would tell them just how they were going to shock and awe their opponents by coming from behind and stealing the win. "So. Any way you can get a few days off next June?"

Levi shrugged. "It's possible. Why?"

"I need you to be my best man. June eighth. Faith and I are getting married."

Levi didn't blink. "Holy crap."

"Yeah." Jeremy grinned sheepishly. "She said yes. I was a nervous wreck, but she said yes."

Yeah, right. Faith Holland had probably been planning their wedding since the day she'd met Jeremy.

His buddy was blathering on about who'd be in the bridal party, and Levi suddenly held up his hand. "Jeremy," he said. "Just one second, okay?"

"Sure."

To ask or not to ask. That was the question. Levi glanced around. O'Rourke's was almost empty; two people at the bar, two more at a table. Connor was behind the bar, tallying up receipts.

"What is it?" Jeremy asked.

"You're getting married," Levi stated for clarification.

He nodded. Levi didn't say anything, just looked. Maybe lifted an eyebrow. Jeremy swallowed, then forced a grin. "Yeah. So?" He wiped his forehead, suddenly sweaty, and that was clue enough. If he was this nervous, then maybe he was just waiting for someone to bring it up.

"I guess I was always under the impression that you were..." Levi waited, hoping Jeremy would supply the word.

"I was what?"

Shit. Levi took a deep breath and held it. "That you were gay, Jeremy," he said very, very quietly.

Jeremy's face didn't change for a long second. Then he took a deep breath. "No! Uh...I don't think so. I mean, everyone has...thoughts. But just because..." He looked away. "No. I'm not. I'm not gay." His voice was hollow.

Levi didn't say anything—what do you say, after all? "It would be okay if you were."

Jeremy looked back at him, and something crossed his face. The truth, maybe. Then he shook his head a little. His eyebrows drew together, and he looked at the table. "I love Faith."

Right. Jeremy certainly was wrapped around Princess Super-Cute's little finger. Levi looked at his friend, who'd been so loyal and decent and constant. He exhaled, nodding. "Okay. My bad."

Again, that thing flickered through Jeremy's eyes, but he put on his game face and smiled. "Well, whatever. If you'd be my best man, that'd be great."

"Sure. If I can get the time, I'm in."

"Excellent! Faith will be thrilled."

Probably not. "Is she around?"

"No, sorry to say. She and her sisters went to the city to shop for wedding gowns and all that. Girls' weekend. Anyway, my parents are giving us the house after the wedding; they're ditching me for San Diego, but it's all good. Can't see that Faith would want her in-laws around all the time, you know?" Jeremy kept talking, firmly back in the role of doting fiancé.

Levi told himself it wasn't any of his business. If Jeremy wanted to marry Faith, he could. But, hell, you had to wonder. How Jeremy could marry a woman he didn't know how to kiss.

You had to wonder how Faith could not know.

You said your piece; now shut up, his brain told him. *Be a good friend. Be a good best man.*

He almost pulled it off.

CHAPTER NINE

FAITH STOOD AT THE TOP of Rose Ridge and looked down through the woods. Once, this area had been fields, and Faith's ancestors had grazed cows up here. In the hundred years since, maple and oak trees had taken over, as well as ferns and moss. Today, a cold front had moved through, bringing heavy-bellied clouds over the lake and a chilly wind. Rain couldn't be far off.

Down below, she could see Ned driving the grape harvester down in the Tom's Woods chardonnay vines, could catch the hum of the engine when the breeze stopped. There was a certain smell to late summer; the air was so sweet with the scent of grapes, but there was a hint of melancholy in the air, too, as the leaves prepared to die their beautiful deaths and the earth prepared for winter.

As she did each time she came home, Faith wondered how she'd ever left. San Francisco seemed like a distant dream life compared to this.

Blue Heron was to the Hollands what Tara was to Scarlett O'Hara. You were from *here,* and here defined you more than you knew. History and family were as much a part of the soil as the dirt itself, and every Holland felt the bond right into their bone marrow.

As the youngest of the four Holland kids, Faith often felt like there wasn't a place for her in the family business. Jack was the wine-making, chemistry genius, could talk for hours about yeast and sugar fermentation till people begged him to stop. Pru was the farmer, tromping through the fields, strong as a linebacker. Honor…well, everyone knew Honor ran the world. Her sister barely stopped working to breathe; every issue came to her, whether it was restocking the gift shop, going on sales calls with their distributors or doing a charity event. She handled all the marketing and sales for the vineyard and did her job beautifully.

And then there was Faith, the child who hadn't had a place waiting for her, the only one who hadn't focused her education around viniculture. There were only so many people who could run the roost before they started eating their young.

She'd played up here as a child, sat in the old stone barn and pretended it was her house. Had tea parties with imaginary friends, made fairy houses and lay in the grass, sheltered by the rocks, staring up into the blue sky, wondering how she could tame a hawk or fawn. It was so magical to her then, she could just about hear the soft footfalls of a unicorn or hobbit. Of all the places on their land, the vines and the fields, the woods and the falls, this had been the most special to Faith.

And now, finally, she could contribute to the family business. It felt good. Just because she was the youngest didn't mean that this place wasn't part of her soul.

Blue nudged her hand and dropped his tennis ball. "Again?" Faith asked. He didn't answer, just stared at her, willing her to throw the ball. "You got it, big guy," she said, hurling the ball into the woods.

Faith had spent the morning at the library, taking photos of the courtyard off the children's wing, measuring, taking notes. It was a sweet little space, and she intended to make it great. Flowering trees (she was already shmoozing the nursery for donations), a winding path, a water installment, because she loved the sound of gushing water (who didn't?). And then, for the centerpiece, something really special, though she didn't know just what yet. She had to spend a little time there first and feel the mojo before she decided. One of her clients in San Francisco used to laugh at her for lying down on the ground of any given project, but, hey, he kept hiring her for more jobs, so clearly it worked.

Just this morning, Faith had probably seen a dozen people she knew: Lorelei from the bakery on the green; her old classmate Theresa DeFilio, and her parade of children, following her like beautiful, dark-haired ducklings. Faith's old Sunday school teacher, Mrs. Linqvist, who still made Faith feel guilty. The football coach's wife. Jack's high school girlfriend. The nurse from Jeremy's office.

As for Jeremy himself, she'd be seeing him tomorrow night.

Faith took another breath, and, as ever, the uniquely sweet smell of the Finger Lakes air—grapes and grass—calmed her. The smell of home.

Blue was back, but he raced past her, woofing joyfully around his tennis ball.

"Hey, Faith."

"Hey, Pru! What are you doing here?"

"Just figured I'd come have a look, see what you were doing up here." She threw Blue's tennis ball into the woods. "About time Dad green-lighted this. All the other vineyards have been doing weddings for years." She took off her hat and ran a hand through her salt-and-pepper hair.

They were quiet a moment, the beauty of the gray day solemn somehow.

"How are you, Pru? You seem a little down."

Her sister sighed. "I don't know. Maybe I'm just tired. Early harvest and all that. Dad's driving me crazy, as usual." She glanced over at Faith. "Also, I feel like Carl and I are living in a porno these days. Sex, sex, sex, all the time."

"Oh! How thrilling!" Faith glanced at her sister's face. "Oops. Not thrilling?"

"First it was just hints, you know? Like, did I want a bikini wax, or could we talk dirty. Then…" To Faith's horror, Prudence's eyes filled with tears. "Shit, Faith. I don't know. The whole bringing sexy back…you know that song? By that cute boy?"

"Yeah, I know it," Faith said grimly.

"Who is he again?"

"Justin Timberlake."

"Right. "Bring Sexy Back" or something. Well, I didn't know sexy was gone. Now Carl wants me to be all creative. You know what he brought back from Costco last week? Eight cans of whipped cream, Faith. Eight."

"That's a lot," Faith said. Time to swear off dairy.

"And it's having the opposite effect. Right? Like, the storm of love I used to have has dried to a mist, because all of a sudden, plain old marital brevity isn't good enough. Oh, and the other day, Abby walked in on us, and she's not speaking to me at the moment. Last week, Faith, I had a mammogram, you know?"

Faith looked up sharply. "Is everything okay?"

"Sure! But I was looking *forward* to it! Like, that was my special alone time, just me and the boob squisher. I didn't have to talk dirty to Carl or wear Vulcan ears—"

"Oh, boy."

"—or deal with the kids, Dad wasn't asking me questions and Honor wasn't up my butt. The mammogram people were running behind, so I got to sit there in a bathrobe and read a magazine and it was the best time I've had in ages! Even when my boob was in the machine, I said to the woman, 'No, no, take your time,' and I *meant* it!"

"Pru!" Faith pulled her sister into a hug, and Blue, panting, joined in the comfort, nosing against the two of them, whining. "Oh, honey. Maybe you just need some time away."

"I know that, Faith!" she barked. "But I can't. We've got harvest, which is seven days a week till it's done, then we have the ice wine harvest, then it's the stupid holidays, and really, why did Baby Jesus have to be born in December? Because March is wide open! I'm just saying."

"I think Jesus was actually born in—you know what? It doesn't matter. You *should* get away for a few days. Alone. I'll drive Abby wherever she needs to go, and make dinner for everyone or whatever you need. Really, Pru."

Her sister straightened up and wiped her eyes on the sleeve of her shirt, then scratched Blue behind his ears. "It's a nice thought," she said. "But I can't."

"Well, you can. You're choosing not to. Don't be a martyr, Pru."

"Please. You sound so California. And being a martyr is our family motto." Her sister wiped her eyes again. "Let's change the subject. Show me what you have in mind for up here. Come on. Chop, chop. I don't have all day."

"Sure." Faith led her sister into the woods proper. The path was overgrown, but it was there. A squirrel chastised them from a tree branch overhead, and the smell of rain was thicker now. Blue led the way, his tail waving.

"I haven't been up here in years," Prudence said behind her. "Always too busy, I guess."

"Do you remember the barn?" Faith asked, holding a branch back so her sister wouldn't get whacked.

"Not really."

"Well, here we are."

They stood in front of what currently didn't look like much: the rock walls of the old barn, which had been built in the early 1800s and burned when Teddy Roosevelt was President. The roof and interior had been destroyed in the fire, as well as the wooden doors, leaving a wide gap in the wall.

Faith went inside, Pru on her heels. "Huh," her sister said.

Three walls of ragged stone surrounded them. The floor had long been taken over by forest grass and moss, and lichen had coated the rock walls. But the best part was—to Faith's mind, anyway—that the lake-facing wall had crumbled, opening the space up to the most amazing view. Thanks to the steepness of the hills, they could see the tops of the trees in front of them. Past that were the fields of grapevines, the white buildings of Blue Heron—the New House, the tasting room, the barn where the wine aged in tanks and casks—and then more fields and woods, and finally Keuka, the Crooked Lake itself.

"So how would this work for weddings and such?" Pru asked.

"Well, this would be the space. You could get about seventy-five people in here, give or take. I'd level off the floor but maybe keep it grass. Then we'd build a cantilevered deck, so you could stand out there like you were on the prow of a ship, ten, fifteen, twenty feet off the ground as the floor extended out. Maybe take down a tree or two and open up the view."

"What if it rains?" Pru asked.

"That's the magical part," Faith said. "You can get clear roofing material, and if Dad wanted to get really fancy, we could take the roof on and off, depending on the time of year or forecast. A fireplace over here for some ambience, build a little stone terrace out here for cocktails. Wouldn't it be beautiful? So you'd be under the stars, dancing on air, all this beauty around you." She looked at her sister. "What do you think?"

"Frickin' amazing," Prudence said. "Wow, Faith! You can do all that?"

"Sure! I'd make a parking area back there on the ridge, widen the path down here, get the doors replaced. You'd come in and boom—magic."

"Parking? Kitchen? Electric?"

"I talked to the building officer about permits, and she doesn't see a problem. We'd just need to dig a trench, lay down some PVC, run electric up from the road. The old well might still be usable. Over there, see that area? That's where the milking shed was. The caterers could set up in there."

And if it looked anything like what she had in her mind's eye, it would be incredible, one of her most intricate projects as a landscape architect yet…and, finally, her contribution to the family business. Her little stone playhouse, transformed. "Think Dad'll like it?"

"Dad would like the Superdome if it made you stay home, Faithie. And I already love it," Pru said, putting her arm around Faith. "Mom would be proud."

One of these days, those words wouldn't kick her quite so hard. One of these days.

The rain that had been threatening began to fall, pattering gently. "Come on, I'll give you a ride," Pru said. "My truck's at the cemetery."

Halfway between the old barn and the vineyard buildings was the family cemetery. Seven generations of Hollands, from the soldier who'd fought in the Battle of Trenton with George Washington to the most recent burial—Mom.

Prudence cleared away some wilted flowers from Mom's marker. *Constance Verling Holland, age 49. Beloved daughter, wife and mother. Always a smile in her heart.*

"You ever come here to talk to Mom?" Pru asked.

Faith blinked. "Oh, sure," she lied.

"Me, too. Dad comes all the time, of course." She straightened up. "Hey, thanks for listening."

"You bet. That's what sisters are for."

At that moment, Pru's phone buzzed. She looked at it and pressed a button. "Hi, Levi, what's up?" she asked.

At his name, Faith felt her skin prickle. She'd have to get used to it, she guessed. The guy was everywhere.

"She did what? Where? Is she okay? Right. Right. Okay, I'll be there in ten minutes." Pru's face was white.

"What happened?" Faith asked, her heart galloping in fear.

"It's Abby. She was jumping into the falls. Drunk. With two boys." Pru glanced at Faith. "She's okay, but Levi's got the three of them down at the station. Will you drive?"

Moments later, they were in the tiny police station. There was Abby, teary-eyed and defiant, sitting at Levi's desk. Thank God, she seemed fine. Levi was there as well, and Everett Field, for whom Faith used to babysit. No sign of the boys in question.

"Baby, are you okay? Are you an idiot? I can't believe you'd do something so stupid!" Prudence barked.

"Really, Mom? You're gonna tell me *I'm* stupid? Who's got a thing for Dr. Spock, huh? You and Dad, that's who. *That's* stupid."

"It's *Mr.* Spock, okay?" There was an aborted snort from Emmaline, who'd been a year ahead of Faith in school. "And we're talking about an underage girl getting drunk and doing stupid, dangerous, life-threatening things with boys. I thought you were smarter, Abby!"

Faith glanced at Levi, who looked quite intimidating, his face in a slight scowl, arms folded across his chest. If he flexed his biceps, that shirt was going to rip, which she probably shouldn't be noticing right now. Behind him, Everett imitated Levi's pose. Didn't have quite the same effect. He smiled at her and gave a little wave, then remembered he was an officer of the law and resumed frowning.

According to Levi, Abby had been talked into showing Adam Berkeley and Josh Deiner the falls on the Holland property. Josh had brought a six-pack, so he was in the most trouble, as was the package store employee who hadn't carded him. The kids had each had a couple of beers, then jumped off the rock into the water, swimming and goofing around, when a lost hiker came upon them and correctly guessed that they were underage. Levi had scared the bejesus out of them by showing up.

"I may puke," Abby muttered, swallowing. Levi nudged the trash can closer to her with his foot, his expression unchanging.

"You know your uncle Jack broke his arm out there," Pru went on. "And what you were going to do with those boys, I have no idea!"

"We weren't gonna have sex!" Abby wailed. "If they'd even tried anything, I would've bitten everyone."

"You're drunk. I can't believe my little girl is drunk," Pru said, her voice baffled.

"And you're a sex addict," Abby said.

"Underage drinking is against the law," Levi said, his voice mild. "What you were doing was stupid, Abby. Your mother is right. Two boys, one girl, stupid. And that gorge is dangerous. A hiker broke his neck out there last year, and it took us four hours just to get him out. He's paralyzed for life."

Abby's eyes filled with tears. "Everyone hates me," she said, then promptly puked into the garbage can, making Everett gag in sympathy.

"Levi, can I take her home?" Prudence asked, and Faith's heart gave a tug. Poor Pru looked years older.

"Absolutely," Levi said. "I'll come by tomorrow."

"Okay, baby," Pru said, holding Abby's hair away from her face. "Let's get you home. We'll deal with this when you're sober."

"Like you're so perfect," Abby sobbed. "Auntie, didn't you ever do anything stupid when you were my age?"

Why yes, honey, as a matter of fact. Faith cleared her throat and didn't look at Levi. Her face felt hot. "Well, sure. But there's stupid, and then there's life-threatening. Let's go home and clean you up, and you can enjoy your very first hangover."

"Am I gonna be arrested or something?" Abby asked, looking at Levi.

"Go home and sleep it off, Abby," he said. "All three of you kids will have to do some community service. But don't you ever do something like this again, you got it? Josh Deiner is not someone you want to hang out with."

"Okay," she muttered, tears dripping down her cheeks. "I'm sorry. I'm sorry, Mommy."

"Let's get you home. Your father's going to have a fit, you know."

This brought on more sloppy crying. Faith sighed and grabbed Abby's backpack.

"It was so great seeing you," Everett whispered, beaming. "Want to have a drink sometime?"

"No! I mean, sure, to catch up, but not romantically, okay? Because I babysat you." Faith smiled firmly.

"You know, I used to think about you when I—"

"That's enough, Everett." Levi's voice was calm.

"Right, right! Sorry, sir!" Ev looked at Faith again. "You look great." He blushed, and she couldn't help a smile.

"Faith."

Levi's voice made her jump.

"Yes?"

"Give her a talk. She obviously worships you."

For the first time in a long time, it seemed like Levi was looking at her with something other than contempt. And you know…a man in uniform…with those big, brawny arms… Her knees felt abruptly weak. "Okay. Thank you, Levi."

And she forgot, at least for a little while, that Levi was the one who ruined her wedding and outed the man she loved.

CHAPTER TEN

NATURE HAD PULLED OUT all the stops the morning of Faith and Jeremy's wedding. The sun shone over the lake, burnishing it a deep, aching blue, and it seemed that every flower and tree was at its most beautiful as the limo drove from the Hill down to the village square. Faith wore a Cinderella dress, the tight, beaded bodice catching the light and throwing rainbows through the car, the tulle skirt so puffy that it almost obscured Abby, who was chattering with excitement. Prudence looked strange and beautiful out of work clothes, her eyes crinkling in a smile. Both her sisters wore pink, Faith's favorite color, and Colleen, as maid of honor, had a dress slightly deeper in shade. Faith hadn't wanted to choose between her sisters, so Colleen had gotten the nod.

"You girls," John Holland said, his eyes damp. "So beautiful."

Faith realized she was clenching her bouquet. She wasn't nervous. Well, a little. But not about marrying Jeremy, of course not. No, it was probably just stage fright. There'd be three hundred people at the church, after all. So yes, it was probably just that. Once she saw Jeremy, those nerves would disappear.

He'd called her last night to tell her Levi had been delayed in Atlanta and would have to meet them at the church, not to worry, he'd be there.

"That's good," Faith had said. The truth was, she

wouldn't have minded if Levi got stuck and missed the entire wedding; she hadn't seen him since high school, and she wasn't really looking forward to that bored, condescending air he always had around her. Then again, surely all that childish stuff was done. She was about to become his best friend's wife, after all. Besides, no negative thoughts would be allowed on the night before her wedding. "It'll be great to see him," she added. Points for positive attitude.

Jeremy hadn't said anything.

"Honey? You still there?" she whispered.

"I just wanted to tell you that being your husband is everything I've ever wanted," Jeremy said, his voice husky.

"Oh, Jeremy," she whispered. "I love you so much."

That's what she should be thinking of on this beautiful June morning. Not the tremor in her stomach. Maybe she was just missing her mom, because what girl didn't want her mother on her wedding day, to exclaim and shed a few tears…and, if the case called for it, to reassure.

From a place dark and deep inside her, something roared.

Nope. No. Uh-uh. It was just stage fright. She was, by far, the luckiest woman in the world. *Being your husband is everything I've ever wanted.* Come on! Those were words she could take to the bank! Nothing could be wrong when a man said words like *that.* This was marital gold.

The limo pulled up in front of Trinity Lutheran, the stone church where the Hollands had gone for generations, and the tourists who were wandering on the green stopped to look as the wedding party got out. "You're so beautiful!" one woman called. The photographer snapped her picture as she bent to kiss Abby's cheek, a picture that would go on to win a prize in a national photography contest later that year.

Then, holding on to her father's arm, Colleen fluffing her dress, Faith went into the church to marry the man she'd loved since the first day she'd met him, when, like the hero in a movie, he'd carried her unconscious form in his strong arms. Okay, that sounded creepy, but it hadn't been. It had been wonderful, or so she was told.

There he was, standing on the altar, so handsome in his tux, tall and manly. He was smiling at someone, maybe one of his patients, because half the town had flocked to him, never mind that he was barely done with his residency. Levi had made it, she noted; he looked older in his dress uniform. He was shorter than Jeremy, his hair sticking up a little in front. His face was somber; he must've been tired from all his traveling. Faith couldn't help thinking it'd be nice if he could fake a smile. It was her wedding day, after all, and the man looked as if he was at a funeral.

Pachelbel's Canon in D began, and Pru started down the aisle. Honor turned, and, so uncharacteristically, hugged Faith. "Love you," she whispered, then started down herself, followed by Colleen and then Abby.

Pachelbel stopped, then, and the wedding march began.

Faith's heart rate tripled. She tried to keep her eyes on Jeremy, felt her face stretching in a smile, but damned if she didn't feel...wrong.

Just nervous, her brain lied.

It seemed like the entire town was there, looking at her: Dr. Buckthal, her neurologist, and his wife. Theresa

DeFilio, one of the truly nice girls from high school, a baby on her shoulder, handsome husband at her side. Jessica Dunn, yawning. Laura Boothby who'd done such an amazing job with the flowers. Ted and Elaine, smiling brightly. Connor O'Rourke. Mrs. Johnson and Jack in the front row. So many people. Way too many.

When Reverend White asked who gave this woman in marriage, Dad answered, "Her mother and I," and the congregation sighed with the bittersweet beauty of his words. Daddy kissed her cheek, tears in his eyes, and shook Jeremy's hand, leaning in to give him a one-armed hug. "Take care of my baby," he said, then went to his seat.

Jeremy's hands were clammy. "You look so beautiful," he whispered, his lips pulling back in something like a smile. His gaze bounced from her to somewhere over her head.

He wasn't nervous. He was terrified.

A floating feeling enveloped Faith, almost like the auras that preceded her seizures, but different, too. Faith could hear her own breathing, rather than the words of the minister, the readings—one by Jack, one by Jeremy's cousin Anne. The wedding seemed to slow into endlessness. It hadn't seemed so long at the rehearsal. Honestly, it was the longest wedding in history! Why hadn't they gotten to the vows yet? She couldn't look at Jeremy and focused on the readers instead, on Reverend White, on her bouquet.

Maybe it *was* the epilepsy. Faith tried to wrestle her faulty brain into order, to press each detail into her memory. Enjoy the day, that's what everyone told her, but, hell, it seemed like she might be on the verge of that dark, epileptic hole. She'd been religious about taking her meds. Hadn't had a seizure in three years. *Please, not that, not now.*

The seizure didn't come, but the sense of doom pressed in on her like hot lead.

Now the minister was talking about marriage and the seriousness of two people pledging their lives together. Faith couldn't concentrate. She just wanted to say her vows and be Jeremy's wife. She wanted to promise to love him all the days of her life, because she *would.* He was the One. Just a few more minutes, and it would be official, and *please,* get this over with, was this a normal way to be feeling, couldn't they just fast forward to the part where people were throwing birdseed?

Reverend White finally stopped blathering. He looked out over the congregation, and Faith looked, too, all those smiling faces, her dad looking so proud, her grandparents beaming. Almost there. Almost there. She looked back at Jeremy. His face was oily with sweat, his hands damp and hot, clenching hers.

"Before we begin the vows," the reverend said, "does anyone know of a reason these two should not be wed? If so, speak now, or forever hold your peace."

Her heart was now beating so hard she could feel the separate chambers rolling and squeezing.

No one said anything.

The reverend smiled. "I didn't think so. In that case—"

"Jeremy." The voice was so low, it might not have actually been spoken. But, no, Jeremy flinched.

It was Levi. "Jeremy. Come on."

What? Why was he *talking?* He looked so damn solemn in that uniform. So…authoritative. Why did he have to come? Why couldn't his plane have been late?

Jeremy's breathing was jagged. The sheen of sweat

grew, droplets beading on his forehead. He licked his lips and swallowed, then opened his mouth to speak.

"No," she whispered.

"Faith," Jeremy said, squeezing her hands so hard he was crushing them.

"No." She forced herself to smile. "I love you."

Pain ripped through his eyes, eyes that had only ever before smiled at her. "Honey, I...I have to talk to you."

A murmur went up from the congregation, and from the corner of her eye, Faith could see her father's mouth opening in shock, Elaine—Elaine, who loved Faith like a daughter—gripping Ted's arm.

Faith's legs were shaking, her dress quivering with the movement. "Jeremy, let's just finish this," she whispered.

"Is there a problem?" Reverend White asked, his bushy eyebrows coming together.

"No!" Faith answered, her voice cracking. Oh, Lord, she was going to faint. "There's not."

Jeremy swallowed again, his eyes filled with tears. "Faith," he said again, and her knees did buckle then.

"Let's go," Levi said, taking Faith by the arm. "Downstairs, you two." He towed her off the altar, the train of her dress tugging with its weight. Jeremy followed.

There was a staircase right by the altar. "What the hell are you *doing?*" Pru asked, and then the voices of the guests rumbled and echoed in the church. Down the stairs they went, Levi's hand inescapable. He was a bully. He was ruining everything.

"Jeremy," she squeaked, looking back. Her fiancé didn't meet her eyes.

Levi pushed through the door at the bottom of the stairs. The church basement was dim and smelled like

chalk. Four or five metal folding chairs sat huddled together. Bible Study or AA or something. Levi let go
of her arm and then guided Jeremy a few paces away,
leaving her standing alone.

"What's going on here?" It was her father, thank
God, and Colleen and her sisters and Jack, and Jeremy's parents, too. Her father came to her side and put
his arm around her, and she sagged against his shoulder. "You're ruining their wedding, Levi!"

Yes! He was supposed to be the best man, not the
ruiner of weddings. How dare he? You know, she had
always wished Jeremy had had a different friend. She'd
never liked Levi Cooper. He was too...secretive. And
confident. And he'd never liked her, especially after
that one stupid kiss.

"Hang on a sec," Levi said.

He and Jeremy were talking, Jeremy's voice panicky, Levi's lower, calmer. Then Jeremy nodded; Levi
gave his shoulder a squeeze, nodded, then turned to
the group.

"Jeremy and Faith need a little time alone," he said.
His eyes stopped—not on Faith, but on Mr. and Mrs.
Lyon.

"Oh," Elaine said, her voice very, very soft. "Oh, dear."

"Faith?" Dad said. "Do you want us to stay?"

She looked at Jeremy, who loved her. Who'd called
her last night to say everything he ever wanted was to
be her husband. "It'll be okay. It's fine, Daddy."

"I'll be right on the other side of that door," he said.
"Call if you need me."

Everyone left, slowly, uncertainly, glancing back at
Faith. She sank into a metal chair, Jeremy sitting across
from her. And Levi, damn him, walked a few feet away

and stood with his hands behind his back, staring at the floor, looking like a stone wall.

"Does he have to stay?" Faith whispered.

"I…I'd like him to," Jeremy whispered back. "If that's okay."

She looked into his eyes, which were so dark they were almost black, and which had always seemed so happy—with her, with life. Smiling seemed to be his natural expression, and everyone commented on it, that big, ready grin of his.

No smiling now.

She sensed the world was about to end.

"Faith," he said, his voice soft and broken, "I want you to know that I do love you, so much." He took a breath and looked at the floor. "But I can't marry you."

"Why?" she asked, her voice squeaking. "Are you sick? I don't mind, I'd stay with you, that's the whole point, in sickness and in—"

He looked back up, his gaze slamming into hers. "I'm gay."

The two words seemed to float around her for a few seconds, meaningless, before they hooked into her brain. She sucked in a quick breath and jerked back, and started to speak. It took a few tries; her mouth was making odd little noises, her lips trying and failing to form words. Finally, she stopped, gave her head a quick shake, and tried again.

"No, you're not. You're not gay."

"I'm so sorry." He looked…old.

"You don't have to be sorry! You don't! Because you're not. You aren't. You can't be."

He hesitated, looking at the floor, folding his hands together loosely, his beautiful doctor hands. There should've been a wedding ring on the fourth finger of his left hand by now. There *would've* been if Levi had kept his mouth shut.

Jeremy took a deep breath. "I didn't…acknowledge it, and I really thought I could… I mean, for a long time, I honestly didn't know. I didn't. I just thought those feelings would go away, and with you, it was like proof that I wasn't—"

"Stop! Shut it, Jeremy. My God." Okay, she was hyperventilating a little. "You are not gay." She took a steadying breath. "You have the worst taste in clothes I've ever seen in a man. I had to teach you how to dress. Remember those mom jeans you thought looked good on you? They were horrible! You have no sense of style whatsoever. If it weren't for me and Banana Republic—"

"Faith, I   "

"No! Plus, you're a terrible dancer! I mean, we had to take six lessons before you figured out the box step, Jeremy! And—and—and you played football! You were really good at it, too. You played *football,* Jeremy! You were the quarterback!"

He put his hands on her knees, on her beautiful dress, on all that poufy fabric, and his happy, beautiful face was so old and tragic now, oh, God. "I know," he said, his voice rough. "And I thought, when I met you, that I'd sort of click into place. I really did love you—"

"You *do* love me! Don't put that in the past tense!" she cried, her voice shrill. "You said you wanted to be my husband! You said so on the phone last *night,* Jeremy!"

"Take it easy," Levi said.

Faith whirled around. "Shut up, Levi!" she barked. "If you have to be here, at least shut up!" He looked back down at the floor and obeyed.

Faith took a breath, then another, and looked into Jeremy's eyes. "I *know* you love me," she went on more steadily. "I know that more than I know anything. How can you be saying all this?" She lowered her voice. "Did Levi make a pass at you or—"

"No! God, no," Jeremy said. "Levi has nothing to do with this. You're the only one I've ever been with, Faith. Ever."

"See? Then you're not gay. You're just not. We've been sleeping together since sophomore year of college!"

A horrible thought occurred to her. That maybe dating a guy who said he loved you but waited two years to get into your pants...oh, shit.

"Faith, when we're...together," Jeremy said, very, very quietly, "I have to...um..."

At that moment, the door opened and Jeremy's great-aunt Peg came in. "I just have to use the ladies' room," she said. "Don't worry, I won't listen to a word. Faith, darling, you look so beautiful. And, Levi, is it? Oh, I love a man in uniform! Thank you for your service, sweetheart."

"Uh...you're welcome," Levi said. "Thanks for your support."

Good God. This was just bizarre enough to be a nightmare. You know what? It might be. She *prayed* it was. The great-aunt in the loo, Jeremy being gay...come on! It had to be a dream. *Please, God. Let me wake up in my bed and have this be a dream, and Jeremy and I will still get married. I can tell him about this dream, and we'll laugh and laugh about it. Please.*

The details, though. The smell of chalk, the cold chairs. The gleam on Levi's shoes, his crew cut.

Jeremy's bowed head.

Finally, Great-Aunt Peg emerged. "See you upstairs!" she said, waving merrily.

"You were saying?" Faith said. Her voice was sharper now, harder. "When we're together, you have to *what,* Jeremy?"

He grimaced. "I have to think of…other things. Even though I think you're beautiful and—"

"What things?" she said. "I think I deserve to know what *things* you had to picture!"

"Faith, this probably isn't—" Levi began.

"Shut up, Levi! What things, Jeremy?"

He looked wretched. Utterly miserable. "I have to picture Justin Timberlake."

Oh.

Okay, that was a showstopper. The case for Jeremy's heterosexuality took a serious hit with that one. "Justin Timberlake?"

"'Rock Your Body.' The video."

Her mouth was open, she realized. She closed it. The JT song echoed in her head, taunting. Those damn white hoodies everyone wore.

Oh, no.

Thoughts bounced and zinged through her head, not quite registering. Her makeup must be ruined from crying. The dress was itchy. They wouldn't have their first dance together. They weren't getting married.

"You're really gay?" she whispered.

He looked up and nodded, his eyes were full of tears, too, and it was idiotic, but she wanted to comfort him. "I thought that I…that I wasn't," he said. "I wanted a wife—*you*—I wanted kids, I wanted a life like my parents have, but…I…yes. I am."

He covered his eyes with one hand and bowed his head. From the first time she'd laid eyes on him, Faith had known he was special and gentle and wonderful. From that first second on, she'd loved him. He had never, ever let her down, never found her lacking, never spoke to her in anger or looked at her in contempt.

Jeremy Lyon was, above all things, a good, good man.

Without quite intending to, she reached out and stroked his smooth black hair, cut short for this day.

He looked up, his misery so obvious that it wrenched her heart, the heart he was breaking.

"It's okay," she whispered. "It's all right, sweetheart."

"I'm so sorry," he said again. "I'm so, so sorry, Faith."

He leaned in close, so his head was touching hers, and they sat there another moment or two—or an hour, the uneven sound of Jeremy's breathing as he cried, the soft pat of tears as they fell from Faith's eyes to her dress. The reality of the future pressed down on Faith, the weight almost bearable at first. Her beautiful wedding wasn't going to happen. No honeymoon in Napa, lounging around in bed with this beautiful man. Oh, God, the weight was pressing on her chest harder now. No black-haired children running through the fields of Blue Heron…no life with Jeremy, the only one who'd ever seen in her something that was special and rare and precious.

Jeremy had been proof that she was forgiven. But now there was nothing. There'd be nothing now.

"I guess we should call off the wedding, huh?" she said, and he gave a half laugh, half sob, then stood up and pulled her against him, pressing her face against his hard, muscled shoulder, and she hugged him as hard as she could, her throat aching with the sobs she wouldn't let out, because it would break Jeremy to hear that, and she loved him too much to do that. He was the love of her life.

"I'll leave town," he said, his voice cracking. "I—I can move. I won't stay here, Faith. I won't do that to you."

But he was the town doctor. Elaine and Ted had loaned him the money to buy Dr. Wilkinson's practice. She'd helped him redecorate the waiting rooms, bought him the iconic Norman Rockwell prints, filled out the online forms so he'd have up-to-date magazines. Six months in business, and he was already thinking about hiring another nurse, because that's how popular he was.

Already her head was shaking. "No. You're not going anywhere. Don't do anything. Just…you know what? Let's not do anything yet, okay?" Her breath was starting to hitch. "Let's…we'll just…talk later." Panic lapped at her feet, her knees, threatening to pull her under. She was going to lose it if she had to stay here another second. "This is all going to be fine, but I—I think I should get going," she managed, looking at his chest. She risked one more glance at his face, and, oh, God, it really did feel like her heart was being ripped apart.

"Faith, I wish things were different," Jeremy whispered. "I'm so—"

"I have to go now," she said. She took a breath and bit her lip hard, and her voice came out in a whisper. "Bye." There was a world of heartbreak in that one small word.

Into the bright sunshine that was an affront now, then into the dark cave of the limo. Some kind blankness was settling around her, thank you, God, and then Daddy was there, holding her against him, and her sisters, and Mrs. Johnson, who gripped her hand and said nothing. Jack was taking care of the guests, someone said, and Jeremy was talking to his parents.

She still had her bouquet.

No one said anything as they drove home. Blue, the half-grown Golden retriever she'd adopted from the rescue league a few months ago (because she was going to be *married* and therefore could have her own dog), greeted her joyfully, jumping up on her dress, and who cared now? Up the stairs—the photographer had taken her picture here just about an hour ago, back in the olden days.

Her bridesmaids—former bridesmaids—were close on her tail.

"Here," Honor said once they were in Faith's room. "Let me help you get undressed."

"I think—I think I'd like to be alone," Faith said. Wow. Her voice sounded so strange.

The three of them swapped a glance. "You're not gonna kill yourself or anything, right?" Pru asked.

"Good God, no. Just…just give me a little while."

Surprisingly, they obeyed, closing the door quietly behind them. Faith sank onto her bed, the tulle skirt puffing around her like dandelion fluff. There was her big red suitcase, all packed for the honeymoon, the tickets to San Francisco peeking out of the side pocket.

Hello Kitty ticked away the minutes from the bureau. She could hear the rumble of her father's voice through the open window as he talked to someone. Mrs. Johnson was banging around in the kitchen—distress cooking, they called it when she was upset. From down the hall came the sound of Abby's sobs—poor kid. Jeremy wouldn't be her uncle, though she'd been calling him that for months now. Bragging about it.

Faith drifted over to the mirror and stared at her reflection. Her mascara was smudged under her reddened eyes, and her lipstick was gone. Face utterly white. But her hair had come out really great.

You know what else? She'd dieted for two months to get to this weight, even though Jeremy assured her he loved her just the way she was. Jeremy, who was gay. Gay men liked curvy women. There you go. Shoulda known.

This morning, Faith had been the luckiest girl in New York State, if not the universe. Everyone thought that, especially her. Now, at 12:44, she was the woman who didn't know her fiancé was gay.

How could she not have known? They *slept* together. A lot! Okay, well, maybe *not* a lot, not as much as she would've liked or as much as her friends seemed to sleep with their boyfriends, but they'd been in college, hello? In separate states! And then in grad school, also in separate states! And then, this past year…well, still not so much.

Justin Timberlake.

Holy futtocks.

All this time, she thought they were happy. All this time, Jeremy, her wonderful, sweet, thoughtful Jeremy, had carried this secret alone.

Well. Levi knew. She guessed he'd told *Levi*.

She stood up and started to take off her wedding dress. It was impossible. All those damn little covered buttons and loops…Jeremy was supposed to have unbuttoned them, slowly, lovingly, and you know, yeah, she'd thought that once they were married and getting pregnant would be a joy and not an oops, their sex life would take off. It had always been fine. It'd been fine! But marriage, she'd just known, would only improve it.

Here she'd been lying naked with Jeremy Lyon, totally in love, believing him when he said she was beautiful and perfect, when he'd been thinking of Justin Timberlake dancing around in a hoodie. And while that was an entirely appealing image, the man she *loved* shouldn't have been cramming it into his head to block out *her*. You know what? Justin Timberlake wasn't even that good. Totally average. How *dare* he occupy Jeremy's mind during sex?

Faith's phone buzzed. Goggy, said the screen, featuring a photo of her scowling grandmother. Faith let it go to voice mail. A minute later, the phone chirped with a text. She looked. Pick up the damn phone. A second later, Goggy's face scowled at her again.

It'd be easier to talk to her grandmother than dodge the calls. Goggy was a slab of granite when she wanted to be. "Hi," Faith said.

"Go on your honeymoon," Goggy said firmly. "Get out of here for a while."

Faith was silent. At the moment, she couldn't imagine standing up, let alone getting on an airplane and flying across the country.

"Do it, Faith," Goggy said, her voice more gentle. "Spend a little time away from home, see the world."

The words were horribly familiar, cutting right into the middle of Faith's heart.

"You have the tickets, right? Use them. Go to San Francisco, honey, and just be away from all of this."

If that wasn't a rope, Faith didn't know what was. "Okay," she whispered.

"I'll drive you." Goggy sounded triumphant, but she was the type who never quite managed to hit forty mph on the highway.

"That's okay. You stay here. I'll get someone else. And, Goggy…" Faith's voice broke. "Thank you."

"I'll call you tonight, sweetheart."

Goggy was right. She couldn't stay here. Jeremy couldn't leave, and she couldn't stay. Jeremy was her next-door neighbor, albeit a mile down the road. She'd see him everywhere.

And at this moment, that thought was unbearable.

Add to that, Manningsport had 715 people in it. Everyone now knew that Faith Holland was too stupid to realize her fiancé was gay. *Nope, I didn't suspect,* they'd say. *Not the way that kid threw the ball…but I didn't* sleep *with him, either! Heh heh heh!*

Her zombielike state shattered abruptly. She grabbed her suitcase and yanked open the door, flew down the stairs, her dress rustling against the family photos, knocking them askew.

Justin Timberlake. She *hated* Justin Timberlake.

Just as she got to the bottom, a quiet knock came at the front door. She jerked it open, out of breath.

Ah. The *other* man she hated. Levi Cooper, Wedding Destroyer. "You," she hissed.

He was still in his dress uniform, his chest full of ribbons and medals. Mr. Hero. "Jeremy sent me to check on you."

"Take me to the airport," she ordered.

His eyebrows rose, crinkling his forehead a little. "I don't know about that."

"Do what I say, Levi," she said.

"Listen, you're probably not—"

"Shush. Just take me there."

Her father came up on the porch. "Faith, sweetpea, I was just coming to check on you. How are you, honey? This is such a shock, I don't know what to—"

"Daddy, I'm going to San Francisco. Okay? I'll call you when I land."

"Wait a second, sweetie, slow down," he said, glancing at Levi. Why? Why glance at the guy who ruined her wedding and kept Jeremy's secret, huh? "I think you should stay here, baby, with your family. This is a tough, tough day, but we'll get you through it."

"I'm going to San Francisco. I have tickets," Faith said.

"Faith—"

"I—I—I—I have to get out of here, Dad," she stammered, the hyperventilating starting up again. "I'll just go to San Fran. Remember Liza? My friend from college? She lives there, so I won't be alone. I'll call her. She's really fun. Okay? Call you later."

"Now, Faith, this doesn't seem like a good idea."

"Daddy, I *need* to get out of here. I'm going."

"All right, all right. Settle down. Just…if you want to go, give me a minute, and I'll pack some things and go with you. Okay?"

"No. I'm going alone. Right now. I have to get out of here or I'm going to lose my shit, Dad."

Her father looked startled. *That's right, Daddy,* she thought irrationally. *Don't mess with me right now.*

"Well, I'll drive you. Don't be silly, baby."

"No. He'll take me. Won't you?" She narrowed her eyes at Levi, wishing looks really could kill.

Levi cleared his throat. "Is that all right, Mr. Holland?" he asked.

"Don't ask him," Faith snapped. "I'm giving you an order, soldier. Get to it."

"Watch it," he muttered.

"Faith, it's not his fault," her father said. She turned her eyes on him, and he actually held his hands up in defense. "Sweetie, I really think you need to take a few days at least—"

"I'll call you when I land." She kissed her father's cheek, and the horrible weight crushed down again. "I love you, Daddy," she whispered. "I'm so sorry about all this. I'll pay you back." The tears threatened again. No, no. Not now. Bottle and cork. She could fall apart later.

Then she tromped down the porch, stepping on the hem of her dress and tearing it. So what? She should burn the damn thing, right along with her own white hoodie (which had been a gift from Jeremy, ack!).

There was Levi's car, a cheap rental with Michigan plates. She got in, stuffed the stupid dress down and gave Blue a few pats on the head as he tried to climb in with her. She wished she could take him. Hang on. She *could* take him. Dr. Buckthal had told her that some dogs could sense an oncoming seizure, and she'd had Blue registered as a service dog, more because she wanted to be able to take him with her wherever she went than because she thought she might need him. But he was registered all the same.

"Wait a second," she said and went inside the house. Her sisters were there, Coll and Mrs. J., too, murmuring, asking, talking, but it was all white noise. She rummaged in the file drawer where she kept Blue's records, and voila. Grabbed the paper, turned to the rest of them. Everyone was talking, offering advice, pats, trying to hug her, but they were like birds, fluttering around her head, and she waved them off.

"Look," she said, her voice wobbling. "I'm gonna go to California for a few days. Maybe take that honeymoon solo, I don't know. But I love you all, and I'm so sorry about this…fiasco. I'll call you, but right now, I have to get out of here."

"Let me drive you, Faithie," her brother said, his voice so kind that her eyes swam again.

"I'll come with you," Pru offered.

"Nope. All set. Thanks, though." She grabbed Blue's leash, figured he could eat hamburgers until she bought him dog food, then went back out to the car, where Levi was waiting. Blue leaped in the back, smiling and wagging, and thank God the dog couldn't speak, because honestly, if someone else said something kind or nice to her, she was going to lose it.

Levi Cooper would not be nice to her. She could take that to the bank.

The rat bastard got in, started the car and gave her father a wave. She waved, too, her head fizzy with adrenaline.

She'd fly to San Francisco, stay at the Mark, where she and Jeremy had been booked for four nights, their wedding gift from his parents. Liza could come, and they'd drink the honeymoon champagne, and, hell, maybe they'd take that Napa wine country tour, too.

She didn't look at Levi, and he didn't talk. Too bad he hadn't been stricken mute on the altar.

She stared out the window, cushioned in a bitter fog. Occasionally, people would see that she was wearing a big white dress or that Levi was in his dress blues, and they'd beep their horns and wave. Her face felt carved out of stone.

After an eternity or so, they got to the swooping Buffalo-Niagara Airport, so oddly beautiful, and went in. People congratulated them. She didn't answer. For the first time since her mother died, she didn't try to be nice to anyone. Just showed her ID and her ticket and passed through the gate, getting some odd looks from the screeners. Guess they hadn't seen a jilted bride yet. "My fiancé turned out to be gay," she said to one. Blue woofed and wagged his tail.

"Oh, wow," the woman said. "You didn't know?"

"No. He did, though," she said, jerking her chin at Levi. Then she put on her ridiculously pretty shoes, grabbed her carry-on—damn, it was heavy—and went to the waiting area at her gate, which was only about ten yards away, and sat down. Looked at the clock. Seven hours till her flight. Maybe she'd have a seizure to pass the time. Stress brought them on sometimes. It'd be better than sitting here, having to think about Jeremy. Just the thought of his name caused a sob to heave in her chest. Blue flopped down on the floor, wagging his tail as a toddler passed him.

Levi was talking to someone. *You're not a ticket holder, asshole,* she thought. *So, there.* But, no. He was telling the screener all sorts of things, scraps of his words floating to her—*wedding fell through, her friend, don't want her waiting alone.*

Her *friend.* What a crock that was. But Mr. Hero got through; who could turn down a guy in uniform, home on leave from the war on terror? He came toward her now, his eyes resigned, mouth in a straight line.

Before he got to her, Faith wrapped Blue's leash around the chair leg and got up and went to the ladies' room, dragging her suitcase with her. The handicapped stall was the only one big enough with this ridiculous dress. She reached back and yanked at the buttons, yanked harder, tearing a few loops, then wriggled free, hopping, banging her shoulder against the wall. Out of the white merry widow and stockings, out of the beautiful white shoes that peeped so endearingly from under her skirt. She'd packed all sorts of cute under-wear, adorable bra and panty sets, silky short nighties. Pretty little outfits for daytime, lovely dresses for those romantic dinners she and Jeremy wouldn't be having.

She changed into some yoga pants, a tank top and sneakers—she'd been planning to exercise on her hon-eymoon to keep the extra pounds off, not be one of those wives who immediately began letting herself go the sec-ond the wedding was over. Oh, no. Not her.

Then she wadded up her dress and banged out of the stall. Paused, debating whether or not to stuff it into the trash. What does one do with a wedding dress when one has been jilted? Yes, Martha Stewart or Miss Man-ners or Amy Dixon, what does one do? One certainly doesn't want to preserve it for one's daughter, not when one won't be having a daughter any time soon, since one's fiancé is gay.

She remembered calling Jeremy after she'd bought the dress. Daddy had taken all of them to Corning, to a beautiful bridal shop, and the very first dress she'd tried on had brought tears to his eyes. She'd called Jer-emy to tell him mission accomplished, and he'd said, his voice warm and loving, that he knew she'd be the most beautiful bride ever, because she had the most beautiful heart. (Gah! How could she have thought he was straight?) Then she'd talked to his mom, to tell her all the details, and Elaine had been so touched that she'd cried.

Oh, lordy. There were those strange choking noises again.

She didn't throw the dress away. She couldn't. In-stead, she walked out of the bathroom, the dress under her arm, dragging the suitcase behind her. Levi was watching the door, talking on the phone, to Jeremy, no doubt. Because *those* two had no secrets. He hung up as she approached.

"Do something with this," she said to Levi, shoving her dress against his chest and continuing on to a row of hard plastic chairs where her dog waited.

In six hours and forty-three minutes, she'd be out of New York.

Levi sat next to her, stowing her dress under his chair. "Can I get you anything?"

"No, thank you. How long have you known?" She didn't look at him.

Levi didn't answer for a minute or two. Finally, she kicked his foot and glared at him. He looked bored. How dare he look bored? The bastard!

"I guess I always knew." Blue rolled onto his back, letting them know he was available for tummy-scratching any time.

"Really. You knew from the minute you met him."

"Pretty much."

"How?" she demanded, looking at his face. "Did he try to kiss you, something like that?"

"Nope."

"But you just knew."

"Yep."

"And you never said anything?"

Levi shrugged. "I asked him about it once. He said he wasn't."

"Really? Well, what about *me,* Levi? Did you ever think to say something to me? Huh?"

He deigned to look at her, his green eyes expressionless. "People believe what they want to believe."

"Well, you know what?" she said, her voice rising. "You should've tried. I love Jeremy! I love him! I'm so in love with him, it kills me! Don't you get that?" Blue barked, backing her up. Blue loved Jeremy, too. Great. Another victim in the war.

"I believe you," Levi said. "Maybe you could quiet it down a little, though, huh?"

"Why? Am I embarrassing you? Am I making a *scene?* Don't you know what it feels like to have your heart ripped open? Do you have any idea? My whole life is gone! You took that away! You just had to say something, didn't you? You had to open your mouth!"

Then she was crying, so hard she was choking, and she jammed her hands into her hair and bent over, the sounds coming out of her alien and horrifying. How would she get over Jeremy? What kind of a life was she going to have without him? Already she missed him so much it was as if someone had shoved a hot poker through her heart. Blue nudged against her, and she buried her head against her dog's neck.

She felt Levi's arm around her shoulders and shrugged him off. Like she'd allow him to comfort her.

"I hate you," she managed to say, the words strangled on her sobs.

"Yeah, well, win some, lose some," he muttered, folding his arms and sighing.

"Just go."

"I told Jeremy I'd stay."

And, of course, Jeremy wouldn't want her here alone. Because even now, he was trying to take care of her. Even now, Jeremy still loved her. And was gay.

The crying was endless, as if she was being punched in the chest with each breath, tears pouring out of her eyes, which Blue licked away, whining. People probably thought she was mentally unstable; she sure as hell felt that way. Her rational thoughts were just distant pings;

it seemed like she was being sucked under by waves of grief and shock, barely able to breathe.

Levi got up—probably to ask someone for a tranquilizer—and returned with a roll of paper towels. "I couldn't find any tissues," he said, taking his seat once more. Blue had given up and was sleeping, his head on her foot. She grabbed the roll and blew her nose, then took a few more and mopped at her face. The tears kept falling.

And now Levi was looking at her with those eyes of his that always seemed to be so bored with her. "Look, Faith, I know this is hard for you. But would you rather be married to a gay man?" he asked calmly.

"Yes! In the case of Jeremy, yes! You didn't do me any favors, you know."

"Yeah, well, I wasn't thinking of you," he said, glancing out the window.

"No. You were being the world's best friend, outing Jeremy on the altar during our wedding. Well done, Levi. Really. Maybe you'll get another medal."

"Faith," he said, "let me ask you a question. What were you thinking during the wedding? Because your face was as white as your dress, and Jeremy was sweating blood. It was a disaster waiting to happen. And if it did, he never would've left you."

"We would've made it work."

"That's ridiculous. You both would've been trapped."

"You can shut up now." Her jaw ached from clenching.

"Someday, you'll be glad you didn't marry him."

"I'm thinking about kicking you in the nuts, Levi. Shut. Up."

Finally, he did. Her eyes stung from tears, and more

tears kept flowing. The paper towel she'd used to wipe her face was smeared with makeup.

Soon, she'd be away. She'd be away from horrible Levi, away from the town where everyone was talking about her, away from Jeremy and his beautiful eyes and happy face.

She wasn't sure when she fell asleep, was only aware that her eyes were burning, her head heavy. At some point, she slid down in the chair, and there was something under her cheek. A hand on her shoulder.

She woke groggily. Someone was shaking her gently. "Time to go, Faith," a voice said.

Levi. Right. Her head was in his lap. She sat up, wincing. Felt as if she'd been beaten with a golf club. Blue was on his feet, tail wagging. "I took him out about an hour ago," Levi added.

"Passengers in first class may begin boarding," the airline person was saying. "This is American Airlines flight 1523, direct to San Francisco. First-class passengers, please begin boarding."

Thank God. She stood up, adjusted her shirt and ran a hand over her head. She'd forgotten to take her hair down; it was still in the complicated and beautiful twist from this morning.

Levi stood as well, and she managed to look as far as his chin. "Tell him I'm doing all right, okay?" she said, then tightened her grip on the dog's leash.

"Lie, you mean?" he said, with a small flash of a grin.

She didn't return it. "Yeah." She took the handle of her suitcase and started over to the gate.

"Faith?"

She looked back at him.

His brows were drawn, his face serious. "I'm sorry things didn't work out the way you wanted."

Said the man who ruined her wedding. "Take care of yourself, Levi," she said wearily. "Don't get hurt over there."

And with that, she and her dog boarded the plane.

CHAPTER ELEVEN

FAITH STOPPED OUTSIDE of Hugo's and did a quick pass of her hair, licked her dry lips and tried to ignore the stomach cramps that had been knifing through her since she woke up at four this morning.

There he was. She could see him through the restaurant's glass door, standing by the maître d's desk, waiting for her. His hair was shiny as a crow's wing, like his mom's, his back to her, as he was talking to someone. Oh, crap, it was Jessica Dunn. Great. No one made her feel less attractive than Jessica, who probably had never even heard of Microfiber Slim-Nation undergarments.

Faith had dressed for the occasion, oh, yes. One does not meet one's gay ex-fiancé without looking fantastic. Her cutest San Francisco dress, a bright yellow confection with good seaming and tulle flowers bunched along the hem. In SF, it had seemed like sunshine itself; now, seeing Jessica dressed in black skinny jeans and a black V-neck sweater, Faith felt like a giant kindergartener. Well. At least she had on slutty shoes.

Now or never, Faith, her brain instructed, sounding like Mrs. Linqvest, who'd often whipped out stories of Eve's pain in childbirth to better terrorize the kids. Faith opened the door, the handle cold in her damp palm.

Jeremy turned around, and his eyes went soft. "Hey," he breathed.

"Hi there, stranger," she said, her voice sounding

false. Then she hugged him, and oh, crikey, he felt so good. Three and a half years apart, and she remembered everything about him, how they fit together, her cheek against his shoulder, the hard, smooth muscles of his back, the soft brush of his hair against her cheek, the smell of Old Spice (again…how could he be gay and wear Old Spice? Or had that been a clue?).

She'd loved him so much. The best man she knew… and the man who'd lied to her for years. Who'd allowed her to think they'd have everything.

Faith pulled back and gave him a smile, which shook a little at the corners. Jeremy's eyes were wet, too.

"You got even more beautiful," he said a little unsteadily.

The words caused the lump in her throat to swell. "And you haven't changed a bit." But he had, a little. There was a sadness around his eyes, and a few very appealing crow's-feet had sprung up, making him even more handsome.

"Hi, Faith," Jessica said, a tinge of impatience in her voice, like she'd had enough of the reunion.

"Hi, Jess. Nice to see you."

Jess cocked an eyebrow. Really, she and Levi had been the perfect couple. Maybe they could go into business. Condescending Looks, LLC. "Come on, I have your old table for you." She led them through Hugo's to the table by the window. Jeremy held her chair, just like old times. Jess handed them menus like she was giving out Oscars, then asked if they knew what they wanted to drink.

"How about a bottle of the Fulkerson dry Riesling?" Jeremy said. "Got any left?"

"We do."

Jeremy smiled at Faith. "They beat us out of the

platinum last year. Don't tell my parents I ordered it. They'll kill me."

A twinge of nervous irritation zipped through her. The man had left her on the altar; now he wanted to joke about wine like they were old chums. Out on the lake, boat lights winked and bobbed. The hum of the restaurant patrons made the silence between them a little less awkward.

Her lessons on dressing well seemed to have stuck with Jeremy; he looked like a model for Ralph Lauren now, a red V-neck sweater over a cream-colored button down, dark washed jeans. His hair was a little shorter than it used to be, and it suited him.

"So Levi told me he's seen you a couple times," he said.

"Yes. Good old Levi," Faith said, managing to keep the snark out of her voice. "You two are still close?"

"Oh, yeah." Jeremy put the napkin in his lap, then took a deep breath. "I've been really nervous about seeing you," he admitted. "I woke up at four this morning."

So they'd been awake at the same time. Funny, that.

"It's been a while," she said, surreptitiously wiping her damp hands on her napkin.

Jeremy pressed his lips together. "I guess I was a little worried about how you'd feel. If you'd slap my face or throw your drink at me."

"Hi, Dr. Lyon!" called a plump woman with pinkish hair. "My knee is so much better! It should be, with all the fluid you drained out of it!"

"Oh, good, Dolores. Glad to hear it."

"Two hundred cc's! I think I hold a record!" the woman said gleefully.

"Could be." He glanced at Faith. "Sorry. Where were we?"

"Drink-throwing and slaps," she said. "Thanks for the ideas."

Jeremy gave a crooked smile and rubbed his chin. "Can we get that out of the way? Do you hate me?"

"No, Jeremy. Of course not. I told you that, right after the wedding. A few times. More than a few."

"Yeah, you did," he said. "But that was in the early days. I thought maybe as time went on, you'd get…I don't know. Angry. You never wanted to see me when you were back in town, so…"

There was a long pause. "I needed to get over you," she said as quietly as she could. "It wasn't because I hated you. It was because I loved you."

His eyes filled again, and he nodded.

"Hey, Doc!" someone called. "Oh, lord, you're with Faith! Hi, Faith, honey!"

"Hi," Faith said. Clearly, meeting in public had been a bad idea. "I have no idea who that is," she murmured.

"Joan Pepitone," Jeremy murmured. "Big Frankie's mom."

"Are you two getting back together?" Frankie's mother asked.

"No, Mrs. Pepitone," he said. "Just having dinner."

"Okay, then," she whispered. "I'll leave you two kids alone."

"Anyway," Faith said. "It wasn't anything but—"

"Here we go!" Jessica announced, sticking the bottle in Jeremy's face so he could see the label.

Jeremy nodded, and Jess began uncorking the bottle.

There were times when Faith really hated all the rituals that went along with wine. Jeremy picked up the cork; it wasn't crumbly. Jessica poured him an ounce; he swirled and smelled it, then nodded. Jess poured Faith a glass, then Jeremy, then started reciting the specials.

"Jess, if you don't mind, we'll let you know when we're ready, okay?" Jeremy said, smiling up at her.

"Sure, pal," she said. "Take all the time you want."
She gave Faith a look that wasn't nearly as warm as
the one she'd just leveled at Jeremy and finally left.
Couldn't have been more than a size four, just in case
she wasn't already a pain in the butt.

Faith straightened out her cutlery, then took a sip of
wine, smiling awkwardly at Jeremy. He smiled back.
All smiles, all the time.

"Jeremy," she said quietly, looking down at her plate,
"I think the hardest part of everything was that you let
it go so far."

He was quiet for a minute, idly swirling the wine in
his glass, staring at it like it was the Rosetta stone. "I'd
never imagined a life that didn't have me as a straight
guy," he said. "I loved you. How could I be gay if that
was true?" He sighed. "I should've talked to you. I
just—and I recognize the irony here—I didn't want to
hurt you. When I did let myself acknowledge that we
didn't have a normal relationship—"

"By which I assume you're talking about Justin Timberlake?" she interjected. She now hated all JT songs
on principle.

He had the grace to look ashamed. "Right. At those
moments, I thought…" He sighed. "I thought, well, you
seemed happy enough. It wouldn't matter if we just kept
going on the way we had been."

Faith let that sink in. "So because I was too dumb to
notice anything was wrong, it was okay to pretend to be
straight." A burst of white-hot anger flared in her heart.

Jeremy's face changed. "No! Not like that, Faith.
Just…if you were happy, then I was. Because I did love
you. I still do. I hope you believe me."

The flare extinguished.

"I do," she said.

They sat for a few minutes. Funny, how she'd never felt uncomfortable with Jeremy before. Ever.

"Was it hard?" she asked. "Dealing with everyone's surprise?" she asked. They'd talked about it in those first few weeks, but he'd always shrugged it off, more concerned with her, both of them trying to assure the other they were fine.

"It was hard being without you," he said. "Every time something good happened, you were the one I wanted to tell. And every time something bad happened...well, a couple times, I was already calling you before I remembered we weren't together."

"Me, too," she said, her voice wobbling. Dang it. She dug in her purse for a tissue, but Jeremy was already handing her a handkerchief. "This is very sentimental, isn't it?" she asked in a shaky voice, and they both laughed a little. She wiped her eyes and tried not to look at him.

The murmur and hum of the diners around them filled the silence.

Faith's heart sat heavy in her chest. Like road kill, like a dead, stiff porcupine. Okay, that was a *really* pathetic image. Even now, the dead porcupine was resurrecting and giving her a reproachful look—*I was just sleeping, dummy*—but yeah, kind of. For eight unwavering years, she'd adored Jeremy Lyon. For the past three, the argument could be made (and made well) that he'd still been the most important man in her life.

It was really time for that to change. She'd kept a few secrets of her own, even from him. And maybe those were just as important as his had been.

"I realize how wrong it was for me to lie to you, Faith," Jeremy said, staring at the table. "I used you so I could be the person I wanted to be, not the person I was, if that makes any sense. I'm more sorry about that than anything."

"I might've done some of that, too," she admitted.

"But you never lied."

"Maybe not." Then again, maybe so.

He looked at her, his eyes solemn. "I have this fantasy," he said. "That you forgive me. That we become really close again. All the feelings I had for you, Faith... I wasn't faking that. I was crazy about you." His voice broke a little. "I've missed you so much."

Well, hell. She couldn't just leave him there, hanging. Faith reached over to grip his strong, smooth hands, bittersweet memories sliding through her like a river. His face as he saw her dressed for the prom, the way he always leaned forward a little when she was talking, as if he was afraid he'd miss a single word. The way he brought flowers to the airport when she came home from college, hugging her so hard he'd lift her right off the ground, the inevitable "aw" of a few onlookers.

"Of course we can be friends, Jeremy," she said. "Of course."

Maybe this was what she needed to get on with her life. For three and a half years, she hadn't been able to find a meaningful relationship. Maybe being here, being around Jeremy, was the final piece of the puzzle.

"You guys ready to order?" Jessica was back, and clearly no more conversation would be tolerated till their dinners had been chosen.

They ordered and ate, talking about ordinary things—Ted and Elaine spent most of the year in San Diego. Lyon's Den was run by a manager and had been featured in the *Times*. Jeremy's practice was bustling; he saw patients who were newborns, patients in their nineties, and, clearly, he was doing what he was meant to do. She brought him up-to-date on the Holland news, her plans for the barn and library.

The time had come to ask the awkward question. Faith realized her toes were curled in her slutty, painful shoes. "Are you seeing anyone?" Faith asked, and Jeremy's face took on that hint of sadness again.

"No. I, uh…no. I had a, um, a friend in the city about a year ago, but not anymore. The long-distance thing was too hard." He looked out the window. "I'm so busy, I don't see how I'd find someone. Dating websites, maybe. I don't know. I keep thinking someone will just show up one day. Maybe. Or maybe I'm destined to be single, which would be okay, too. I don't mean to sound pathetic. I'm very happy."

"You *do* sound pathetic," Faith said. "You sound like Bob Cratchit after Tiny Tim dies. 'I am a happy man.'"

He grinned. "How about you, Faith? Anyone special?"

"I've dated here and there," she said. *Still haven't slept with a straight guy, though that is definitely something I'd like to cross off my bucket list.*

"But nothing…serious?" Jeremy asked, and she could tell he was hoping she'd say yes.

She shook her head. "A good man is hard to find." She hesitated, then told him about her last date, Clint and his kid calling her whore, and by the time she was done, they were both laughing so hard they were crying.

"It's so good to be with you again," Jeremy said, wiping his eyes.

"Right back at you," she said, and her heart gave a twist. She *did* love Jeremy, and she always would. They could be friends. Real friends, honest this time around. Because men like Jeremy…they just didn't make them like that anymore.

"Hey."

Faith startled a little. Crap, it was Levi, like an irritable grammar school nun about to whack their hands with a ruler. He still wore his uniform, gun and all. He gave her a five on the Boredom Scale, his eyes glancing over her and dismissing her in a nanosecond.

"Levi! Have a seat, buddy," Jeremy said, letting go of her hand. "Faith and I were just catching up."

"So I see." He paused. "Faith."

"Levi." She mimicked his solemn tone, but he didn't seem to notice.

Jeremy beamed. "Sit down. You want something to eat?"

"Yeah, join us, Levi," Faith said, narrowing her eyes just a little. He wouldn't sit down. He disliked her too much.

He sat. Next to Jeremy of course, the better to level that *God, you're so uninteresting* look at her, now a seven. Faith smiled at him, making sure to wrinkle her nose like a Disney princess. His look shot up to a nine and a half. Already, his fingers were drumming on the table, ever itchy where she was concerned. Good. Let him itch. Let him have an infestation of fleas, perhaps, or a festering, scabby rash.

"My grandmother baked some brownies for you, Levi," she said sweetly, tipping her head and tucking some hair behind her ear. "Since you were so helpful with the flying squirrels."

"He lives to serve," Jeremy said, grinning. Levi gave Jeremy a wry look, which slid right off his face when he returned his gaze to Faith.

"Well, she's a huge fan, Levi. If you ever wanted a girlfriend, I'm convinced she'd leave my grandfather for you." Another sunny smile, which failed to illicit any reaction at all, though Jeremy laughed.

Jessica came over. "Hey, Levi, how you doing?" she asked, messing up the chief of police's hair.

"Hi, Jess."

"You want something to eat?"

"No, thanks. I'm not gonna stay," Levi said.

Thank God for small favors, Faith thought. "So are you two...together again?" she asked, glancing up at Jessica.

"Oh, hell, no," Jess snorted. "We broke up in high school."

"Well, you were always on and off—" Faith began.

"Yeah, well, people change," Jessica said, a smile not quite masking the sharpness in her voice.

"It was always just physical, anyway," Levi said, giving Jess a wink, a slight smile pulling his mouth up in one corner. "Right, Jess?"

Hello. Captain Testosterone still had it, Faith had to admit. That look was equivalent to half an hour of dedicated foreplay—green eyes all sleepy and knowing, that faint smile promising all sorts of thorough attention. Not that she was...it wasn't like she...what was the question again?

"Faith? You want dessert?" Jessica demanded.

"Oh! Um, no, that's fine," she said brightly, hoping no one noticed her burning cheeks.

"Gotta go," Levi said, standing up. He punched Jeremy's shoulder, leaned in to kiss Jessica on the cheek, then glanced at Faith. Good Lord, he wouldn't kiss *her,* would he? Should she offer her cheek, just in case? But Jessica was standing in the way, and if he wanted to kiss her, he'd have to—

Yeah, never mind. He was leaving. "Bye, Levi!" she called merrily. "Always so great running into you!"

She didn't miss Jessica's eye roll as she padded away. Well, who cared? Levi and Jessica were two people she'd never managed to win over.

"Where were we?" Jeremy asked, and she turned her attention back to him.

WHEN SHE GOT HOME THAT NIGHT, Goggy and Pops were still awake, alas.

"Your grandfather won't go to bed," Goggy announced, crossing her arms over her ample bosom. She looked like an angry pink pigeon, wrapped tightly in the fleece robe Faith had given her for Christmas.

"Your grandmother won't, either," Pops said from the den. "How was your date, sweetheart?" He came into the kitchen and bent to kiss her cheek.

"Yes, how was it?" Goggy asked, squeezing her hand, not to be outdone in the affection department.

"It wasn't a date," Faith said, spying the plate of brownies Goggy had made earlier. She took one, not because she was hungry, but because Goggy had made them for Levi. "But it was good to see Jeremy again."

"Those are for Chief Cooper," Goggy said, a hint of reproof in her voice.

"I know, but they looked so beautiful, I couldn't resist," Faith said.

"Let me get you some milk, sweetie." Mollified, Goggy leaped to the cupboard for a glass. Pops tried to sneak a brownie, too, but Goggy slapped his hand. "Those are for Levi! Not for you!" she said. "Faith, sweetheart, do you want another one?"

"So, Pops, it's nine-thirty," Faith said. "Why are you

up?" Her grandfather, being a farmer, did tend to go to bed around eight each night. "You feeling okay?"

"You know what it is?" Goggy said. "It's that *woman,* that German, on *Project Runway.* He's making a fool of himself, watching a show for a *German* woman who's a third his age!"

"So? I'm allowed to look. I'm not dead yet."

"Too bad, isn't it? When are you going to do me a favor and—"

"So, listen, you two," Faith said loudly. They quieted. "It's obvious that you don't need me around here, checking on you. I'm going to find a place of my own until… well." *Until I go back,* she was about to say.

But she'd never planned to stay in California forever. No one was getting any younger. Abby'd be off at college in two years; Goggy and Pops were old, if still filled with piss and vinegar.

"Who said we didn't need you? Of course we need you!" Goggy said firmly. "You should stay with us."

"She's a grown woman, Elizabeth," Pops said. "She can do what she wants. And aren't you the one who sent her all the way to California?"

"So what? She needed to get away! Her *heart* was *broken,* you doddering old man. I didn't mean she should stay away forever. Did I tell her to do that? No! This is her home."

"Well, maybe she wants to spread her wings a little without you nosing into her business," Pops said.

"Okay, okay," Faith said. "No more fighting."

"We weren't fighting," Goggy said. "We were discussing."

"Right. Let's watch *Project Runway,* okay? But I am moving out."

"I don't know. A single girl on her own? Someone

could break in and slit your throat as you're sleeping," her grandmother said.

"Thanks for the thought, Goggy."

"You should get married. Oh! You know who's single? Levi!" Goggy made a clucking sound of triumph. "That wife of his left him! I bet he's lonely. You could marry him! Is he Lutheran?"

"I don't know, but he's not my type," Faith said easily. "Come on. I hear Heidi Klum."

She herded her grandparents into the den and sat between them on the couch.

Marry Levi. Right.

CHAPTER TWELVE

"I DON'T SEE WHY YOU GIRLS needed me to drive you," Faith's father said as they pulled into the parking lot.

"Because we need you to protect us from disgusting men, Mr. H.," Colleen said. "Though if you'd marry me, I wouldn't be reduced to Singles Shooting Night."

"Please, Dad. We'll both feel better if you're here. And Coll, no more proposing to my father, okay?"

The plan was to get Dad out in the world of senior citizen singletons and show him that there were women who weren't quite as, er, carnivorous as Lorena. Two days ago, Honor had caught the woman in Dad's bedroom, going through Mom's collection of antique perfume bottles. When Honor confronted her, Lorena said she'd gotten lost on her way back from the bathroom, which didn't explain why she was making a list. This had resulted in a phone call from Honor, saying that if Faith wasn't up for the job, she'd do it herself.

But Faith was trying. She wanted nothing more than for Dad to find a nice woman, though it was still shocking that after nineteen and a half years, someone like Lorena had wormed past his shield. Tonight, she'd opted for the more personal route, completely unable to imagine her beloved dad with StillHotGranny or NotDeadYet, the most recent listings on eCommitment/SeniorLove.

And so, Singles Shooting Night (*Ages 21 to 101!* the

ad had merrily announced) here in Corning, which got Dad out of town and might make him a little more relaxed...he'd always tended to blush and mutter around interested women (except Lorena—again, probably because he was so clueless). And sure, Faith had it in the back of her mind that maybe, just maybe, she'd meet a sweet and wonderful man. One who looked like Jake Gyllenhaal, maybe. Or Ryan Gosling. She'd take either. Or both. Why not? A girl could dream.

As for the whole weapons aspect of the evening, well. There wasn't much in terms of singles events around here, if you didn't count setting a fire to a hay bale so the Manningsport Volunteer Fire Department would come out, which Suzette Minor had done last week. According to Ned, Suzette had then been asked out by Gerard Chartier, so maybe there was something to be said for arson. But Singles Shooting Night had a certain metaphoric truth, Faith thought. You'd aim, fire and hit or miss. *We met over a Glock, and she nailed the target right in the face, and I just knew.*

"Game faces on, people," Colleen said as they got out of the car. Dad grumbled but followed her inside, removing his cap and running a hand through his silver hair.

"Daddy, don't forget you have to talk if a lady approaches you," Faith said. "Be nice."

"We should've brought Lorena," Dad said. "I think she's interested in getting married again."

"Oh, she is, Mr. Holland," Colleen said. "She's got her eye on you, don't you know."

"I wouldn't say that," he said, smiling fondly.

"Does she put out?" Colleen asked.

"Coll! Come on!"

"I— We...ah, we don't...well, she's fun and all, but...

uh, here you go, girls." He held the door to Zippy's Gun & Hunting and then went inside. Plenty of people crowded into the shop, Faith thought. Lots of white hair.

"Hello there," a man said to Colleen's boobage, which was on excellent display, as ever. He was around seventy, and Colleen smiled slyly. She'd often voiced the opinion that she had the makings of an excellent kept woman or trophy wife.

Faith had to give the organizers credit: at least there'd be something to do in addition to the usual chatter/interrogations that went on at singles events. Kill each other, for example. She tried not to sigh as Coll wandered off.

Her parents had grown up together, childhood friends, dating since tenth grade, when Dad had caught Mom's shoe at a church dance—the boys had lined up on one side of the room, the girls on the other, and the girls had been told by the reverend to throw one shoe, then find the boy who caught it and dance with him. Mom had admitted to hurling her Ked at John Holland "like Don Larsen throwing to Yogi."

Then again, maybe they weren't the best example.

Colleen returned. "I already have three phone numbers," she said. "So old school. Two of those guys don't even have a Facebook page."

"Well, you're tapping into the artificial hip crowd, Coll, what do you expect?"

"You see anyone for you?" Colleen asked, peering around. A man wearing overalls—but no shirt—leered at them, but Coll just laughed and said, "In your dreams, pal. Eesh. Avert the eyes, Faith. I don't think he's wearing underwear."

By and large, the attendees were female and over fifty. She and Colleen definitely stood out. There were…let's see…seven men, not counting Dad. Speaking of, her father approached. "Sweetie, what should I do?" he asked. "Two women have already asked for my phone number."

"Oh, great!" Faith said, patting his arm. "Very flattering. Maybe you should meet one of them for coffee. I'm sure they're very nice."

"I don't think so. I'm not really interested in dating."

"Dad, Lorena is circling you like a great white. I think *she* thinks you're dating."

Dad gave her a confused look. "No. She's just fun. A nice person. Very vivacious."

Faith paused. "Dad, we're pretty sure she's after your money."

"I have no money. I have four children instead."

"She was cataloguing Mom's perfume bottles."

"Oh, those things. Your mommy sure did love them. I thought they were dust collectors, myself, but…" His blue eyes softened at the memory, and Faith's heart tightened. She *had* to find him someone else. He deserved it.

A woman edged closer. Nicely dressed, age-appropriate. Faith gave her a tiny nod and turned back to her father.

"Dad, if you think Lorena's fun, maybe you'll like talking to other women who don't discuss thongs with your teenage granddaughter."

"Did she do that?" Dad asked, suitably shocked.

"Ask Abby."

"Give someone else a shot, Mr. H.," Colleen said. "See what you got. Oh, that guy is giving me the eye. Back in a flash." Colleen dashed off to another septuagenarian, this one with a walker, and tossed her shiny hair.

"Hello there! I'm Beatrice," said the woman who'd been eyeing dear old Dad. Attractive, lively, smiling.

A contender, in other words. She spoke to Faith, rather than John. "Aren't you beautiful! I love red hair."

Nicely played, Faith admitted. Go straight for the child. "I'm Faith, and this is my dad, John. He's a widower."

"Oh, I'm so sorry for your loss," Beatrice cooed, her eyes sparkling with delight. "I'm divorced, three kids, four grands."

Dad didn't answer, so Faith gave him a hearty nudge to the ribs. "Oh, uh, I'm…uh hello. John. John Smith."

"Dad," Faith muttered.

"I have several children myself," he said. He was sweating already. Faith stepped discreetly away, pretending not to see Dad's pleading look.

Colleen intercepted her near the refreshments table. "The guy was impotent. I mean, come on. I'm willing to overlook certain things, but that? No. Says his heart condition prevents Viagra, so thus ends our courtship. Oh! Faith, check *that* out. If the flip side is half as good as what we're seeing, I think we've found your soul mate. *That,* my friend, is a great ass. Do you concur?"

"I concur most heartily."

The man was not old, nor did he have a walker. Score two points. Jeans (yes, she checked out his ass first, what else was a girl to do when presented with that side of a man?), a green T-shirt, the sleeves tight around his gorgeously muscled arms. Broad, solid shoulders. Short dark blond hair.

An icicle sliced through the warm curls of lust that were starting in her girl parts. He turned toward them. Yep.

"Oh, my God, it's Levi!" Colleen exclaimed. "What's he doing here? Don't tell me he's cruising these pathetic singles things?"

"I hate to point it out, but we're cruising these pathetic—"

"I know, but I've seen up close how that man has to fight off the hordes of hungry females in our town."

Faith glanced at her. Colleen was unabashedly, er... open about liking sex. "You and Levi ever...?"

"Oh, no. He's too young for me."

"He's our age, Coll."

"I'm aware of that, Faith. No, I like them broken in."

"That sounds filthy."

"Trained. I like them trained."

"That's worse." Faith grinned.

"Okay, I'll stop. Hey, Levi, come on over, bud!"

"No, don't, Colleen, you know he never... Hi, Levi."

"Ladies."

Colleen put a hand on his arm. "Levi, we're looking to get laid."

"Colleen," Faith groaned.

Her friend ignored her. "Can you hook us up with the hottest men here? I like them fifty, fifty-five plus. Don't mind a little beer belly. Missing limb is okay, as long as it was lost heroically. I don't want some dumb ass who cut off his own hand chopping wood."

"Got it," Levi said. "Been through the population of Manningsport, Coll?"

"Don't be catty. Seen anyone who might be Faith's soul mate?"

"I'm just here to keep my dad company," she muttered.

"Which is not to say we weren't just checking out your ass," Colleen added.

"And you, Levi?" Faith asked, feeling the heat prickling not just her cheeks, but her throat and chest, too. "Looking for Mrs. Cooper the Second?"

He gave her a long, unblinking stare. A nine on the scale, sort of a *So this is what hell is like* look. "I'm the instructor," he said.

Great.

"Hey, Levi," her father said, having extracted himself from Beatrice of the voracious eyes. "How you doing?"

"Good, thanks. The girls say you're…"

"Let's not talk about it," John suggested.

"Fine with me," Levi said. "I need to get started."

"Sure, sure, do your thing, hottie." Colleen smacked him on the shoulder, then mugged for Faith as he walked away. "I would ride him like a Brahma bull if he were twenty years older."

"Colleen, you're a hoot," Dad said, chuckling.

"If I said that, you'd drop dead of a heart attack," Faith pointed out.

"True enough," Dad said. At least he seemed more relaxed.

"Okay, people," Levi called. "Welcome to…" He glanced at his clipboard, then sighed. "Target Practice for Singles." His eyes stopped on her, and even from five yards away, she could feel his disdain. "I'm Levi Cooper, your shooting instructor for tonight. Who here is familiar with guns?"

LEVI HAD SUSPECTED THIS GIG was a bad idea. Once in a while, he taught gun safety classes here, so when Ed, the owner, had called him, he said sure. It paid four hundred dollars, and with Sarah's textbooks costing as much as a pony, four hundred bucks wasn't bad for two hours' work.

He hadn't expected to see the Hollands here, that was for sure. Or Colleen. She, at least, was fun. Faith, though…she had some bug up her ass. For some reason, she was telling every woman there that he was single, too. "Oh, Levi's wonderful," he overheard her say to a woman who looked much like his drill sergeant. "So sensitive. Also, a war hero. I know. We went to school together. Sure, he loves older women."

"Partner up, folks," Levi called. "Faith, old buddy, why don't you come over here?" It was only fair, really, that she get the guy in the overalls who'd opted not to wear a shirt tonight.

"Gosh, you're pretty," the guy said.

"And you should wear a shirt," she said easily. "Really. Okay? Next time, wear clothes." She smiled at the guy, who got the idiotic look of a man in love. Or a drunk. Slack jaw, blurred vision.

"You've fired a gun before, Faith, haven't you?" he asked her.

"I have. Hand her over, Levi. I'm feeling a little trigger happy tonight."

"You can shoot, too?" Shirtless said. "The perfect woman."

Levi almost smiled as he walked up and down the line, instructing the amateurs on how to hold the gun, what kind of kickback to expect. Colleen had some old dude eating out of her hand, and the man certainly wasn't complaining. One woman didn't want to wear ear protection because it would mess up her hair. Honestly.

"I don't know a thing about guns," said one lady, grabbing his arm, the better to squish her boobs against him. "Can you help me with my stance?"

"Sure. Like this." He demonstrated the proper firing stance—legs slightly spread, arms out, elbows bent, both hands wrapped around the gun. "Keep your thumbs together, your trigger finger here. Got it?"

"Can you stand behind me, and put your arms around

me to make sure I'm doing it right?" She gave a wriggle of anticipation.

"No, ma'am. Sorry."

She frowned. "Please? Pretty please? I'm Donna, by the way."

"Sorry, ma'am. We have rules."

"That woman said you're ex-military," she murmured huskily, jerking her chin down the line at Faith. "I won't lie. I find that very hot." She trailed a finger along the bottom of the crossed swords of his 10th Mountain Division tattoo, making his skin crawl.

"I have to move on." He glanced at her partner, who was doing a finger stick to check his blood sugar. "Good luck, sir."

The sound of gunfire still made him flinch a little. Another good reason to be here. Desensitization.

After the target practice, the participants were supposed to sit down and talk in eight-minute segments, then move on. Like anyone would need eight minutes to tell. Nina, his ex-wife, had been a helicopter pilot who'd picked up his patrol during a messy skirmish, and ten seconds into their conversation, he'd already known they'd be sleeping together. Three days later, he'd been thinking marriage, kids, a little house back home.

Then again, Nina had dumped him thirteen weeks into the marriage.

Whatever. Target practice was almost over. In an hour, Levi could lock up and go home, and hopefully sleep better than he had last night, although gunfire wasn't the best sound to have echoing in your head before bedtime. Maybe he'd bake some cookies for Sarah.

He stopped to check on a couple who actually seemed to be having fun, gave the guy a tip on aim and moved on. John Holland was in the next lane. He wasn't shooting, though. He was being hunted, practically pinned against the wall.

"Feel them," said the woman who'd claimed him as partner. "They're just like the real thing. I said to myself, 'Carla, do you want to have droopy old boobs for the rest of your life?' This was my sixtieth birthday present to me. Implants, double D, peanut oil. Go ahead. Take a squeeze."

"Hey, John," Levi said. "Could you give me a hand with something?"

The man leaped at the chance. "Thank you, son," John breathed. "God, I miss my wife."

"Don't give up yet." He glanced at his chart. "Okay, yeah, this lady seemed nice." They approached another woman who was firing with great efficiency. "I'd be gay for Ellen," she was telling the man she was with. "She has a *great* ass."

John's face turned a shade whiter.

"Moving on," Levi said.

"This was my daughter's idea, and I just don't... I think I'm going home. Do you see Faith and Colleen?"

Levi glanced down the line, where Faith was leaning against the wall in the last stall, Shirtless pouring on the charm. She saw Levi and gave him a subtle finger. "Know what?" he said. "It seems like she's having a great time. Colleen, too. How about if I drive them back?"

John nodded. "That'd be great, Levi. Thank you." With that, he hurtled for the door.

A little while later, the guns, ear and eye protectors stowed, the now-unarmed single people sat in the shop area of the gun range. The walls were lined with rifles, locked glass cases housing ammo and pistols. Metal chairs had been brought in, and the single people sat facing each other in a long line. It looked like visiting hours at a prison, minus the phones.

"Have you seen my dad?" Faith asked him as he walked past.

"He left," Levi answered, not pausing. He heard her squawk and turned around. "I'm driving you and Colleen home."

"Or I could," Shirtless Joe offered.

Levi leaned against the wall and checked his phone. Four texts from Sarah. I have 0 friends. Can u come get me?

Feel sick was the second.

Stop being an ass, u can't make me stay here was the third, and the fourth was simply I hate u.

Sighing, he stepped into the hallway to call her back. Got her voice mail. Honestly, why had he bought her a phone if she just used it for texting?

"Sarah, stop being such a drama queen, okay? You can come home on Columbus Day. You need to make some actual human friends." He paused, picturing her at a party with a bong and a bag full of Ecstasy. "Or just study more. Keep up those grades. All right? I have to go." He paused. "Bye."

Ten seconds later, his phone buzzed. Still hate u. And ur 1 2 talk. Get a life & stop obsessing about me. U need 2 get laid.

Inappropriate, he texted back. Oh, and by the way, he'd *love* to stop obsessing about Sarah, but she texted or called at least ten times a day. Would it be wrong to strangle her? Probably.

Levi rubbed his eyes. The truth was, both of them needed to get a life. These past two years, with Nina leaving and Mom's cancer…it'd been rough. And he and Sarah were closer because of it. But when your family shrinks to two, it got to be a little hard sometimes, the only shoulder for Sarah to cry on.

The door opened—Colleen. "Hey, Chief. Come on in here. Let me practice on you."

"Sounds so dirty, O'Rourke."

"In your dreams, Cooper."

"In my dreams, definitely," he said.

"Ooh, wanna talk dirty? Bet I could win." She raised her eyebrows and grinned.

"You would," he acknowledged. He liked Colleen, one of the few who'd never treated him differently after he'd come back. Her brother, too, and Jeremy. And Faith, now that he thought of it, though Faith had an edge to her he didn't remember. It was better than Princess Super-Cute.

Colleen towed him back in the room and gestured to one of the empty metal chairs.

"Just sit there and look pretty," Colleen said, taking a seat. "Let's pretend we don't know each other. We're supposed to ask three questions each. I'll go first."

"Of course you will," he murmured.

"What's your favorite food?"

"Cheeseburgers made at O'Rourke's," he answered.

"Oh, good answer!" she said, clapping. "What's your favorite color?"

It was such a girl question. Did he even have a favorite color? Blue? Red? "Green," he said.

"Super. And last one, what's your favorite position?" She gave him a leer, and Levi just smiled. "Well, points for trying," Colleen said. "I was gonna write it in the bathroom stall at the bar. When are you gonna start dating again, Levi?"

"Three questions was all you got."

Someone's watch or phone beeped, and all the

women got up and shifted. Colleen blew him a kiss. He nodded back. The next woman was the one who'd stroked his tattoo. Her questions were, *Do you believe in love at first sight, have you ever spanked a woman* and *what's your favorite color.* His answers were no, no and red.

"Okay, ask me anything," she said.

Levi sighed. "Um, what's your name?"

"Donna. I already told you that." She gave him a huge smile and squeezed her arms together, making her leathery cleavage swell. "Want to come back to my place and work on that spanking?"

For crying out loud. "I think it's still my turn for questions. Uh, what's your favorite color?"

"Pink! I'm actually wearing pink underwear. Want to see?"

"Still my turn. What are your views on the Mideast peace talks?"

"I think everyone should totally get along, don't you? Want to go out sometime?"

Mercifully, the timer sounded again. "Nice meeting you," he said.

Faith sat down in front of him. The night just kept getting better. "Oh, my gosh," she said to the departing lady. "I think he likes you! He was just checking out your ass."

"Shut it, Faith," he muttered.

"Really?" the woman said. She slapped her own butt and winked at him.

"Looks like you made a friend," Faith told him. "That's so you, Levi. Such a friendly person."

"Do you have three questions?"

"I do, actually. Not that I want to date you, of course."

"Yes, I remember."

That got her. Pink rose in her cheeks (and neck…and chest, there was the mighty rack again, showcased in a red V-neck, and really, there was nothing like a red-head in red). She unfolded a piece of paper. "Have you ever been in prison?"

Okay, well, at least it wasn't his favorite color. "No."

"Have you fathered any children, and are you involved in their lives if so?"

"No kids."

"How many women have you slept with?" She gave him a knowing look. "If you can count that high, that is."

The number wasn't as high as his reputation, apparently. "Pass. Next question?"

"Can you provide me with your social security number so I can run a background check on you?"

"Hard to believe you're still single." He lifted an eyebrow at her, and she folded up her list, making a huffing noise.

"Don't crinkle your forehead at me, Levi Cooper. Questions like this cut through the garbage. Who cares if you like moonlit walks or love old movies or if you're married or gay or live in your mother's basement?"

She had a point. "I hate old movies," he said.

"Me, too. They're so schmaltzy. Give me a horror flick any day."

"I like horror movies, I don't live in my mother's basement, I'm not married and I'm not gay," he said.

And all of a sudden, an electric current seemed to hum between them. She seemed to feel it, too, because her cheeks flushed, and her eyes seemed to soften. *You need to get laid,* his brain reminded him.

Shit. *Not* with Faith Holland and all her baggage. No matter how much his body was starting to growl.

"Exnooze me," came a baby voice, and Levi jumped as something nudged his ear. It was Donna, and holy hell, she had a puppet on her hand. A pig, waving at him. "Do you wike animoos? I wuv dem!" Her voice changed back to normal. "I do puppet shows at children's parties. I love kids, don't you? I'd like to have a few."

Faith smiled at him, the timer sounded, and both women went on to someone else.

So FAITH HADN'T FOUND her future husband. She hadn't really expected to, but she'd gotten three phone numbers for Dad and would begin screening tomorrow. The night wasn't a total bust.

Levi drove in manly silence all the way home; she asked him to take Route 54 instead of Lancaster Road, but he hadn't asked why; just grunted and done as she requested.

You know, for a second there, she could've sworn that something had passed between them. Maybe. Whatever it was, imagined or not, it had vaporized almost instantly.

"This was *such* a good idea," Colleen said. "Sugar daddy, here I come."

"I just feel bad that my father left," Faith said.

"I just feel bad that you won't let me marry him," Coll returned. "Wouldn't I make a great stepmother?"

"He'd be dead in a week," Faith said.

"Levi, did you find anyone? That lady with the tattoos, she was kinda hot."

"Or the puppeteer," Faith couldn't help adding. "Very kinky."

"I was just there as the instructor," he said.

"Well, you should find a nice girl," Colleen said. "I'll be on the lookout."

"No, thanks."

Colleen sighed dramatically. "Faith, his heart was broken when his evil wife left him. We have to help."

"Do we?" she asked. "He seems to want to be left alone."

"Correct," he said, glancing in the rearview.

Pretty eyes. Levi Cooper definitely had pretty eyes.

She kind of hoped Levi would drop Colleen off first. Why, she didn't know, but the thought of being alone in the car with Levi Cooper made her knees tingle.

But, no. Geographically, the Old House came first, and sure enough, Levi pulled into the driveway. She said goodbye to Colleen, thanked him for the ride, then stood, watching them back out, oddly jealous that Colleen would have three more minutes in the car with Chief McYummy.

CHAPTER THIRTEEN

"FAITH, SINCE YOU'RE NEW, why don't you get us started off, honey?" said Cathy Kennedy, the leader of Women's Bible Study.

"I thought it was my turn," said Carol Robinson, one of the power walkers Faith had almost hit on her way into town a few days ago. Honestly, the six of them walked abreast, like they *wanted* to end up in the hospital.

"Well, Faith is new, so let her have a turn."

Faith smiled. Cathy was *definitely* a contender for Dad's girlfriend. Last night, Lorena of the Leopard Print had been at dinner again, and Faith had been summoned by an urgent call from Honor, who'd had a wine tasting over at The Red Salamander. Sure enough, Lorena had innocently been rifling through the desk in the den while Dad read the paper, oblivious. When Faith had asked if she could help her find something, Lorena had said she lost an earring last time she'd been there. "That woman is going to rob your father blind," Mrs. Johnson had growled when Faith had gone into the kitchen, banging a pot to reinforce her point.

So, yeah. Where better to find a nice woman than Bible Study? Only one of the three candidates from Singles Shooting Night had held up; one didn't like children, and the other seemed to have a gambling problem. Number Three was still under investigation, but she lived kind of far away.

"We're at, let's see, now, Exodus, chapter four, verse twenty-five. Go ahead, Faith," Mrs. Kennedy said.

"Thanks, Mrs. Kennedy," Faith said, looking at her Bible. "Um…okay, here we are. *'Then Zipporah took a sharp stone, and cut off the foreskin of her son*—oh, crikey, are you kidding me?—*and cast it at his feet, and said, 'Surely a bloody husband art thou to me.'* Am I in the right chapter?" Horrified, she glanced around at the other women.

"Perfect!" Cathy said. "Shall we discuss?"

"Was the baby crying?" Carol asked. "You slice off his little foreskin with a rock and throw it on the ground, I want to know what the baby's doing."

"Might not have been a baby," Lena Smits observed. "Sometimes those boys were fifteen, sixteen years old when this happened."

"I doubt it," Mrs. Corners said. "My grandson won't even let his mother hug him. I doubt he'd let anyone circumcise him with a rock."

"I doubt it, too," Faith said, suppressing a dry heave. Surely, God would see how selfless she was being—senior citizen matchmaking *and* Bible Study rolled into one—and reward her with not only a pleasant stepmother, but also a nice husband and several cute babies. *Any time now, Big Guy,* she thought.

And speaking of marriage…the last time Faith had been in Trinity Lutheran's basement, she'd been wearing a wedding dress.

Well. No point in crying over spilled champagne. She wasn't here to relive her aborted wedding day. She was here to pick up women.

Cathy Kennedy, sure. She'd been widowed a long

time. Janet Borjeson was also single, though Honor had made disapproving noises when Faith had mentioned her. But still. She noted their names in the margin of the Book of Exodus.

"What do you think, sweetheart?" Goggy asked.

Faith jumped. "Um, about the circumcision?" And really. Was there something wrong with *Let the little children come to me?*

Goggy frowned. "No, honey. Barb's thinking about a breast reduction. She's had back pain for years." Barb nodded in agreement.

First foreskins, now boobs. "Go for it. I hear you'll be really perky afterward."

"Exactly," Barb said. "Thanks, Faith. You're a doll, you know that?" She smiled. "You know, my grandson is single, honey. Shall I give him your number?"

Faith suppressed a shudder. Barb's grandson had escorted her in, a living cliché for serial killer—shuffling feet, thinning hair and the creepy, unblinking gaze of Mark Zuckerberg. "Oh, that's sweet of you, but, no. I, uh…no, thank you."

"She's still heartbroken over Jeremy Lyon," Carol Robinson announced.

"No, I'm not," Faith answered. "We're friends."

"How *could* you get over him?" Cathy said. "All that and a doctor, too. Did you know he actually had me laughing during my annual you-know-what?"

The topic switched to Jeremy's gentle hands, and then to the new sneakers Carol had bought at seventy percent off during her trip to the outlets.

After an hour or so, which seemed to be spent discussing ungrateful grandchildren and knee replacements, and *not* Moses in the desert, Bible Study finally broke up. "This must bring back terrible memories for you," Carol said. "This was the exact spot where Jeremy broke up with you, isn't it?"

"It is, Mrs. Robinson. Thanks for bringing it up." She kept her eye on Cathy, hoping to casually mention Dad.

"You poor thing! It must've been horrible! Did you really have no idea?"

"I didn't. Big surprise, right? How about that Zipporah, huh? Interesting woman."

Carol would not be deterred. "I understand you not wanting to date Bobby McIntosh, but you *are* looking for a husband, aren't you? Your grandmother said you are."

"No, no. Not really. Well…sort of, but, no." Faith shot her grandmother a look, but Goggy was busy discussing the delicacy of Norine Pletts's lemon bars and making the argument that pastries that good could only be from Lorelei's Sunrise Bakery while Norine simply smiled in enigmatic silence. And dang it! Cathy Kennedy had just walked out the door.

"Well, my son's brother-in-law is single. You want his number? Want me to have him call you? He has a glandular problem, so he sweats a lot, but he's very nice. So I'll tell him to call you. Good! Okay, bye."

"That's all right, Mrs. Rob—" But Carol was gone, power-walking efficiently away.

Faith approached Goggy, who was still drilling Norine about her baking techniques. "Well, if you didn't use baking powder, Norine, then how are they so flaky? Answer me *that.*"

"Family recipe," Norine said, smiling at Faith.

"Goggy? I'm gonna start unloading the car, okay? See you when you're done here. But take your time."

Goggy's face took on a tragic expression as she turned to her fellow Lutherans. "Oh. That's right. She's *leaving* me, you know. She's...*moving out.* She could've stayed with us, but, no, these *young* people, they all need their *space.*" She sighed mournfully, invoking a Greek chorus of disapproving murmurs.

"Bye, ladies! Thank you for letting me sit in." The disapproval turned to hugs and pats and admonitions to watch herself crossing the street and to lock her doors at night so her throat wouldn't be slit.

She made her way out of the church basement and blinked in the bright sun.

It was one of those perfect, late-September afternoons, clear and cool, the air tart with the smell of changing leaves and pumpkin soup from the little lunch place down the square. A line of preschoolers, all holding onto (or tied to) a rope, made their way across the street. It was a Wednesday, and while a few folks wandered up and down the street, peering into the windows of Presque Antiques and Unique Boutique, it was mostly quiet.

Two days ago, Faith had asked Honor if she knew of any apartments that might be available. Five seconds later, Honor had Sharon Wiles on the phone. Not only was there an apartment available, it was the model, the only one in the building still not rented *and* furnished, when would Faith like to move in? Faith had to hand it to her; Honor knew everything and everyone in this town.

In the back of the car were two suitcases, a few boxes of miscellaneous kitchen stuff Goggy insisted she couldn't live without, and Blue, sitting up, disgusting tennis ball in his mouth, head tilted as if trying to use mind control so she'd throw him the ball.

"Hi, sweetie pooch!" Faith said. "Do you love your ball? Is it so slimy and delicious? It is?" Blue chuffed agreeably, wagging his tail. Sharon Wiles hadn't been crazy about the idea of Blue, but she couldn't deny that he was beautiful, well behaved and, yes, technically a therapy dog. Hey. It got him into restaurants.

Faith heaved a box out of the back and made her way over to the Opera House, the dog on her heels. Her new domicile was very conveniently located just off the square and directly across from Lorelei's Sunrise Bakery. Also, there was a new chocolatier that Faith very much wanted to support. But first, she'd settle in, put a set of new sheets on the bed, make some coffee, unpack her clothes. Goggy would be coming over, too; she wanted to make sure the new apartment was clean enough.

For a second, Faith pictured her mom helping her move. In Faith's mind, Connie Holland had aged beautifully, wore jeans and a T-shirt and Converse sneakers. They'd laugh and rearrange the furniture, something Mom had loved to do. Then they'd get some cookies from Lorelei's and just talk. Maybe about Jeremy. Faith had wondered a thousand times if Mom would've been able to tell.

And all that might've been possible, Faith reminded herself, if it hadn't been for her own self.

"Come on, Blue," Faith said, opening the door. Up the wide staircase to the third floor, her dog following, ball in mouth. Her apartment was 3A, which overlooked Lorelei's. Thank you, Jesus, she'd wake up to the smell of bread. She shifted the box and fumbled in her pocket for the keys.

The door to 3C opened, and there stood Levi Cooper in uniform. His forehead crinkled in a frown. "What are you doing here?" he asked.

Blue leaped over to Chief Grouchy and dropped the ball. When Levi didn't understand, the dog picked the ball up again and dropped it. Repeated, not caring that Levi was staring at Faith like a python eyeing a mouse. Whatever little bonding nanosecond they'd had at the shooting range was obviously a figment of her imagination.

"Levi. What a lovely surprise. Are we neighbors?" Faith kept her tone bright and chirpy, but a blush was prickling its way up her chest. Granted, housing options were limited—the Opera House was the only apartment building in town, but come on.

"Are you moving in?" Levi asked.

"You can tell that? It's astonishing. How did you know? Here, hold this." She didn't wait for an answer, just shoved the box at him.

"You're moving in."

"It's like you're psychic. Thrilling, really. You should stop scowling. You'll need Botox before you know it."

Blue was still dropping and redropping the ball, trying to clue in the dopey human. Faith had the door open now and reclaimed the box. "See you around, neighbor."

She went into the cute little apartment, set the box down and then looked out the peephole. He was gone.

So Levi Cooper lived in 3C. That was okay. Free country and all that. They'd probably never see each other. Which was fine. Okay, yes, they'd see each other sometimes.

She wasn't sure how she felt about that.

Blue was sniffing the corners. The dog had a point. This was their new place, at least for a while; Sharon had let her do a month-to-month rental, since some income was better than no income.

And the apartment was lovely. The floors were the original, narrow birch planks, soulfully scuffed from a hundred and fifty years of use, now polished to a high gloss. The actual theater part of the opera house was on the fifth floor; Faith imagined the third floor had been a workspace for set-making or costume storage or the like. From the front windows, not only could she inhale the glorious smells coming from the bakery, but she also had a glimpse of Keuka and a very nice view of the green.

The kitchen had granite countertops and an island, as well as a built-in wine rack. There was a tiny study where she could set up her computer and stalk potential mates for both her father and herself. And work, of course. In addition to the barn and the library courtyard, she'd had a request for a design from another vineyard across the lake, and two private homes.

The door opened and in came Goggy, holding a tiny box, and Levi, holding two much larger ones. "Look who I found!" Goggy crowed. "Levi Cooper, our chief of police!"

"I know who he is, Goggy," Faith said. "Thanks, Levi."

"You're welcome," he said, setting the boxes on the table. "Anything else I can do, ladies?"

"Oh, you've been wonderful!" Goggy said. "Hasn't he been wonderful, Faith?"

"So wonderful."

"Have a good day, then," he said, smiling at Goggy. Not her, of course. Then he was gone.

"Thank you for doing this with me," Faith said, giving the old lady a hug.

"Oh, honey, I love being needed," her grandmother responded, her soft, wrinkled cheeks flushing a lovely shade of pink. "Thank you for asking me. I never had a girl, you know."

"I do know." Faith's smile widened; Goggy often

dropped well-known facts as if she was revealing them for the first time. "So you and Pops will be okay without me?"

Goggy turned the hot water on and began filling the sink. She didn't believe in dishwashers. "We'll be fine," she said. "It was nice, having someone break up our routine."

Guilt cartwheeled merrily through Faith's heart. "I'll stop in every day," she said.

"Oh, you don't have to do that. I understand," Goggy said. She opened the first box and started setting glasses in the hot, soapy water. "I envy you. I wouldn't mind having a nice new place like this and living by myself, either. Starting over."

Faith looked at her, surprised. Not something you'd expect from an eighty-four-year-old woman. Or maybe it was exactly what you'd expect.

"What's it like, being married for so long?" Faith asked, opening another box.

"Oh, I don't know," Goggy said. "Sometimes I feel like your grandfather has no idea who I am. I'm sure *he* thinks he learned everything there was to know in the first week we were married, and there's been nothing new since. But there is! Sometimes I want to tell him about a book I've read or something someone said in church, and he barely listens."

Faith made a sympathetic noise. "You got married when you were so young," she said. Her grands had known each other only a month before they got married. Back when you did stuff like that.

"Don't I know it," Goggy said.

"You must've fallen in love right away."

Goggy snorted. "Hardly, sweetheart. He had land,

we had a little money, he'd just come back from the service, and our families approved."

"Did you love him?"

Goggy's face hardened. "What's love, anyway?" She
scrubbed a glass so hard Faith feared for its future.

"Want to sit down, Goggy?" Faith asked. "Let's have
some coffee and talk."

Her grandmother looked at her, her eyes soft. "That'd
be nice, honey. No one thinks I have much to say these
days. Just you."

Faith made the coffee, grateful for the Keurig and
its speed. She set Goggy's cup down in front of her and
sat down next to her grandmother.

"I was engaged to a boy who died in the war," Goggy
said, and Faith choked, she was so surprised. Goggy
patted her idly on the back. "His name was Peter. Peter
Horton."

Peter, Goggy said, was the boy from down the street,
the milkman's son. His mother was British, which made
him seem very glamorous. They'd had an understand-
ing—Peter would go off to war, "because that's what
people did back then, Faith, no matter if you were rich
or poor. Even Hollywood actors went to war." Upon his
return, they'd marry.

He died in France, and Goggy hadn't much cared
much after that. John Holland, why not? She did want
to have children. And there weren't so many options
for women back then.

"But I still think of him, Faith," Goggy said now, her
voice quiet and gentle. "Sometimes, I'll be doing laundry or going up the stairs, and I wonder if he'd even
recognize me. I wonder if we'd have been happy. I think
we would have. He'd bring me flowers he'd picked in

a field, and write me poems, and sneak looks at me in church."

"He sounds wonderful," Faith said, wiping her eyes on a napkin. Her chest ached, knowing Goggy had once been so sweetly courted, so in love.

"He was." Goggy was quiet for a minute. "Your grandfather, he never tried very hard. I was a done deal." Goggy glanced at Faith and reached over to squeeze her hand. "So I understand how you must feel about Jeremy, in some ways. The love of your life won't be the man you end up with, and you'll always compare the two."

"Well, I hope not," Faith said. "But, Goggy, I'm so sorry. That's such a sad story. Why didn't you ever tell me?"

"I don't know," she said. "No one wants to hear an old lady's stories." Goggy sighed and then rose to her feet with surprising vigor. "Let's get cleaning. This place looks well enough on the surface, but those cabinets could be hiding a world of germs."

FAITH WOKE UP AT THREE in the morning with an idea.

The first event at the Barn at Blue Heron would be an anniversary party for her grandparents. She could have the place done in time, or at least mostly, and she'd organize a big party for them, and maybe Goggy and Pops would remember some good times. Some love. Surely you couldn't be married for six and a half decades and not love your spouse.

Poor Goggy. How hard it must've been, moving on from that idyllic love to something so utilitarian with Pops, wondering what life would've been like if Peter had come home from the war. Dad, too, faced with so many days without Mom, his life so different from the one he'd imagined.

She wished she could call Jeremy, hear his kind voice. Maybe her grandmother was right...she'd never find someone to love who measured up to her first love. Just like Goggy. Just like Dad.

Crap. She seemed to be crying a little.

Blue gave a soft snort, then wagged his tail in his sleep. The moonlight was sweetly unfamiliar, cutting into her room in slices of cool white. From the kitchen came the sound of the refrigerator cycling on. Otherwise, it was quiet.

She may as well get up, check the production schedule for the barn. She padded barefoot to her office, Blue following dutifully, his ball in his mouth, then flopped down at her feet as she sat at her desk, as if they'd lived here for years instead of hours. Faith rubbed her foot through his thick fur, earning a croon of appreciation from the beastie.

You couldn't be too lonely with a dog. That was for sure. Faith turned on her computer, then noticed something.

The apartment smelled like chocolate.

Now, *that* was nice. And a little odd. Maybe the bakery was opening already? As the computer warmed up, Faith went to the front windows to check. Nope, Lorelei's windows were dark.

She went to the door and opened it a crack. The hall was dark, but there was a band of light coming from under the door of 3C, and the smell of chocolate was stronger here. Blue poked his head out, too, and licked his chops.

Levi was baking.

Baking at 3:17 in the morning.

CHAPTER FOURTEEN

Two WEEKS LATER, all Levi wanted was to get into his apartment without Faith's big dog leg-humping him in the hall, pour himself a beer and watch the Yankees win. It had been a very long couple of days; he was trying to train Everett, but the kid had a mind like a sieve. Nevertheless, Levi was letting him be in charge tonight, no matter how unsettling the thought was.

"You call me if there's anything you're not sure about, okay?" he asked. "And you keep that gun holstered. If I hear you took it out without my direct consent, you're fired. I don't care who your mother is."

Everett beamed. "Roger, Chief. Don't worry about anything." He put his feet up on the desk, missed and fell out of his chair.

Levi suppressed a sigh. "I'll check in later."

"You're a control freak, did anyone ever tell you that?" Emmaline said as she pulled on her raincoat. On her desk was a book entitled *Taking Control of Your Life: How to Change a Dead-End Job into the Career of Your Dreams*.

"Looking for a new job, Em?" he asked.

"Looking to get yours." She gave him one of her classic looks, half amused, half irritated.

Levi held the door for her, then bent his head against the foul weather. Even though it was only October, it had gotten cold all of a sudden, and the earlier rain had turned to sleet. The sidewalk was already slick. Lucky for him, his commute was roughly fifty yards. He walked with Emmaline, who lived right across the way in a pretty little bungalow next to the library. There was some work going on there—right. Faith Holland was doing something to the courtyard.

"Thanks for walking me home. Now go. Get away. Leave me. Shoo," Emmaline said as she unlocked the door. "And don't obsess over Everett. He needs experience, and if you keep hovering over him like a worried mother, he'll never learn."

"Have you thought of running for president?" he asked.

"I have, but I don't photograph well. Try to have a good night, Chief."

A night alone. It should be something he looked forward to. Sarah had shown up Tuesday night, claiming to be sick. Homesick, yes, but physically sick, no. Plus, she'd *hitchhiked.* With a cop for a brother! Said her car hadn't started, so she'd gotten a ride with the Hostess deliveryman. This had required Levi to lecture her on the dangers of that *and* the idiocy of saying she didn't want to go to college. "What are you gonna do if you stay here?" he'd asked sharply as he'd driven her home the next morning. "Wait tables? Be a bartender up at one of the vineyards? Don't you want more, Sarah?" She'd answered by staring out the window, tears leaking out of her eyes, making him feel like an utter shit. She hadn't even said goodbye when he'd pulled up in front of her dorm.

Then there'd been a wreck on Route 54…no fatality, but for the grace of God—Josh Deiner, the same kid who'd gotten Abby Vanderbeek drunk. The wreck had resulted in the kid losing his license, which brought on a huge hissy fit—he was a rich kid, not used to the rules applying to him.

And then there was Faith Holland, living across the hall from him. It was…distracting. He'd only seen her a few times, but each time, it seemed harder to shake off.

"Hey, Chief! Nasty night, isn't it?" Lorelei called as she locked the front door of the bakery.

"It is. You be careful on the roads, okay?"

"You bet." She beamed, then dug her car keys out of her giant purple purse. He waited till she got in her car, then watched as she drove up the street. She fish-tailed slightly as she turned, but she only lived about a mile out of the village, not up the Hill, where conditions would be worse.

He opened the door to the Opera House. If there was an accident tonight, he'd definitely have to go out; Ev wasn't up for handling that yet. That being said, Levi hadn't had more than two nights off in a row since he was hired.

Maybe Nina's leaving wasn't such a mystery, after all.

He pushed the thought from his mind. His wife hadn't left because he'd worked too much; she'd left him because she was an adrenaline-junkie chopper pilot.

Levi opened the ornate brass mailbox—bills, a movie from Netflix—then headed upstairs. Faith's door was open, and he hesitated, almost hoping she'd come out and…hell, do what, he didn't know. It just seemed like a long night in front of him all of a sudden.

Something pressed against his leg. Blue, the big dope. "Go home, pal," he told him.

He went into his apartment, only to have the dog head-butt the door, probably hoping for some special time with his leg. Levi changed into a flannel shirt and jeans, putting his uniform in the hamper. Life in the military had made him become a little obsessive about neatness, something his mom and Sarah had found quite funny, as he'd been the typical teenage slob before. Not anymore. The apartment was neat as a pin, especially now that Sarah was away. He always cleaned her room after she left, since God knew she wouldn't make a bed on her own.

He called Lorelei; she'd made it home just fine, but, yes, it was slick out, and he was an angel for checking on her.

Levi hung up, then opened the fridge, took out a bottle of Newton's Pale Ale and surveyed his dinner options. Lots of leftovers; cooking for one wasn't easy. Plus, there was a vat of sauce and meatballs; he'd made it for Sarah on Tuesday, since that was her favorite. Just because he didn't want her to drop out of college didn't mean he didn't love his little sis.

There was the thud against the door. Blue again. Beautiful dog, but dumb as a fern. The dog was whining now. Another thud.

Levi opened the door and stared down at the dog. "What?"

Blue looked up and whined.

"Holland, your dog's out," Levi said. Her door was still wide open.

There was no answer.

"Faith?" He went into her apartment. "Holland, you here? Oh, shit."

Faith was standing at the kitchen counter, plucking at her sweater. She looked confused.

If memory served, she was about to have a seizure. "Faith? You okay?"

She didn't turn. The dog barked once, and Faith

crumpled. Levi yanked her toward him so her head wouldn't hit the counter and eased her onto the floor. She was already jerking, poor kid, muscles stiff, jaw clenched. He turned her on her side in case she threw up. Her eyes were open and vacant, and out of reflex, Levi looked at his watch. 18:34:17. Time the seizure in case it lasted more than five minutes, that was protocol. He wasn't an EMT for nothing.

He'd seen Faith have a seizure four or five times in school. Somehow, it was scarier now that he was the adult in charge. Her fingers were splayed and rigid, her back arching with the force of the spasms.

Blue paced back and forth, panting and whining. "It's okay, buddy," Levi said, his hand on Faith's shoulder as her arms and legs spasmed. "She'll be fine."

18:34:42. Still seizing. What else should he say? *Speak reassuringly to the victim,* the nurse used to say, and the whole class knew who the victim was. "You're okay, Faith," he said. "You'll be fine."

18:35:08. "Doing great, Holland. Don't worry. Your dog is here." Well, that was dumb. "Me, too. I'm right here."

It was oddly quiet, the seizure, just the sound of her shoes rubbing against the floor, the sleet pattering against the window, the sound of her hard breathing. "Hang in there, Faith."

Shit. It couldn't be fun, having your body and brain rebel against you like this. Her muscles were tight and clenched under his hand, her right arm out in front of her face as if shielding herself from a blow. "Don't worry, sweetheart. Almost done." Not that he knew anything.

18:35:42. Maybe he should call her dad. As a member of the volunteer fire department, Levi knew there wasn't anything a call to 911 would do; they'd give her oxygen, which did more to make them feel better than because she needed it. No, she was breathing fine, if hard. No blueness to her face or lips. Dr. Buckthal had done an in-service for Emergency Services last year— Marcus Shrade had a TBI from a car accident, and had grand mals a few times a year. The doc said a seizure would end when it ended. Hopefully soon. Helluva way to get a workout.

Okay, she was stopping. 18:36:04. Her arms and legs stilled, and he could feel the tension start to seep out of her, see her practically sink into the floor as the misfirings in her brain stopped and allowed her muscles to relax. Blue lay down next to her and put his head on her leg.

"Faith? You okay?" He smoothed some hair off her face. She wasn't shaking anymore, but she was still out of it. *Postictal,* that was the word, staring straight ahead. The dog's tail started thumping. "You're in your apartment, Holland. You had a seizure, but you're doing fine." She blinked and swallowed but didn't answer. He fished his phone out of his pocket and found the Hollands' number on it. "Hey, John, it's Levi Cooper. Listen, sir, Faith just had a seizure. Lasted about ninety seconds."

"You saw the whole thing?" John asked, his voice sharp with concern.

"Yes, sir. Anything in particular I should do?"

"Is she awake now?"

Levi saw that he was stroking Faith's hair, the red strands impossibly silky. "Faith? How you doing?" She swallowed and looked up at him. "Your dad's on the phone. You want to talk to him?"

She blinked. "My dad?"

"Yep. She's coming around, sir." He held the phone to Faith's ear, and she reached up, her arm wobbling a little.

"Hi, Daddy," she said. "Um…I…I don't know." She closed her eyes and frowned. "I'm fine. I think Levi… I don't know. Okay. Here he is."

Levi took the phone back. "Anything I should do?" he asked.

"I'm coming right down," her father said.

"The roads are pretty icy." He paused. "I can stay with her, or take her to the hospital, if you think she should go."

"I don't wanna go anywhere," Faith muttered. "I'm tired."

"She says she's tired," Levi added.

John sighed into the phone. "How bad are the roads?"

"Bad enough to stay put. What does she need?"

"A nap. Someone to keep an eye on her. That usually does the trick. Damn, she hasn't had one of these in a long time."

Faith seemed to be sleeping. "I can stay with her for a while," he said. "I live right across the hall."

Her father hesitated. "You sure?"

"Absolutely, sir."

John sighed. "Okay. I'd appreciate that. If you could call me when she wakes up, that'd be great. Generally, she sleeps for a little while, seems a little groggy, but otherwise, she's fine. She probably missed a few doses of her medication. But if she seizes again, call me right away."

"You got it. I'll check in later."

"Thanks, son. You're a good kid."

Levi put his phone on the counter. "Faith? You awake?"

"I'm tired," she said without opening her eyes.

"I'm gonna pick you up, okay?"

"I need to lose fifteen pounds first."

He felt the start of a smile. "I can manage." He slid his arms under her and lifted her up. Okay, she wasn't a wisp of a thing, she had a point. She sure smelled good, though, sweet and warm. Her head settled against his shoulder, her hair brushing his chin.

The dog trotted into another room, tail waving, and Levi followed. Set her down on the unmade bed and took off her shoes. "Thanks, Levi," she murmured, her voice distant.

He pulled the covers over her. Blue jumped up and put his head on her hip. Faith reached out to pet him without opening her eyes. "I'll be out here if you need me," Levi said.

"Okay." Her eyes were closed, lashes a dark smudge against her cheeks.

Levi reached out to smooth her hair again, but he stopped himself. She was awake now. Sort of.

He went into her living room; her apartment was more or less the same as his, minus one bedroom. Unlike his, though, hers looked…homey, which was strange, because she was just back for a little while, so far as he knew. Nevertheless, one wall had been painted fire-engine red, and there was a red-and-purple throw on the couch. A bookcase held a couple dozen books, some photos and keepsakes. A women's magazine was open on the coffee table, as well as a giant red mug with a sunflower painted on it. Her kitchen counter held a vase of yellow flowers. The wine rack was filled, he noted. As it would be, if your family owned a vineyard.

A gust of wind sent sleet crackling against the window, making him jump a little. It always surprised him, how innocent a gun could sound, like firecrackers. Or sleet.

Time to be useful. He picked up her cup and went to the kitchen. The dishwasher was full of clean dishes. Taking care to be quiet, he unloaded it, figuring out where things went, then wiped down her counters. Folded the blanket on her couch. Turned on the TV, found the YES Network, saw that the Yanks' game had been canceled due to rain. Clicked around for a little while, then turned the TV off. Pulled out his phone and called Everett.

"How are things going, Ev?"

"Great, Chief! Um, we had one call asking for help on how to put the battery into a smoke detector—that was Methalia Lewis, and lucky for me, I have the same kind, so I was able to walk her through it just fine, Chief."

The pride in Everett's voice was obvious. "Good job."

"Thanks, Chief!"

"Anything else comes up, just give me a call."

"Roger that, Chief Cooper. Over and out."

Seemed like the good people of Manningsport had exhibited some excellent common sense thus far and stayed off the roads tonight.

He looked in at Faith, who was sleeping with her arm around the dog. She might be hungry when she woke up. Going back to the kitchen, he checked her fridge. A bottle of white wine, an open Pepperidge Farm chocolate cake box, a roll of Pillsbury Dough cinnamon rolls, and a jar of artichokes. Cooking wasn't her thing, apparently. He went back to his apartment, grabbed the container of meatballs and sauce, as well as a box of linguine, and took it back to Faith's. She'd been asleep for about an hour now.

What to do. Levi drifted over to the bookcase. There was a sock monkey with pink button eyes and a pink bow. A little red vase, a tiny metal chicken. He couldn't, for the life of him, imagine collecting such clutter. A Derek Jeter bobblehead. Here was a framed photo of her family at Pru and Carl's wedding. Looked like Faith had been the flower girl—she was maybe nine or ten in the picture, holding a bouquet of flowers. Pru looked the same, except for some gray hair, and Carl did, too, though he'd thickened over the years. Mrs. Holland had been a knockout, same red hair as Faith, smiling at the bride, her arm around her husband. Jack looked sheepish, Honor pretty. A Golden retriever sat obediently next to Faith.

He put the photo down and went onto the next one. Faith and a friend in front of the Golden Gate Bridge on a foggy day, both of them laughing. Another showed Faith in work boots and jeans and a flannel shirt, standing in front of a fountain.

And here was a photo of her and Jeremy. The two of them at the beach, arms around each other. Interesting that she kept that on display.

He put the photo down and saw her next keepsake— a glass bowl of white beach stones. There, on top, was a little chunk of rose quartz, no bigger than a nickel and shaped roughly like a heart. He frowned, then picked it up and held it to the light.

"Someone gave me that after my mom died. Left it in my locker at school."

Faith had changed into some pajama pants (red with Dalmatian puppies all over them) and a Blue Heron sweatshirt.

Blue bounded over to him and tried to mount his leg. "Blue, get off," Faith commanded, and the dog obeyed.

Levi put the rock down. "How do you feel?"

She took a deep breath and tilted her head. "I'm okay. A little groggy. So I had a seizure, huh?"

"Yeah."

Her cheeks reddened. "Sorry you had to be here."

"You should be glad, Holland. You could've hit your head on the counter if it weren't for me." He folded his arms and raised his eyebrows expectantly.

She gave a little smile. "Wow. A hero yet again."

"Actually, your dog came to get me. Kept head-butting the door."

"Really?" Faith knelt down and opened her arms, and the dog bounced over to lick her face. "Blue! You're such a good boy! Good dog!" She kissed him on the head and looked up at Levi, grinning. "Technically, he's a therapy dog, but he's never been put to the test. I guess he's got more going on than I thought. Yes, you do, Mr. Blue! You're brilliant!"

She looked so…happy. Bright as a new penny, his mom used to say, and the saying seemed to fit. Levi cleared his throat and looked away. "So all this stuff… Are you staying?" he asked, gesturing at her bookcase.

"My roomie sent me a box of stuff. It may be a sign that her honey's moving in for good. And some of that is from my dad's house. The books and stuff."

She hadn't answered the question. "Are you hungry?" he asked.

"Starving."

"Good. I brought dinner."

"A multitalented babysitter." She smiled.

A distant warning bell clanged somewhere in his brain. Faith's hair was tangled, makeup smudged under her eyes. The baggy sweatshirt wasn't doing her any favors—gave her the same shape as a side of beef, and somehow she radiated sex all the same.

"Call your father," he ordered, going back into the kitchen to start the water for pasta.

It was impossible not to overhear. "Hi, Daddy, I'm fine," she said, and he wondered if girls ever outgrew the need to call their fathers *Daddy* instead of plain old *Dad*.

For about a week, Nina had thought she might be pregnant, though they hadn't planned on it, and Levi was surprised at how happy the idea had made him. Pictured a daughter right away. But it had been a false alarm, and when Levi had suggested maybe they should toss the birth control and give it a try for real, she'd clammed up. Informed him of her re-enlistment two weeks later.

"I feel great, don't worry," Faith was saying. "I know, I know. I forgot to get it refilled, but it was a day or two at most…I know, Dad, I'm really sorry. No, don't come down, it's nasty out there. Good thing the grapes are in, huh? Yeah, he's here. Sure. Love you, too." She padded into the kitchen and handed the phone to Levi. "He wants to talk to you."

"Hey, John."

"Levi, I was wondering if you could possibly keep an eye on her tonight," John said, the worry in his voice from earlier still present. "She skipped her medication for a couple of days, and if she has another seizure, she shouldn't be alone."

Levi hesitated. The warning bell clanged again. "Sure. No problem."

"I'm so sorry to ask you this, but you're right, the roads are a sheet of ice. I tried to get down the driveway and slid right off onto the lawn."

In a truck with bald tires that had last been serviced in the '90s, most likely. "Don't come out, sir. It's fine."

"You sure you don't mind?"

"Not at all."

John sighed. "I owe you one. Kids. They age you. Okay, Levi. Thanks again."

Levi hung up. "Looks like my babysitting gig just got extended. We're having a sleepover."

"No!" Her face went bright red. "You don't have to stay, Levi. Really. I'm fine. I missed my meds for two days, but I'm back on them, I'll be fine. See? They're right here." She opened a cabinet and shook a prescription bottle at him. "You can go home. I've never had two seizures on the same day."

"I'm staying."

She gave a huffy sigh. "Fine, bossy. Want some wine?"

"As opposed to cake or cinnamon rolls?"

"Chief Cooper! Have you been snooping in my fridge?" She grinned again. "I don't blame you. I'd do the same at your place. What people have in their refrigerators says a lot about them."

"Really."

"Mmm-hmm. I bet yours is immaculate. The four food groups, leftovers put in matching Tupperware."

He stirred the meatballs and sauce. "You're correct."

"See? It matches your anal-retentive personality."

"So what does yours say about you? You've got a half-eaten cake in there, wine, rolls from a can and an unopened jar of artichokes."

She smiled. "It says I go out a lot, make the occasional bad choice, enjoy life and live spontaneously. Do you want wine or not?"

"No, thanks. Come on, let's eat."

They sat at her kitchen table, Blue shooting them hopeful glances, his head on his paws. "Thanks for this, Levi," Faith said, glancing at him with another blush.

"Nothing better to do on a night like this." The words came out wrong. Her face flushed a deeper shade.

She took a bite of her food. "Did it freak you out? Jack filmed me once, so I know what I look like."

He looked at her for a second, saw a little flash of worry in her eyes. "It didn't bother me. Looks like it might be…uncomfortable, though."

"It's not. Or if it is, I don't remember. They're… blank spots."

So she wouldn't remember that he'd called her "sweetheart." That was probably a good thing.

She didn't say anything more, other than to compliment him on the meatballs. The sleet and wind kept up, and while it had made him a little jumpy before, it now felt…safe.

When he and Faith had been in sixth grade, they'd had this really crappy science teacher. Mr. Ormand, was it? The guy hated kids. Every day, he'd single out a student and just eviscerate the kid, mocking him or her for getting an answer wrong or missing a step in the lab. Didn't matter if you were getting a D or an A; if a kid was smart, he'd mock that, too. "I guess we know *everything,* don't we, Miss Ames? You must be a genius! Class, we have a genius among us! Isn't it *thrilling?*"

Then one day, Faith had raised her hand and asked about studying for an upcoming science test, and Mr. Ormand had said something like, "Perhaps you could read the *textbook,* Miss Holland? Perhaps *that* might help?" his voice dripping with customary sarcasm. And much to the shock of everyone, Faith had snapped back in the exact same tone, "Or perhaps you could actually *teach,* Mr. Ormand? Instead of sitting there *complaining* about how *dumb* we are?"

There'd been a collective gasp, and Faith was ordered to the principal's office. But as she'd left the room, Levi had muttered, "Nice job, Holland," and winked. She'd looked at him, and he'd have thought she'd be scared, getting in trouble for the first time that he could recall. But instead, she'd grinned, and for that second, he'd thought maybe Faith had a little bit of bad in her. Maybe she wasn't quite the Goody Two-Shoes she always seemed. Also, she already had boobs. Just another thing to appreciate.

Not long after, Faith's mother had died in a horrific accident. The guidance counselor had come in and told them not to ask questions, but Faith's father had wanted to make sure everyone knew she'd been in the car, had had a seizure and mercifully didn't remember anything.

When their homeroom teacher had instructed them to write her a note, Levi couldn't. What did you say to a kid who woke up trapped in a car with the broken, lifeless body of her mom? "Sorry?" Everything had sounded pathetically small. The teacher had glared at him, so he'd scrawled a few lines on a piece of paper, surreptitiously stuffed the note into his pocket and passed in a blank page instead.

When Faith had come back to school after a few weeks, she was a ghost of the cute girl who'd sassed their mean teacher. She'd been popular before, but her mother's death shot that into the red zone. Everyone had flocked around her, fighting to be the one to sit next to her, to give her their Twinkies or have her come over to their house after school and pick her first to be on their team in gym class.

Levi had done none of those things. Hadn't gone to

her mom's wake, hadn't picked her for his team, hadn't said he was sorry. For some reason, he couldn't. He'd just…ignored her. He'd been an adolescent boy, not an age group famed for emotional insight.

But one day when he'd been fishing in the stream behind the trailer park, he'd spied something gleaming on the shore. He'd brought it to school the next day, and then, after he'd wrangled a detention from Mr. Ormand for not passing in homework, when the halls were empty and Levi was the only one around, he'd taken the little treasure from his pocket, wrapped it in a scrap of rough brown paper towel and shoved the rose quartz rock through the air vent in Faith's locker.

A rock she'd kept for almost twenty years.

There was an odd pressure in his chest.

"You want to watch TV?" he asked, clearing her plate.

"Sure. Maybe a movie? Netflix came today."

"What have you got?"

"A zombie movie. Supposed to be very gory."

He glanced at her, surprised.

"What?" she said. "They can't all be romantic comedies."

If Levi wasn't mistaken, Netflix had just sent a very gory zombie movie to his mailbox today. "Sounds good," he said, tidying the kitchen.

"You'd make a great housekeeper," she commented, settling onto the couch with her blanket.

"In addition to babysitter and chef, you mean?"

"Exactly." She smiled at him again as he sat in the blue chair, feeling a little awkward, at least at first. But Faith was a movie talker, it turned out, and didn't need him to carry on an entire conversation. "That girl only looks dead. Ten bucks she bites the cute cop. And there you go. Ten bucks, Levi. Oh, come on now. He's hiding under the bed? Has he *never* seen a horror flick? They always find you there."

And as the sleet pattered against the windows, eventually changing to rain, and as the zombies killed everyone in great sprays of blood and fire, Levi couldn't help thinking this was one of the best nights he'd had in a long time.

WHEN FAITH WOKE UP in the morning, Blue was not the only one in the room with her.

Levi Cooper, police chief and babysitter extraordinaire, was sitting in the chair next to her bed. He'd taken Dad at his word; though she'd argued and yes, whined a little, he'd dragged the chair in here nonetheless and kept watch, ever the good soldier.

A tired soldier, too. He was asleep, his head tipped back against the chair, arms folded. And what arms they were. Her girl parts purred as she stared. The lower half of a tattoo showed where the thick muscle curved—*10th Mountain Division.* His dark blond hair was rumpled, sticking up in front a little bit.

Oh, man. Levi Cooper was really, really…*hot.* She'd managed to put that out of her head for quite a long time now. For more than a decade, she hadn't allowed even one thought about his hotness, and really, how had she avoided it? The Man. Was. Delicious.

Even in sleep, his face held a slight scowl. But his eyelashes were straight and long and unexpectedly sweet, and his mouth was…yeah, okay, that was a nice mouth, full and sulky, and really, she should not be thinking these thoughts. He'd seen her in full blown seizure mode—oh, hemorrhoid—and he'd been nice enough to do her a favor (or do her father a favor, if you

wanted to be technical). So fixating on his hotness…
that was a one-way ticket. Because she knew what she
looked like during a seizure (thank you, older brother):
like one of the zombies from last night, stiff and jerking, possibly drooling for that extra dose of sex appeal,
eyes wide and scared, snorty little pig noises thrown
in for flair.

Faith looked at Blue, who was eyeing her from his
half of the bed. "Stay," she whispered, then slipped out
from under the sheets. She went into her bathroom and
started at her reflection, flinching a little. Hair matted,
crustiness in one eye, mascara smudged, a crease running down one cheek courtesy of her pillowcase. She
pulled her hair into a ponytail and washed her face mercilessly, then brushed her teeth. There. At least she was
clean now. Oh, the sweatshirt. Nice touch. And let's not
forget the doggie pajamas. One could practically hear
the bass of porno music pulsing.

Well. It was Levi, after all. He wouldn't be thinking
porno, not with her.

It was funny; she hadn't had a witnessed seizure
for a long time. Two times, she'd had them in Jeremy's
presence, that first time when he'd carried her to the
nurse, and another time, when he'd been visiting her in
college. He'd always treated her like a spun-sugar fairy
princess, almost like her epilepsy made her more attractive (which she hadn't really minded, to be honest).

But Levi…it didn't seem to sway Levi one way or
the other. He could've made her feel like an idiot last
night, and he was gifted in that department, after all.
But for some reason, last night had been oddly…fun.

"Right, Faith," she muttered to her reflection. "Why
don't you have seizures more often, huh? The entrée to
a good time—epilepsy."

"You okay in there?"

She jumped at the sound of Levi's voice. "Yes! I'm fine. Thank you! Out in a sec." Pulling her hair out of the ponytail, she fluffed it, then rolled her eyes at herself. Kind of a lost cause at the moment.

She opened the door to find him standing there. "Do you always eavesdrop on women in the bathroom?" she asked, inching into the hall.

"You feeling all right?" he repeated, glancing at his watch.

"I'm fine. Thanks again, Levi. I'll tell my dad what a good boy you were."

He narrowed his eyes at her, but maybe there was a gleam of amusement there. No smile, of course. This was Levi Cooper, after all. "See you around," he said.

"Okay. Thank you again. Sorry for the inconvenience."

He didn't move, just stared at her impassively.

Then he closed the small distance between them and kissed her.

She wouldn't have believed it if there wasn't proof, but nope, no, he was *definitely* kissing her, his lips firm and, oh, wow, really good at what they were doing, and his big, bulging manly arms slid around her, pulling her against his solid, warm frame. One hand cupped the back of her head, his fingers sliding into her hair, and Faith's mouth opened in a bit of shock, and holy moly, he was frenching her, tasting her, and she melted against him in a purely primal—oh, yes, *primal*—reaction. Her arms slid around his lean waist, hands sliding up the smooth, hard muscles of his back, his skin hot under the thin cotton of his T-shirt, his mouth moving against hers.

Then the kiss was over, and she was panting in shaky

gasps, as if she'd run all the way up to the barn. Her eyes needed a second to focus, and her legs wobbled.

Levi did not look similarly affected. He blinked. Twice. "I didn't see me doing that," he said, frowning down at her.

"Oh, well, you know…you could do it again," she breathed.

He stepped back. "I don't think so." He ran a hand through his hair, making it stand up even more.

"Excuse me?" she said.

"Yeah. That was a bad idea. That was a mistake. I definitely shouldn't have done that. Sorry, Holland."

She just stared at him for a minute. Nope, he was serious. Dead serious, from his expression.

Men. Just…men! Was there ever going to be a normal man in her life? Huh?

"Out you go," she said, shoving his hard chest. "Bye! Thank you for everything, you jerk. And you know what?"

"What?"

"Nothing. Get out." She hustled him to the door, opened it and waved. "Bye."

Levi stepped into the hallway, and Blue bounded out as well, then attached himself to the horrible man's leg. As goes the slutty owner, so goes the slutty dog. "Blue, get back here!" she ordered. Her dog obeyed, and she took one more look at Levi's expressionless face. "Have a nice day."

Then she slammed the door. Opened it and slammed it again, just in case he missed the point.

CHAPTER FIFTEEN

THE GOOD NEWS WAS, the barn was going beautifully.

The arborist had come in and removed five trees, which opened up the view just enough. She'd hired Crooked Lake Landscaping and a very cute Irish stone-mason (married, sigh) to work on the parking area, a wall along the path and the retaining wall. Samuel Hastings, a Mennonite carpenter, and his son would build the deck that would extend out over the hill. The electric had been run, and things were clicking along.

Faith was doing a lot of the work herself. That wasn't usually the case; as the designer, most of her work was done at a computer, figuring out things like water run-off rates and soil retention. But this was Holland land, and the barn was her baby. Faith wanted to filter the dirt and help build the rock walls, dig holes and loosen root balls, and hear the sound of hammers ringing out over the hill.

She'd been working a lot. At the library, studiously not looking across the green to the police station. At the other vineyard. Up here at the barn.

As for Levi—he'd nodded at her three days ago as their paths crossed at O'Rourke's. She'd glared; he'd said nothing.

"So you must see Levi a lot," Jeremy said, practically reading her mind.

"Not really," she answered, shoveling some gravel

from a wheelbarrow to line the path that led to the barn's entrance. Jeremy had come up on his lunch hour, bearing a glorious Cubano sandwich from Lorelei's. Things were still a little awkward since their reunion, but, hell. He was such a good guy. And he brought food, so...

"Oh," Jeremy said. "I thought you lived across the hall from each other."

"We do." Her tone must've hinted at Panty Twist Supreme, because he didn't pursue the subject further.

"This is going to be amazing," he said, gesturing with his own sandwich. "I've already told Georgia to start referring people here. We get a lot of requests for weddings, but you know. A tent is nothing compared to this."

"Thanks, ba—buddy." She'd been about to say *babe*. Old habits.

He picked up the tennis ball and fired it into the woods, putting his quarterback arm to use. Blue bounded after the ball joyfully. Faith wondered if her pet remembered Jeremy, who could throw farther than anyone.

"One of my patients asked about you yesterday," Jeremy said. "He wants to surprise his wife with a water garden, and I told him that'd be a piece of cake for you."

"Thanks," she said, hefting another shovelful of gravel and tamping it into the path. "I hope he calls."

"Have you thought about staying here permanently?" Jeremy asked. "I imagine you'd have clients by the dozen." He offered her some potato chips, and she took a few.

"I want to stay," she admitted. "I've been here a month now, and it's hard to think about going back to California. I see my dad and the grands almost every day, have dinner with Pru and the kids once or twice a week. Colleen and I hang out all the time… I wonder how I lived without everyone for three years."

You included, she didn't add. But Jeremy's friendship, this new phase of it…that was becoming important, too.

"But I do have a very nice life back in San Francisco," she added. "Can't just forget that. I pitched a job in August, and it's supposed to move forward soon. So we'll see."

Jeremy fired the ball into the woods again for the never-tired Blue. "You're different now," he said. "You're really…solid."

"Pick another word, quick." She smiled as she spread another shovelful of gravel onto the path.

"Sorry." He grinned. "Confident in who you are."

"Better, better."

"So what's on your mind? You seem a little distracted."

Levi's on my mind, Jeremy. I may want to kill him. That, or handcuff him to the radiator, rip off his clothes with my teeth and have my way with the man. "Oh, just work stuff," she lied.

The memory of that kiss had been replayed roughly a thousand and eight times in Faith's brain, usually around three in the morning. Twice in the week that had passed, the smell of chocolate had crept into her apartment, and it was maddening. So close and yet so far, across the hall and baking. Way too adorable an image to pursue. Almost as adorable as the sight of him sitting by her bed, asleep, all rumpled hair and long eyelashes and beautiful arms.

This was her problem: falling for emotionally unavailable men. For one night, Levi had been nice to her, one lousy (well, okay, one excellent) kiss, and yes, her panties were in a snarl.

She dug into the gravel with more strength than was necessary. Call it a workout.

"I heard you and Colleen went to a singles thing," Jeremy said. He hesitated. "Are you…interested? In dating somebody here, I mean. Or maybe you're seeing someone already?"

"No. Nope. I'm not. Not even a little." Okay, she didn't have to be so emphatic. "Why?"

"Well," he said, throwing the ball for Blue once more, "maybe this is just me trying to soothe my conscience, but…think you'd like to be fixed up?"

"I'd love it," she said instantly.

"Really?" Jeremy asked.

"Absolutely. How well do you know him?"

"Not that well. He's my accountant." Jeremy paused. "He's very good-looking. And honest."

"Sold! Give me his number, I'll call him right now."

Blinking a little, Jeremy passed over his phone.

Five minutes later, Faith had a date for that very night. Maybe this guy wouldn't be gay, married or view kissing her as a huge mistake.

And wouldn't that be a nice change.

SHE AND BLUE STOPPED at the Old House, regretting it the second she walked into her grandparents' back hall. "It's coo-pon," Goggy was saying, her voice laced with steel.

"I like cue-pon," Pops said defiantly. Oh, lordy. Perhaps Faith could sneak out, undetected. She glanced down at Blue, whose doggy brow wrinkled at the sound of the bickering grands.

"We never said it like that before," Goggy said. "Why

are you changing it now? You sound ridiculous. It's so pretentious." Faith turned to leave, stealthy as a ninja.

"Cue-pon," Pops said. "Faithie-bear, is that you? Come on in, honey!"

Busted. "Hi, guys! Oh, cookies! Can I have one?"

"Of course you can," Goggy said. "Take three. Sweetheart, how do you say coupon? Hmm? It's coo-pon, isn't it?"

"I've heard it said both ways," Faith said, opting to play Switzerland in this horribly important discussion. Moving out had definitely been the right choice. She took a bite of the cookie. Oh, yeah. Snickerdoodles. Three might not be enough.

"See, I'm French Canadian," Pops said. "We say cue-pon up North."

"Your parents came over from Utrecht! You had a great-uncle who lived in Quebec for a year. That doesn't make you French Canadian!"

"Cue-pon." Pops grinned, winking at Faith. The man was adorably evil. "How's the barn?"

"It's going to be rather gorgeous, if I do say so myself."

"Of course it is, with you doing it." Goggy pushed the plate of cookies toward her. Her grandparents had flown out to see the dedication of the Douglas Street Park and been simultaneously stunned and smug at her work (as well as concerned about her throat being slit in the big city).

The phone rang, and Goggy hurtled to answer it. "Oh, Betty, hi," she said, taking the phone into the living room.

"So, Pops," Faith said. "I was hoping to talk to you about your anniversary."

"Anniversary of what?" he said, pouring some of

the sauvignon blanc that had won the vineyard a silver medal last year.

"Your wedding anniversary. It'll be sixty-five years next month."

"And still I walk this earth, shackled to your grandmother by the chains of marriage." He winked and poured her a glass, as well. Cookies and wine…looked like those fifteen pounds wouldn't be going anywhere.

"Yeah, okay, but you love her, of course," she prompted.

"Love, shmove," he answered. "Love is for you young people."

"How can you be married for sixty-five years and not love your wife?" She smiled, hoping to encourage him.

"I don't know," Pops said, giving a cookie to her dog, who swallowed it instantly. "I'm cursed?"

"You're a horrible old man, that's what you are," she said, fixing his collar. "Admit it, Pops. You love Goggy."

"I love this wine, that's what I love. Do you like it?"

She took a sip. "Lemon, honeysuckle, a smidgeon of burnt marshmallow."

"That's my girl."

"Anyway, I thought your anniversary would be a great way to dedicate the barn. A Holland family event, and such a milestone. I know Goggy would love it."

"You want to throw us an anniversary party?"

"Absolutely! The leaves will still be beautiful, we could invite all your friends and colleagues, and it'd be a great way to have everyone see the new venue. The Barn at Blue Heron, the nice old Holland clan. What do you think?"

"I think I should get a Purple Heart and a week's vacation, alone, that's what I think."

Remembering the story of Goggy's tragic first love,

Faith sighed. "Pops, I think it would mean a lot to Goggy. A long marriage is something to be proud of—"

"Or terrified of," he said.

"—and Goggy deserves a special night. Don't you think so?"

"Oh, I don't know. We don't generally like that sort of fuss."

"What sort of fuss?" Goggy asked, coming back into the room.

"It's about time," Pops grumbled. "I'm starving. It's ten after five already."

"I was telling Pops," Faith said firmly, "that I thought it'd be nice to throw you two an anniversary party."

"What does he think?" Goggy said after a beat, as if her husband wasn't seated a foot away.

"Who needs a party?" Pops snorted. "Too much money."

"I'd love it," Goggy said instantly. "What a nice idea, sweetheart! Aren't you wonderful to think of it." She gave Pops a dirty look, then smiled at Faith. "Want to stay for supper? You look too thin."

Oh, grandmothers! "No, Goggy, but thanks. I have to go, actually. I have a date."

This caused some coos of delight from Goggy, who felt she was owed more great-grandchildren, and fast, as well as some grumbles of warning from Pops about the evil natures of men.

Faith kissed them both, then headed for home. She was meeting Ryan Hill at O'Rourke's, which would allow Colleen to check out the guy, as well as allow Faith to get the nachos grande. Two birds, one stone, a possible husband.

But first, Faith thought as she came into the Village, a macchiato from Lorelei's. She tied Blue to the lamppost and went into the bakery, where she was immediately presented with the solid back of Manningsport's chief of police, who was just placing his order. "Medium coffee, please, Lorelei. Cream, no sugar."

"You got it, Chief," Lorelei said with her customary smile.

"You sure you want cream?" Faith asked, a trifle loudly. Chief Asspain turned and gave her a four on the Boredom Scale—*What's your name again?* Didn't stop her knees from giving a traitorous wobble. "Because you might *think* you want cream, but then you taste the coffee, and you decide you don't really like it, after all. Cream might be a bad idea. Or a big mistake."

"It won't be," he said, giving her an odd look.

"Wow. You're so decisive today, Levi! But are you sure? Because if you end up not liking the coffee, its feelings might be hurt."

"What are you babbling about?" he said.

"Indecision. Poor impulse control. Waffling."

The four grew to a six: *I can't believe I still have to talk to you.* Lorelei handed him his coffee. "There you go, Chief! Oh, hi, Faith, I didn't see you there! How are you? What would you like today?"

Screw the coffee. Granted, she might go into sugar shock, but some fortification was called for. "I'll have a chocolate croissant and a small hot chocolate, please."

"You bet!"

"How about a slab of chocolate cake with that?" Levi suggested. "Maybe a candy bar on the side?"

"Aren't there criminals who need to be brought to justice somewhere, Levi? Hmm?"

He was still staring, his forehead slightly crinkled. "Is this about the other day?" he asked.

"What other day?" she snapped.

"Look," he said, "that…moment…was a mistake, and I'm sorry."

"Women love to hear that. No, really. It's so flattering."

"I'm not trying to flatter you. I'm just telling you the truth. It was a blunder, and I regret it."

"Keep it up. I might swoon."

Lorelei was done and rang her up. Faith handed her a five. "Thanks, Lorelei," she said, taking her goodies. "Chief Cooper. Have a lovely day."

He didn't bother answering, but his irritation was palpable.

It was deeply satisfying.

CHAPTER SIXTEEN

TWO HOURS LATER, Faith walked into the warm Friday night roar that was O'Rourke's and went straight to Colleen, keeper of all information. "He's here," Coll said, "third booth in the back, adorable, nice manners, hint of a Southern drawl." Her friend grinned and pulled a beer for Wayne Knox. Looked like the volunteer fire department was having a "meeting." Gerard, Neddy-bear, Jessica Does and Kelly Matthews were all grouped on one side of the bar, howling with laughter.

"How do I look?" Faith asked her.

Colleen leaned over the bar and gave Faith's shirt a tug to show more flesh. "There. Work the assets, girlfriend. Am I right, boys?"

The males of the fire department agreed heartily. "Can't go wrong with boobs," Everett Field said.

"I babysat you," Faith returned.

"I remember. I think about it all the time." He received a hearty slap on the back from Gerard Chartier, his comrade-in-ogling.

"Get going," Coll said. "Jeremy's already over there, chatting him up."

"Jeremy's here?"

"Yeah. He and Levi usually come in on Fridays."

"Their weekly date?" Faith couldn't help asking.

"I must say, Levi is looking über-hot these days," Coll said. "Those arms! Honestly, he comes in wearing a T-shirt and I actually have an orgasm. Here's your white wine spritzer, Mrs. Boothby." She ignored the disapproving glare from the florist. "Your dad is also here," Colleen added, "speaking of men who—"

"Oops! There's the line, don't cross it." Faith went to the far side of the bar where her father was talking to— oh, hemorrhoid, to Levi. "Hi, Dad. You look nice." He did—he was showered, for one, and wore a rugby-style shirt rather than his usual tattered flannel.

"Hello, sweetpea," Dad said, giving her a one-armed hug.

"Faith," said the police chief.

"Levi." Amazing how he could irritate her just by saying her name.

"You're on a date, I hear," Dad said.

"I am," she said. "Hopefully it won't be a mistake. Or a bad idea. Or a blunder."

Levi sighed and stared into the middle distance.

"I'm sure it won't be," her father said. "Well, you go have a good time, honey. I'll be here if you need me."

"Thanks, Dad." She dropped her voice to a whisper. "Are you here alone?"

"I'm meeting Lorena."

"Oh." She tried not to flinch. So far, she'd screened and dismissed the women of eCommitment/SeniorLove, and her efforts to engage Cathy Kennedy in conversation about her sainted father had fallen with a thud. "Okay, well…there are other fish in the lake, Dad."

"What kind of fish?"

"Fish who don't wear cheetah-print bras with see-through shirts and ask what your bank balance is," she said, referencing Sunday's dinner conversation, which had caused Mrs. Johnson to growl audibly.

Dad still looked clueless. "Never mind, Dad. Just don't get married without checking with me first."

Her father laughed. "Listen to her, Levi. Half the time I have no idea what she's talking about."

"I know the feeling," Levi said.

Ooh. "Well. My date awaits."

"Have fun," Levi said.

"Yes, honey, have fun!" Dad said. "I'm ready for more grandchildren. Just keep that in mind." He pinched her chin. "Levi, don't I have the prettiest daughters?"

"You do," he answered, his glance flicking over Faith, pausing for just a microsecond on her boobage. "Got your list?" he added.

Faith didn't deign to answer (but, yes, it was in her purse). She took a calming breath and went to the third booth. There was Jeremy, looking utterly beautiful, talking to Ryan, she assumed.

"Faith!" Jeremy jumped up, kissed her cheek, his smile as warm and bright as if it had been years since they'd seen each other and not hours. "You look beautiful, as always. Let me introduce Ryan Hill, my accountant."

Ryan was *adorable.* Go, Jeremy! Dimples, honey-colored hair, blue eyes. He stood up and shook her hand, smiling. "Great to meet you, Faith." And he had a drawl! Colleen was right! Oh, sigh!

"I'll leave you two alone," Jeremy said. "Have a nice time!" He grinned happily and wandered off toward the bar.

"Super guy," Ryan said.

"Absolutely," Faith agreed.

"So you two were engaged, he said?"

"Yes," Faith admitted, glad to have it out of the way. "We met in high school, before he, um…came out."

The waitress, one of the many O'Rourke cousins, came over, bringing Faith a glass of Blue Heron's dry Riesling, courtesy of Colleen, who waved from behind the bar. Ryan asked what was good here, and Faith recommended the nachos grande, which she hadn't had since Tuesday and was hence suffering serious withdrawal. "Sounds great," Ryan said. "If you like them, I'm sure I will, too." Oh! Southern charm!

They exchanged pleasantries until the food arrived—jobs, college, where they grew up—and not a red flag to be found. In fact, Faith was feeling the tingle, oh, yeah. Ryan's cuteness, combined with Jeremy's recommendation, had her feeling truly hopeful for the first time since Clint Bundt, the Lying Liar of Lie-Land. No, Ryan was definitely her best prospect since gay Rafael (who'd just texted her a picture of the hors d'oeuvres choices they were considering for their wedding, wanting her opinion).

Definitely better than Levi, who was an ass-pain.

Nope. Not another thought of Levi would be entertained tonight, no way.

As if reading her mind, Levi looked at her from across the bar, those sleepy green eyes causing certain parts of her anatomy to tighten in a hot, slow clench.

Damn. Colleen was right. Levi Cooper was sex on a stick. Sex against the wall, on the floor, on the table, on…other naughty surfaces…dirty, sweaty, delicious sex…not that Faith had any firsthand experience with that. But she could imagine it, quite graphically, in fact. Especially while staring at the man in question.

Oopsy. Her mouth was slightly open, and she was possibly a little flushed. She forced herself to look at her date, who smiled politely.

Right. Concentrate on the perfectly nice man who

actually seems to like you, Faith. "So," she said. "Let's cut to the chase. I'm the youngest of four, two sisters, one brother. My dad is sitting at the bar over there, so don't get fresh. I love my job, my grandparents, Ben and Jerry, and my dog, who is, I should tell you up front, the greatest canine the world has ever known."

"Can't wait to meet him," Ryan said. "Keep on going, Miss Faith."

She smiled. "Well, in my free time, I like to eat out, I do Pilates—" well, she *intended* to do Pilates, one of these days "—and I love violent, scary movies and romantic comedies. I'd like to be in a serious, committed relationship with a man who's not married, not a deadbeat dad, has a job and isn't gay. With me so far?"

"Are you kidding?" Ryan said with another fantastic dimpled smile. "I'm halfway in love with you already."

"Get outta town, you big liar," Faith said. Yay, Jeremy! She grinned, just happening to catch a glimpse of Levi. He was watching. *That's right! Suck it up, Chief,* she thought, finishing her wine. "Your turn, Ryan."

"Not so fast, there. Jeremy tells me you have a list," Ryan said. He tore off a hunk of nachos and held it up to her mouth. Huh. Feeding her already? Was that icky, or adorable?

Adorable, Faith, adorable. Still, a bit awkward, since the sour cream was a little drippy. But still. A good sign (she hoped).

"I do have a list," Faith said, wiping her mouth. "It's sort of…Machiavellian."

"Sounds fun." Ryan gave her a steamy look.

"Really?"

"Mmm-hmm. Give it to me, baby."

"Oh…yeah, okay, I can do that." She paused. "Now?"

"Sure."

"Okay." She opened her purse and took out the well-worn list. "This is just the big stuff, you know, to make sure I shouldn't run screaming from the bar."

Another dimpled smile. "Please don't, Miss Faith."

He was *so* cute. "Okay, so…have you ever been in prison?"

"Not yet."

"Yay! You have an A so far. Next question: Have you fathered any children, and do you pay child support, if so?"

"No kids. Not yet."

Another excellent answer. *Not yet,* implying that he wanted them in the future. He was an A+ now.

"Okay, last major question, and then we can get into things like moonlit walks and old movies—"

"I love old movies. And moonlit walks."

Well, you couldn't have everything. "How many women have you slept with?"

Ryan had to think about that one. "Uh…ten?"

Ten? Ten! That seemed like a lot. Then again, if you figured he was thirty-two years old (thank you, Google), and say he'd first had sex around age seventeen (because with those dimples, he wasn't getting out of high school a virgin), that was fifteen years of single heterosexual male having sex. So—Faith did some quick math in her head—that was 0.667 women per year. Which sounded very weird but maybe wasn't that many? Even if it sounded like a *lot* of people?

"I had a pretty serious girlfriend right out of college," he said in his adorable drawl. "Figured we'd get married, you know? But she left me, broke my heart." He gave her a puppy dog look. "Since then, I just haven't been able to find the right person."

Okay, okay, that was tolerable. Sort of. But still. Ten.

"No diseases, by the way," he added.

Granted, she'd need medical confirmation. Should she ask for his doctor's name now, or wait? Maybe waiting would be good.

She glanced over at Levi, who was no longer looking at her. Fine. Let him ignore her. "Thanks for answering my questions, Ryan. You're very tolerant."

"You're quite welcome. Hey. You wanna get our first kiss over with?" He smiled. "I find it makes things more relaxed, without us having to worry about how that'll go."

"Um...okay." Another glance at Levi. You know what? Yes. Let him see her kissing someone else. She leaned over the table, moving the nachos first (wouldn't do to have guacamole on the boobage) and gave Ryan a quick kiss on the lips, then quickly sat back down.

Was there a tingle? Too fast to tell. A quick glance at Levi, who was lifting his beer glass. Damn it. His *arm* made her tingle.

"That was very nice," Ryan said. "A little sting from the jalapenos, but I kinda liked it. Sweet, with a little bite."

"That's me," Faith said.

His expression became rather wolfish. "*Real*ly."

"Well, I don't actually know, but...it's sort of me, maybe." Flustered, she took a bite of nachos. Hannah O'Rourke (or possibly Monica) brought her another glass of wine, bless her.

"So I have a list of my own," Ryan said.

"You do? That's great!" Kindred spirits. Made her feel less freakish.

"You ready?"

"Sure." She sat back and smiled. "Fire away." She took a bite of the nachos.

Ryan grinned. "Do you like being spanked?"

She sucked a bit of jalapeno into her lung and wheezed. "Excuse me?" She coughed (and coughed, and coughed), then took a sip of her wine. "Um...I can't really say. I've never been...spanked."

"So you're a spanking virgin?" He licked his lips.

"I— You know, I think that book everyone was reading last year? That may have given the wrong impression. You know, about women wanting to have violence perpetrated against them. So. That's off the table."

"How about handcuffs?"

"Again...uh...not a lot of experience. And not seeking any." Crap. Was there a way to keep this date from going down the toilet faster than her black wraparound sweater? Her brain groped around for a solution and came up empty.

"Do you like being submissive? Would you have a problem calling me Master?"

"No, and yes. That's really not my thing, Ryan. Maybe we can shift course here, huh?"

"Hey." The puppy dog look returned. "I answered your questions. It's only fair."

Faith took a slow breath. It'd be so nice to just walk away now. She could. However, she really didn't feel like seeing the look on Levi's face if she did. "Fine. Go for it."

"Great!" Ryan clapped like a little kid. "Would you like it if I locked you in my boudoir for twelve hours and only left you a glass of water?"

"Do men have boudoirs? Because that's a very girly term to me. And no. I'd get very hungry."

"I see. I suppose I could slide some slices of baloney under the door."

"Baloney? I'd need more than that."

"Maybe some American cheese?"

"No," Faith said. "I would require a gourmet pizza with shrimp, mustard and pesto from The Red Salamander, a bottle of chardonnay, and at least one pint of Ben & Jerry's Peanut Brittle."

"I see."

"Also, I wouldn't let you lock me anywhere. I'd kick you in the nuts if you tried that, buddy."

"Oh! Awesome!" Ryan beamed. For the love of all that was holy… "What if I came in dressed as Zorro with absolutely nothing on under my cape?"

"You look nothing like Antonio Banderas. I would have to reject you. I imagine I'd laugh." Jeremy was going to have to pay for this, oh, yes indeedy. And speaking of the town's beloved doctor, where was he? "Hannah? Can we have the—"

Ah, hell. Levi was looking at her, a slight smirk on his face. And even if Ryan was a pervert with a terrible imagination, at least he was into her. "Never mind," she told the girl. She turned her gaze back to Ryan of the Debauched Dimples. "Next question."

"Great! Okay, say you were my cleaning woman, and you were on your hands and knees in my kitchen and I came in. What would you say?"

"I'd say, 'Why is this floor so filthy? Can't you learn to lean over the table?'"

"And I would say, 'Take off the uniform, Cinder-Slut, and put your skills to other uses.'"

Faith folded her hands. "I would say, 'No, sir, I will not! I require that you hie unto the market and buy me the Clorox Cleanup I asked you to get last week.'"

Ryan looked a little confused. "Uh…then I'd say, 'Do as I say, serving wench!'"

"No, no, that won't work," Faith said, "See, I'm the

cleaning lady, not the serving wench. Now I lost my character's motivation. Scene."

"You're not doing this right, Faith," he said, a sulky note in his voice.

"And you're a fairly unimaginative perv," she returned. "The maid is the best you can come up with? Yawn."

Ryan's phone buzzed. "I have to answer this," he grumbled.

"By all means," she said. Someone plunked into the seat next to her.

"Hey, Pru!" Faith said. "How's it going?"

"Great. Got a quick question for you. Am I interrupting?"

"Not one bit." Ryan was muttering into the phone, his hand cupped around it so she wouldn't hear.

"Okay, well, here's the thing. Carl's sexting me."

"Wow. I... Wow."

"Check this out. What color panties r u wearing? Do I tell the truth? Because I think it's the ones with the squirrels riding their little sleds. Or should I make something up?"

"Um, you know, do what you think is best," Faith said. More wine would be called for very soon.

"Tell him you got on a red thong, and you want him to take it off with his teeth," Ryan offered, pausing in his phone conversation. "Or even better, tell him you're not wearing any panties at all. And that you'd like to play serving wench and master when you get home."

Prudence stared at him. "This is your date?" she asked Faith.

"Sorry to say, yes, he is."

"I have to go," Ryan said. "My mama has a wax ball in her ear. Faith, what do you say? Wanna hook up? The ear will only take a minute, and it's easier with two people, since she needs to be restrained."

"I'll take a pass," Faith said. "Good luck." Ryan threw a few bills down on the table and left, grumbling about the lies of erotic fiction.

Pru was texting. "Being sexy is exhausting," she said. *"I'm wearing a thong,"* she narrated. *"Come and get it, big boy.* You know what I miss, Faith? My periods. At least then, I'd have a few days off. And when a woman yearns for her periods, that's a sign that the end of days is coming." Her phone chirped, and she paused to read. "Ah, shit. Look at this."

She shoved her phone across the table so Faith could read. am deeply disturbed. be more careful with the send button, for the love of god. will accept gifts to undo the psychological damage just inflicted. xox your son, Ned

"I think I might divorce Carl if this keeps up," Pru said. "Okay. Gotta go screw my husband. Sorry your date was an ass. Talk tomorrow." Her sister kissed her on the cheek and left.

Faith slid out of the booth. Jeremy was gone, apparently, but Levi was still at the bar, and Dad, as well as Jack now, too. And speaking of Dad, he seemed to be having a good time…and with a woman! Oh, with two! How thrilling! Cathy Kennedy, chooser of odd Bible verses but otherwise quite nice, and another woman Faith didn't know. Levi said something, allowing a faint hint of a smile cross his face. Faith's girl parts gave a sudden, hard tug.

"Sweetpea! Over here!" Dad called, and wasn't he in the most jocular mood tonight! At least one of them was having luck with the opposite gender. She went to her dad, who slipped an arm around her, and smiled broadly at her potential stepmother.

"Honey, you remember Mrs. Kennedy, right?"

"Of course I do, Dad. Nice to see you again, Mrs. Kennedy. I had a great time at Bible Study the other day."

"Call me Cathy, sweetie. This is my wife, Louise."

Hemorrhoid! Why were all the good ones gay? "Very nice to meet you, Louise," Faith said, trying not to sigh.

"You're going to Bible Study?" Jack muttered.

"With Goggy," she muttered back.

"Trying to get the house in the will?"

"I think I've earned it, don't you?"

"Wasn't that the most interesting verse?" Mrs. Kennedy said. "Boys, we were discussing the history of blood rituals in the Old Testament. Circumcision, human sacrifice, that sort of thing."

"Makes me a believer," Jack said.

"This verse was about circumcision with a flint stone," Faith added, giving her big brother a look. "You wonder why some traditions die out. I mean, flint was good enough back then…why fix it if it ain't broke?"

"So how was the crop this year, John?" Mrs. Kennedy asked, and Dad started on his favorite subject.

"How was your date, sis?" Jack asked.

"Wonderful," she answered, as Levi was in hearing range. "Very charming guy." But Levi wasn't looking at her; instead, he stood up and opened his arms as his sister approached. Sarah Cooper dropped her backpack and went right to her brother, hugging him tight.

"Thank God I'm home," Sarah said. "I thought my brain would explode."

"From an entire week at college?" Levi said.

"Listen, G.I. Joe. You have no idea how hard it is."

She rested her head on his shoulder, and Levi kissed her hair, and the gesture was so unexpectedly sweet and natural that Faith found herself…softening. Levi might be a pain in the ass, but his sister loved him. Jack, on the other hand, had only done things like film her seizures and hide in her closet with a knife when she was nine.

"I can't imagine you giving me a hug in public," she told him.

"Me, neither," Jack said. "You're so irritating."

"No, I'm not," she said, grinning. "I'm your favorite sister."

"Only because you used to live three thousand miles away," he said. "These days, it's a toss-up."

"Well, even if you wanted to hug me, I'd never let you, because you smell funny and don't know how to eat in public and—oof!"

Jack had grabbed her in a bear hug, lifting her off her feet. "God, you're heavy," he grunted. "Lay off those Girl Scout cookies."

"Shut up and put me down," she said, smacking him on the head.

Dad was watching with a smile in his eyes. "You're so much like your mom," he said.

The words, intended as a compliment, made Faith's smile slip.

"Thanks," Jack answered. "I get that a lot." Then he noticed Colleen smiling at him, and his grin disappeared.

"Don't be scared, Jack," Colleen said. "I only bite on request."

"Well, I'm heading home," Dad said. "Jack, you ready?" Her father tousled Faith's hair. "'Night, sweetie. Oh, hi, there, Sarah, how are you?"

"Hi, Mr. Holland," she said. "I'm fine, how are you?"

"I'm going, too," Faith said, her heart sinking a little. Another crappy date. Ah, well. At least she hadn't
wasted too much time running a background check.
She'd go home, cuddle with Blue, call Jeremy and give
him the report, then discuss how he'd make this up to
her. "Have a good night, everyone."

"Hey, Faith," Sarah said. "Um…do have a second? I
was wondering if I could talk to you. About San Francisco?"

Faith glanced at Levi who was on the phone, then
back at Sarah. "Sure, honey."

"Your nephew? Ned?" Her cheeks blossomed with
color. "He was telling me you'd been out there a few
years. Do you like it?"

A crush, how sweet! "I love it out there. It's gorgeous."

Levi shoved his phone back in his pocket. "Sarah, I
have to go on a call. You want to come?"

"What is it this time?" Sarah asked. "Another chicken
under the porch?"

"It's actually a possum in the Hedbergs' basement.
Their dog went crazy, which scared the cat out the window, so now they're afraid a coyote will eat the cat."

"Isn't there animal control in this town?" Sarah
asked.

"Yes, but the guy's old, and it's past ten."

"I'll pass. Meet you at home." She turned back to
Faith. "So, did you like living away? I just can't imagine living anywhere but here. I mean, I remember how
you were, um…left at the altar. Maybe you went because you… Oh, jeesh. Sorry if I'm bringing up bad
memories or whatever." Sarah grimaced.

"No, no, that's fine. Common knowledge." Alas.

"Faith, can I talk to you for a minute?" Levi said.

He didn't wait for an answer, just took her by the arm and towed her away. The simple touch made her entire arm buzz with heat. Levi's green flannel shirt made his eyes look darker, and crikey, he had big, manly hands. So…alpha. Colleen said big hands meant—

These lustful thoughts will send you straight to hell, her conscience chided in the sharp voice of Mrs. Linqvest.

"So, listen," Levi said.

"Yes, sir, Chief Cooper."

"Sarah's got some serious homesickness going on. Trying to drop out of college and move back here. I'd really like her to get an education. So if you two are talking about living away, I'd appreciate it if you encouraged that. I don't want her to end up here because she never gave anything else a chance." He ran a big hand through his hair, and Faith's inner slut gave a moan. She remembered that hair, the soft, silky—*I'm serious,* said Mrs. Linqvest. *Knock it off.* He shoved his hands in his pockets, the fabric of his shirt straining against those thick, masculine arms.

Faith cleared her throat. "No, I get it. Everyone should live away from home, at least for a while."

His eyes came back to hers. "Exactly."

His eyelashes were *awfully* nice, long and straight and blond.

"You go get that possum," Faith said. It sounded vaguely sexual, for some reason. *Yes, Levi. Get that possum. Don't stop getting it. Get it good.* Mrs. Linqvest got out the ruler. "I'll hang out with your sister. We can walk home together."

"Thank you."

The words caused a warm, liquid rush through her

knees. "You're welcome," she said, her voice a little husky.

Then he turned and left, raising his hand as someone called a good-night to him.

BY THE TIME LEVI GOT BACK from the call (the possum having been flushed out through the hole in the stone foundation, the hole temporarily patched with the help of young Andrew, and the cat found safe and sound, much to the sobbing relief of the Hedberg girls), O'Rourke's was mostly empty. "Did my sister go home?" he asked Colleen, who was wiping down the bar.

"Faith said they were going out on the beach," she said. "Don't know if they're still there."

"Thanks."

Levi went out the back door, past the parking lot where he'd pulled Faith from the window. That seemed like a long time ago. He wouldn't mind seeing her in that black bra again, that was for sure. Or out of it.

Shit. He shouldn't be having those thoughts again. Faith was...well, she wasn't his type. Too—too much, that was all. Too ~~delicious edible~~ complicated. He should *not* have kissed her that morning. That had been really, really stupid. Hadn't planned it, that's for sure, but one kiss, and he'd felt an almost violent rush of lust slam into him, heavy and thick and immediate. Her mouth was so soft—all of her was so soft, like a bed you could sink into—and the smell of her, as inviting as cake warm from the oven, and when she'd made that little sound, he'd nearly lost it. Pulled back because if he'd kissed her another second, he'd have done her against the wall.

And that kind of thing, that got a little...out of control.

Faith was, first and foremost, Jeremy's ex. What-

ever the circumstances, Jeremy was her first love, and
Levi didn't like the thought of being runner-up to his
best friend. And secondly, there was that overwhelm-
ing sense of being lost in the moment, being oblivious.
He didn't like that. He'd felt that twelve years ago when
he'd kissed her, a kiss that had erased common sense
and loyalty and whatever else that mattered.

And thirdly…she wasn't even here permanently. John
Holland had told him he was hoping Faith would stay in
Manningsport. But the truth was, she had a whole life
back in California. Once before, he'd fallen in love with
a woman who'd left him. He shouldn't charge head-on
into doing it again.

Not that he was in love with Faith Holland.

The town beach was actually a little park—grass and
some flowering trees, a few benches, a boat launch, a
dock and a tiny sand beach at the edge of the lake. Stars
dotted the sky, but no moon was out, and it took Levi's
eyes a moment to adjust to the darkness after the pinkish glow of the streetlights. There were Sarah and Faith,
sitting on a bench, their shoulders touching, looking out
over the dark water. Their backs were to him, so they
didn't see him approach across the grass.

He stopped at the sound of Sarah's laugh. Hadn't
heard that for a while.

"No, but seriously, I know how you feel," Faith said.
"My mom died when I was young, too."

"How old were you?"

"Twelve."

"Sheesh. That sucks."

"Yeah. Car accident."

"So no time for goodbye?"

"Right."

Sarah chewed that over. "I guess at least I had that."

"Both ways are tough. There's no getting around it. It's so hard."

"Do you still think about your mom?" Sarah asked.

"Oh, yeah," Faith said. "Every day."

Levi did, too. Every day, some thought of his mom would cross his mind—her energy, her total lack of self-pity. Even when she was doped up on morphine, she'd make him and Sarah laugh.

There was an unusual tightness in his throat.

"There are days when I'm so sad, I don't think I can even get out of bed," Sarah said now, her voice small. "All I want is my mom, and I have to go to classes and listen to all that stuff, and it just seems so shallow and meaningless, when I'd trade in everything for just another regular day with her." His sister's voice broke, and Faith put an arm around her.

"I'm sorry, honey," she said. Nothing else, just that. She stroked Sarah's hair in an unconscious way, idly, her head tipped against Sarah's. Just petted her hair and let his sister cry.

"I know I should get over it," Sarah said. "It's been more than a year."

"Well," Faith said, "you don't really get over it. You just learn to carry it better. And the only way to do that is to do the regular things. Get out of bed. Go to classes. Try to be normal, and pretty soon all that grief you carry…it gets easier."

"That's what Levi says," Sarah said after a minute. "I guess he's not always a dope, then."

"Most of the time, he is."

"Yeah, I'd agree with you there." There was a smile in Faith's voice.

"I just…I feel her more when I'm here," his sister said. "That's why I don't want to be at school."

A pain stabbed Levi's chest. Why didn't his sister tell *him* that? Why did she whine about hard classes and her lack of friends if that wasn't the real issue?

He thought he might know the answer.

Because he didn't let her.

"Do you ever talk to her?" Sarah asked.

"Oh, sure," Faith answered. She was lying, Levi thought.

"Does she ever answer? Like, do you ever think her spirit's with you or something?"

Faith was quiet for a few seconds. "Yeah, I do." Another lie, telling Sarah what she wanted to hear. "How about you?"

"Definitely. Levi just looks at me funny when I say that, but I feel her around sometimes."

"Well, he's a guy. They're pretty thick." There was another smile in Faith's voice, and Levi felt the corner of his mouth tug.

"Total cement," Sarah said.

"Lead."

"Exactly." Sarah straightened up and blew her nose. "Were you homesick when you first left?"

"Oh, yeah. I missed this place so much it actually hurt. I had a stomachache for weeks."

"I know!"

"But, Sarah, if you stayed here and passed up on the chance to live away and be your own person, rather than Levi's little sister…wouldn't you always wonder what you missed?"

Good girl, Faith.

"I guess. I mean, theoretically, I do want to go to college and stuff. Live away, at least for a while. But it's hard."

"I know, honey." Faith was quiet for a minute. "You know the saying. Everything worthwhile in life is hard."

"Yeah. Levi quotes it on a daily basis." Sarah stretched her arms over her head. "I should get home." She turned, and, seeing him there, gave a little shriek. "Jeez! Levi! You shouldn't just stand there like a serial killer! Say something next time!"

"I just got here, so settle down," he said. "You two ready to call it a night?"

Faith stood up and brushed off her skirt. "Chief. How was the possum?"

"Feisty," he said. Her white shirt glowed in the darkness. "Walk you home, girls?"

"So what's your favorite thing to do in San Fran?" Sarah asked, trotting backward so she could see Faith as they walked up Lake Street, and Faith talked about the weather, the flowers, the food, the views. She made it sound like the best place on earth.

"Maybe I'll go there for a semester," Sarah said. "My school has swap programs with a bunch of colleges."

Well, hell.

"It's a great city," Faith said. "Definitely look into it. If I'm still there, we could get together."

They walked past the now-quiet green, the shops dark. "Look up there," Faith said, and sure enough, a light was on in her apartment, silhouetting her dog as he stood with his paws on the windowsill. "Hi, Blue! Be there in a minute," she called.

Levi held the door, and Faith's hair brushed his chin as she went in, enveloping him in that smell. He followed her up the stairs. Great legs.

"Thanks for hanging out," Sarah said as Levi unlocked their door.

"Oh, honey, it was really nice," Faith answered.

"Sorry if I was a total drag."

"You weren't. Are you kidding?" She smiled and opened her own door, and her dog bounded out, dancing with joy.

"Hi, poochie!" Sarah said, bending to pet him. The dog licked her chin and whined. "Aw, what a sweetie you are!" She scratched his ears, then straightened. "Good night!" With that she went inside.

Levi didn't follow. He waited till the door closed instead, just looked at Faith, who'd reached inside her door and gotten Blue's leash. She bent over and clipped it on, giving him a glimpse of the mighty rack, then straightened up.

"Yes, Levi?" she said, sighing.

Then damn if he wasn't kissing her again, but there he was, his mouth on hers, a surprised little squeak coming from her throat. His hands cupped her face, and part of his brain barked out something about how stupid he was. The rest of him, however, was all for it. Her lips were soft and pliant, and, yeah, she was kissing him back.

Then she gave him a hard shove, and he stepped back, feeling blurry and slow.

"So what is this, Levi? You're just going to blindside me with a kiss every once in a while?" she whispered.

Blue jumped against her like this was the best idea he'd ever heard, his tail whacking against the wall. She gave the dog an idle pat, but she looked mad. He couldn't blame her.

"Sorry," he said.

"You're so damn confusing," she hissed. "Really. I mean, I get the impression that you can't stand me, then after my seizure, you were incredibly nice and helpful, then you kiss me, then you ignore m—"

Ah, hell, he was kissing her again. If nothing else, it did shut her up. And he liked her mouth doing something other than yapping at him. Soft and sweet and hot. He drew her against him, and she didn't resist. Instead, her hands slid into his hair, and she kissed him back, that sweet little noise coming from her once more. Then she let go.

"Stop it," she whispered against his mouth. He obeyed. Her eyes were wide and blue, and she looked a little dazed.

"Thanks for talking to my sister," he murmured, forcing himself to step back.

"You're welcome," she said after a beat, licking her lips. God, he wished she wouldn't do that. Just made him want to instead. She swallowed. "I, um…I have to walk my dog."

"Okay."

She walked down the hall, stopping to glance back at him. And because he didn't know what to say, he just looked at her, that soft, pretty package, her silly strappy shoes and now-messed-up hair and happy dog.

Then she went down the stairs, and he leaned against the wall, wondering exactly what the hell he was doing.

CHAPTER SEVENTEEN

"ARE YOU SURE YOU don't want an entire case?" Faith asked. "Wine makes such a great present, the holidays are coming up, and your friends will know you were thinking of them while you were on your trip." She smiled and leaned on the counter of Blue Heron's beautiful tasting bar.

"I can't resist a pretty girl," said the man. "Sure. Why not? Make it three cases. Best Riesling I've tasted."

"I'm gonna tell my dad you said that," Faith said. "You'll make his entire week. And how about the cab you liked? The one you said had blackberry undertones and a hint of tobacco? You have a great palate, by the way."

"All right. Great idea. I'll save that just for me, though."

"I like a man who treats himself right," Faith said with a wink, handing the order to Mario, who'd run the cases out to the guy's car.

Years of practice had shown Faith that flirting worked wonders when at the tasting bar. Honor used to lecture her about it, but no one had had a better record than Faith until Ned had come of age. At the moment, he was with a gaggle of fiftysomething women, clad in sturdy sneakers and matching, eye-bleeding pink sweatshirts that proclaimed them as "Phi Beta Bitches."

She took the guy's tasting glass to the sink. "I just

sold four cases to one man," she murmured as she passed her nephew. "Suck it up, sonny."

"Ladies," Ned said, "my aunt here doesn't think I can sell as much wine as she can. Help me prove her wrong. I'm throwing myself on your mercy."

"Whore," she whispered, patting his shoulder.

"I learned from the best," he returned.

It was fun to be back in the tasting room, especially with Ned. This was Honor's domain—she worked out of a big office in the back, running the sales, media and distribution, and running them well. But whenever Honor was around, Faith felt slightly out of place. This morning, though, Honor had called, saying that Chipper Reeves had sprained his ankle, and could Faith please pour for the afternoon. And even though it meant pausing in her work on the barn, she didn't want to say no. Honor so rarely asked her for help.

"Thank you, beautiful ladies!" Ned called as the Bitches left. "Eight cases, by the way," he added to Faith. He took a cloth and started wiping down the counters, taking advantage of the break in traffic.

"Yeah, but my per capita ratio is still much higher. Guess you're not quite as cute as you think, Neddie dear."

"I don't see how that's possible," he said. "I have a mirror, after all."

"And speaking of cute," she began.

"Nice transition, Auntie."

"Thanks. Speaking of cute, you and Sarah Cooper? Is there cause for concern? Do I need to lecture you on safe sex, or just point out that her big brother is a decorated war veteran who can hit a moving target from five thousand yards?"

"Are you serious?"

"No, it's just a line from a movie. But you don't want him mad at you, do you?"

"Levi's skill with a gun was definitely a consideration at first," Ned said sagely, stroking his chin. "But Sarah's cute little ass soon rendered me incapable of rational thought—"

"You did not just say that. I'll have to kill you now. It pains me."

"—and she's pregnant with triplets. Congratulate me."

Faith stared at him.

"Okay, fine," Ned said. "The truth is, we text a little sometimes and play Words with Friends."

"That does sound more like you," Faith admitted. "Are you part of the reason she wants to come home so much?"

"Oh, I don't think so. She crushing on me, and who can blame her?" He ducked as Faith swatted him. "I do like her, don't get me wrong, but she's a little young yet."

"See? Just when I think I should drown you in a bucket, you come up with something really sensible." Faith paused. "Just don't let the crush get too out of hand, okay? They can really hurt."

"Does this great wisdom come from the shards of your own broken heart, Auntie, or—"

"You know what? Get the bucket." She turned as a couple came into the tasting room. "Hi, there! Welcome to Blue Heron."

"Faith? Can I see you a minute?" Honor stood in the hall that led to the offices.

"I got this," Ned said. "What can I pour for you guys this afternoon?"

Faith followed her sister past the conference room

and offices that were kept (and seldom used) by Dad, Jack and Pru.

Honor sat behind her beautiful, frighteningly organized desk, a gorgeous piece of walnut and oak made by the same carpenters Faith had hired to do the deck for the barn.

"How are things?" her sister asked briskly.

"Great. Uh, how are things with you?"

"Just fine. Have you found Dad a suitable woman yet?"

Faith snorted. "That sounds...well, never mind. Um, not quite. I'm working on it. I'm casually introducing him to a gardener today, and I have a date set up with someone from eCommitment next week."

"Good. We don't want someone like Lorena taking Dad for everything he has."

Faith felt the odd impulse to stand up for the woman. "You know, Honor, maybe it's one of those opposites-attract situations. He seems to really like her."

"She just asked him for a loan of ten grand, Faith. For a boob job in Mexico."

"Mexico?"

"She knows a guy." Honor raised her eyebrows.

"Well, maybe Dad can decide for himself. It's his money."

Honor sighed. "Do you know how much it takes to run this place, Faith? Let me put it this way. Two bad weather years in a row, and we'd be in the red."

Faith chewed on her lip. "Right."

"So you'll try a little harder?" Honor suggested, tapping a key on her sleek Mac.

Faith wasn't sure what else she could try, short of eBay. "I— Yeah. I'll try harder."

"I won't see you till the party," Honor said, typing

in a staccato burst. "I have to be in the city for a couple days." There was but one city if a person was from the Empire State. Or Jersey, for that matter. Or Connecticut.

"That's nice," Faith said. "I mean, nice that you're getting away for a couple days."

Honor made a noncommittal noise.

"Do you like it? Those business trips?" Faith asked.

Her sister stopped typing and looked up. "Yeah. I do," she said. "It's nice to...well." She shook her head, and Faith felt the sharp knife of regret she so often felt around her sister.

"Nice to what?" she asked.

Her sister shrugged.

"Be your own person?"

Honor looked up, surprised. "Exactly."

Faith smiled. "Not just a Holland of the Holland family, where everyone already knows everything about you."

"Yes." Honor stared at her for a second, then smiled, and Faith felt such a rush of love, she almost hugged her sister. Instead, she just smiled back, feeling her throat tighten a little.

"Can you keep a secret?" Honor asked.

Wow. "Sure."

Honor hesitated. "I've... Well, I've been seeing someone. It's getting serious."

"What?" Faith barked, then covered her mouth with both hands at her sister's grimace. "Honor!" she whispered. "Wow! I didn't know that! Who is he? What's he like?"

"He's...he's *that* guy. The one we mere mortals only get to admire from afar."

Good heavens. Honor was actually blushing. "Except you got close up?" Faith suggested.

Her sister bit her lip and smiled. "Oh, yeah."

"So he's...the one?"

Another dreamy smile was her answer.

"Are you planning to introduce him to the family?"

Honor nodded. She looked so pretty, dumbstruck with love. "He's coming to the anniversary party."

"Wow. So it *is* serious, if you're gonna...unleash the Kraken and all that." Sure, she loved her family, but en masse, they could be a little terrifying.

"Yeah."

Faith grinned. "This is great, Honor. I'm so happy for you."

"Just don't say anything yet, okay? To Dad or Jack or anyone. You're the only one I'm telling for now."

Faith paused. Honor, confiding in her. "I won't say a word."

"Thanks, Faithie."

It had been a long time since Honor had called her that.

Her sister seemed to snap out of her fog. "I need to get back to work. I'll see you when I get home. If you need any help with the party, let me know." She paused. "I went up to the barn the other day, and it's really beautiful, Faith."

And now a compliment! Whoever this guy was, Faith would have to thank him. "Thanks," she said, her voice a little husky. "Well. Have a good trip. Call me if you want. You know. Just to chat."

"If I have a second, I will." Honor smiled and began typing again.

Faith left the office and went back down the hall to the tasting room, which was now empty. She saw Ned through the window, putting a case of wine into the couple's car. Good. A quiet moment.

That was—by far—the most intimate and friendly conversation she'd had with Honor in nineteen years. Maybe, now that Honor had more in her life than the vineyard and Dad's care and feeding, they'd be close. Maybe…just maybe…Honor would finally forgive her for Mom.

Honor never could talk about the accident. Dad had held Faith at the hospital, rocking her, telling her she wasn't to blame, she couldn't help having a seizure. Jack had been horribly gentle and kind, saying at least Faith hadn't died, too, and Pru, who'd been in her twenties at the time, did her best to fill the maternal role for Faith. Everyone seemed to recognize the terrible cost of being alone in the car with her dead mother; Faith had had nightmares for a year, had even wet the bed a time or two, hadn't talked much for months. She didn't have to do homework for the rest of the school year. Everyone was kind…except Honor, whose eyes held a message that Faith could read all too well. *You killed our mother.* And the thing was, it was true, though Honor didn't know to what extent.

But Honor was a good daughter. A martyr, sure, but completely solid with their dad. Faith may have been Daddy's little girl, but Honor had been Mom's favorite, always more mature, more adult than the rest of them, despite being third out of four. She and Mom had had a special bond, and after Mom died, it seemed like Honor couldn't bear to be in the same room with Faith.

But maybe this was a turning point. Maybe—just maybe—Faith could get her sister to like her again.

When her tasting room duties were finished, Faith spied her father, who was sampling the homemade wine Gerard Chartier had brought him for his opinion. "Not bad," John said. "Nice with a rare steak." Blue circled, dropping his ratty tennis ball suggestively. Dad picked it up and tossed it without pausing in his discussion of the different kinds of yeast Gerard could use. Dear old Dad. With his baseball cap, aging flannel shirt and purple-stained hands, he wasn't the most dapper of men, but he was certainly the best.

"I see my little princess over there," Dad said finally.

"Hi, little princess," Gerard called with a grin.

"Hi, Gerard," she said. "Save any lives lately?"

"No, but I can carry you down a ladder if you want," he said.

"Don't tempt me. Dad, got a sec? I wanted to show you the barn."

"You bet, baby. See you, Gerard." Her father picked up Blue's hideous ball and held it high. "Who loves his ball? Do you love your ball?" he said, causing Blue to freeze with elation at the word. Dad threw the disgusting thing past the storage barn, and Blue streaked off, caught it midbounce and returned immediately.

"He could play for the Yankees," Dad observed.

"Can't hit to save his life," Faith said. "So, uh, did Levi tell you about how good Blue was when I had my seizure?" she asked. Sure, it was a blatant attempt to bring up his name, but no one else was as unsuspecting as dear old Dad when it came to being pumped for information. She hadn't seen Levi since he'd kissed her the other night. Hadn't heard him out in the hall, either. Had stopped short of pressing a glass against his door, but only just.

"He did. Said Blue came to get him. Who's a good boy? Huh? Do you love Faithie? Do you love her? You do?"

There was something about Blue that made everyone a cheerful idiot, Faith observed as her father put the ball in his own mouth. "Dad. So gross."

He took the ball out and threw it up the hill. "So I finally get to see this place," he said, putting his arm around her as they walked.

"You haven't been sneaking peeks, have you?" The final week was when a project really took shape, and Faith had wanted to surprise her father.

"No, sweetpea. I have three daughters. I'm excellent at following orders."

They hiked up the hill, past the golden-leafed vines, up to the cemetery. Dad took off his hat and put his hand on the granite of his wife's headstone. "Hey, Connie," he said, his voice so full of love that Faith felt tears prick her eyes. "We all miss you so much, honey."

He glanced at Faith. "Hi, Mom," she said obediently. *I'm so sorry.* It was her customary thought, lodged like iron in her heart. She waited as her father brushed a couple of leaves from the grave, his face in its familiar sad and handsome lines. *Please help me find him someone,* Faith prayed. Would Mom want that, though? Faith thought she would, but then again, she was no expert on what her mother had wanted.

Dad stood, and they continued up the hill, talking about the grapes that would be left on the vine for the ice wines, and his prediction that it'd hit seventeen degrees before Thanksgiving. "Gonna be a cold winter," he said.

"You smelly old farmers have a way of predicting those things," she said, earning a grin. "Okay, we're here. You ready to be dazzled?"

Dad had been up two weeks ago to check the progress; the stonemasons had been working on the rows of rock walls in the parking area, and Samuel had been putting up the railings around the decking. But since then, the path and the beds had been completed, and today, Jane Gooding, an organic farmer from Dundee, was bringing in the plants. Faith wanted to take one more look before the holes were dug, maybe rearrange a few things, before committing to the final layout.

And, yes, Jane Gooding had been vetted as a potential date for Dad. She was in her mid-fifties, loved the outdoors, understood plants, had a master's in botany as well as her master gardener certificate. She was long divorced, had dated here and there, had one grown daughter and was quite outgoing and attractive.

A home run, in other words.

Jane was unloading plants from the back of her truck. She stopped and waved as Faith approached. "Hello there!" she called, smiling. Attractive wrinkles creased her face, and she shoved a bit of curly blond hair behind her ear, leaving a streak of dirt. Totally Dad's type. Bet *she* didn't own an animal-print thong.

"Hi, Jane," Faith said.

Dad was staring open-mouthed at the barn. "Sweetheart! This is amazing! It happened so fast!"

"I aim to please," she said, her father's pride warming her. "Jane, this is my father, John Holland. Dad, Jane Gooding, who owns Dundee Organic Gardens."

"Pleased to meet you," Dad said, shaking her hand. "You have a nice operation over there. I've driven past but never stopped in."

"Well, we can't have that!" Jane said. "Drop in next time you're around. I'll give you the tour." She smiled at him, then turned to Faith. "It's all here. You ready?"

"You bet. Dad, do you have time to help us out?"

"Sure, sweetpea. I just can't get over this! Nice work, honey."

Faith's goal in the barn had been to make it look completely unlandscaped and artlessly natural. The beds around the building were bordered with deceptively sturdy, uneven rock walls. A rusty old wagon wheel, a relic from the barn, leaned against the base of a two-hundred-year-old maple tree, and six old milking containers lined the rock foundation. Seven different varieties of moss and ferns, all indigenous, sat in pots, waiting to be put in the soil. A thousand daffodil bulbs would be scattered in clusters along the foundation, which would make it flippin' gorgeous next spring, and a fairly mature sweet wisteria was already planted by the sliding wooden door, which Samuel had rebuilt beautifully. Faith had painted it periwinkle blue yesterday.

Her little playhouse of old was glorious. She'd saved the barn from becoming just a pile of rocks, created this beautiful place where so many happy memories would be made. Still, a lump came into her throat at the memories of sitting on the moss, pretending to pour tea in acorn caps, trying to tame a chipmunk, leaving a ring of daisies as a gift for the fairies. Such happy times.

Well. Dad and Jane seemed to be getting on like a house on fire, Faith noted. Gardening. So much better than a singles event.

She got to work. Faith always felt like she was a midwife when she planted something, coaxing the plant out of its container, loosening the roots, gently placing it into the carefully dug hole, then filling in the gaps with soil. The dirt on her hands, the rich, dark smell of damp earth, and now, the satisfaction of seeing her design come to actual life… There was nothing like it. The sun beat on her hair, and sweat dampened her

T-shirt despite the cool air, the sound of shovels and birdsong making the afternoon utterly perfect.

Three hours later, they were done.

"That went fast," Dad said.

"Right," Faith said, rolling her eyes at Jane, who smiled. "That's because you missed us prepping the soil last week. That's the hard part."

"It's so pretty, honey. Your grandparents will be amazed."

"Wait till you see it at night, Dad. The lighting is the best part, maybe."

"Well, I should go," Jane said. "So nice meeting you, John! I'll see you at the party, I imagine?"

"You sure will. Nice to meet you, too," he said, blushing a little, but he shook her hand and waved when she started up her truck. "So, she's coming?" he asked Faith

"Sure. You always invite the people who worked on a project, Daddy. It's classy."

"Oh, so we're classy now?"

"Yes. Which means I get to pick out your clothes for Saturday."

The party had the potential to be fantastic, Faith thought as she tidied up a few things. Goggy and Pops would soften toward each other, remembering old feelings, perhaps. Dad would have an almost-date with a very nice woman. Honor would whisper conspiratorially about her new love. Maybe she could get Jack to dance with Colleen, though the odds were low on that. But since she'd clearly backed a winner with Jane, maybe her next project would be her brother.

And maybe Levi would dance with her. Her knees wobbled at the image, the memory of his hard muscles, his heat pressed against her. Probably not, but it sure was a nice thought.

She snapped out of her fog and put the shovel in the shed. Whatever the case, the anniversary party would be a special night. A magical night.

ON SATURDAY EVENING, Faith was resisting—barely— the urge to strangle her grandfather.

"What the hell is this?" he asked, dangling the suspicious food in front of his face.

"Just shut up and eat it," commanded her grandmother. "It's party food. Don't be such a pain in the ass."

Make that strangle both grandparents.

"*You're* the pain in the ass," Pops retorted. "You've been a pain in my ass for sixty-five years."

"No fighting, kids," Ned said. "This is your party. Don't make us sign you into the home just yet. Pops, it's a shrimp. It's wrapped in prosciutto, that's all."

"What the hell's prosciutto?" Pops asked.

"It's like extra-fatty bacon," Faith said. "You'll love it."

Okay, so the night was not exactly *magical*. Not yet, anyway. She could still pull it off…if she drugged Goggy and Pops.

The Holland family had come up to the barn for a special dinner before the big party, since only hors d'oeuvres would be served at the event, and God forbid her grands missed a solid meal. Or Prudence. Or Dad. Or Jack. Honor was here; her mystery man was not, and when Faith had asked about it, *sotto voce,* Honor gave her an icy look as an answer. Mrs. Johnson was also irritated with Faith, since Faith hadn't asked her to prepare the dinner but to be a guest instead, which had somehow insulted her.

"You look really handsome tonight, Pops," she said,

smoothing some of the more fascinating eyebrow hairs away from his eyes.

"Thanks, sweetheart. Maybe I'll get a dance with my special girl, what do you think?"

"If I'm the special girl in question, the answer is yes. But don't forget," she added, whispering, "you and Goggy have a dance first."

Pops grimaced.

"You do," she said firmly. "And you have your speech, right?"

"Oh, yeah," he said. "That's right here." He tapped his jacket pocket.

"Hello, hello," came a voice. It was Jane, the gardener, dressed in a long, shapeless, greenish-brown cotton dress. "Oh, dear," she said. "Am I early?"

"Party starts at seven," Pru said, her voice even louder than usual.

"No, it's fine," Faith said. "Come and join us."

"I'll come back later," Jane said. "This is so embarrassing."

"Not at all. We'd love to have you." She introduced Jane to the family, earning suspicious looks from Goggy, who didn't see anything wrong with her son staying a widower for a few more decades, as well as from Abby, who was sulking because she'd been made to change into something "less whorish," according to Pru. Carl was also missing, though Faith had wised up and not asked why.

"Very nice to see you again," Dad said with an adorably shy smile.

"You, too, John," Jane said, tilting her head to smile back. Jane and John. So cute.

"Please, sit down," Dad said, holding out a chair.

"Thank you." She looked around. "Um, is this…all?"

Jane asked, surveying the shrimp and pasta dish Faith had ordered from the caterers. "I'm sorry. I'm a vegan. A rawist, actually."

Life without cheeseburgers? So sad. "Right. Um, I'll find you something." The caterers should have a veggie platter somewhere.

"And what is a rawist, my dear?" Pops said, turning on the charm (the better to irritate Goggy).

"I only eat raw food," Jane answered.

"Why?" Mrs. Johnson asked. "Are you sick?"

"Oh, no, it's by choice. For health reasons," Jane said as Faith intercepted the vegetable tray from one of the servers. "Thanks, Faith. This'll be perfect." She took an impressive handful of baby carrots and began shoving them into her mouth like popcorn, crunching madly. And another handful. And some celery. Her mouth worked faster than a wood chipper, Faith thought.

"You eat raw meat? That can't be good for you," Goggy pronounced.

Jane paused in her crop decimation. "I don't eat meat. Raw vegetables and fruits only."

"What about bread?" Abby asked.

"Nope. Gluten is poison for me." She picked up another handful of carrots and started chainsawing through them, little flecks of orange flying from her lips. "You should try it. I have literally no mucus issues anymore. And I'm never constipated."

Dad had that *hide me* look on his face, and Ned was choking with laughter. Jane did have very strong-looking teeth, Faith noted. The veggie platter was supposed to serve twenty, but at the rate Jane was going, she'd polish that off, then start on the table, which was hopefully gluten-free.

"Faith," Pru said, draining her wine, "where's Colleen and the hard stuff? You did say we were having an open bar, right?"

Yes, where were Connor and Colleen? Faith checked her phone. No messages. She sent a quick text, asking if they needed help. It was getting to be crunch time. She excused herself and started putting the centerpieces on the tables, which had been covered with pale blue tablecloths.

Prudence approached, a shrimp in each hand. "The place looks beautiful," she said. She was wearing dress pants and work boots, as well as a low-cut white sweater. An impressive purple hickey stood out on her throat.

"Thanks," Faith said. "So things are good with Carl?"

Pru shrugged. "Yes and no. I kicked him out."

"What? Why?"

"We did it the other night, right? Good old married sex, nothing fancy. Finally, right? Then he says he wants to film us—"

"What?"

"Right. So he's staying at his mother's. Figured it'll shake him up a little."

Faith nodded as if she understood. "Um…you have a big hickey, you know."

"Really? Damn it. Should've looked in the mirror, I guess. Anyway, nice job here!" She poured herself another glass of wine and drank it like it was water.

The DJ asked where he should set up, and Faith directed him to one corner. Then, after two more questions from the caterer had been answered, Faith adjusted the light under the maple tree, fixed the door, which was sticking, and found Pops's lower denture plate in a gooey nut cookie. She worked the teeth free as Goggy had a fit that Pops was eating nuts when his gastroenter-

ologist specifically said not to. As Jane was eating half
her body weight in roughage, Faith asked Mrs. Johnson if she might have any more vegetables, earning a
glare from the housekeeper and some dark mutterings
about people having evolved enough to cook their food.
Faith took that as a yes, ran down to the New House,
raided the fridge, cut up red peppers, carrots and broc-
coli, then cleaned the kitchen at lightning speed, because Mrs. Johnson hated anyone to leave a mess in her
workspace. Then she power-walked back up the Hill,
in heels, managing not to drop a single pepper slice.

Magical. Yeah, right. She was sweating, how magical
was that? And the guests were just starting to trickle in.

Honor appeared at Faith's side. "Lorena's here," she
growled. "I thought you took care of that."

"I didn't invite her. I guess Dad did."

"Check out that dress, Faith."

Lorena was currently kissing Pops on the cheek,
bending over the old man, who clearly didn't mind.
And the thing was, Lorena's dress…the woman had to
weigh somewhere around two hundred pounds and was
sixty years old if she was a day but, for some reason
that went against nature and God's law, had chosen to
wear a skin-tight rubbery black dress. No back. White
granny panties, though, clearly visible.

Faith's breath left her in a rush. "That's—I…gotta
give her points for, um, confidence. Maybe Dad *should*
pay for that boob job. Wow."

Honor was not amused. "You said you could find
him someone, Faith. That other woman, the gardener, is
talking about how often she poops, and here's Lorena,
dressed like Lady Gaga. Can't you do better?" Before
Faith could answer, Honor walked away.

With a sigh, Faith went over to say hello to Lorena.

"Hello, sweetie!" Lorena boomed. "And just who do we have here?" She was glaring at Jane, who sat next to Dad.

Jane paused in her chewing. "I'm a friend," she said, looking Lorena up and down.

"A friend? A friend of who?" Lorena asked, her expression lowering.

"A friend of *whom?* Is that what you mean?" Jane smiled tightly and took another celery stick.

"Cat fight," Ned murmured as he walked past Faith, phone in his hand.

Next time Faith felt the urge to throw a party, she'd ask Pru to duct tape her into a chair.

And things hadn't even started.

CHAPTER EIGHTEEN

LEVI PULLED ON HIS suit jacket, the one usually saved for weddings or funerals. The whole town had been invited to old Mr. and Mrs. Holland's anniversary party, the police chief included. He hadn't seen Faith much since the night he'd kissed her. Last weekend had been Columbus Day, and what with Sarah home and all the tourists, the biplane show out on the lake, the wine tasting on the green, the wooden boat parade, he hadn't had a free minute. Not that he knew what he'd do with it, to be honest.

On Monday night, he'd driven Sarah back to school, stopping at Target to get her some stuff to make her dorm room more homey, pillows and girly stuff like that. Then he'd taken Sarah and her roommate out to dinner. Seemed like they were getting along just fine, those two girls.

As he'd said goodbye to his sister, he'd tried to find something to say about their mom, something similar to what Faith had said, but nothing sounded right, so he'd just given her fifty bucks and told her to study hard. Drove back to Manningsport and tried to chop away at the mountain of paperwork on his desk at the station, even if it was ten o'clock at night.

Thought about Faith.

Yeah, she was…delicious. He was a guy, he was straight, she was luscious and lived across the hall from him. Also, she smelled good. And though he'd once viewed her as an irritating puppy of a person, she was…more.

That didn't mean he wanted to date her. He wasn't sure he wanted to date *anyone* right now. His divorce wasn't even two years old.

He should really stop thinking about her.

Levi drove up the Hill and turned into Blue Heron's driveway, where a line of cars was heading up the long dirt road that bordered one of the fields. There was a tasteful new sign with the gold and blue vineyard logo on it: *The Barn at Blue Heron, 0.4 miles.* As ever, it amazed him how much land the Hollands owned.

At the top of the ridge, a field served as a parking lot. Rock walls divided it up, the walls looking as if they'd been there forever, though Levi was pretty sure they were new.

"Levi, hey!" Jeremy approached from the field. Living next door, he must've walked over.

"Hey, Jer. How's it going?"

"Very well, my friend. How are you?"

Levi had heard from Emmaline that Faith and Jeremy had been at O'Rourke's the other night, laughing it up. The news had caused a ping of jealousy to echo through him. Which was stupid, of course. The two of them had a history. Everyone knew that.

Didn't stop that pinging, though.

People were streaming toward a path flanked by two maple trees, which were lit from the bottom by small spotlights, casting the yellow leaves in a warm, golden light. The path was wide, a stone wall running along one side, little copper lamps lighting the way. A wood thrush called, and farther away, an owl hooted. Somewhere in the distance was the sound of rushing water.

Suddenly, Levi recognized where they were. He'd been here before. Twelve years ago, he and Faith had eaten lunch about a hundred yards from here, over by the waterfall.

"Have you ever been out here?" Jeremy asked like a fricking psychic or something. "There's a nice place to swim."

Ah. So Jeremy had been here, too. Well, sure. He was the one who dated Faith. "I don't know. Maybe," he said. Then they rounded a slight curve in the path, and both men stopped.

"Wow," Jeremy breathed.

The structure in front of them was both modern and old—the old stone barn, topped with a clear-paneled roof, glowing from the soft lights inside. All around, trees had been lit from below—white birch and silver maple, beech and hickory. There were flower beds, but it wasn't fussy or precise; it was kind of…magical. Like something out of a fairy tale.

"Levi, Jeremy! So glad you could come!" John Holland greeted them at the big barn door, which was lit with copper lanterns. Two women flanked him; one in what appeared to be a brown paper bag; the other in, ouch, best not to look. Right. Lorena Creech, who'd been sniffing around Faith's father in recent weeks. "Come on in, see what our Faith has done. Phyllis! How are you! The walk wasn't too bad, was it?"

"This is unbelievable," Jeremy said as they went through the barn doors.

Inside was quite possibly even prettier. Lamps made from Blue Heron wine bottles had been fastened to the stone with iron brackets. More wine bottles, the necks cut off, sat on the tables, filled with what looked like wildflowers. People milled about, pointing and exclaiming.

The far wall of the barn was missing, and a two-level deck cantilevered out over the hill. There were more tables out there, and people admired the view, which stretched out past the lighted trees, over the fields and all the way to the lake.

"Levi! I clocked a speeder going past my house at sixty-two miles an hour," barked Mrs. Nebbins, who owned her own radar gun and phoned him about three times a week. "When are you going to set up a speed trap on my road?"

"I was out there yesterday," Levi said.

"Well, you need to give more tickets. Or maybe put out some spikes. That'd slow people down, let me tell you."

"Phyllis, you just get more beautiful, if that's possible," Jeremy murmured, kissing her cheek.

"Oh, Jeremy, you liar!" she said. "Have you seen Faith? Is it hard? Is she still in love with you? She probably is, poor thing. Listen, my knee is out of whack, and those exercises you gave me didn't work, so I stopped doing them."

"Really? How long did you do them?"

"Two days."

"That's just insulting," he said. "Come on, complain away, I've got all night. But I want to see that deck." He escorted the crotchety old lady away, grinning over his shoulder at Levi. Too bad the guy was gay. He was so good with women.

Levi got a glass of seltzer water and wandered around. The barn smelled of freshly cut wood, grass and food. Lorelei from the bakery was putting some flowers on top of a chocolate cake; she waved and smiled. Colleen manned the bar, which was made from stone and topped with a huge slab of wood. Suzette Minor, she of the mysterious noises and slutty nightgowns, gave him the eye from over the rim of her wineglass. Where was Gerard? Last he heard, they were seeing each other. Levi nodded, turned and bumped into Faith.

"Hey," he said, grabbing her arms to steady her. Her skin was cool and smooth.

She blushed, the color rising from the neckline of her red (have mercy) dress, up her throat and into her face. "Levi," she murmured.

Her hair was up tonight, and long gold earrings swung from her ears. As she looked at him, she bit her lower lip, and the action sent a jolt of electricity straight to his groin.

"Hi." He realized he was still holding on to her and let go. "Haven't seen you around."

"No."

The air seemed to thicken and pulse between them. There was that smell of warm cake, and, not for the first time, Levi had a sudden image of doing Faith against the wall.

"Faith! Your grandfather just spilled his drink on me," Mrs. Holland said, breaking the moment. "And have you seen that Lorena? The outfit! Doesn't she have a mirror? Oh, hello, Levi, sweetheart. Faith, do you have something to blot me?"

"I— Yep. Sure, Goggy." She led the old lady away. If she looked over her shoulder, Levi thought, the wall would be a definite possibility.

She looked, tucking a strand of hair behind her ear.

Then her father went over to her, and Faith nodded, said something. She finished with her grandmother, kissed her on the cheek, then found a waiter and pointed him in someone's direction. Poured a glass of wine and handed it to Mrs. Robinson, laughed at something she said.

And even though she was clearly doing a thousand things at once, taking care of a half-dozen people in the space of a minute, she looked back at him once more. Then, after a second, she smiled.

This time the jolt hit him in the chest. Faith Holland, smiling at him, not too far away from the spot he'd kissed her for the first time, all those years ago.

"She's such a natural at this, isn't she?" Jeremy said approvingly, having made his way back from the deck. "And this design! Gorgeous. She's already had seven bookings for weddings here next summer, Honor told me."

"Hey, Levi, hi, Jeremy!" Abby Vanderbeek bopped over, as well as Helena Meering. Helena had just gotten her license and had already received a ticket and a stern lecture from the chief of police, which had only made her giggle. "Want to eat with us?" Abby asked.

Helena smiled and stroked her own hair in that weird way girls did. "I see you didn't bring a date, Chief Cooper."

"Inappropriate, Helena," he said. "Where are your parents?"

"You just look lonely, that's all," Helena said. "Besides, boys our age? So boring and immature."

"I'll be your date, ladies," Jeremy said.

"Aren't you gay?" Helena asked.

Abby took Jeremy's arm. "Gays make the best dates, Helena. Everyone knows that."

Faith, he noticed, ended up sitting with Jeremy and her niece, as well as a couple other members of the Holland family. Levi chose a seat at a table with the very nice Hedberg family. Andrew, who was about nine, was unfortunately fascinated with Levi's military past and grilled him mercilessly.

"Did you ever kill anyone?" the kid asked.

"Andrew," his mom chided.

"I only shot at bad guys," Levi said, his standard answer. "You should come by the station, Andrew. I'll let you sit in the back of the cruiser."

"Really?" the kid said. "Awesome!"

Levi excused himself and went to get another glass of seltzer from the bar. Then someone whistled, and everyone turned their attention to the front of the room, where Faith stood, microphone in hand, looking pretty damn delicious.

"Thank you for coming, everyone," she said. "My dad is too shy to say anything—" this was met with a ripple of laughter "—so he asked me to do the honors. I'll start by saying how happy we all are that you could make it tonight to celebrate my grandparents' sixty-fifth anniversary." There was a round of applause.

"God bless 'em!" boomed Lorena of the unfortunately backless dress. "Hope they're still getting it on! Go, seniors! Whoo-hoo!"

Levi'd have to make sure she wasn't driving.

Faith gave a pained smile. "Uh, okay, Lorena. Anyway, we also wanted to have you see the Barn at Blue Heron, which is available for any type of special occasion. This was the milking barn back in the 1800s, and it burned down in 1912, when my great-grandmother sent my great-grandfather here to sleep after they had a fight. I guess Great-Grandpa knocked over a candle, and that was that. He barely made it out, the story goes, and you can bet he never made my great-grandmother mad again." There was a warm laugh from the audience.

Levi glanced at Jeremy, who was sitting a few tables away. He was smiling, his eyes glued to Faith, looking like a man in love.

"I'm really grateful my dad gave me the chance to make this space into something new, and there's no better way to christen it than with my grandparents' milestone. So thanks, everyone, and without further ado, my grandfather would like to say a few words to his beautiful bride."

The guests gave an *Aw,* then clapped as old Mr. Holland went over to Faith. "Thank you, sweetheart," he said, chuckling. "I guess not many people can say they've been married sixty-five years. But I have been." He paused, looking out at the guests with a smile. "Where did I go wrong?"

There was a round of laughter.

"People say to me, John, I don't know how you do it. And I tell them just look at my wife. She's got the face of a saint! A Saint Bernard, that is!"

Levi glanced over at Mrs. Holland, whose expression was thunderous (and actually, yes, did resemble the jowly dog).

Faith darted out and whispered something to her grandfather, but he just shook his head, and took a few steps away from her. "Faithie here wants me to dance with my wife," he said, "but how can I? She's got two left feet, and I've got a ball and chain!"

"I'll dance with you, sweetie!" Lorena called. That rubbery dress…good God. She went up to old Mr. Holland. "Put on some music!" she ordered. The DJ complied, and the opening chords of "SexyBack" came booming over the speakers.

"Now you're talking!" said Mr. Holland, and, to Levi's horror (and the horror of every living creature, he imagined), Lorena began gyrating her flat, aging ass against Faith's grandfather, who put up his fists in classic white-guy style and bobbed in time to the Justin Timberlake song, which Levi had always liked. Until now.

Faith darted out again, her face pained. "Stop the music, please? Lorena, take your seat, okay? Please? Could you just…go over there? Thanks." She grabbed the mic out of her grandfather's hand. "Okay, thank you, Pops. Go sit down." She pushed her hair back and tried to smile. "Um, well, there's a lot to be said for having a sense of humor, right? Dad? Would you like to say something?"

Her father shook his head.

"No? You sure? Okay. Um…Goggy? How about you?"

"Does anyone know a divorce attorney?" she said, her voice good and loud.

Faith winced. "Okay. Right." She took a deep breath. "You know what? I stayed with my grandparents for a couple of weeks recently, and here's the thing. They might not be the most, um…romantic couple in the world, but they do take care of each other." She paused, looking at her grandparents. "Pops might not bring Goggy flowers, but he puts her cup out every night, the tea bag right in it, one teaspoon of sugar, so that in the morning, all she has to do is add water."

Levi used to set up the coffee for Nina. Same idea, he guessed.

"And, um, my grandmother," Faith continued, "she cooks dinner every night. Makes Pops watch his cholesterol and stuff like that."

"Nights like tonight, I wonder why," Mrs. H. said, getting a laugh of her own.

"So maybe my grandparents aren't the poster children for love. But they've farmed this land all their lives, never sold off a piece, even when times were hard, even when the whole crop was lost in a hailstorm or the year when it rained so much the grapes rotted on the vine." She turned to her father. "They raised my dad and helped him with us kids after my mom died." She paused. "Maybe love isn't just a bouquet of roses once in a while. Maybe it's just sticking it out, when it's hard, when you're mad, when you're tired."

The place had gone quiet. "Goggy, Pops, I picked a special song for you two. 'And I Love You So' by Perry Como, your favorite, Goggy." Faith raised her glass. "So, folks, um…to my grandparents. Happy anniversary, Goggy and Pops."

"Hear, hear," murmured the guests.

The DJ started the song. Mr. and Mrs. Holland stayed put. "This is when you dance, Pops. Goggy."

They didn't move.

Suddenly, Lorena Creech lurched to her feet, knocking her chair over. "You're what?" she screeched, pointing to the woman in the paper-bag dress. "You're not his date! *I'm* his date!"

Yep. Definitely getting her keys.

"Wow," Faith said. "We are certainly entertaining tonight. Uh, enjoy the music, everyone." She gestured to the DJ, who cranked up the volume, then put the mic down and walked out of the barn.

Poor kid, to have done all this work and have the night ruined by badly behaved adults. Nevertheless, a few couples were going out onto the dance floor.

Levi went over to the Holland table. "What do you mean, we're not dating?" Lorena was saying to Faith's dad. "Of course we're dating!"

"I'm so sorry for the misunderstanding," John said, wincing. "We're not dating. I'm sorry."

"As you should be," Mrs. Johnson said. "Your children have been telling you what this woman was up to for weeks, but do you listen? No. You don't."

"He's got better taste than you," murmured the paperbag woman, which made Lorena swell.

"Do you have a ride home, Mrs. Creech?" Levi asked, trying not to look directly at her. "I don't want you driving."

"I'll call a cab, Mr. Uptight. And don't worry. I never drink and drive."

"I never drink at all," said the other woman, her voice prim.

"No, I bet you don't!" Lorena said. "Too busy talking about your mucus production! That's it. I'm leaving. John Holland, you've broken my heart."

"So sorry," John said, wiping the sweat from his forehead. "Um, also, Jane, I'm not dating anyone. Sorry."

"Well, for heaven's sake," the bag lady said, tossing her napkin on the table. "Why was I invited, then? I'm leaving, too. What a waste of time."

"At least you got fed, didn't you?" Mrs. Johnson said. "Not that it was enjoyable, watching you lay waste to three pounds of raw vegetables, mind you. And, John, you are an idiot when it comes to women. Shameful."

The two women left, and the clueless DJ started the Perry Como song for the second time. Levi bent down to talk to Mr. and Mrs. Holland. "Listen, you two," he said. "Faith worked really hard on this party. Why don't you dance together and show her you appreciate it?" He gave them his sternest police chief stare.

"Who'd want to dance with him?" Mrs. Holland snipped.

"My arthritis is killing me," said her husband.

"Better move around a little, then," Levi said. "For Faith, if not for anything else. She adores you two."

There was a moment's silence.

"Fine. Let's get it over with," Mrs. Holland said. "He's right. Faith did all this for us, you ingrate."

"I'm not ungrateful. I love what she's done."

"Prove it," Levi said. "Get up there."

"Fine. My suffering continues." Mr. Holland sighed. He stood up and extended his hand. Mrs. Holland took it.

The song started for the third time, and as the old Hollands assumed the position, Levi was almost sure they were smiling.

Faith was nowhere to be seen.

FAITH HAD FOUND A PLACE under the deck where she was fairly sure she wouldn't be found. The grass was cool and damp, but who cared? Better to hide here and get grass-stained than go back to the party. If she *was* found, she might stick a fork in someone's eye.

She took a long pull from the bottle of wine she'd appropriated.

Though she knew it was pointless, Faith let herself imagine what tonight would've been like if her mom were here. That she'd have tilted her head against Dad's shoulder and whispered something to make him laugh. There'd be no need for Lorenas or vegan zealots, and, somehow, Mom would work her firm magic on Goggy and Pops, would help Honor relax, laugh with Pru, dance with Jack, and maybe, just maybe, have some words for Faith, too.

The grief slipped around her like a heavy cape, enveloping her. She didn't deserve to miss her mother, but, dear God, she did.

"Hey."

Faith jumped. "Hi, Levi," she said, surreptitiously wiping her eyes. Her achy heart sped up.

"Drinking alone?" he asked.

"Yep. Tonight, I think it's more than justified."

Levi sat down next to her. "So this has been…" His voice trailed off.

"Terrifying?" she suggested, taking another pull. "Because really, what other word works here?"

"Memorable." There might've been a smile in his voice, but it was too dark to tell.

"*Memorable*. Your word is better."

"Were you crying just now?" he asked, his voice quiet.

For some reason, his question made her throat tighten again. "A little."

He didn't say anything to that. Didn't say anything at all, and it was kind of nice, just having him there at her side. She felt chilly all of a sudden. Wondered what he'd do if she leaned her bare shoulder against his.

"They're dancing, you know," he said after a minute.

She shot him a look. "Really?"

"Yep."

"Oh. Good." She looked back at her hands. The waterproof mascara was not tearproof.

From up above came the shrill and adorable voice of young Michael Jackson. Footsteps thudded more or less in time to the music, indicating that people were dancing.

"This place is beautiful, Faith," Levi said, and all of a sudden, Faith's toes curled in her shoes, because… well, because he'd come to find her.

"Thank you," she whispered, turning her head to look at him in the faint light. Damn. Levi Cooper in a suit. She couldn't say she'd ever seen him in one before, aside from his dress uniform. His hands were clasped loosely in front of him and he was looking at her. "Are you having a nice time?" she asked.

"I am now."

The words caused a tightening low in her belly. "You look very handsome, Levi."

He did. Those sleepy eyes definitely held a slight smile now. At least, that's what it seemed like. He leaned so that his shoulder bumped hers, and the small gesture made her entire body feel warm. "And you look very pretty, Faith," he murmured.

"Thanks."

He looked at her a long moment, then reached over and touched the silky hairs at the back of her neck, studiously, a slight frown coming to his face, as if he'd never touched that spot on a woman before. Faith swallowed as her entire side broke out in goose bumps, her muscles turning liquid. He stared at the spot he was touching, his lashes catching a bit of the light from outside. The Boredom Scale didn't exist now.

His mouth was so close. She could just lean in and kiss him, feel that perfect pressure, that thrilling moment when the kiss would deepen and she'd feel his tongue slide against hers.

Yes, if she worked up the nerve, Faith could kiss Levi Cooper, the boy she'd known most of her life, the boy who'd never liked her.

But she didn't move, hypnotized by that gentle touch on her neck. He could do that all night, and she'd sit here and not want anything more.

Except she did.

"Come on," Levi said. He stood up and took her hand, pulling her to her feet, and led her out from under the deck to the barn's entrance. "Take a look at that." He stood behind her, not touching her, but close enough for her to feel his warmth.

Her grandparents were dancing; Michael Jackson had finished, and the Rolling Stones were singing "Beast of Burden." Dad was dancing with Honor, Colleen with old Mr. Iskin, Pru with Ned, Abby with Helena, both girls laughing.

And Goggy and Pops were dancing, too. Dancing, and smiling as they talked.

Faith felt a smile come to her own face. She'd done it. It looked…wonderful. Magical, even.

"You wanna get out of here?" Levi asked, and his breath was soft against her neck.

The party would last maybe another hour. The caterers would take care of cleanup; everyone had already been paid; she'd be up here tomorrow, anyway. Her job was done, in other words.

And Levi Cooper was asking her to go somewhere with him, and there was a promising look in his eyes… she suddenly, desperately wanted do something about that.

"Okay," she whispered.

CHAPTER NINETEEN

THE WHOLE SEDUCTION thing…easier said than done.

They'd been home for eighteen minutes, and the only one seeing any action thus far was Blue, who'd attached himself to Levi's leg the second they came through the door. Luckily, she'd asked Eleanor Raines from downstairs to walk the beastie; Ellie fell over herself to worship him on a number of occasions, so Blue was all set for the night. Good thing the dog was here, because conversation wasn't exactly flying.

Levi was sitting on her couch, having successfully ended the humping session (well, Blue's humping session) and was now scratching the dog's ears as her pet stared at him worshipfully, tennis ball in mouth. Faith herself was leaning against the counter, drinking a glass of ice water.

Maybe she'd been wrong about Levi's intentions. Was it possible, she wondered, that Levi had no idea she wanted him to, ah, *do* her? If he did, how come he was just sitting there? How exactly did people proceed? Should she just announce it? God, she was nervous! Heart zipping away, hands shaking slightly, stomach in knots. Where was that warm melting sensation from before? Hmm?

What to do, what to do. She and Jeremy had had dozens of conversations on the topic before doing the deed, but obviously, theirs wasn't the typical male/ female dynamic.

The facts were that Levi had kissed her. Twice. Three times, if she counted back a decade or so. And there was the neck stroking. Also, his sister had called nine minutes ago, and he'd let it go to voice mail.

Okay. Faith was gonna go for it. Sort of. In a way.

"Let's get this party started, shall we?" someone said, and oh, hemorrhoid, it was her very own mouth that had formed those ridiculous words.

Levi gave her a long look. "Really?"

"Shut up, Levi," she said, her face hot. "You want to get it on or what? Oh, God, I sound like such a slut. You know what? You can go. No hard feelings. *America's Next Top Model* is having a marathon, anyway."

Blue barked, wagging happily. It was his favorite show.

Levi got up. Faith's heart rate tripled. Oh, yes, yes indeed, he was coming over. To her, or to the door? Oh, lordy, to her. There was a very faint, possibly imagined, smile playing around his mouth, and his eyes had that sleepy, incredibly hot look. He took the glass out of her hand and set it on the counter. Just the brush of his fingers against hers made her knees tingle and weaken. She inhaled the smell of his soap—Ivory, maybe? Who knew? He smelled good. *Focus, Faith, focus. A heterosexual male is standing in front of you. Do something about that.*

She didn't. She appeared to be frozen. Well, there was some dried cuticle that could use picking. How about that? That'd be fun. Easier than this. She really didn't know what she was doing, man-wise. Maybe *America's Next Top Model* would be the best option, after all.

Levi put his hands on the counter, trapping her without touching. He was maybe an inch away from her, all bristling testosterone and heat. Faith swallowed, the noise gunshot loud.

"I'd rather stay," he murmured.

Then he closed the tiny space between them, his body a hard, warm shock, and his mouth found hers.

And it would've been great, except, you know, sex was looming.

She tried pursing her lips, and crap, that didn't feel right. What was she supposed to do, exactly?

"Relax," Levi said, and she realized he'd stopped kissing her, and she was standing, clenched as tightly as new rope.

"Right," she said, licking her lips. *Unclench, unclench.* She loosened her fists. "Okay. I'm trying. Go ahead. Kiss me again."

He raised an eyebrow. "You sure?"

"Yes. Please. Please kiss me." Great. Now she was begging.

His eyes were half closed now, those beautiful green eyes, and he leaned in, his hard, muscled arms pulling her against him. Then his lips were against hers, more insistent this time, and Faith tried to kiss him back, but she couldn't quite breathe.

He sighed and pulled back again. "What's the problem here, Faith?"

"I don't have a problem," she snapped. "Maybe you have the problem. Maybe you're not as great a kisser as you think. Or maybe I'm worried you'll hate yourself in the morning. I mean, you've kissed me twice now with absolutely no follow-up, so maybe you're the one with the problem. Jeez."

He stared. Blue flopped on the floor, belly up. The clock ticked. Futtocks, this was awkward!

"How many men have you slept with?" Levi asked.

Busted. "Uh, counting you?" she said, feeling her chest practically burst into flame with a blush.

His forehead crinkled with that incredulous look she'd seen so many times in their high school years. "We haven't slept together, Faith."

"No, I know that. You have a point. Can't argue with that." She closed her eyes briefly. *America's Next Top Model* was looking better and better.

"So not counting me, how many?"

Faith nodded as if considering the question, glancing at something safer than Levi's face. The fridge, or the bowl of green apples that had looked so pretty in the market but had tasted so sour in reality. Should really throw those out. "Let's see," she said. "Um…one."

Her heart seemed to curl in on itself in embarrassment.

He didn't blink. Even his eyelashes seemed disdainful.

"One," he said.

"Yep."

"You've only slept with Jeremy?"

"You are correct, sir." Her face was hot enough to fry an egg. Not that she had anything to be embarrassed about. Chastity was a good thing. Being fastidious about one's choices in life—an excellent quality.

This night was not going as planned.

"Look," she said, perhaps more sharply than she meant. "Since Jeremy, I just never met anyone who… I mean, it's not like I didn't— There were a couple guys who…" She took a breath and forced herself to look at Levi directly, who was waiting, that *look* still on his face. "I didn't want to sleep with someone just for the sake of it," she finished.

Words that would make a man run. Especially someone like Levi, who seemed like the type to *absolutely* sleep with someone just for the sake of it.

The truth of the matter was, Faith had wanted to be in love first. For eight of the past eleven years, she'd only ever imagined sleeping with one man, after all. Sex was far too intimate to do with someone she didn't love. Gay or not, Jeremy *had* loved her and, God knew, she'd loved him back.

She wasn't in love with Levi. And Levi certainly wasn't in love with her.

This was ridiculous. Of all the men she might pick, Levi was not a likely candidate for husband/father of her adorable children. A) he barely liked her. And B)... well, who knew what B was. Hot or not (well, he was definitely hot), he was probably not the guy to—

He reached up and cupped her cheek with one hand and studied her, his expression unreadable—eyebrows drawn, the slight, omnipresent frown on his face. Faith swallowed, her throat dry.

"Do you want to sleep with me, Faith?"

The question took her by surprise. His voice was low and gentle, and Faith felt a tug low in her belly. "If you don't mind," she whispered. He smiled the slightest bit, then ran his thumb over her lower lip, and she drew in a shaky breath. Then he pulled out the clip that held her hair up, causing it to tumble down in a sweep. Slowly, almost carefully, Levi bent his head and kissed her neck, his arms going around her, and, oh, mercy, his mouth was warm and gentle, and a rush of molten gold seemed to flow through her limbs, heavy and electric.

Her bones seemed to soften, and her head tipped back, her breath suddenly ragged.

Her hands didn't know what to do. Levi took one in his and kissed her palm, then flattened her hand against his chest so she could feel the slow, hard thud of his heartbeat. And this time, when his mouth touched hers again…this time it was right. His hands moved through her hair, then down her back, pulling her against him, and, oh, he was as solid as granite, utterly dangerous and absolutely safe. Her mouth opened in a sigh, and he took advantage, tasting her, and the hot golden feeling was stronger now, pulsing hard. Her hands slid against his ribs, feeling the play of muscle against skin, and his kiss became deeper, more insistent, hotter. Faith's knees loosened dangerously, a little moan escaping her throat.

Then Levi pulled back, and it took Faith a minute to open her eyes. Her breathing was ragged. So was his. His eyes…*bedroom eyes*. That was the term.

"You sure you want to sleep with me?" she said, her voice breathy.

He smoothed some hair away from her face. "I'm sure."

She bit her lip. "Okay, then. Take me to bed."

"I was thinking against the wall."

"Good God!" she blurted. The golden heat surged hot, hard and heavy. "Okay, fine, whatever you think. You're the expert here."

His smile was slow, and it made the throbbing hotter, stronger. Then he bent and picked her up so that her legs wrapped around him of their own accord, and Levi Cooper did what he said he was going to do.

THEY DID END UP IN BED, and bed was good, Levi thought. The wall had gone well until Faith's dog kept dropping his ratty old tennis ball at their feet, and she started to laugh. Besides, given that Faith had never been with a straight guy, he wanted to give her the whole experience, as it were. She was worth exploring, her body lush and soft, all pink and cream, and she made the most gratifying little noises, and had done a fair bit of exploring herself, her hands sliding over him, her mouth soft and sweet.

And when they were done, and her eyes were wide and her cheeks flushed and her skin damp with sweat, he rolled on his back and pulled her against him, a fierce sense of…something…swelled in his chest.

Even she was quiet. "So, was this, um…pretty typical?" she asked eventually.

No. "Pretty much," he answered, his fingers playing in her hair. *Now why'd you say that, dumb ass?* his brain scolded.

Because he didn't want too much too soon. That was all. He was being careful, and careful was smart.

The dog decided it was bedtime, too, and jumped up, draping himself over their feet. "Do you mind him?" Faith asked.

"He's fine."

She propped herself up on her elbow and looked at him. "Do you need to go?"

He blinked. "Kicking me out?"

"No. I just…I didn't know if you wanted to spend the night. If you do, I have to take off my mascara and hide my, uh, undergarment."

"I've seen your undergarment. I've also seen combat armor that looks more comfortable."

"Is this your pillow talk?"

"Is this yours?"

"Don't crinkle your forehead at me, Levi. I'm new to the game here."

He felt a smile threaten. "You're pretty good for a rookie."

"Shush." Here came the blush. He turned and pressed a kiss on her shoulder. Her blush deepened.

"You're pretty and soft and you smell like cake. How's that?" he asked.

She smiled a little. "Cake?"

"Yes. Edible."

That flustered her. She pressed her lips together and looked away, still a little spooked around him. "So, are you staying?"

"Do you want me to?"

Her gaze flickered to his and away again. "Okay. If you want to."

He could've claimed ten things, nine of them true, that would've gotten him home. He was on call. He had paperwork. Emails to answer. A grant to finish. He could take a cruise through Manningsport, just to let the good citizens know he was out there. He probably *should've* used any one of those because there was sex, and then there was spending the night, and this was way too early to spend the night.

"Sure," he said.

"You really want to stay?"

"Yes. Now be quiet and go to sleep."

She looked at him another second, unconvinced, and he felt a pang of remorse. He picked up a strand of her hair and gave it a gentle tug, then pulled her head back down to his shoulder.

"Levi?"

Women. Always with the talking. "Yeah?"

"Thanks for doing me."

He laughed. "You're welcome. Did you have fun?"

"What do you think?"

"You made a lot of noise. That's generally a good sign."

She raised her head to look at him, her coppery hair falling half over her face. "Well, well, well. Look at that. Levi Cooper, smiling."

And sure enough, it seemed he was.

Then she kissed him, hesitantly, sweetly, then less hesitantly, and nobody went to sleep for a long while.

Except the dog.

CHAPTER TWENTY

LEVI COOPER HAD washboard abs.

Not that Faith was ogling or anything. Okay, she was *totally* ogling. So was Blue, for that matter, still hoping Levi would throw the ball ten or five hundred times.

But Levi was asleep, so ogling was allowed. Plus, how could a woman drag her eyes off that perfect, beautiful body? His arms were ridiculously male, heavy and thick with muscle, his chest solid and broad. And those abs…rippled and hypnotic and magically perfect.

Yes. Levi Cooper was a sparkly unicorn of wonder.

Granted, Jeremy had been gorgeous. Movie star, NFL chiseled handsome, and, yes, Faith had loved looking at him, too. Then again, he hadn't known what to do with her.

And Levi most definitely had. Hand to God, yes.

Sex with a straight guy—*definitely* the way to go. Especially *this* straight guy, because, much to her surprise, he hadn't just been hot and, er, competent, he'd been… sweet. There was really no other word for it. And Levi Cooper with ruddy cheeks and sweaty hair and beautiful arms, asking her if she liked what he was doing… crikey! She was getting turned on just thinking about it.

Time to go. Blue needed a walk before she jumped Levi again. She pulled on some clothes, then slipped out of the bedroom with Blue. Realized she was grinning. Kinda felt like skipping.

She set up the coffeepot and turned it on, then grabbed Blue's leash, causing her dog to freeze in wonder before springing for the door. "Yes! We *are* taking a walk! I know! It's so exciting, isn't it?" she whispered (because she had a beautiful man sleeping in her bed, had she mentioned that?). She opened the door and Blue bounded out, whimpering in excitement.

Sarah Cooper was standing in the hallway.

"Do you know where my brother is?" Sarah blurted, her face creased with worry.

"Oh, honey, yes, I do. He's, uh…he's in there." Faith nodded back at her place.

"I called him last night, but he didn't pick up," she said.

"Shoot. I— He's…sleeping."

Sarah's expression changed from worried to astonished. "Holy heck," she said. "Did you guys do it? Are you sleeping together?"

"Um…maybe your brother should answer that."

"You *are!* You're doing my brother. OMG, where's my phone? I have to tweet this."

"Calm down, Sarah," came Levi's voice. The man himself came out of her apartment, his dress shirt untucked. "If you tweet this, you're dead."

"Dude, I'm completely supportive. Faith is much nicer than G.I. Jane. I approve."

"Super," Levi said. Faith smiled at Sarah, grateful. Always good to have family on your side.

Levi tucked in his shirt. Too bad. He looked better naked. "What are you doing home, anyway?" he asked his sister.

Sarah's eyes widened. "Levi! This was the weekend you *allowed* me to come back, remember? The weekend I wasn't *forbidden* to come."

Levi took a short breath, held it, and then said, "Right. So get inside and stop bothering Faith. I'll be right there."

"I'm not bothering her," Sarah said. "We're bonding. In case I'm gonna be an aunt sometime soon."

"Sarah. Go. Inside. Now." There was a fascinating knot in his jaw. His sister obeyed, pulling a face at Faith as the door closed.

"Don't be mad at her," Faith said.

"I'm not," he said. Jamming his hands in his pockets and ignoring Blue's whimpers of adoration, Levi finally looked at her. "Hi," he said, his voice just a soft scrape.

A two-letter word, and she was a mushy puddle. "Hi," she whispered.

"How are you?" he asked.

"Fine. How are you?"

His eyes dropped to her mouth. "Also fine. But I have to go." He looked as somber as somber got.

"Okay."

"I'll see you."

"Yes. As we live not too far from each other." She bit down on a smile.

"Right." Only then did he seem to realize she was joking, which he acknowledged with a raised eyebrow. Then he grabbed her, eliciting a squeak, and gave her a hard, fierce kiss, and before she could even respond, let her go. "See you around, neighbor."

With that, he was gone.

"YOU HOT BITCH," Colleen breathed the next evening, her eyes full of admiration. "You slept with Levi Cooper? Get outta town! Tell me everything. How many times did you—"

"Okay, whoa. Easy, girl." Faith sat back in her seat

at O'Rourke's, which had just opened. She hadn't seen Levi since The Night, though she'd smelled chocolate again at three this morning. Today, though, his car wasn't at the station or in back of the Opera House, so she assumed he'd driven his sister back to school. Not that she was stalking, though, yes, she had just followed Sarah Cooper on Twitter.

"I want every detail," Colleen said. "You owe it to me. My friend got it on! I'm so happy!"

"Yay! But could you just lower your voice a teensy bit? That'd be great."

"No one's here, pet."

"Your brother might come in any second."

"He doesn't count. Right, Connor?"

"That's right." Connor appeared from the kitchen. "Hi, Faith. Glad you're getting some."

"Thanks, Con. And thank you, Colleen, for not telling me your brother was lurking."

"What color dress should I pick out for the wedding?" Colleen asked. "You definitely owe me another gig as maid of honor, since Jeremy ripped me off the first time."

"You know what? He's the—" Faith looked around (the early crowd was trickling in) and lowered her voice to a whisper. "He's only the second man I've slept with. So let's just slow things down."

"I know he's the second," Colleen said. "That's my fault. I regret buying you adult toys."

"Shh! Come on! I don't want your brother to know all this stuff!"

"Well, it's true," her friend said, taking a long pull of coffee. "I'm sure you would've gotten laid long before now. Three years is too long."

"I'd have to agree there, Faithie," Connor called.

"You two. What a team." Ah, well. It was just Coll and Con, the two-for-one special.

"So how was it?" Colleen asked.

"I'm only telling you if you keep your voice down."

"Fine," Colleen whispered. "How's this?"

Faith smiled. "It was…" She smiled. "It was amazing."

"Yes! This is great! Con, it was *amazing*."

"Yay."

Colleen sighed happily. "So, are you engaged, are you dating, or was this a one-time bang-a-palooza, never to be repeated, are you friends with bennies… what?"

Faith paused. "I don't know. We're definitely not engaged."

Colleen gave her a knowing look. "You're in love, aren't you?"

"No."

"Sure you are. I know you. You wouldn't have had sex with him if you weren't."

"I'm not. He's… I mean, he's… It could happen, I suppose." Her face was getting hot again. "Look, here's my dad. Please don't hit on him or tell him I'm getting a little some-some or give him anything with jalapenos, because he's got acid reflux."

"Oh, Jack is here, too. Hooray."

"Be merciful, Coll."

"They're kind of early, aren't they?" Connor asked, looking out from the kitchen door. "I don't usually see Jack before seven."

"I'm screening a date for my dad. Dad will eavesdrop, then give me the thumbs-up or down."

"You Hollands are so cute."

The afternoon after the party, while Levi had been

busy with his sister, Honor, Pru and Faith had had an intervention with Dad. Honor had served as Head Inquisitor, Mrs. Johnson banging pots and slamming drawers in the kitchen to underscore the theme of disapproval. Dad had admitted that he'd enjoyed Lorena's "wacky ways," as well as the distraction of having someone new to talk to but hadn't believed she was as attached as his children had warned. He had no intention of seeing the vegan gardener again and said he'd try to be open to dating someone. Maybe. Possibly. And, yes, he'd do what they told him from now on.

Faith was immensely relieved.

"Jack," she said, "brother mine, don't think I didn't notice you skulking off from the party the other night."

"Don't think I didn't hear you left with Levi."

"He drove me home," Faith said, feeling her face practically burst into flame.

"Is that what you kids are calling it these days?" He gave her a cuff. "Spare me the details, okay? Pru is bad enough. Pru is horrifying, come to think of it."

A half hour later, Faith was seated in a booth, the same one where the accountant had tried to talk dirty to her. Accountants. Were they all pervy? At any rate, Dad was in the next booth, already sweaty, pretending to talk to Jack, who was reading the paper.

Because internet dating *was* the most effective way to find someone, Faith had given it another shot (avoiding StillHotGranny). She reposted a profile for her dad, admitting immediately that she was his daughter, acting as first-round screener. Tonight, she was meeting a woman named Maxine Rogers, who'd answered all questions appropriately.

Faith was just digging into the plate of nachos grande

and a glass of beautiful Riesling, which had the nicest tangerine notes and went perfectly with dinner, when Maxine approached.

"Faith?"

"Hi! Maxine, right?"

The woman smiled broadly. "Yes. How are you, dear?"

She was very tall, which hadn't come across in the photos. Her hair was black (had to be dyed, but it was a nice job, too, very shiny, unlike Lorena's Sharpie look), and her makeup was expertly applied, especially her red lipstick, which was bold and rather dashing. Maxine had put in some effort, in other words, and it worked. She was nicely dressed, especially notable since she had to be nearly six feet tall. Faith noted that her dad had turned his head the slightest bit to check her out.

"It's wonderful to finally meet you," Maxine said. Her voice was pleasantly low-pitched.

"You, too," Faith said. "You're so nice in your emails."

"Oh, sweetheart, you're an angel to say so." She settled back against the booth. "I think it's very kind what you're doing, helping your father find love again. Just so sweet."

It really was, Faith thought. "Would you like some nachos?"

"Thank you! Aren't these gorgeous," Maxine said, taking a healthy chunk. Good. Faith hated being the only female who really ate.

Colleen approached the booth. "Can I get you— Oh! Hi. Uh, I'm sorry, I didn't…see you come in. Can I get you something to drink?" she asked Maxine.

"Faith, what are you drinking, honey?" Maxine said, and Faith already liked her immensely.

"Coll, what am I having?" she asked. "Maxine, Colleen is my oldest friend."

"Nice to meet you," Maxine said, offering her hand to Colleen.

"You, too. Um, Faith is drinking…the uh, the Bully 2011 Riesling, right, Faith?" Coll gave her a pointed look.

"That's right. It's delicious," Faith said. "Tangerine overtones, a little straw flavor, very smooth finish."

"Sounds delicious," Maxine said, smiling. "I'll have that."

"I'll bring it right over." With that, Colleen was off.

"So, you don't have children, is that right?" Faith asked.

"No, sadly I never did. But I have four nieces and six nephews, and I adore them all, as well as their kids. I like to think of myself as an Auntie Mame type."

"That's so nice. I have a niece and nephew myself. And you're a bookkeeper?"

"Yes. I love numbers, love making sense of things. I always have."

Faith sat back and listened as Maxine told her about life in rural Ohio and how she'd come to the Finger Lakes on vacation, then decided to move to Penn Yan after she'd had a windfall. "It was one of those things, Faith," she said. "I was doing fine, don't get me wrong, but I must've had some kind of angel on my shoulder, because really, who wins a hundred thousand dollars with a scratch-off? I asked myself, what do I want to do for the rest of my life? And this place above all others was the one that spoke to me."

Colleen brought over the wine. "Faith, can I see you a second?" Colleen asked. From the kitchen came a crash and a yell. "Shoot," she said, and dashed off.

Maxine was passing every test. Manners, funny, open, warm, told a good story. She was financially secure, had an active social life, loved fishing, tennis and cooking. Faith's hopes rose. At the very least, she could see Dad dating this nice lady occasionally. For one indulgent moment, as Maxine was telling her about her trip to Montana last summer, Faith pictured her in the New House for Sunday dinner, laughing her husky laugh, charming everyone. Even Mrs. J.

Maybe Levi would be there, too.

"I'm sorry," she said. "I didn't hear what you just said." What the heck. She already felt like she and Maxine were old friends. "I just started seeing someone myself," she whispered. "I'm a little distracted."

Maxine's face lit up. "I wondered why a pretty girl like you was still single," she whispered. "Tell me about him."

"It's very new," Faith whispered, feeling the heat rise into her cheeks. "He's very…" Her voice trailed off. *Hot. Intense. Great in bed. Delicious.*

"Oh," Maxine said, smiling in a wonderfully conspiratorial way. "One of *those*. I get it."

Faith felt like giggling. Two glasses of wine, only nachos since noon. "Anyway, back to you, Maxine. What do you like to cook?"

Her phone vibrated, her cue to go to the bathroom. "I'm so sorry. Excuse me for one second," she said, sliding out of the booth.

Jack met her at the entrance of the restrooms. "Dad says it's a go. He likes what he's heard so far."

"Yes!" Faith said, elation rising up like a geyser. Finally, she could look at Dad and see a happy man, rather than a lonely widower doing his best.

"This is so weird, Faith. I feel like we're pimping out our father."

"No, we're not! Don't you see, Jack? Dad could get married again. He could stop missing Mom and be happy."

Her brother gave her an odd look. "I think he'll always miss Mom, even if he did remarry, and he's not unhappy, Faith."

"Well, you're next, so be nice to me or I'm throwing you to Colleen, and the hyenas will pick over your bones."

"So, love is in the air, huh? Since Levi, ah, drove you home?"

She couldn't help a smile, remembering the other night.

"Oh, God," Jack said. "Sorry I asked." He walked back to his table.

Faith took a minute to use the bathroom. Her cheeks were flushed. She looked a little…dreamy. Maybe Levi would come over tonight and shag her silly, since Sarah's Twitter feed said he'd dropped her off and all.

The stall door opened, and Jessica Does came out.

"Oh. Hey," Faith said, abruptly turning on the water. Didn't want Jessica to think she just came in to gaze at her reflection.

And, oh, crap. Jessica was Levi's old girlfriend. Would that come into play?

"Hi." Jessica washed her hands, too.

"How are you?" Faith asked.

"Fine. You?"

"Fine."

With that, Jessica reached past Faith and grabbed some paper towels from the dispenser, her movements so sharp that Faith actually ducked. "Jesus, Holland," Jess said, rolling her eyes. "You think I'm gonna slap you or something?"

"No, no. I didn't. I just…"

"Whatever. Bye."

Jess was gone, ever the princess of manners. Didn't matter. Dad's potential wife was out there.

Faith's phone buzzed. It was a text from Colleen, for God's sake. Faith had nothing against phones and texting, but really. Colleen was in the same building. She opted not to read it but speak to her friend instead. Maxine, a live human, was waiting for her, after all. Faith opened the door and went out, only to see her father standing there.

"I really like her," Dad said. "She seems really nice. Tall, isn't she?"

"Mmm-hmm. Great clothes."

Dad smiled. "I noticed that, too. Your mom was quite snazzy, too. Like you."

This time, the guilt punch wasn't quite so strong. "Thanks, Daddy."

Her dad folded her into a hug. "I appreciate this, sweetpea. I really do. You're awfully good to your dear old dad. So maybe I'll swing by the booth, pretend I just dropped in, how's that?"

"That's great."

Maxine was delicately nibbling on a nacho when Faith got back.

Huh. Nail polish, definitely a professional mani, but there was something…

"There you are! Hello again." Maxine smiled.

Her phone buzzed again. Colleen, being a pain in the butt. Still, two in one minute, it must be important.

She clicked the "view" button. The message consisted of one word. She-male.

Huh?

Oh.

Oh, no. No, no. Faith glanced at Maxine.

Oops.

"Faith, honey!" Oh, futtocks. It was Dad. "I haven't seen you all week," he said, winking to make sure she knew he was lying like a four-term senator. "How've you been?"

"Hi, Dad," she said in a faint voice.

"Oh! How nice to meet you!" Maxine said. "I'm Maxine. You have an absolutely *wonderful* daughter."

"I couldn't agree with you more," Dad said, sliding next to Faith. "And two more like her, I'm happy to say."

Faith's brain was white with commotion. She thought back frantically to the eCommitment profile she'd filled out for Dad...she *had* clicked on *man seeking woman,* right?

"Hi, everyone."

Holy crap, it was Honor. So not good.

"Sweetheart!" Dad said.

"Hello," Maxine said.

Honor looked at her, then did a double take. "Oh. Um...hi. Sorry. I'm Honor. I...I didn't realize...um, I didn't mean to, uh, interrupt." She gave Faith a look that was simply incredulous.

"So, Maxine," Dad said. "I had no idea Faith was meeting you tonight. What a happy coincidence. I just happened to drop in, and now you can meet two of my daughters! How nice!"

So the old fox had decided to go for it, laying it on quite thick. "Dad," Faith said, "Um, Honor has to speak with you, right, Honor?"

"Absolutely. It's kind of important, Dad."

"Sweetie, we live in the same house," he said. "We can talk later. Sit down. Don't be rude."

"Very nice to meet you, Honor." Maxine beamed. Nice smile. Faith sighed. "You know, John, I think it's lovely that your daughters are so involved in helping you find someone," she said. "Really, girls. Your concern is so touching."

"Yeah," Honor said. "I... Thank you."

"My son is here, too, somewhere," Dad said. "Oh, there he is, at the bar. The big good-looking one."

"Takes after his father," Maxine said.

"Jack! Come over here," Dad called. "Maxine, I hope you don't mind. It's a small town, and O'Rourke's is our little hangout."

"I love Manningsport," Maxine said. "I've been here before, actually. Prettiest town in New York, I think."

"It is, it is," Dad said, nodding approvingly. He looked at Faith and gave her a little wink, as clueless as she'd been.

Jack approached. "Hey, Dad," he said. "Hi, I'm the son." He stuck out his hand to Maxine, who shook it. Jack's eyes widened. "That's some grip," he said, glancing in horror at Faith.

"I have one more daughter who's not here," Dad said, beaming. "But you've met seventy-five percent of my offspring. And since they're the most important things in my life, I guess it's good to get that covered."

"A beautiful family," Maxine said. "But I'm afraid *I* have to go. Too bad I didn't know you'd be popping in, John! I have a dinner date with the lovely old gentleman who lives next door to me, and he barely gets out, so I'd feel terrible if I was late. But I hope we can see each other again!"

"I think that would be great," Dad said.

"Yeah, no, that's…that's great," Faith said. "Um, it was so nice to meet you."

Jack and Honor murmured in agreement, their faces a bit pained.

Maxine got out of the booth and grabbed Faith's hands. "Thank you, sweetheart," and, yeah, *husky* wasn't quite the right word to describe that voice.

"Take care," Faith said. She kissed Maxine's cheek, getting a bit of stubble.

"John, wonderful meeting you. Have a lovely weekend." She tilted her head and waved, then off she went. Faith sat back down.

"I *really* liked her," Dad said. "Good job, Faithie. She's lovely."

"Dad," Faith said. "I, uh…Maxine is not going to be your girlfriend."

He paused. "Why?"

Honor shook her head and sighed.

"Well," Faith began, hoping to break this gently. "Did you notice anything about Maxine? Anything at all?"

Her father frowned. "She's tall."

"That's it, Dad. Run with it," Jack said, taking a long pull of his beer.

"Um…very warm and well spoken. Pretty."

"*Pretty* is not really the word here," Jack said. "Wouldn't *handsome* do better?"

"Sure. I guess so," Dad said.

Honor sighed, and turned to look at their father. "Dad, Maxine is a man."

Dad blinked. "What?"

"She's a man, Dad."

"No, she's not."

"Oh, but she is," Honor said, taking a nacho covered in cheese.

"But she—"

"No, Honor's right," Jack said. "It's a boy." His shoulders started shaking in a silent laugh.

"Oh," Dad said. "Uh…oh. I see." Then he bit his lip and started laughing, too.

Honor rolled her eyes. "Colleen, can I get a very strong martini?" she called. "Bone dry, three olives." She looked at Faith. "I'll give you this, Faith. She was better than Lorena."

"So you kids *don't* want a stepfather, is that correct?" Dad said, wiping his eyes with a cocktail napkin, and though Faith laughed along with them, that familiar feeling of guilt twisted in her stomach.

She still hadn't made things right.

CHAPTER TWENTY-ONE

"I THINK IT'S FANTASTIC that you guys are together. Really. You're perfect for each other." Jeremy beamed at them like a proud parent.

Faith made a noncommittal noise, looked in her wine and tried not to cringe. Levi, she imagined, was doing something similar, though of course he was too stoic and manly to cringe, but inside, he'd be cringing, too.

They were at Jeremy's for dinner—a celebratory dinner, he'd said, because the two people he loved best in the world were shtupping each other. He seemed to be the only one celebrating, however, and it was quite possible he was a little *too* happy, which was rather grating.

Jeremy had figured it out during what had become their weekly lunch at Hugo's. Levi had come in for something or another, wearing a gun and looking *incredibly* smokin' alpha protector, and she'd fought the urge to wrap herself around him like a python. "Gotta go," he'd said, and Faith had muttered goodbye, and the second Levi was out of earshot, Jeremy's eyes had widened. "You two are *doing* it, aren't you?" he'd whispered gleefully.

Yes. They were. But it was a little early to be thinking thoughts like *perfect* or even *together.* Levi was hard to figure out. On the one hand, he'd come to her apartment door six out of the eight nights since they'd first slept together. And the sex was *great.* She honestly hadn't known sex like that really existed outside of Ryan Gosling movies. Skyscraping, mind-blowing, tunnel-of-light great. Before and during sex, and immediately afterward, it felt as if they had something going on, something—she barely even dared to think the word—*special*.

Otherwise, not so much. She'd dropped by to see him the other day at the station; he'd asked, "What can I do for you, Faith?" with a completely straight face, like she wanted to discuss her parking tickets (which she really should pay…sleeping with the police chief hadn't prevented him from ticketing her car in the forty-five seconds she'd been double-parked in front of Lorelei's).

Then last night during nooky, he'd put a hand over her mouth, smiling. "You'll wake the neighbors," he'd said.

"Don't stop," she'd whispered.

Hmm. Now that she thought of it, that had been their longest conversation. Levi had been working constantly—there'd been a small crime spree in east Manningsport. He'd gone up to Geneva to have dinner with Sarah (and hadn't asked her to come…which was fine, but still, she really liked Sarah, and if she and Levi were in something, it'd be nice to see his sister more. Right?).

So tonight was their first "date," not that it had been either of their ideas. It was the brainchild of Jeremy— Jeremy, who was dressed in black jeans, a blue striped shirt, untucked, and yellow river man's sweater with four buttons unopened at the neck. Good old Banana Republic.

Levi, on the other hand, wore faded jeans with a tear in the knee, work boots and a flannel shirt, and despite her growing irritation with the man, it was getting hard not to rip open that shirt and take a bite.

But so far, Levi had barely said two words to her. Make that one. He'd said *hey* when he came in the door, half an hour after he was supposed to be there.

"I should've thought of this years ago," Jeremy now said. "Faith and Levi. Levi and Faith." Again with the beaming.

"Well, years ago, *we* were together, Jeremy," Faith said, a trifle testily. Levi said nothing. She resisted the urge to elbow him in the ribs.

"Right, right! But you two have, you know…chemistry."

Faith rolled her eyes. At the moment, the only chemistry she was feeling was acidic. She glanced at Levi, who gave her a six on the Boredom Scale. Nice. Then again, she may have been misreading his glances. Then again on top of that, she was, thus far, nothing more than a booty call.

"Whoops. Let me check the potatoes," Jeremy said now. He got up, all male grace, and went into the kitchen.

And still Levi said nothing.

"Am I just a booty call to you?" she whispered.

"What? No," he answered tersely.

Wow. Two whole words. "You haven't taken me out yet," she countered.

"I've been working."

Ooh. Three words now. "Sure."

The Boredom Scale jumped to a nine. "Faith, four houses have been broken into in the past ten days. I'm the police chief. I like my job. I have to *do* my job in order to keep it. I'm sorry I haven't—"

"You know what? It's fine."

"I hate that word," he grumbled.

Faith gave him a pointed look. "Oh, I'm so sorry, Levi. Please forgive me."

"What bug is up your—"

"Shut up, he's back."

Levi sighed, that typical male *women are such pains* sigh. This time she did elbow him in the ribs. "Jesus," he muttered.

"No, it's just Jeremy. But close," Faith shot back.

"So tell me everything," Jeremy said. "How did you guys get together?"

"It's purely sexual," Faith said.

Jeremy laughed. "You're so cute."

"It's true. I'm adorable."

"You are." He smiled at her. "Isn't she, Levi?"

"Yeah. Adorable." At that moment, his cell rang. "Chief Cooper," he answered, his face losing that bored affect as he listened. "Okay. Yep. I'm on my way." He stood up. "Sorry, guys, I have to go. An attempted break-in at the Hedbergs' house. They think their dog scared off whoever was there."

"Have fun," Faith said, taking another sip of her wine.

He looked down at her. "I don't know how long I'll be."

"Whatevs, honeybun."

Levi looked at Faith another minute. "Bye," he said, then leaned in and kissed her, and just like that, her heart softened.

"Be careful," she said.

"Will do." Then he left, and she and Jeremy were alone in the beautiful living room of the Lyon house, a fire crackling in the huge stone fireplace, wine and cheese on the coffee table.

She already missed Levi. Even if he was just her life-size sex toy.

"So," Jeremy said. "You and Levi. How's it going?"

She tucked her feet under her and took another sip of the wine (an oaky chardonnay with an overstated buttery texture, to be honest). "I don't really know," she said.

"The air crackles between you two. It does. It crackles."

Faith snorted. "Crackles with irritation, maybe."

"Well, you like him, right?"

Faith had to think about that one. "I like him sometimes. And, once in a great while, I think he likes me. I mean, I know he likes me in *some* ways—"

"He does. Of course he does. You're wonderful."

Faith put her wine down. "Can you stop with the compliments, Jeremy? It's driving me crazy."

He sighed. "Okay, yeah, I'm a little…" He paused. "I'd really like to see you happily settled with someone. And I love Levi like a brother. So I'm sorry if I'm a little overly invested here."

"I'm sorry, too," she said. "I didn't mean to snap at you."

He smiled, that easy, generous, ready smile that won over patients in a heartbeat. "It's okay. I think I'm owed some snapping." He paused. "I still feel bad that I couldn't give you what you wanted, Faith."

"It's okay," she said. "Water under the bridge."

Being here in his beautiful house, where she'd been hundreds of times, the fire, the wine, the elegant furniture and many family photos…she'd been so close to living this life. To having Jeremy, the heir to this vineyard, the town doctor, the guy who was everything she'd ever imagined having in a man.

The man who loved her with all his heart but had to picture Justin Timberlake to do the deed.

It occurred to Faith that she'd never thanked Levi for stopping her wedding.

She took a sip of her wine, which was improving with oxidation. "Can I ask you something about Levi?"

"Of course! I mean, nothing that would betray our brotherly bond and all that." Another smile.

"What was his wife like?" Faith asked. She'd been dying to hear about her, but as she and Levi hadn't done more than some X-rated acts, she hadn't had the chance.

"Nina, Nina, Nina," Jeremy said, swirling his wine around. "Nina Rodriguez. She was *unbelievably* pretty."

"Hey! A little loyalty, please?"

"I take it back," he said. "She was so ugly. In an unbelievably pretty way." He grinned. "She looked like J-Lo."

"Ouch."

"Well, she was also the one who broke his heart."

Crap. She'd been kind of hoping for a marriage of convenience situation with an upcoming and heartfelt declaration from Levi that only now did he understand the true meaning of love, yadda yadda. Too many romance novels or something. "They were only together for a little while, right?"

"Well, they knew each other in Afghanistan. She was—is—a helicopter pilot. Total kick-ass."

"Right." More wine was definitely called for. She took the bottle from the ice bucket and poured herself a second glass. "Was she nice?"

"Not the word I'd use. She was hot. Sorry, she was," Jeremy said. "And she was funny. Great smile, seemed very smart. But nice? Not sure about that."

Unfortunate that she had to ask Jeremy about these things instead of the man himself. Jeremy, however, would talk. "Did they live together first or anything?"

"Nope. Levi had to go to some Army thing in Fort Drum, and he came back with her, asked me to come to the Town Hall and there she was. They got married right then and there, with just his mom and sister and me." Jeremy smiled at the memory. "He was totally smitten. Couldn't take his eyes off her. He was so…smug, you know? Like, yeah, look at me, married to her."

"You're giving me a cramp, Jeremy."

He grimaced. "Well, obviously it didn't work out. Nina was fun, she was gorgeous, but she was edgy, too. It was tough, because it was one of those situations where you could see that his heart was going to be crushed. No one was really surprised it didn't last."

"Except him?"

"Exactly." Jeremy paused. "He adored her, she couldn't wait to leave. Just not meant for small-town life, I guess. Or marriage. And Levi, meanwhile, had practically named their kids."

Faith knew that feeling. She and Jeremy actually *had* named their kids. "And that was a year ago?"

"More than that. Maybe a year and a half? Yeah, because it was June and we had the biplane show on the lake. He walked around like someone had hit him in the head with a baseball bat."

Faith sighed. "Well, this sucks, Jeremy, because from the sound of it, she's the love of his life, and I'm a booty call."

"How long have you guys been together?"

"Eight days."

Jeremy laughed. "I'd give it a little time, sweetheart." He stood up and picked up her wineglass. "Let's eat. I have some beautiful steaks and twice-baked potatoes *and* coleslaw, all your favorites, not to mention grape pie from Lorelei's. We can watch a movie if Levi's late. I have *The Devil Wears Prada.* I watched it last night, too, and I swear it gets better every time."

"I can't believe I ever thought you were straight." She took his hand and let him pull her off the couch, then followed him into the kitchen.

THE HEDBERGS HAD COME home to find the back door open and called Levi, rather than go inside in case the burglar was still there. Smart. He made the family wait as he took a walk-through. No intruder. It looked like Katie's room had been tossed, but she said it was as she'd left it. Andrew gazed at him with wide-eyed adoration, firing off questions about bad guys, guns, robbers and whether or not Abraham could be trained to attack.

After that, Levi walked around the house, looking for signs of a break-in—screens knocked out, footprints in flower beds, damage to any of the doors. Christine, the oldest of the three kids, admitted it was possible she hadn't closed the back door when she'd left that afternoon.

"Sorry to have bothered you for nothing, Chief," Mr. Hedberg said.

"No bother. You did the right thing by calling," he said, scratching Abraham's ears. "That's what I'm here for, and especially with the other burglaries, you shouldn't hesitate. It's good you have a dog, though," he added. "Very effective deterrent, aren't you, boy?" Abraham had wagged to show that yes, he was an excellent watchdog.

"We should give Abraham a steak," Andrew suggested. "Right, Chief Cooper? Can I be a cop when I grow up?"

"Sure," Levi said.

"Or a soldier! So I could kill the bad guys."

"Hopefully all the bad guys will be gone when you grow up," Levi said, feeling the familiar awkwardness. Then he shook hands, told the family to have a good night and took a cruise through the neighborhood. Pru and Carl lived up the street, so he pulled into their driveway and knocked on the door. Abby answered.

"Hi," she said, her face lighting up. "Wanna come in? Hang out?"

"Sorry, Abby, I can't. Are your parents home?"

Her face darkened. "They're 'taking a nap,' okay?" she said, making quote marks with her fingers. "Like I'm four and believe that. My father's living at my grandmother's house, but he comes over for conjugal visits. The noises, Levi. No matter how loud I turn up the TV, I swear I can still hear them. I cannot *wait* to go to college."

He suppressed a grin. "Well, the Hedbergs thought someone might've tried to break in, but there was no sign of anything missing. Even so, make sure the doors are locked, and you call me if you hear anything."

"First of all, I know everything already. Katie just texted me. And secondly, I'm not exactly the type to go investigating things that go bump in the night. I've seen all the horror movies."

"Right." He gave her his best cop look. "And how are you? You keeping on the straight and narrow?"

"Oh, sure. Mmm-hmm." She was texting as she spoke. Irritating.

"Make sure you do, Abby. One act of stupidity can have long-lasting implications."

"Wow. I'll totally think about that. Thanks. You've changed my life."

"Don't be a twit," he said.

"I'm posting that you said that on my Facebook."

"I mean it, Abby. You don't want to get pregnant or—"

"Oh, hey, I just remembered something! I'm *not* your sister! I have plenty of adults to lecture me, okay? Don't be one of them. Just give me one of those hot looks instead, how about it?"

"Have a good night, Abby."

"That'll do." She held up her phone and clicked. Great. He'd be on her Facebook page in seconds.

No, she wasn't his sister. She might end up as his niece, however.

Oh, shit. Where had that thought come from?

He backed out of the Vanderbeek's driveway. Thing was, yeah. He wasn't the tomcat type. It'd be nice to get married, have a couple kids.

But this time, he had to pick wiscly. Nina had said she loved him (though looking back, she said it in the same tone that she used in saying she loved pizza). Said she was ready to settle down. Liked the idea of small-town life. She figured she'd get her master's in education, become a teacher. Yes to kids.

That had lasted three months.

He picked up his phone and called Sarah. "Hey. What are you doing?"

"Nothing. Studying. How are you?" There was an eagerness in her voice that bespoke loneliness. He could hear music in the background.

"I'm fine. You alone?"

"Yeah. Chem test tomorrow. My slutty roommate's with her boyfriend."

"I thought you liked her."

"She's a slut, Levi. So what's up?"

"Just checking on you."

There was a pause. "Thanks," she said, her voice small.

"I need advice," he said, surprising himself.

"Really?" Her tone was much happier all of a sudden. "Why? Did Faith dump your sorry ass?"

"No," Levi said, a smile threatening. "I'm just wondering if I want to be…I don't know. Runner-up." He winced, not sure he should be telling his sister this.

"Why would you be runner-up? Oh, the Jeremy thing! Right! I got it." There was a rustle. "Tell me everything."

"There's nothing to tell."

"Is she still hung up on him?"

Levi hesitated. "I don't know."

"Ask her."

"Right."

"Do it, dummy! Just ask her. Then kiss the stuffing out of her, and she'll definitely pick you. Straight trumps gay every time."

Levi laughed. "Got it. How are you? Doing okay?"

She sighed so hard it practically ruffled his hair. "Am I allowed to say no?"

He hesitated. "You're still adjusting, that's all. You'll love college before long."

"Whatever."

"Not whatever, Sarah. You have to give it some effort, though." He tried to think of what Faith would say. "It's okay to be homesick. But don't let that take away all the good things." There. That sounded pretty good.

"Whatever, Sigmund. I have to study." Her voice was deflated.

He sighed. "Okay. You're smart, you'll do great."

"Thanks." Barely a grunt now.

He hung up, bemused. College was supposed to help with her grief, not make it worse. He didn't like knowing she was lonely.

A sign told him he'd driven out of Manningsport, across the little stretch of Osskill and into the town of Bryer. Looked like his subconscious had taken him for a little ride. A left at the intersection, two miles down, a right. This was the fourth time he'd been here. Funny how familiar the drive was.

Nice neighborhood, built in the late sixties. Ranches and Capes, big yards, smallish houses, all very wholesome. Great place for trick-or-treating, unlike the trailer park, where things could be a little dicey. When he was seven, Jessica's dad had offered him a can of Pabst. From then on, Levi's mom had driven him and Jess into the Village on Halloween. That had ended when they were nine. They'd each just happily accepted a regular-sized Mr. Goodbar (his favorite) and were leaving the porch of the giant old Vic when a voice came from the window. "Who was it?" the man asked.

The woman—Mrs. Thomas—answered, her voice sharp, "It was a couple of those trailer park kids. I wish their parents wouldn't drive them here. They take advantage."

Levi's face had grown hot, and Jess…Jess had looked as if someone had just punched her in the stomach. Without thinking, he'd thrown his candy bar in the bushes, then hers. Taken her pillowcase and dumped it all right there, then did the same with his, even though the McCormicks had been really nice, complimenting him on the zombie makeup and telling him he'd almost given them a heart attack, he was so scary. They'd told Jess she looked beautiful.

Mrs. Thomas had broken her hip last spring, falling as she got out of the shower, and Levi had knelt on the floor next to her, the first person on the scene. He'd covered her up with a bathrobe so the firefighters wouldn't see her naked, and she'd cried as he did it, telling him he was so kind. He told her not to worry, wondering if she realized that the kind cop had once been one of those trailer park urchins who used up the treats meant for better kids.

Levi slowed the cruiser, then pulled over. There was the house, a dark blue ranch with rhododendrons and a big maple tree, complete with swing. Lights were on in the living room, shining through the big window. A child's bike lay next to the mailbox, half on the street.

There was his father's wife, coming into the living room, handing someone a glass. His father, most likely. Their TV was on. Levi had never met the woman his father had married…only a glimpse of her twice before. She had fluffy blond hair and was on the skinny side.

There were no lights on in the bedrooms, which indicated the boys were asleep. Strange to think he had two half brothers. He'd never met them, didn't know their names. He'd seen them the first time he'd come down the street, playing in the driveway with their Matchbox cars. They were young. That was about all he could see. He hadn't parked that time, just kept going, careful not to look too hard.

Levi's watch beeped. Ten o'clock. He could be with Faith right now, and all of a sudden, the desire to see her closed in on his chest like a vise.

But before he left, he got out of the car, walked over to the bike and moved it so it wouldn't get run over.

Twenty minutes later, he was back at Jeremy's enormous house. "Sorry that took so long," he said.

"Hey. Faith's asleep," Jeremy said, pointing.

Sure enough, she was, her head on the couch pillows, a soft-looking blanket over her.

"Is she okay?" he asked, fighting a small pang of jealousy. A movie played softly on TV, something with that famous actress, the one who won all the Oscars.

"Just tired," Jeremy said. "How was the call? Don't worry, she sleeps like the dead."

"I know." Well, he knew that he could kiss her good-bye in the mornings and not have her so much as stir. Then again, he'd managed to wake her a time or two in the middle of the night, and done his best to make her sleep-deprived.

"Right, right. Of course you do. You want some food? We saved your steak."

We. "I'm good." He sat down in the chair, looking at Faith.

"So, are you guys serious?" Jeremy asked softly.

Levi took a breath and held it for a second. "We've slept together a couple times, Jeremy." Six nights of the past eight, spent in the little apartment that looked as if she'd lived there for years.

"She's not really the type for a casual relationship, you know," Jeremy said.

"Listen, single gay guy, I can take it from here, okay?" He raised an eyebrow at his friend, who smiled.

"Yeah, I understand. But maybe I could give you a little advice?"

"I'm good." The questioning look stayed on his friend's face. "Fine," Levi said. "Knock yourself out."

Jeremy adjusted the blanket around Faith's feet. "Little things mean a lot to her. Tell her she looks pretty or notice if she's wearing a new dress. Talk to her. Bring her flowers."

"Flowers. Got it."

"And don't be sarcastic. She's fragile."

"I actually think she's pretty tough," Levi said, his words tight.

"It's an act."

"Is that right?"

"I think so. I know her very well." Jeremy smiled, and for a nanosecond, Levi felt like punching him.

"Well, if the advice portion of the evening is done, I think I'll take the delicate flower home," Levi said.

"Sure. I didn't mean to be a dick or anything. I just want you guys to work."

And that was the thing. Jeremy was a damn prince.

"Got it. You wanna wake Sleeping Beauty?"

"Faith," Jeremy said in a loud voice, shaking her feet. "Faith, honey, time to wake up. Come on, now. Wake up."

Nothing from Faith, who appeared to be in a deep coma. "Faith. Come on." Jeremy was practically shouting at her now.

"Maybe a bucket of ice water?" Levi suggested.

"What? I heard that. Don't throw anything at me," Faith muttered. "I'm here. What day is it?" She struggled into a sitting position, frowning. Then she saw him, and her face softened. "Hi."

That urgent feeling of wanting he'd had at his father's house, the need to be with her—not necessarily to sleep with her, though that would be nice—but just to touch her, have her close…that feeling was back. "Ready to go?" he asked.

"Okay." She leaned over and kissed Jeremy on the cheek. "Thanks for dinner. Sorry I fell asleep."

"Oh, don't worry. It was like old times." He smiled. "Levi, let me pack up your food."

When they got back to the Opera House, Levi followed her into her place. "Hi, handsome!" she said to her leaping dog. "Who's a good boy? Hmm? Give me two minutes, and we'll take a you-know-what." She went to the kitchen and got a glass of water, then scootched up onto the island counter, swinging her feet. "I take it you're staying over?" she said, pink staining her cheeks. She didn't look at him.

Levi didn't answer. Instead, he walked over to her and wrapped his arms around her and just lay his head against her chest. Felt some of the tension drain from his muscles as he breathed in her warm, sweet smell.

"You okay, Levi?" she asked softly.

"Yep."

"What took you so long tonight?"

He imagined telling her about his father's other kids, the happy little family he wasn't part of. Maybe throw in some of the jealousy thing with Jeremy. Didn't really see the point, all that talk about problems and issues and whatnot.

And, to be honest, he wasn't sure he wanted her to know. Her, or anyone. "It just took a while, that's all," he said. He could stay here all day, against Faith's gorgeous rack, listening to her breathe. Kinda perfect.

Except for one thing. "Faith?"

"Mmm-hmm?"

"Your dog's trying to impregnate my leg."

She laughed, the sound rich and warm. "You'll make beautiful puppies together."

"Let's take him for a walk."

"And come back here and fool around?"

"Sounds like a plan." He looked into those dusk-blue eyes. "You want to go out with me tomorrow? On a date?"

Her smile was a sight to see.

CHAPTER TWENTY-TWO

THE MANNINGSPORT PUBLIC LIBRARY was closed on Saturday afternoons, but Faith had the code. Levi probably did, too, but he stood back and let her punch it in.

There was something magical about being in a library when no one else was around, she thought as they went through the darkened rooms to the children's section. That, and Levi's strong, calloused hand holding hers as the rain pattered on the roof. Holding hands for the first time. Funny, the sweet shock of such a small gesture.

"So it's all done, then?" Levi said as she opened the back door to the courtyard.

"All done. The dedication is Wednesday night." She paused. "Maybe you'll be there?"

"I hope so," he said.

His answer, while noncommittal, made her cheeks prickle with a blush just the same. "Well, here it is. Take a look around."

The courtyard had been a bit of a challenge, since the space was so small. Previously, it'd had a cement bench and an anemic flower bed of red geraniums (cemetery flowers, Faith always thought), as well as a germ-laden birdbath. Few people had ever used the space.

Now, watching Levi take in her work, Faith felt a warm swell of pride. In each corner was a Japanese maple tree, chosen for their manageable size and gorgeous foliage. Next week, Julianne had said, the kindergarten reading group would be making wind chimes to hang in the branches, and Topper Mack had already made four birdhouses, miniatures of the library.

In between each tree sat four mahogany and chestnut benches, made by Samuel Hastings. Faith had kept the carpenter busy this fall. Each bench had been donated by a founding family of Manningsport—the Hollands, of course, the Mannings, the Meerings and the van Huesens. The southern wall had no window and, since it got the sun all day, had made the courtyard stifling; this was the wall where Faith had designed a sleek waterfall that ran in a smooth, fluid sheet, the sound soft and soothing.

In the bulk of the space, Faith had created a circular path lined with low boxwoods and paved with old brick, which led to the object that, in Faith's opinion, made the courtyard great: a life-size, bronze statue of Dr. Seuss, reading a copy of *The Lorax* as the furry little creature looked on.

Levi stood there now. "Dr. Seuss, huh?" he said. His hair had darkened in the light rain. "Why him?"

"Because he's the greatest children's author in the world," she said. "In my opinion, anyway. The library board seemed to agree."

"*Happy Birthday to You* was my favorite," Levi said, brushing a fallen leaf off Dr. Seuss's foot. "I used to read that after—I read that a lot."

"After what?" Faith asked, pulling her jacket closer.

He glanced over. "After my father left," he said after a pause, looking back at the statue.

Right. She'd always known Levi's dad wasn't in the picture, but he'd never mentioned it before. Her heart tugged, picturing Levi as a little boy, reading the joyfully exuberant book to counteract the misery he must've felt. "How old were you?" she asked.

He didn't answer. "This is really nice, Faith," he said after a minute. "The kids'll love it."

Looked like the subject of his father was off-limits. "Thanks." She paused. "The idea was to take a space that no one really saw and make it beautiful. Get people to appreciate what nature has to offer, get them away from their phones and computers and take a breath and listen to the birds and the water and just…be."

"Is that what all your projects are supposed to do?"

She shrugged. "I guess so. Yes." Now that she'd said it out loud, it sounded a little dorky. Dorktastic, maybe. Hopefully.

Levi was looking at her steadily. "You hungry?"

"Sure," she said. "Want to go to O'Rourke's?"

"Nope," he said, coming back to reclaim her hand. "A picnic. I checked with Honor, and she said the Barn at Blue Heron was free."

Twenty minutes later, they were hiking up the hill. Levi held a good-sized brown bag with "Lorelei's" stamped on one side, as well as a blanket. The late October rain had petered off to a drizzle, and it was incredibly romantic, a Saturday afternoon picnic on a chilly autumn day.

Despite the fact that she'd worked on the barn for six solid weeks, the sight of it was still a small shock. The plants had withered from the cold—it'd been thirty degrees last night—but it was still beautiful. Leaves had gathered on the roof in one corner; she'd have to come up with a ladder and take care of that.

Levi spread out the blanket on the floor of the barn, then got to work, grabbing kindling from the little alcove next to the fireplace. Once the fire was blazing, he sat down. "Hungry?"

"Starving. Feed me, Chief."

He smiled then, just a little, and Faith's heart gave a sweetly painful tug. Levi Cooper didn't smile enough. She'd like to change that.

The wind gusted around them, sending puffs of smoke from the fireplace once in a while. They sat on the blanket and ate Lorelei's beautiful sandwiches, roast beef and horseradish mayonnaise with sharp cheddar cheese on a hard roll, egg salad with dill on a thick rye. A bag of potato chips, two bottles of iced tea. And, for dessert, chocolate cookies, thick and dark and chewy. Faith closed her eyes as she chewed. "These are proof of a loving God," she murmured. "Lorelei should be canonized."

"She didn't make them," Levi said.

Faith opened her eyes. "Really? Oh! Are these the source of that heavenly smell at three o'clock in the morning?"

He nodded, looking, for the life of her, a little shy.

"Good job, big man," she said. "I should tell Barb at the newspaper. 'Chief Cooper's Baking Secrets' or 'War Hero Secretly a Midnight Baker.'"

"Don't you dare." There was that almost-smile again.

"Why? The townspeople would love it. Don't hide your light under a bushel, Chief Cooper."

"Hush, woman. Close your eyes and eat another. You're fun to watch."

She obeyed, trying not to think of her thighs and the effect these cookies would have. It was worth it. When she opened her eyes, Levi was looking at her, his face solemn, two lines running between his brows. His eyes looked gray today, same color as the sky.

"I'm sorry I called you a tease that day," he said. "You weren't."

The memory knifed into her heart. That day, when he'd given her the kiss that had so stunned her, not far from this very place. She swallowed the cookie in a lump. "That was a long time ago, Levi."

"I know. But I've been thinking about it, a little. Thought about it a few times over the years." He looked at the fire. "It wasn't my finest moment. I'd just kissed my best friend's girlfriend, and I wanted someone to blame. I'm sorry."

"Thanks," she whispered. The fire popped and hissed. Shoot. Now or never. "Levi, is this a relationship, or are we just fooling around?"

Because if it wasn't a relationship, she'd better lasso her heart and bring it back to the stable, since it was obvious that thing was galloping away.

He looked at her with some difficulty, it seemed. "I don't know. Are you staying in town?"

"I...I have to take care of some things first. I want to stay, though." More than ever now.

He hesitated, then nodded.

"So we're...friends?"

"Is that what you want us to be? Friends?" He wadded up the paper bag and tossed it into the fire.

"I've wanted to be your friend my whole life," she said, her throat abruptly tight.

He looked at her sharply. "Why?" he asked. His face was in its familiar solemn lines, forehead slightly crinkled with a question.

"I don't know. You were... I don't know." And she didn't. He'd been one of the cool kids, of course, but there was something more to him. Something different. "There was one time, when I had a seizure. Maybe

third grade? Yeah, because Mrs. G. was our teacher."
Levi nodded. "And what I remember when I came out
of it was you, telling people to back off and stop staring." She looked at him, and his face was gentle now.
"Do you remember that?"

"No."

"Well. I do, obviously. But other than that, and especially when I was with Jeremy, you never seemed to
like me."

She looked down at the string edges of the blanket.
Quite fascinating. Faith braided three of them together,
then found her hand covered by Levi's.

"I like you now, Faith."

She looked up to see him smiling, just a little. "That's
good."

"Feels like we're more than friends, though."

There was the rush of golden heat, fast and heavy.
She nodded.

He pulled her against him, and the nice clean smell
of him, soap and smoke, made her chest ache. There
was a little bit of dried leaf on his flannel shirt, and
she brushed it off, her heart feeling fragile and new in
her chest.

Then she kissed him. His mouth was firm and
smooth and so, so good at what it was doing, and that
golden heat filled her, making her warm and slow and
lazy with its sweetness.

And heck, there was a fire and a blanket and a beautiful man, and now rain pattered on the clear roof of the
barn, and if there was a better place to make love, Faith
didn't know what it was.

A good while later, the patter had turned into a
steady rush, blowing the last of the leaves onto the roof.
Blue lay on his back in front of the fire, dreaming of

being a ball boy at the U.S. Open, his paws twitching. Faith was against Levi's side, her head on his shoulder, warm and sleepy from the heat of the fire and her man's warmth.

Yep. Her man. That worked.

"Can I ask you a question?" Levi's voice was just a rumble in his chest.

"Sure."

"What's it like to have a seizure? You don't have to answer if you don't want to," he added.

"No, it's okay." She tucked a bit of hair behind her ear. The question was familiar. "At first, I have what they call the aura. I get worried, like something really bad's about to happen. Doomsday bad. I can feel my body doing things—I know I pull at my shirt, and I feel almost panicky, and then I just…check out."

"What's that like?"

"I don't know. It's just…empty." She ran her hand over his smooth skin, feeling the muscles underneath. "What's funny is how people act afterward. Or during, I guess, but I only see them afterward."

"How do they act?" he asked.

"It depends on the person. You were pretty good. Kind of perfect, actually."

"I get that a lot." There was that lovely smile in his voice.

"I'm sure. Especially from the over-eighty crowd."

"Correct. How do other people act?"

She thought a minute. "Well, when we were little, Jack would stay away from me, like I was about to burst into flames. Except, of course, for the time he filmed me for a Boy Scout badge or something. My mother almost killed him. Pru was pretty good. Honor…it's funny, Honor would cry."

"Honor cries?"

"I know." She smiled.

"How about your parents?" he asked.

"Well, Dad would look like I'd died and come back. He'd be totally spent and relieved. I think it was harder on him than on me. And my mom would be…well." Faith stopped. The rain was harder now.

"Mom would be what?"

"She'd be mad." It felt sacrilegious, saying something negative about her dead mother.

Levi rolled over to look at her. The frown lines and crinkled forehead were back. "Your mother couldn't have been mad at you because you had a seizure, Faith," he said.

"No, I guess not. Mad that I had epilepsy, mad at the universe maybe. But it used to seem like she was mad at me." She gave a small shrug. "But no, she probably wasn't."

"Can you imagine being mad at your kid because she had a seizure?"

The image of a little girl with sleepy green eyes came to her, so clear that she sucked in a breath, then cleared her throat. "No. Anyway. Let's change the subject." She paused. "My turn for a question. How'd you do in Afghanistan?"

His eyes changed, as if a door had closed. A second ago, they'd been gentle and kind…now, there was nothing in them. "I did fine."

"So you don't talk about the war, then."

He didn't say anything for a second. "I just don't know how to answer when people ask that question."

"How many tours did you do?"

"Four."

"All in Afghanistan?"

"Yep."

She paused. "Were you ever scared?"

"Sure."

"Is that where you met your wife?"

"Yes."

He didn't say anything else. Faith waited. Waited a little more. "You can tell me about it, you know," she said.

"About what?"

"Whatever you wanted. What you had to do over there, how you feel about it, or your wife, your mom, your father...whatever you want."

He sat up and started dressing. "There's really not much to tell."

Looked like the intimacy portion of the afternoon had ended. "Well, if the mood ever strikes to go into a bit more detail, I'm just saying you can, if you want to."

"I don't." His movements were sharp and hard.

"Yes, that's coming through loud and clear."

"Well, not everyone sits around feeling the feelings, Faith."

"Is that a jab at me?"

He stopped buttoning his shirt. "No."

"Do you have bad dreams?" she asked, unable to stop. "Is that why you bake in the middle of the night?"

He didn't answer for a long minute, his smile gone. "Yes," he said eventually.

She waited for more. Nothing came. She waited some more. "You could wake me up, too," she said. "If you're sleeping over, that is."

He looked at her solemnly. "I don't have those dreams when I'm with you."

The words went straight to her heart—a gift, even if he didn't seem to realize it.

His phone rang. Dang it all—just when they were getting somewhere. He groped for the evil little device, and honestly, wasn't Everett ever on? "Chief Cooper. Hey. Sure, what's up? Yeah, okay, I'll be there in ten minutes."

Faith suppressed a sigh. She shouldn't complain; the guy *was* the police chief. "I have to go," he said. "Alice McPhales thinks there's a man in her woods."

"Right." Mrs. McPhales, her Girl Scout leader. Seemed like her Alzheimer's was worsening; Faith had gone over the week before to cut back her plants for winter. The sweet old lady had made her tea but had forgotten the tea bag, so Faith, not wanting to upset her, had just drunk the hot water. "Want me to come with you?"

Levi glanced up at the clear ceiling. "No, it's really pouring. I'll just tramp around in the woods and reassure her."

"I don't mind."

"It's fine. I'll see you at home." The word *home* had never sounded nicer.

Tiling her chin up, he looked at her steadily. "I had a really nice time with you today."

"Thanks. Me, too."

"Walk you back to your dad's?"

"No, that's okay. I'll get this all cleaned up. Put out the fire and all that."

He kissed her quickly, and again more slowly, then left her alone with the sound of the rain and the smell of wet leaves and wood smoke.

WHEN LEVI LEFT THE STATION after filling out a report or six, it was dark. The rain had blown off across the lake, leaving behind a clear, moonless sky. Lights were on in Faith's apartment, he noted as he crossed the green. He stopped, looking up. It was a skill he was getting pretty good at, this spying—first his father's house, now her funky little apartment. From where he was, he could see part of the red wall, a bit of the bookcase where she displayed all those family photos.

And the rose quartz heart he'd given her.

He should probably cop to that.

There she was, the phone tucked under her ear as she walked, a carton of Ben & Jerry's in one hand— she had six of them in her freezer last time he checked, and not one green vegetable—a spoon in the other. She was laughing, and Levi felt a blade of lust knife through him. He loved when Faith laughed. She had such a girl-next-door face, but when she laughed, she looked—and sounded—like a sex kitten, and the husky sound of her voice seemed to have an electric effect on his groin.

His phone rang, and he jumped, then answered it. "Chief Cooper."

"Little Cooper here."

"Hey, hon, how you doing?"

"I'm good. Got an A minus on my chemistry test."

"Told you so. Good job."

"Thanks for the cookies. I'm getting fat. Fatter, I should say."

"You're not fat."

"So what are you doing?" There was that lonely note in her voice again. "You at the station?"

"Nope. I'm staring up at Faith's windows, watching her."

"Stalker-ish of you."

"Well, I'm a police officer," he said. "We're good at that."

"At being pathetic, you mean? Because that sounds

totally pathetic. You about to burst into verse? 'What light through yonder window breaks' and all that crap?"

"Sounds like a plan."

"Sad. You're still coming up for dinner this week, right?"

"No. When did I say I'd do that?"

"Levi!" his sister barked. "You said you'd come for dinner! Since you banned me from coming home before Thanksgiving, which is still weeks away!"

"Well, I can't come this week. I have a budget meeting tomorrow—"

"What about Tuesday?"

"Tuesday I'm on call."

"Wednesday?"

"Dinner with Faith's family." Shit. He shouldn't have admitted that.

"How cozy," Sarah said, her voice thick with tears. "Thursday?"

"On call again, honey. Come on. I didn't say this week. I said sometime before Thanksgiving, and—"

"You know what? Don't come up. That's fine. I'll make new friends and be happy and you don't have to worry about me at all. Okay? Bye."

"Sarah, don't be so—" Great. She'd hung up. He called her back, but it went right to voice mail. Texted her. Please stop being an ass. He waited. She didn't write back. He waited another minute or two.

With a sigh, he texted again. How about friday?

Seconds later, his phone chimed. fridays great. xoxox

Tucking his phone into his pocket, he crossed the rest of the green. Into the Opera House, up the stairs and straight to Faith's apartment. Knocked, causing Blue to bark wildly.

A second later, Faith answered the door, still on the

phone. Her hair was in a ponytail, and the Dalmatian pj's were topped with a skimpy little tank top that barely contained the mighty rack. She looked, in other words, like the start of a particularly good porno.

"Why, it's Manningsport's hottest cop," she said into the phone, stepping aside so he could come in. "No, not in uniform, alas. Flannel. Has a sort of lumberjack appeal, though. No, I totally agree. Dresses like a straight guy. Well, then again, so did you." She laughed merrily. "Hi," she whispered to him. "It's Jeremy."

"Yeah."

"He's doing the one-word answer thing," she said into the phone. "No, he's scowling. It works." She held the phone out to him. "Jeremy wants to talk to you."

Levi didn't want to talk, not to Jeremy, not to her. He took the phone, clicked it off and tossed it onto the chair, then wrapped his arms around Faith, slid his hands down her generous ass, pushed her against the wall and kissed her smooth, beautiful neck, then licked the same spot.

Blue began trying to get in on the action, so, without releasing her, Levi turned, grabbed a pillow from the couch and tossed it on the floor. Blue took the hint. Then Levi slid his hands up her front, feeling her nipples harden under his palms. "You like this shirt?" he muttered, his lips just below her ear.

"Not really," she whispered, her voice shaky.

"Good." He grabbed the neckline with two hands and ripped it open, and without further ado, she wrapped herself around him and gave as good as she got.

CHAPTER TWENTY-THREE

LEVI HADN'T EXPECTED to see Jeremy when he and Faith went for dinner at her father's house.

He was already a little itchy with the whole family thing. He'd had dinner with the Hollands a time or two over the years, but he never could shake that feeling he'd had as a kid—the big house on the Hill, off-limits except when the doors were opened to the great unwashed. The sight of Jeremy there, acting like a son-in-law, made it worse.

"Hey," he said tightly as Jeremy greeted him with a clap on the shoulder.

"Good to see you, buddy," Jeremy said. "Glass of wine?" He didn't wait for an answer, just sauntered away.

"Oops. Mrs. Johnson is flagging me down," Faith said, slipping off herself. The housekeeper gave him a death stare, then melted back into the kitchen.

Under normal circumstances, Levi liked the Holland family quite a lot. But now that he was Faith's… whatever…it was a lot more awkward. Jack gave him a pained glance, then returned his gaze to his beer; Ned and Abby were bickering over by a window seat.

Jeremy returned and handed Levi a glass of wine, seeming as comfortable here as he was at his own place down the road. The fact that he'd left Faith at the altar seemed to have been forgiven. Levi mentally chastised himself; the elder Lyons lived in California, and the Hollands were as close to family as Jeremy had around here.

"Hi, Levi," Honor said, emerging from the kitchen. Her voice was neither more nor less friendly than always.

"Hi," he said. "How are you?"

"Heard you're banging my sister," she said.

"Uh…I'll let her respond to that."

"My father's ready to kill you. Beware." Honor went over to her dad and handed him a glass of wine. John glanced at Levi and gave him a steely nod.

Right. Well, to the kitchen it was, then.

"I fail to see how this is sexy," Prudence was saying. "I look like a plucked chicken."

"Why you would do such a thing, I don't want to know," Mrs. Johnson said, opening the freezer and handing Pru a bag of peas. "You girls today are a terrible mystery."

Pru put the bag on her crotch. For the love of… "Hey, Levi!" she said amiably. "Got a bikini wax today. I do not recommend it. The pain was unbelievable! I swear the woman was enjoying it, all that ripping and tearing. Shoot, these are cold! I might be getting frostbite."

You'd think that four tours would've steeled him for such a mental image. They didn't. "Hi," he murmured.

"Mrs. Johnson, say hello to Levi," Faith said, coming over to his side.

"Good evening, Chief Cooper," Mrs. Johnson said. "What are you doing in my kitchen?"

"He's here for dinner." Faith slid her arm around his waist, her warm, sweet smell coming to him. "He's my honey."

Her honey, was it? Sounded kind of…nice.

"Which does not answer the question of why he's

standing right in front of the salt potatoes when they're nearly ready. Shoo, Chief! Get out!"

"Thanks for the peas, Mrs. J.," Pru said. "Want them back in the freezer or what?"

"Throw them away, child!"

"Fine, fine," Pru said, walking like a cowboy after a hard day in the saddle. "Waste not, want not, I always thought."

"Oh, Goggy and Pops are here!" Faith said, abandoning Levi yet again.

The housekeeper gave him another glare. "Well? Go. What are you waiting for?"

An eternity later, the Holland family, Jeremy and Levi were jammed around the dining room table. Old Mr. and Mrs. Holland, John, Pru, Ned and Abby, Honor and Jack. And Faith, flanked by Jeremy and himself.

"Faith, we *never* see you anymore," Mrs. Holland said.

"I was over yesterday," she said.

"You young people. Always so busy."

"So what? She should be busy. Before she knows it, she'll end up trapped for sixty-five years," Mr. Holland said.

"Dad, knock it off," John said patiently. "Jack, pass the bread, will you?"

"Jeez, Ned, stop it!" Abby barked. "Mom! He's kicking me under the table!"

"Ned, for crying out loud, you're a legal adult," Pru snapped. "Don't make me get up to hit you. I'm totally chafed."

"College, college, college," Abby chanted, putting her fingers in her ears. He smiled at her, only to have her glare back at him. He'd just given her the sentence for her foray into underage drinking: twelve hours of community service.

His head was starting to ache from the din of approximately six separate conversations in which everyone spoke at once and no one listened. He glanced at his watch, wondering how long they'd have to stay.

"Levi, just what are your intentions toward my daughter?" John asked abruptly.

"Daddy," Faith sighed. "Come on. We talked about this."

"So?" John stared expectantly. "I think I have the right to know what your plans are. Faith is my daughter. My princess."

"Yeah, Faith, where is that crown, by the way?" Jack asked, taking more potatoes.

Pru snorted. "Honor, did Dad ever call you his princess? I'm pretty sure I was never called princess by anyone."

"I believe only Faith holds that title," Honor said.

"Girls, don't be ridiculous. You're all three my princesses. Levi? Answer the question."

"I intend to date her, sir," Levi said.

"Whatever that means these days," John grumbled.

"It means sex," Abby added, getting an elbow from her mother. "What?" she asked. "How can I not be aware of it when you and Daddy are doing it all the time?"

"Well, Faith," said Mrs. Holland, "I think you should date a long, long time. Your grandfather took me for two walks before we were married. I wish I'd gotten to know him first, rather than count on my parents' judgment."

"So you guys were an arranged marriage?" Abby asked, perking up.

"More or less," Mrs. Holland said. "You think I would've married him if my parents weren't—"

"Dying to get rid of her?" Mr. Holland interjected.

"—pressuring me to marry him for his land."

"Well, your mother and I were a love match, kids," John said loudly, clearly trying to drown out his parents. "Love at first sight, as they say."

"Like Faith and Jeremy," Abby said. Levi felt his jaw locking. Jeremy smiled and said nothing.

"Abby, why are your panties in a twist?" Faith asked.

"Levi's making me clean the tourist restrooms, that's why! I screw up one time, and I have to clean bathrooms!"

"Guess you shouldn't go drinking with idiot boys, then, huh?" Ned said.

"At least I wasn't sleeping with anyone, Ned! I read your texts the other day. You and Sarah Cooper are so cute."

Levi felt his hackles rise.

"We're only friends," Ned said, his voice panicky.

"Do not distract my sister, Ned," Levi ground out. "And do not sleep with her."

"No, no. I wouldn't. Abby doesn't know what she's talking about. She's an idiot, right, Abs?"

"Can everyone just settle down?" Honor said calmly. "Levi's our guest tonight. Let's save the reality of Holland family life for another time. Dad, Levi's dating Faith, he's her first boyfriend since the gay ruined her for other men, she's thirty years old, and you already have one spinster daughter, so get over it." She picked up her fork and took another bite of potatoes.

"She's right," John said after a minute. "Sorry, Levi. I just… She's my daughter, that's all. I want the best for her."

"Understood." His watch must be broken.

"So," John continued, "who planted those chrysan-themums on your mother's grave?"

"I did," Honor said.

"Beautiful color, honey." He sighed. "Hard to believe it'll be twenty years in June."

There was a moment of silence.

"How's the dating going, Dad?" Jack asked.

"Since the transvestite, you mean?" he answered, which went right over Levi's head. He supposed he should be grateful. "Well," John continued, "I think I've given it a good shot, but I'm probably happier alone."

"Oh, Dad, no! Don't give up," Faith said. "You said that the lady from Corning was really nice. Please give me another chance!"

"Just don't let Lorena back in the house," Jack said. "That woman makes my testicles retract."

"Preach it, Uncle J.," Ned murmured.

"I'm fine on my own," John said. "Don't worry, Faithie."

"Grandpa, you live with a daughter and a house-keeper. You're not exactly on your own," Abby said.

"Exactly. I have Honor and Mrs. J. and all you kids." His eyes grew distant. "Connie was the love of my life. You only get one of those, and you can't replace it just because you want to."

THEY WERE FINALLY ABLE to leave a decade or so later (after Jeremy had kissed Faith robustly on each cheek *and* hugged her. Levi was seriously considering punch-ing him). Faith, though, had been a little…wan.

The full moon turned the landscape blue and white, casting wide shadows of the house, the trees. "Thanks for asking me to come tonight," Levi said, holding the car door for her.

"Oh, sure," she said. "You're welcome. Sorry if it was…a lot."

"It was nice," he lied. "Did you have fun?"

"You bet."

Seemed he wasn't the only liar in the car. She was quiet on the short drive home, quiet as they went into the Opera House, quiet as she unlocked her door. "Do you want to come in?" she asked.

He leaned against the door frame, frowning. "Is everything okay, Faith?"

"Sure. Of course it is." Her eyes didn't meet his.

"Seems like something's the matter."

"Nope."

Something was very much the matter. "You feel okay?"

"I'm fine."

"Have you been taking your meds?" he asked.

"Yes. Want to count them and make sure?" Her voice was sharp.

"No." He looked at her another minute, ignoring Blue, who was nosing his leg for a little lovin'. "Maybe I should stay at my place tonight," Levi said.

"Okay. Thanks for coming tonight. Um…sleep well." She kissed him on the cheek and closed the door.

Well, shit. He'd screwed up somehow. Maybe he hadn't talked enough. Maybe…he hated this next thought…maybe Jeremy was on her mind. Obviously, Jeremy wasn't exactly a rival, but he was still her buddy, still completely at home with her family, still here if she wanted to fall asleep on his couch. Love at first sight, love of her life. You only get one of those, according to John Holland.

He went into his own apartment, which suddenly seemed very bland. Sure, he had his own family photos here and there. But he didn't collect little treasures the way Faith did, didn't keep too much from the past. He was a guy, after all.

A guy who was in trouble with the woman across the hall for reasons unclear to him. She'd pried some information out of him the other day up at the barn, had seemed intent on digging, and now she kinda wasn't talking to him.

Time to bake cookies.

When Levi was little, most of their desserts had come from a Hostess box, especially after Sarah arrived on the scene. But his mother had this one recipe, and she could whip a batch together in seconds, it had seemed. Levi's job had been to put the ingredients on the table, then stand back and watch, and maybe lick off the rubber spatula.

He took out the flour, the squares of unsweetened chocolate, sugar, vanilla. Eggs from the fridge.

A knock came on the door. He answered it, and there she was. "Hey," he said.

"What do you know about my mom's accident?" she asked.

He blinked. "Uh…you want to come in, Faith?" She did. "Sit down," he said, and she obeyed, perching stiffly in the middle of the couch cushion, like she'd forgotten what a couch was for. He sat down in the chair opposite from her and leaned forward.

She didn't look right.

"So did you ever hear anything about it?" she asked.

"Sure. The guidance counselor talked to us."

"What did you hear?"

"Uh…he said you guys were T-boned, and your mom died right away."

"Is that all?" Her eyes were bleak.

Levi ran a hand through his hair. "You had a seizure, right? You didn't remember anything. The fire department had to cut you out. We weren't supposed to bring it up."

She nodded. Kept nodding. Hadn't really looked at him since she came in.

"Faith, are you okay? You don't seem—"

"I didn't have a seizure. I lied about that. I told my father I did because I didn't want to tell him the truth."

The oven ticked as it preheated. "And what was that?" Levi asked.

"I made her crash."

Those four words seemed to be torn out of the deepest part of her. Her face didn't change, but her eyes were desolate.

"How'd you do that?" he asked as gently as he knew how.

"I was mad," she said. "I didn't want to talk to her, and she turned around, because I was sitting in the back. She asked me if I was okay, and I didn't answer." Faith swallowed. "She thought I was about to have a seizure, because I space out before one, as you know. So I let her think that. And then we got hit." Her face was white, her bloodless hands knotted hard in her lap.

"Faith, you can't—"

"She wanted to leave my father."

Ah, shit. "She told you that?"

"Yes."

That wasn't how Levi remembered Constance Holland from the few times he'd seen her. She'd seemed to be the Disney Channel's version of a mom—pretty, happy, wisecracking and capable.

Or maybe he was confusing her with his mom.

"That's why I didn't answer her." Faith's voice was hollow. "She kept talking about how it'd been a mistake to get married so young, how she always wanted to do more but got stuck with us. I let her think I was about to have a seizure so she'd stop talking. And then we got hit."

The look on her face was like an iron spike going through his heart. "Faith, you were a kid. You can't blame yourself."

"I knew what I was doing. I wanted her to feel guilty."

"That's not the same as wanting her to die."

She flinched. "No. But I'm responsible all the same. When I came back here in September, I thought if I found Dad someone else, maybe I could make up for it. But I haven't. My dad worships her memory—Jack and my sisters do, too."

Yeah, that seemed true. "You never told anyone?"

"No! I… When my father came to the hospital, he was so…broken, and I was afraid he'd stop loving me if he knew. So I lied." She dropped her gaze to the floor. "I just wanted you to know. I don't want you to tell me how it wasn't really my fault. I know what I did."

He didn't know what to say to that.

"You can't say anything," she said, her voice level now, and somehow that hurt his heart more than ever. "I don't want them to know how she really felt."

Levi ran his hand through his hair again. "Why don't you stay here tonight?"

"I'm gonna go home, actually," she said. "But thank you."

"Please stay."

"No, thanks. I'll...I'll see you around." She stood up, and he did, too, pulling her into a hug. She felt cold and brittle, Faith who was all soft and sweet and warm.

"Stay," he said one more time.

"I'm fine," she said. "See you tomorrow, maybe." And with that, she opened his door and went across to her own apartment.

The quiet of the night settled around him.

Faith's mother had been dead for twenty years. That was a long time to keep a secret.

The cookies would have to wait. Levi turned off the oven, grabbed his car keys and headed for the police station.

CHAPTER TWENTY-FOUR

THE DAY HER MOTHER had died had been utterly normal except that Faith had needed shoes.

Faith had always loved being the baby of the family. In exchange for all the fun things the rest of them had done before she was born or when she was tiny, it seemed only fair that she got special treatment. She knew her family viewed her as vaguely cute but somewhat useless. Mom still never asked *her* to start supper…only Honor could do that (and had been doing it for years, as her older sister liked to point out). Jack was in college learning how to make wine and already knew cool stuff like how to fix the harvester and clean the thresher. Prudence was a grown-up, married and everything.

So Faith got to be the cute one. Her parents' attention was spread thin, and Faith used it to get away with stuff…not being a straight-A student, for example, unlike her siblings. Not going to bed on time, because who really noticed? She didn't have to eat all her vegetables, because with four kids over seventeen years, her parents were a little weary of enforcing the rules.

Her epilepsy got her the kind of attention she *didn't* want—the panicky eyes from Dad, the short, sharp orders from Mom. She'd take some benign neglect any day.

But the day she needed shoes would be, she hoped,

one of those rare and special times when she and Mom could do something, just the two of them, like those cloudy, lovely memories from when everyone else was in school, and Faith was her mom's little shadow. Maybe they'd stretch the day out, get some ice cream at the cute place on Market Street.

Instead, Mom had been in a *mood*. "Don't think you can try on every pair in the store, Faith," she said as they pulled into the parking lot. "I have a thousand things to do today. Why you couldn't have told me you needed these last week, when I had to come to this exact same place when Jack was home…"

And so Faith had ended up with a pair of not-bad sneakers, though she hadn't been one hundred percent sure she wanted those and not the cute Reeboks with the pink laces. No time for ice cream, just back in the car. "You can sit in the front, you know," Mom said, a trifle impatiently.

"That's okay," Faith said. She'd gotten in back automatically, accustomed to being low man on the totem pole when it came to the shotgun seat. It was a move that saved her life, the firefighters would say later.

But still, Faith had new sneakers. She always felt as if she could run faster in new sneakers, and gym was on Tuesday. Jessica Dunn was the fastest girl in their class and often made fun of the way Faith ran, and wouldn't it be nice to run faster than Jessica, just once? Not that it was possible, but still…just once.

"Make sure you see the world before you settle down, Faith," Mom said abruptly from the front seat. "I told Prudence the same thing, and did she listen? No. You get married young, and your options are severely limited."

Faith frowned. Why would her mother say something

like *that?* Pru and Carl were so cute. Plus, Faith was an aunt already. Everyone at school had been jealous. Possibly even Jessica Dunn.

Mom glanced in the rearview mirror. "You should see the world when you still can. This is a huge country, though if you asked anyone in the Holland family, they'd probably tell you the earth falls into an abyss if you cross the county line."

"I love it here," Faith objected. She took a new shoe out of the box and stroked the pure white shoelace. Should've gotten pink. Or maybe not. Maybe pink was babyish.

"Yeah, well, you've never seen anywhere else, have you?" Mom asked. "There are other places worth seeing, too, you know. Pru would have to be dragged kicking and screaming off the vineyard, and your brother's already a lost cause, but you and Honor don't have to stay."

Mom's voice went on and on and on. And the thing was, Faith *wanted* to stay. Where else was better than home? She'd already been to New York City on a field trip just a month ago. Levi Cooper and Jessica had gotten caught kissing in the back of the bus, which was bad enough (Faith still played with dolls…kissing? Gross!). The city had been so loud and hot; Manningsport seemed like heaven when they got back.

"There are days when all I can do is think about how nice it'd be to live somewhere else. Wouldn't it be great to live in a city? Seattle, Chicago, San Francisco, all these places I've never even seen. And what does your father do? He laughs when I talk about it." Mom's voice was inescapable. "That's why you should live a little before you settle down. You'll regret it otherwise."

Faith looked out the window. Daddy was perfect.

He never seemed impatient or short. He always said Faith was his princess. And he loved Mom! He picked her flowers! Faith turned her eyes to the scenery outside, where black-and-white cows gazed placidly at their minivan. Leave here? Never.

Mom glanced in the rearview mirror. "It could be just us three," she said. "You, me and Honor. Girl power."

White-hot anger flashed like lightning. Oh, so now Mom was leaving? Fine! They'd be fine without her! And girl power? Is that what she called *divorce?*

"Why are you so quiet?" her mother asked, as if she didn't know.

Faith didn't look away from the fields. No, she didn't think she would answer at all. Mom could suck it up.

"Honey, are you okay?" *Yeah, that's right. Call me honey,* Faith thought. *You should, after all that mean talk.* From the corner of her eye, Faith saw Mom put a hand on the back of the passenger seat to turn around more fully. "Faith?"

Nope. Not gonna answer.

And then there was a slam, so loud it was like an explosion, and they were spinning, and the ground wasn't where it was supposed to be, and the *noise,* the screeching and crashing, they were tumbling so fast it felt like she was in a dryer, arms and legs flopping helplessly, the seat belt hurt, grinding into her shoulder, her new shoe hit her in the side of the face, and God, they were still rolling and bouncing, someone stop that horrible noise, the grinding and crunching, it was *awful.*

And then they stopped, and the noise stopped, too, except a hissing sound and someone's gasping little screams. She was dizzy, on an angle. There was a tree in the car with her, a chunk of the bark gouged out.

They'd been in an accident. That was it.

She was the one making the noise. Faith wrestled her mouth closed and stopped those awful little scream-gasps. Was she still in the backseat? Because the car didn't look like the car anymore, bent around her, torn upholstery, wires and broken glass everywhere. It was crushed around her; the place where her seat belt fastened hidden in twisted metal. She seemed to be on her side, and her chest hurt. She could move her legs, if not see her feet. The door handle was against the ground.

She couldn't get out, in other words.

"Mommy?" Her voice was weak and high. "Mommy?" There was no answer.

"Mom? Are you okay?"

No answer. No sounds at all, not even moaning. "Oh, Mommy, please, please," she heard herself say, and suddenly she was shivering and damp and could smell pee. She'd wet herself.

There. There was her mother's hair, almost the same color as Faith's, a few feet in front of her face, just out of reach. Faith's fingers strained, but the car was trapping her. "Mommy," she whispered, and she didn't like the sound of her voice, not one bit.

Then she looked out the broken windshield, and *there* was her mother, standing in the field, completely unharmed, smiling and beautiful. Thank *God*.

"Mommy, get me out!" she called, trying to pull herself from the mess of the car, tugging on her seat belt strap.

"Don't worry, sweetie," her mother said. "You're fine. I love you!"

Then she blew Faith a kiss. Why was she so happy when they'd just been in an accident? Faith looked back at the hair in the front seat.

It was still there.

When she looked out the windshield again, the field was empty, and Faith understood in a sudden, wrenching tear.

Her mother was dead.

"Mommy," she cried, her voice so thin and ruined. "Oh, Mommy, I'm sorry."

She stopped trying to get out.

No one came to help. For a very long time, the only sound was the birds and the wind. Horribly, the clock on the dashboard still worked, so Faith was all too aware of the time that passed. Fifty-two minutes before someone called out, "Are you okay? Hello? Can you hear me?" She wasn't able to answer, because then she'd have to give the news that Mommy had died. Sixty-three minutes before she heard sirens in the distance. Sixty-eight minutes before Mr. Stoakes from the candy store appeared in the windshield, strange in his firefighter clothes, and said, "Oh, God, no. Oh, no," before he saw Faith looking at him.

Seventy-four minutes when they started cutting with the noisy tools, yelling reassuringly to her, their faces telling the true story.

A hundred and fifteen minutes before they lifted Faith out.

Two hours with her mother's body, two hours spent shivering and sobbing, fading in and out of shock. Two hours of whispering how sorry she was.

When she saw her father's face at the hospital, when she saw how old he'd become since morning, when he'd held her bruised hand, she told him she'd had a seizure and didn't remember anything.

Better for him to think that than to know his daughter was a murderer.

THREE O'CLOCK IN THE morning. The loneliest time, even with an eighty pound Golden retriever taking up two-thirds of the bed.

Since telling Levi, a strange, heavy fog seemed to be pressing on Faith's brain. For twenty years, she'd tried to avoid indulging in memories of her mother, feeling almost like she didn't deserve them. But tonight, images of her mother, good and bad, flickered through her brain like a faulty movie—Mom in the kitchen, ferociously scrubbing the sink after dinner, mad at someone. At bath time, when Faith was really small, laughing as she draped the face cloth on Faith's head. Chastising her over a teacher's comment about Faith being inattentive in class. Clapping for her as she rode her bike around the giant tree in the front yard for the first time. Sitting on the couch, reading to Honor, even though Honor could read by herself. Crying as she folded Jack's laundry before he left for college. Holding baby Ned in the hospital after he was born, her eyes so shiny as she smiled at Pru.

Kissing Dad in the back hall, then laughing, telling him he needed a shower.

Had Mom really been so unhappy? Had she really viewed her life as a mistake, filled with regret and bitterness?

It never seemed that way.

Suddenly, Blue leaped off the bed and raced out of the room. She heard his toenails clicking on the floor, then his bark. Feeling old and weary, Faith pushed the covers back and got out of bed.

A quiet knock came at the door.

It was Levi. "Got a second?" he asked, as if it wasn't the middle of the night.

She looked at him a long minute, then held the door

open. He had a file and a laptop, but her brain felt too heavy to ask why.

"Have a seat," he said, turning on the light that hung over the table, making her squint.

She sat. "Would you like coffee or anything?" she asked, her voice odd to her own ears.

"No, thank you." How oddly formal they were being. He sat down, too, and put the folder on the table, then tapped it, looking at her solemnly. "This is your mother's accident report. It was in the storage place out on Route 54. Took me a little while to find it."

She glanced at it. "I don't…I don't want to look at that, Levi."

"You might." He looked at her, then ran his hand through his hair, frowning.

Blue put his head in her lap and wagged, and she petted his beautiful head, not looking at Levi.

"When you said you were responsible…why did you think that? The guy who hit you, Kevin Hart. He ran the stop sign. So why was the accident your fault?"

She looked at him, oddly wary. His gaze was steady, that slight frown creasing his forehead. "Because," she said, "my mother would've seen him coming if she hadn't been looking at me, and she could've stopped or swerved."

Mom would've swerved into the field, where the cows chewed so placidly. Constance would've cursed at the damage to the minivan, and by supper, it would've become a great story, and Faith could have told her part, about bouncing over the field, the cows scattering and mooing, and everyone would have laughed and patted her hand and not expected her to do anything for cleanup, because she'd had a scare, even though everything had turned out just fine.

It was a scenario she'd pictured ten thousand times. She had a dozen others that ended about the same way.

Levi nodded. "That's what I figured you thought. And it's a logical assumption." He paused. "You remember Chief Griggs?"

"Yes."

"He wasn't the most thorough guy."

She didn't say anything.

"I looked at the report, and it says, right here, *mother distracted by sick child.* But here's the thing. I'd bet that she could tell if you were really about to have a seizure or not. You ever think about that?"

Faith frowned. "No. I mean, you might be right about that, but…no, I'm pretty sure she thought I was."

"Well, I never could fool my mom, and I tried really hard. Anyway, even if she thought you were having a seizure, she'd know that she couldn't help you. There's nothing you can do for a person who's seizing, and you were buckled in, nice and safe. Right?"

"Right."

"So I wondered, even if your mom did think you were having a seizure, would she take her eyes off the road for very long?"

Faith pushed away the memory of her mother's face, peering back at her in those last seconds. "She did, Levi. She looked back at me."

"Right. And what did she say?"

Faith took a deep breath, the air feeling heavy and thick. "She asked if I was okay."

"Do you remember exactly?" Levi looked at his watch.

Of course she did. "She said, 'Honey, are you okay? Faith?'"

Constance Holland's last words. Trying to take care

of her daughter, checking on the child whose selfishness would kill her. It felt as if a knife was stuck in Faith's throat.

"So maybe three, five seconds to say that?"

"I guess."

"I took the report out to the accident site," he said.

A vision of that maple tree, that field, flared in her mind. It was horribly intimate, knowing Levi had been there, that place where she'd sat in her own urine, whimpering for her mother. In all these years, Faith had never gone back to that spot.

"Here's the thing, Faith." He hesitated. "Like I said, Chief Griggs wasn't the most thorough guy. He knew Kevin Hart had run the stop sign, figured your mom was distracted by you and that's why she didn't see him coming. And that was the end of the investigation."

"Do you have a point, Levi?" She was so tired.

"Just…just bear with me. It's a good point. Well worth hearing. Okay?"

She nodded.

He opened up the laptop and hit a key. "I took some measurements based on what was in the report. Things like skid marks at the point of impact and how far your car rolled before it hit the tree, the weight of your car, the weight of Kevin Hart's." He turned the screen so she could see. "This is an accident reconstruction program. Obviously, Chief Griggs didn't have it twenty years ago."

A blade of remembered fear sawed through her. There was the intersection, shown in stark lines. Two car icons, one red and one blue, touched each other. The red icon was bigger, pointing north on the road labeled Hummel Brook. That would be her mom's Dodge Caravan.

Levi pointed to the screen. "Based on the skid marks, she was doing about forty, and Kevin was doing sixty-five. Not forty-five, like Kevin said. But the chief didn't do the math. Kevin left twenty feet of skid marks and sent your car rolling out to that tree. That puts him at about sixty-five."

The fact that Faith had been awake for twenty-one hours, and had told Levi her damning secret, was catching up with her. His words didn't quite make sense to her fuzzy brain. Even her hand didn't seem capable of petting Blue anymore. Her dog flopped on the floor, his muzzle on her bare foot.

"Estimating that it took four seconds for your mom to look back at you—which is a lot of time to take your eyes off the road, but assuming your memory is right—that puts you guys here." He hit a key, and the red car moved back.

Faith looked at the screen with her burning eyes. It was farther away from the intersection than she would've guessed.

"That's two hundred and thirty-five feet away from the intersection. And Kevin Hart, doing sixty-five, ends up here, almost four hundred feet away from the intersection." Levi clicked another key, and the blue car moved back, quite far, on Lancaster Road. "Now you can't forget these." He clicked another button, and round green objects popped up along Lancaster Road.

"What are those?" Faith asked.

"Maple trees. There are—and were—maple trees all along that stretch."

The accident was on June fourth. The trees would've been fully leafed out by then. No doubt about it.

Faith's heart was suddenly thudding fast and hard.

She wiped her palms against her pajama pants and leaned forward, her fatigue forgotten.

Levi looked at her, his brows drawn. "You okay?"

She nodded.

"Good. Now watch this." He clicked another key, and the cars advanced toward the intersection, stopping just before it. "According to you, your mom never saw him coming, because she was looking at you."

"Right."

"But she did see him, Faith. When the chief heard you had a seizure, he just figured she was distracted. He didn't do the math."

It was getting hard to breathe. "I—I don't follow."

"She couldn't have seen Kevin Hart until she was almost in the intersection, because he was doing sixty-five, tearing down the road. And the trees blocked her line of sight. But she couldn't have been looking back at you, because there were skid marks, Faith." He paused, letting the words sink in. "So she did see him. If she'd been looking at you, she wouldn't have hit the brakes."

She never saw it coming. Those words, meant to comfort, had haunted Faith for nineteen and a half years.

Faith stared at the screen. Even here, even with the screen resembling a game more than a fatal car accident, it looked horribly ominous. Her brain couldn't quite compute what Levi was saying. "I—I don't understand."

"She did see him, but it was too late…not because of anything you did or didn't do, but because the trees blocked her view, and because Kevin was coming so fast."

He covered her hand with his, and the warmth made her realize how cold she was. "But I remember…I remember her looking at me, not at the road."

"People's memories are generally unreliable after an

accident. You were looking out the window. You must not have seen her turn back."

The blood seemed to drain into her knees, and a strange floating sensation enveloped her head. "So you're saying it wasn't my fault?"

"Correct."

How could that be true? *Everyone* thought she had some role in the accident. Everyone. Her father had told her hundreds of times it wasn't her fault…but he hadn't known what really happened.

Levi did.

He was still looking at her, his green eyes patient, waiting.

"Are you sure?" she asked.

"Yes."

The news was so enormous, it had to creep slowly into her heart.

Could Levi be right? He just looked at her, solid and patient, a slight frown between his eyes, waiting for the news to register.

"Are you really, really positive?" she whispered.

"Yes."

"So…it wasn't my fault, and it wasn't hers, either."

"That's right."

"Really? You're not saying this just to be nice?"

"I never say anything just to be nice."

He was telling the truth.

Faith pushed back from the table and turned her back on the laptop and on Levi. Went to the bookcase and grabbed the photo of her family…of her mom. No, no, that was too much. She picked up the little pink rock and closed it in her fist, leaning against the window-sill, looking out over the dark street, the quartz digging hard into her palm.

It was weird, then, because she was crying, tears pouring out of her eyes, but her mind was still reeling, as if she'd been hit in the head. Her chest jerked with squeaky little noises, but she couldn't quite catch hold of that news.

Levi was there, then, pulling her against his broad, hard chest, wrapping his arms around her, standing behind her like a rock, and just held her close. She brought one of his hands to her lips and kissed it.

She hadn't killed her mother.

That had to be the truth, because Levi would never, never lie to her.

CHAPTER TWENTY-FIVE

FAITH COULD CRY for a very long time, Levi noted. He was thinking it might be time for a tranquilizer. Unfortunately, he didn't have any.

He'd led her across the hall to his place, because, well, frankly, he had no idea what to do with a sobbing woman, and being on his own turf might help him a little. He got a box of tissues and sat her on the couch, where she continued to cry, burying her face in her dog's neck, sobbing.

Those noises were like shrapnel to the heart, recalling the other time he'd been helpless to comfort her— her wedding day. "Want me to make you something to eat?" he asked, setting down a box of tissues. She shook her head. "A beer? Wine? Whiskey, maybe?"

Another head shake. She grabbed a tissue, blew her nose and kept crying.

Well, hell. He patted her shoulder awkwardly, and she kissed his hand again. Blue put his paw against Levi's leg and licked his hand as well, then put his muzzle on Faith's lap.

A bath. Women liked baths, right? A bath it would be. Also, he could get away from the crying for a second, because it made his insides hurt. His bathroom was needlessly enormous, and it did have a pretty amazing bathtub. Last time he'd used it, Blue had been the beneficiary of all those water jets. He turned on the knobs, checked the temp. Went into his sister's bathroom and found some stuff under the sink—vanilla almond bubble bath, like Faith needed anything to make her smell any more edible—and went back to his bathroom and dumped in about half the bottle. Checked on Faith, who now had a pillow clutched to her stomach.

"Come on, Holland. Bath time."

She looked up at him, so reminiscent of that little ghost who'd come back to sixth grade, that his heart gave a hard tug.

"Levi," she began.

"No talking," he said. He didn't need to hear it, and she didn't have to say it.

A half hour later, Faith's sobs had stopped, though the tears continued to pour out, almost like she didn't notice, starring her eyelashes. Even so, she looked like an old-school Playboy bunny, albeit a very sad one, her hair piled sloppily on her head, bubbles up to her neck. She'd accepted the glass of wine he'd pressed into her hand and was putting a fair dent in it. Her dog sat with his chin on the edge of the tub, slightly wary either of his beloved's mood or the memory of his own stint in this tub.

Levi sat on a little footstool, watching her. Those tears made him want to beat someone up. He wanted to drive to the Holland house, pound on the door and grab John by his shirt and shake him. How could she have thought this accident was her fault all these years? What kind of father lets his twelve-year-old think that she in any way was responsible for a fatal car accident? How could he miss the fact that she felt that way? Didn't anyone *talk* to her? How could she have kept that in for so damn long? Walking around, thinking of yourself as the reason your mother died, carrying that kind of guilt from the age of twelve on… It wasn't right. It wasn't fair.

He handed her another tissue. This was his job of the night, apparently. She blew her nose, then gave him a bleary smile.

"You've been really great tonight, Levi." Her voice wobbled.

"Good." He paused. "Truth is, I have no idea what the hell to do here."

For some reason, this caused a smile, followed by a fresh stream of tears. "Well, you've been wonderful. I'll never be able to thank you for what you did." Her face creased like she was about to start sobbing again, but instead, she rallied and took another swallow of wine.

For some reason, her words made him feel like utter crap.

All those years played back in his head. He remembered that girl from sixth grade and now saw, clear as day, that there was something darker, something heavier about her than simply a girl who'd lost her mom. Saw her being Princess Super-Cute on all those committees that no one else joined, Environment and World Justice and all that crap, maybe trying to make up for something, maybe trying to avoid the secret she carried. Maybe just trying to avoid going home.

Saw her with Jeremy, grabbing on to him like a lifeline, because maybe that's what he'd been. Marry the perfect boy next door, join your vineyards together, somehow create a kind of absolution.

No wonder she hadn't looked a little deeper at Jeremy. He'd been her redemption.

"You want to come in?"

The question startled him. "In the tub?"

She gave a little smile. "Yes."

He paused. "Sure," he said. Pulled off his shirt, then unlaced his boots and pulled them off, followed by his jeans and boxers, then got in behind her, her wet, slick skin sliding against his.

Now is not the time, his conscience barked. *She's in mourning. Or something.*

Well. Faith wasn't crying now. She was quiet, her head against his shoulder.

"You doing okay?" he asked, slipping his arms around her. Impossible to avoid touching breast, so why bother trying?

"Mmm-hmm."

He kissed her hair. Wasn't sure what else to do. She relaxed into him, all soft, warm, wet sweetness. The dog eyeballed him like a disapproving chaperone. Right. Levi was supposed to be comforting Faith, not lusting after her.

She slid around so she was lying on him, causing some water to slosh over the side, and the lust factor shot up into the red zone. Her dog lapped at the puddle on the floor.

"Faith," he said, and his voice was rough, "I can't believe you've thought the wrong thing for so long. Someone should've told you it wasn't your fault."

"Oh, they did," she said. "But they...well, I told them I had a seizure. That's what they meant. It wasn't my fault because I couldn't help having a seizure. And I just couldn't tell them I didn't."

"You should've told the truth, honey."

"No," she said. "I couldn't break my father's heart even more. 'Daddy, I'm sorry Mommy's dead, but she was going to leave you.' No. I couldn't do that." Her eyes were full again.

"I hate this crying stuff," he whispered, and for some

reason, it made her laugh, even as the tears slid down her cheeks.

"Well, take me to bed and make love to me, and maybe I'll stop."

She was unpredictable, he'd give her that. "You sure?" he asked. "I could bake you cookies instead."

"You can bake me cookies after."

"All right then. You're the boss." He kissed her, that soft, pink mouth, then wrapped her legs around him and stood, keeping his mouth on hers, and lifted her out of the tub, resulting in a great rush of water and suds. The dog barked. "Get out, Blue," Levi muttered against her mouth.

Her smiling mouth.

If her tears hurt his chest, for some reason, her smile made it ache all the more.

LATER, WHEN HE'D FOLLOWED her orders and made love to her till she was even pinker and sweeter and her cheek was against his chest, his own heart slowly returning to a normal pace, Levi was aware that something had changed.

When he'd seen that empty, hollow look in her eyes, when she'd looked far older than her years, something had built in him, a sense of urgency and protection and helplessness. For twenty years, she'd been carrying this secret to protect her family, and no one had seen the cost.

He remembered how that little bad-girl streak in her had evaporated after her mother's death. Remembered how he'd judged her as a little shallow, a little boring, when the truth was, maybe he should've looked a little harder, too.

He kissed her hair and held her closer.

"I love you," she said.

He froze. Not that he was moving to begin with, but it seemed his heart and lungs stopped for a good ten seconds.

Now was the time when he should say something back.

It was just that the words didn't come. There were a lot of feelings churning around, but actually putting a name to them…that was harder. He raised his head, expecting to see her waiting for his response, but instead her eyes were closed, that same little smile from before playing on her lips.

"One of these days," she said, her voice drowsy, "you're going to tell me you gave me that little pink rock."

Well, holy crap.

"I used to wonder who gave it to me," she murmured. "Would've bet the farm it was anyone but you." She opened her eyes, looked at him for a second, then closed them again. "But now I see that it couldn't have been anyone else."

Another beat passed. Then he kissed her forehead. "Go to sleep, Holland," he said, then watched as she did just that.

Then, when he was sure she wouldn't wake up, he got up and baked those cookies.

It wasn't like he'd be able to sleep after that, anyway.

CHAPTER TWENTY-SIX

A WEEK LATER, FAITH WAS fairly sure that dropping the L-bomb had been a mistake.

She and Levi hadn't talked much since the night he'd…well, changed her life. That revelation was still so stunning, Faith wasn't sure what to do with it. But the knot that had been in her heart was loosening. Whether or not she should talk to her dad or say something to her sibs, Faith didn't know, but that charred spot in her soul, the one that had always told her she didn't deserve what other people did…it was healing over, pink and new and fragile.

As for Levi and her… Sigh. He'd had to work—a lot, it seemed, even more than before. He visited his sister and fixed something in her car. On the two nights Faith and he had spent together, he'd been called away once and had to take two lengthy phone calls for something or another. She and Levi themselves had talked about very little, just ended up in bed where, admittedly, things felt much clearer. Actions, maybe, if not words.

One night after nooky, she'd told him about walking in on her grandparents the other day, when they were both in the downstairs bedroom; for the life of her, she thought they were getting it on, Goggy saying, "No, it goes in *there,* not like that! Don't you remember? You don't like it there! It's never been comfortable that way!

Push it to the left a little!" But no, turned out they had simply been moving Pops's bed, thank you, Jesus.

Levi had laughed till there'd been tears in his eyes, and the sound had been so wonderful, Faith had wondered how she could bottle it.

But it hadn't escaped her notice that Levi had yet to say "I love you" back.

A clear-cut case of man panic.

And sure, it was a lot—it almost made her cringe when she thought of that night, of telling him her secret, of her Olympic bout of weeping thereafter, followed up by her declaration of love and the assertion that he'd been the one to put the pink quartz rock in her locker all those years ago. It would've been nice, she thought as she made her way to O'Rourke's, if she could've quit while she was ahead. But it was as if once the cork had been popped, she hadn't been able to keep anything in.

But Levi kept showing up. Maybe it wasn't as bad as she thought.

The barn was completely done, the library courtyard had been dedicated, and Faith was finishing up two other jobs. Snow had fallen three times already, and the air was cold and damp. Thanksgiving was coming, and Faith wondered if it would feel different now, now that she knew she hadn't caused the accident, if that aching, omnipresent regret would gentle to simply missing her mom.

Clearly, she didn't want to tell her father that his wife's last words to her had been to hint about leaving him. But maybe if Dad—and Pru, Jack and Honor—knew that it hadn't been a seizure that had caused the accident…maybe something would shift. What, Faith didn't know. She would've talked to Levi about it…but Levi didn't seem up for talking these days. He'd told her he'd be working late tonight, so she was meeting Jeremy for dinner. That would be nice.

She had six jobs lined up for spring—four private homes, two vineyards over on Seneca, and she was pitching to redo the park over by the glass museum in Corning. Already, local landscapers were calling, wanting to introduce themselves and show her their work.

She'd thought about splitting her time between San Francisco and here, but who was she kidding? She was back in the heart of her family. She had her dad, who adored her. Her grandparents, who wouldn't be alive forever. Her niece and nephew, her sisters and Jack, Colleen and Connor. Faith was even thinking of joining the volunteer fire department, since Gerard kept heckling her about it. She had this new phase of friendship with Jeremy, who was loyal and generous and funny. She had the steep and beautiful hills, the cold, deep lakes with their infinite secrets, the quiet woods and gushing waterfalls. She was a Holland, and she belonged to this land.

And she had Levi, who might admit he loved her back.

Why go back when all she'd ever wanted was to stay?

That being said, the architect who'd given Faith her first job in San Francisco had just come through with a job to design a common area for a big condo complex in Oakland. Lots of land, lots of potential. He'd sent her some photos, and right away, ideas had started forming. She could take the job, which paid very well, go back to the city by the bay, pack up her apartment, sell what she didn't want, say goodbye to her friends.

Being away, making something of herself without the goodwill generated by the Holland name, being alone… it had made her stronger. Mom had been right.

But it was time to come home.

So she'd go to San Francisco, end things on a strong note, and then let her heart come back home.

Faith pushed open the door, the heat of the pub most welcome. A two-minute walk, but already her feet were like blocks of ice.

"Hey," Connor greeted her as he pulled a Guinness. "My sister's looking for you."

As the words left his mouth, his twin pounced, dragging Faith into the bathroom.

"And hello to you, too," Faith said. "What are you—"

"This thing with you and Levi…how serious is that?" Colleen asked, her face unsmiling. "You totally smitten?"

"Oh. Yes, actually. Why?"

Colleen sighed. "He's here. With his ex-wife."

Faith felt her mouth drop open. "Wow."

"Yeah. They're in a booth in the back."

"Oh." Faith glimpsed her face in the mirror. Not reassuring. "That's…sucky."

"Figured you should have some warning."

"Thanks."

Well, nothing to do but go out there. It wasn't like she was going to climb out the bathroom window. Not this time.

But she could fix her hair. And borrow some of Colleen's makeup.

AT FIVE-THIRTY THAT EVENING, Levi had been struggling through some paperwork that was endless, repetitious and irritating when the station door opened, and in came Nina Rodriguez, who not so long ago had been Nina Rodriguez-Cooper.

"Hey, stranger," she said with a big smile.

Gorgeous. That was his first thought. Clad in the same skin-tight clothes she always wore if she wasn't in uniform…and why not? She had a killer body.

His second thought was *What the hell?* because really, a little warning might've been nice.

"Do you have a complaint you'd like to register?" Emmaline said, not bothering to keep the bitchery from her voice. She might be a pain in the ass, but she was loyal.

Nina ignored her. She was good at that. "You gonna stop staring and say hi?" she asked Levi, raising a perfect eyebrow and leaning against Everett's desk. Ev, too, had frozen, his eyes on Nina's ass, which, granted, was one of the seven wonders of the natural world, right up there with Faith's rack.

"Hi," he said.

"Hi," Everett echoed.

Nina smiled and pulled up a chair. "I was in the area. Figured I'd stop in and see my favorite cop."

He caught a whiff of the stuff she used in the shower, a musky, flowery scent, and waited for the surge of anger. This was, after all, the woman who'd left him with a hug and a cheery wave after three months of marriage, making him look like an idiot, for one, and breaking his heart for another. Two things he hated.

The anger didn't come. "How've you been?" he asked.

She tipped her head. "I've been fine," she said.

"Glad to hear it," Everett said, his voice faint.

Nina glanced at Ev with that beautiful-woman smile, the kind that said *In your dreams, mister.* Everett only closed his mouth to swallow.

"So we gonna air our dirty laundry here?" Nina

asked. "Or are you gonna buy a girl a drink? The best thing about this town was that little bar, as I recall."

And so Levi stood up, Everett watching in a trance, Emmaline hissing, and took his ex-wife across the square to O'Rourke's. Ignored Colleen's look, as well as the fact that three members of the town council fell silent upon his arrival. Victor Iskin waved, his latest taxidermied cat on the bar in front of him, poised as if to leap while Lorena Creech admired it.

"Town hasn't changed much," Nina observed.

"Nope." He took her to the farthest booth in the back and sat down.

He was flustered. Shitty feeling, that.

They ordered a couple of beers and the nachos grande, which Nina recalled with great enthusiasm. Colleen took their order with another pointed look, kicking Levi's ankle. Nina talked about generic things—the traffic in Scranton, the cow in the road in Sayre. The nachos and beers came, delivered with another kick from Colleen.

And then Nina started with the war talk, which was what soldiers did when they reunited. Levi waited for her to get to whatever point she was here to make. He knew from experience there was no changing of the subject with Nina; she had an agenda, and trying to rush her only drew things out.

Then, finally, after reminding him of their common past in as entertaining a way as possible, she got personal.

"So how's Sarah?"

"She's good," Levi said. Didn't mention the fact that she could've used a sister-in-law this past year or so.

"Is she in college?"

He nodded. "Over at Hobart."

"Good for her! And your mom? Still hates me, I'm sure."

"My mom died a couple months after you left."

Nina's face changed. "Oh, Levi, you ass. Why didn't you tell me? I would've come for the funeral!" She reached across the table and gripped his hand.

"I didn't really see the point," he said, extracting his hand.

She sat back in her seat, her big brown eyes growing hot. "The point, idiot, is that just because our timing was off doesn't mean I don't care about you. Or Sarah."

"Gee. Thanks."

She shook her head. "Man. You are totally furious, aren't you?"

He declined to answer. Looked at her instead. It always made Faith irritable when he stared at her; hopefully it would work on Nina, too.

It didn't. She took a sip of her beer, smiling a little, her eyes still on his.

She was the type of woman who could seduce in seconds. A regular…what was that Greek chick's name? The one who caused the slaughter of an entire city? That one.

Levi took a careful breath. "So why the visit?"

"Never could fool you, could I?" she said.

"Actually, I'd say you fooled me pretty good," he answered calmly.

"Okay. Fine. Let's put it on the table." She leaned forward, boobs practically tumbling out of her skimpy shirt onto the nachos. "This last tour was it for me. I was thinking about you. Thought maybe we could give it another shot."

He waited until Nina huffed and rolled her eyes.

"Look, moron," she said, and he felt an unwilling

tug of affection for her total lack of sentimentality. "We were good together. It was the timing that sucked. I wasn't ready to settle down two years ago. I am now. Simple as that."

"Seems like you're leaving a lot out of that equation."

"So why don't you fill me in?" she said with another sex goddess smile.

I loved you. You left me. You left me when I wanted to have a family with you, when I thought we were happy, and you walked away like I was nothing.

But the feelings behind those words were old and tired, and not worth putting into words.

"Hi."

It was Faith. She looked at both of them, then stuck out her hand. "Faith Holland."

"Hi." Nina took her hand. "Wait a sec, Faith Holland? Holy shit! Jeremy's ex, right?"

"That's right." She looked at Levi, her cheeks flushing. Otherwise, her expression was calm.

"Faith," Levi said, "This is my ex-wife, Nina. Nina, Faith is my…" He looked at Faith, hoping she'd supply the appropriate word.

"Neighbor," Faith said.

Women. You never knew what they were up to.

"Holy crap!" came another voice. "Nina?"

"Jeremy!" Nina jumped up and hugged him hard, like they were old pals. "It's so great so see you!"

Jeremy, Levi was pleased to note, did not hug her back, just gave Levi a look as Nina babbled and grinned.

There'd been one night after Nina had re-upped when Jeremy had invited him up to the house, broke out the twenty-four-year-old single malt scotch and had very thoughtfully gotten drunk with Levi, and Levi had been able to be a normal person, to act not like a cop or a soldier or a big brother or the man of the house, but like a poor slob whose wife had left him.

Levi caught Faith's hand and tugged her into the seat next to him. "Stay," he ordered.

"I'm not your dog," she said.

"Please stay."

There. She squeezed his hand. "Whatever you want, neighbor."

He narrowed his eyes. Now was not the time for sass. She blushed, and for some reason, it made his chest ache.

"Watch it, Chief," she said. "I think I see a smile."

Before he realized what he was doing, he leaned in and gave her a quick kiss on her soft, pink lips.

Which did make Nina stop talking.

"Oh!" she said. "You two are…together. I didn't… wow." She sat down, as did Jeremy, as if they were on a double date. "So, let me get this straight. Levi, you're dating Faith, who was once engaged to your gay best friend."

"Yes."

She nodded appreciatively. "Am I the only one who thinks that's weird?"

"Seems kind of perfect to me," Jeremy said.

Nina grinned, her perfect smile not quite masking her sharklike intentions. "Well, this is awkward, Faith, because I'm here to try to get my husband back."

Faith nodded sympathetically. "Wow, that *is* awkward. But you mean ex-husband, right?"

Score one for Faith. She smiled sweetly, then looked at him, then back at Nina. "That being said, we'll let you guys talk. Jeremy and I were about to grab dinner."

"Oh, my gosh, you two are still BFFs? That's so cute!" Yep. A great white.

Faith smiled calmly. "Yes, we're adorable. Very nice to have met you."

"Same," Nina answered.

Faith slid out of the booth and looked at him. "See you around."

"Okay," he answered, wishing she'd stay.

With that, the cavalry left, Jeremy giving his shoulder a sympathetic squeeze as he left.

"So where were we?" Nina asked.

"We were nowhere," he answered. "You were telling me we should get back together, and I'm about to tell you that won't happen."

"Well, you know what, hotshot?" Nina said, nibbling a nacho with ridiculous sex appeal and a studied casualness. "Your little birdie is right. We have a lot to talk about. Give me a couple hours of your precious time. I'm here for the weekend, at least. Staying at the Black Swan." She raised her eyebrows and smiled at him from around the chip.

The Black Swan was where they'd spent their wedding night.

"Fine," he said. "Get it over with."

CHAPTER TWENTY-SEVEN

SO HIS EX-WIFE WAS BACK.

Faith sighed. Tried not to worry. Failed. Took another bite of Peanut Brittle. Another sigh. She held out the spoon for Blue—it was his favorite flavor—and took another bite for herself. A movie flickered on the TV—one of those stupid old black-and-white movies she didn't like—but it was better than the infomercials for those hellish workouts where the "before" body looked a helluva lot like the one she was in, and the "after" looked way too much like Nina Rodriguez's.

Levi's *wife*. He was mad at her, sure, but he'd loved her once.

Would he want another shot at that? The chance to do a better job? Maybe just to show that he hadn't been wrong about the woman he married? She could see that, understand how Levi, who tried so hard at everything, would want a better result than a quickie divorce in which he'd had no say.

When she was first in San Francisco, Faith would occasionally dream that Jeremy was knocking on her door, confused as to why she wasn't at their wedding. No, of *course* he wasn't gay, where had she been? The wedding disaster…*that* was the dream. She should come with him; everyone was waiting at the church.

Waking up from those dreams had always been like a kick in the stomach.

She wondered if Levi had similar dreams after Nina left.

"She can fly a helicopter," she told Blue, who was staring at the pint of Ben & Jerry's. She gave him another bite.

Levi was home, she knew. She'd heard him come in after midnight, muted the TV and leaped for the door. Waited for his knock, which hadn't come. Saw through the peephole that he was alone.

O'Rourke's closed at eleven. So where had he been?

Faith sighed and got up from the still-muted Bogart movie. Maybe Levi had sent her an email; he never had before, but it was worth checking, even if it did qualify her for Pathetic Female status.

Nothing except a note from Sharon Wiles saying she had a permanent tenant for the apartment, so if Faith could pack up her stuff and be out by the end of the month, that'd be great.

Crap. She liked it here, across the hall from her man. Who might not be her man anymore.

No, no. No reason to think that (yet). Faith shut down the computer and went back to the couch. Fluffed the cushions. Folded the blanket.

This was where a mother would come in very handy. Pru would listen, but she wasn't great with advice, and given her recent marital roller coaster, might well be wearing Vulcan ears and doing her husband. Jack—no. Dad, ditto. Honor's mysterious boyfriend hadn't materialized, and she probably wasn't in the mood to listen to Faith's relationship woes. Also, it was 2:32 a.m.

But a mother...

Faith stopped at the picture of her family on Pru's wedding day, the last one taken of all of them. Next to it was the rose quartz heart. Levi hadn't denied giving it to her, but he hadn't admitted it, either.

Of course it was from him.

Faith picked up the photo.

The tarry guilt she'd felt all these years wasn't easily scraped away. Faith could feel it lurking, waiting for another chance. But there'd been flashes since Levi had unveiled the facts of that day. Flashes of pure memories undimmed by the belief that she'd caused the accident. Memories of her mother's love so pure and bright and strong, they were shocking.

2:47 a.m.

"Want to go for a ride, Blue?" she asked her dog, whose ears pricked up at the magic word. "Want to go in the car?"

FOR TWO DECADES, FAITH had not been on either Lancaster or Hummel Brook roads. It had taken some doing. Hundreds of miles of avoidance. Her heart began thumping as she approached the intersection, and she exhaled shakily as she pulled over and turned off the engine. Rolled down the windows halfway so Blue could have some cold, fresh air.

It was beautiful here, the place her mother had died. The night was clear, the fields bathed in white from the nearly full moon. Faith had been afraid that the land had been sold to a developer, who'd slapped up some McMansions and stuck in a painfully awkward street named Ciderberry Circle or Owl Hollow Lane or some such ghastly moniker.

But no. It was the same.

Blue whined, wagging his tail, eager to go out.

"You stay here, boy," she said, her voice loud in the perfect quiet.

Pretty soon, maybe even later this week, Dad would start the ice harvest, calling up the troops at two o'clock in the morning at the very second the temperature fell to seventeen degrees. But tonight, it was only in the twenties.

Only the twenties. Spoken like a true upstater.

Their car had been broadsided right here. Right in the intersection. Maybe her mom had died on impact, maybe it had taken a few minutes. She hoped with every molecule of her heart that her mother hadn't suffered, but the truth was, she'd never know.

Faith went to the bank that ran along the edge of the road, climbed down. This was where the car had rolled. A long way, all the way to the maple tree. Kevin Hart had been going fast indeed.

Over the years, she'd looked him up on Google from time to time; he'd had a concussion from the accident, and broken the ring finger on his left hand. A college student at the time, not drunk, just driving far too fast on the lonely country road, unaware that during his first semester, a stop sign had been put up at the intersection. The judge had given him community service. He was a civil engineer now. Maybe the kind who studied where stop signs should go.

Faith had never blamed him, not really.

She walked through the field, the brittle grass crunching softly under her feet, and came to the tree that had stopped their car. She remembered that sound, that final crunch, the shiver of the car, the patter as the splintered safety glass let loose.

Running her hand over the rough bark, she felt the smoother place where the tree had healed from the gash their car had left. The wood was still strong and smooth, all these years after that long-ago afternoon when the sky had been so blue.

She sat under the tree, distantly noting the cold, unyielding ground. It was so quiet tonight. No crickets, no coyotes yipping, no night birds. Just the quiet.

Maybe her mother had been planning to divorce Dad. Maybe not. Maybe, Faith thought, her mother had just been having a bad day and vented, inappropriately perhaps, to her youngest child. Maybe, for some reason, she thought her frustrations would be safe with Faith, that for whatever reason, Faith would understand. Maybe wanting more for your child than you had yourself didn't mean you were unhappy.

That was the thing with a sudden death. Some questions would never be answered.

Faith would keep her mother's secret. She'd let the guilt slink away, but she wouldn't sully the memories her family held. The truth was, they all probably knew Constance wasn't perfect; they were all intelligent, sensitive people, more or less. Maybe their beatification of St. Mom was more a choice than ignorance, and each one of them had tiny shards pricking their hearts, memories of Mom's imperfections kept to themselves.

Mom had loved them all. She'd been a good mother, and John Holland had been a happily married man. Nothing could ever erase those truths.

Faith looked over to the spot where she'd thought she'd seen her mom standing that day, telling her she'd be fine.

Mom had been right, hadn't she? Faith had survived the wreck, had turned out pretty well for a girl without a mother. Had found a profession she loved and had become successful, had survived heartbreak, had created a life in a strange city, had become somebody who loved the life she was living.

Too bad Mom couldn't see her now.

"I miss you," Faith whispered.

Then she blew a kiss into the air, the same gesture she thought her mother had made to her, that last time she'd ever seen or imagined her. Connie's kiss for her littlest girl, returned, finally, after nineteen and a half years.

And this time, the heat of tears in her eyes was welcome.

When Blue appeared, having apparently wriggled his way out of the car window, she was glad for his furry head in her lap, his silky ears and big heart.

FAITH APPEARED ON her father's doorstep at seven that morning. She'd gone home, slept for a couple of hours, then awoke twenty minutes ago, sure of what she had to do.

"What's the matter, sweetpea?" Dad asked, ushering her in. "Baby, are you okay?"

"Hi, Daddy, I'm fine. Hey, Mrs. Johnson."

"Heavens, she needs coffee," Mrs. J. surmised. "She, with her hair in a snarl and yet appearing in public."

"This isn't public, Mrs. J. It's home. Is Honor up?" she asked.

"Honor is up," her sister said, coming into the room, dressed for work, hair band firmly in place.

"Good," Faith said. "Um…I need a minute with you all."

"I'll leave you alone," Mrs. Johnson said.

"Oh, stay," Faith said. "It's not like you won't be eavesdropping, anyway."

"You *are* in my kitchen," the housekeeper said with a

hint of a rare smile, "even though this monstrous house has eleven rooms, half of which nobody ever uses."

They all sat around the table, Mrs. J. handing Faith a cuppa joe. "Thanks," Faith said. "So here's the thing."

At that moment, the back door opened, and Pru and Jack came in, bickering. "So what?" Pru said. "Who cares what you think? Just because you're the boy—"

"You sound like you're eight years old," Jack said.

"And you sound like the ass you are. Hey, guys! What's everyone doing here?"

"I live here," Honor said. "As does our father."

Faith waved her hand. "I need to tell you guys something."

"You pregnant?" Pru asked.

"No," Faith said, even as Mrs. Johnson clapped her hands together in joy.

The housekeeper's expression fell back to thunderous. "Is it really out of order?" she said. "Four of you adults now, but only two grandbabies, and they nearly grown at that. It's not fair. The three of you are wretched children, and Prudence, why did you not have more?"

"She has a point," Dad said.

"And back to me," Faith said. Such was the way of family gatherings. She should've emailed instead. "This is important."

"Shoot," Pru said, rummaging in the cupboard. "Where's that mug I made in fourth grade?"

"I'm starving, Mrs. J.," Jack said.

"So eat something, you rude boy," Mrs. Johnson said, cutting a muffin in half for him. "I see hands attached to the ends of your arms. Am I expected to feed you like a baby bird?" She handed him the plate.

"The day Mom died," Faith said loudly. That shut everyone up. Pru sat down; Jack froze with the muffin halfway to his mouth. "The day Mom died," she said in a more normal tone, though her heart began to gallop sickly in her chest, "I didn't have a seizure." She swallowed. "I—I just said I did."

Her siblings exchanged looks. Dad took her hand, which, Faith noted, seemed to be shaking.

"Go on, sweetheart," he said.

She swallowed. "Well, you know how everyone said Mom never saw what hit us? She…she did. She did try to stop. There were skid marks. But the other car was coming too fast. I told you I had a seizure because I thought the accident was my fault."

Another silence.

"Why would you think that?" Dad asked.

Faith drew a slow breath. "Mom asked me something, and I didn't want to answer. Um, I was a little mad at her over something. So she turned around to check on me. I always thought that's why Kevin Hart hit us, because she was looking at me and not the road. But Levi did an accident reconstruction, and it showed that Mom couldn't have seen him until we were almost in the intersection, and then it was too late. Even though she tried."

There was another silence while her siblings, Mrs. J. and Dad exchanged looks.

"Honey," Dad said, squeezing her hand. "No one ever thought it was your fault. Not ever."

"But you thought I had a seizure, and Mom was distracted, and that's why we got hit."

"It was that stupid kid, Faithie," Jack said. "A kid in a muscle car, blowing through a stop sign."

"No one thought it was your fault, Faith," Honor said slowly. She looked at the others. "Did you guys think that?"

Pru shook her head. "Of course not."

"I was actually glad you had a seizure," Dad said slowly. "Because that way you wouldn't have remembered anything."

Silence fell around the table.

"Do you, sweetheart?" Mrs. Johnson asked, reaching out to touch her cheek. "Do you remember the accident?"

Faith hesitated, then nodded. "I… Yes. I do."

"Oh, God, Faith," Honor whispered, her eyes filling with tears. Her sister's arms around her was such an alien feeling that for a second, Faith didn't know what to do.

Then Pru hugged her, too, then Jack, and Dad, and Faith found that she was sobbing.

"I thought you blamed me," Faith whispered, and Honor seemed to know the words were for her. "You were so mad at me."

"Oh, honey," she whispered back. "I was jealous. You were the last one who got to be with Mom. You were with her in the end."

A little while later, when eyes had been wiped and an extra box of tissues had been brought to the table and Mrs. Johnson was making sweet potato pudding for everyone and crying a little herself (though she wouldn't admit it), Dad reached out and put his hand on Faith's shoulder.

"Was that why you stayed in San Francisco?" he asked. "Because you felt responsible?"

Faith took a deep breath. "Maybe a little. I mean, at first, I just wanted to get away from Jeremy. But I remembered something Mom said, about how she always wanted to live somewhere far away. And it just felt… right. Like I was doing what she never got to."

"That's really nice, Faith," Honor said.

"And what now?" Dad asked. "Are you going to stay in New York?"

"You and Levi seem hot and heavy," Pru observed. Dad and Jack winced in unison.

"I'd like to stay," Faith said, her eyes filling again. Home had never felt more precious than it did at this moment, here in the kitchen of the New House, where Mom had cooked and laughed, where Mrs. Johnson had worked so hard to take care of them all these years.

"Oh, crap, another sister," Jack said, sighing, but he messed up her hair.

"I do have to pack up my apartment, both at the Opera House and in San Francisco," she said, wiping her ever-leaking eyes. "Sharon Wiles found a tenant. So I might have to live here for a little while, once I'm back from California. Please don't make me move back with Goggy and Pops."

"Live with me," Pru said. "Carl's staying at his mom's indefinitely. I like having a long-distance marriage. The bathroom is certainly more pleasant. And you know the kids and I would love having you."

"We'll figure out the logistics later," Dad said. "Faith, sweetpea, you look exhausted. Come on, I'm tucking you in."

Her room was filled with some boxes of both her stuff and Honor's, but her bed was the same, made up with a lavender comforter and fluffy white pillows. Faith was suddenly dead on her feet.

Dad pulled the covers up to her chin. "Nice to get to take care of my little girl," he said. He sat on the side of her bed and smiled down at her, and Faith's heart ached with love. He was so familiar, so unchanging—

the faded flannel shirt, the smell of wood smoke and coffee, his grape-stained hands.

"Honey," he said, "this…matchmaking stuff. Did that have to do with what you just told us?"

Faith nodded. "I guess I thought if I could find you someone, it'd wipe away some of my…guilt."

Dad shook his head. "I haven't been paying enough attention," he said. He was quiet for a few minutes as he stroked her hair. "Now you listen," he said finally, "and you listen good. I'm always going to miss your mother, even if I get married again, which frankly, I can't picture. She wasn't perfect, but she was perfect for me, and if there's ever going to be anyone else, that's my responsibility, not yours. When the right person comes along, she will. It'll be my job to notice. You understand?" She nodded, and he leaned over to kiss her forehead. "I'm supposed to take care of you, not the other way around."

Dang. More tears. "You're the best, Daddy."

Her father stood up. "Well. You go to sleep, princess."

"I love you, Dad," she said.

"I love you, too." He paused. "Your mom loved you so much, Faith. You were our little surprise. Our gift."

The words settled around her like a blanket, soft and warm, keeping her company as she fell asleep in her old room.

CHAPTER TWENTY-EIGHT

LEVI'S DAY HAD NOT been good.

First, there was Nina, who'd shown up at his apartment at seven o'clock with donuts and coffee from Lorelei's, which he hadn't accepted (though it had been hard…the donuts were still warm). She'd followed him to the station. Bopped over to the post office, where she'd rented a post office box, to demonstrate her intention to stay, she'd said. Mel Stoakes had come in to say she'd been in the candy store, did Levi know she was back? Gerard Chartier had entered just as Mel had been leaving to report the same news. "Hey, Levi, that hot chick you were married to…she back in town?"

So rather than having her sit next to his desk and interrogate him in front of Emmaline and Everett, he'd said yes to lunch at Hugo's, where hopefully Jess would spit in Nina's food, and reiterated the fact that he had no interest in getting back together with her.

"That's the anger talking, *querido,*" she said, licking her lips.

"It's the brain talking," he replied wearily.

"Ah, but what does your heart say?"

"Same thing. As do the lungs, liver and kidneys. You know as well as I do that you're only back here because you're at loose ends." And that was another thing. Had she come back on leave, he might've believed the sincerity of her words, not that it would've changed his mind. As it was now, he was just a stopgap measure. The second Nina was bored, she'd be off again.

Hopefully, she was bored now.

She wasn't. At the end of his shift, there she was, coming into the station like she owned the place. He hadn't seen this much of her during their entire marriage. Ignoring Emmie and Ev, she plunked herself on the edge of his desk as he shut down his computer.

"Wanna get a drink, baby?" she asked.

"Nina, I really would like to go spend some time with Faith," he said bluntly.

"To make me jealous?"

"No. Because she's…"

"Sweet?" Nina said, pulling a face and batting her eyes.

"Mine."

The word surprised him, and it made Nina freeze. But only for a second. "Fine," she said. "Go to the little princess. Bet she doesn't know what I know." She reached for his belt, right there in front of Everett and Emmaline, but he snagged her wrist.

"You'd be surprised," he growled. "Go back to the city, Nina."

"I'm not going anywhere, baby. But for now, fly home to your little birdie. Just remember, your gay best friend had her first."

There was the Nina he knew. Scratch the surface, and she was meaner than a fisher cat.

He walked across the green, jerked open the door of the Opera House and stomped up the stairs. Heard noises in Faith's apartment, opened the door.

There were boxes everywhere.

She was packing over by her bookcase, her back to him.

Packing, as in leaving. Moving.

Blue leaped over to him and tried to mount his leg. "Get off, Blue," he muttered, and the dog slunk away, clearly wounded. "Going somewhere?" he asked Faith.

"Hey!" She was wearing those ridiculous Dalmatian pajamas. "How are you? How's it going with, um... with Nina?"

"Are you leaving?"

She glanced around. "Oh. Um, I only had this place month-to-month. Sharon Wiles found a permanent tenant. Wasn't happy about the red wall, either, but she said she'd paint that over. Anyway, yeah, I have to get out." She seemed nervous, her hands knotted in front of her. "But after San Francisco."

Coldness filled his chest. She *was* moving. "San Francisco?"

"Right, right. I guess I didn't tell you. You've been, um, otherwise occupied the past few days. Anyway, I have a job in Oakland, so I'm heading back to San Francisco on Monday. It's this really nice common area for a condo complex, great view of the bridge, and while I'm there, I'll—" She broke off, her mood visibly changing. Folded her arms under her chest, tossed her hair back. "Why are you scowling? If anyone has reason to scowl, isn't it me? Since my boyfriend has basically ignored me since his ex-wife popped into town?"

"You're going to San Francisco?"

"Yes, and about the ex-wife and potential reconciliation, maybe you could at least talk to me about what you—"

"For how long?"

She threw up her hands. "A few weeks, Levi."

"How few?"

"Possibly six, hopefully more like four. I'm—"

"Really. And you never mentioned this."

"It came up kind of fast. Why is the branch back up your ass, Levi?"

"How fast?" he said, ignoring the question.

"Um…I pitched the job in August, but I didn't hear until about a week ago, and it wasn't a sure thing until Friday. I would've told you—"

"So you make plans to move to San Francisco for a month, maybe more, but you don't think to talk about this with me."

She stared at him a beat or two. "I guess it was a little hard to find the time," she said, her voice cool. "Since you've been so busy with Nina and the peace talks."

"You could've made the time. And there are no peace talks," he growled. "Give me some credit. She left me. That was the end of it."

"Really nice of you to tell me. Funny, how it's taken you two days to mention this."

"You can't really believe I'd get back with her."

"I have no idea what to believe, Levi! Because you don't talk to me!"

"Said the woman who neglected to mention she's moving back to San Francisco."

She jammed her hands on her hips. "Well, it looks like communication isn't our thing." She was mad now. Good. So was he. Kinda furious, actually.

Twice in his life, Levi had been left. Hadn't seen either time coming. Both times, he'd had to pick up the pieces, jamming down misery, going on with day-to-day life, burying all that hurt, going on as if everything was fine.

He didn't feel like doing that again.

She was glaring at him, waiting—for what, he had no idea. This was too complicated, too difficult, too… emotional. He jammed a hand through his hair. "Okay. That's fine. This wasn't working, anyway."

Faith's head jerked back a fraction. "Wait. What? You're dumping me?"

He shrugged, shaking his leg to dislodge her dog. "Have fun in San Francisco."

Her mouth opened. "I'm coming home after this job, Levi," she said, her voice softer now. "Don't make this into a big deal. It's just for a few weeks."

"You sure?" he said, his voice tight. "Because the first time you went for a few weeks, it turned out to be a few years. Then you come back here, and you decide maybe you'll stay. But maybe not. Maybe this is just a stopgap for you. You're going back to California, and, hell, maybe that'll be so great, you'll change your mind again!" He seemed to be yelling. Not good. Definitely not good.

She tilted her head. "I have to say, your head does seem to be up your ass with that branch right now. You know what I think? I think this is really about Nina."

"It's not."

"Seems like it is."

"It's not."

She threw up her hands again. "Great! Another conversation we can't have. You won't talk about the war, you won't talk about your father, you won't talk about your ex-wife. And here's the thing, Levi. I've already been with a guy who hid some very important things from me. I'm not doing it again, so if there's something you'd like to say, by all means. Go for it."

"Well, I'm not gay."

"I'm aware of that. Still, I would really appreciate it if you could tell me what on earth is really going on here. Blue, for the love of God, get a room, okay?" She kicked the dog his pillow, which the dog happily jumped. "You have ten seconds. One." She grabbed a book and threw it into a box. "Two." Another book. "Three."

"Don't forget the picture of Jeremy," Levi said.

She froze, book in hand. "Really? Are you really going there?"

"Maybe you never got over him. I'd hate to force you to take sloppy seconds with me." Ah, shit. This was bad, and getting worse by the second.

"It's ironic," she said. "You're the one who can't resist the chance to run off to open a jar or save a cat. You're the one with an ex-wife sniffing around. I'm trying to make a real relationship here, but I can't do it alone."

He shrugged. Felt some heat rising to his face that he didn't like one bit.

"You know what?" she said, walking over to him, her eyes narrowed. She poked him in the chest with her forefinger. Hard. "*I'm* the one who said I love you. The fact that *you* didn't say boo was duly noted, Chief Cooper. *You* can't even admit you gave me that damn rock, and I've been carrying that thing around from place to place for decades!" Another poke. "Say what you want about Jeremy—" poke "—but gay or not, at least he knew how to be in a relationship. At least he was willing to commit."

He looked down at her. He didn't like having all these…these…*feelings* churning around. He didn't like fighting.

And he didn't like being wrong.

"Enjoy California," he said.

With that, he turned around and left.

CHAPTER TWENTY-NINE

"HE'S A THERAPY DOG," Faith said, fishing out a tissue and Blue's papers at the same time. "He can ride with me. Persons with Disabilities Act and all that." She wiped her eyes and gave the TSA drone a watery smile.

"Boarding begins in forty minutes. Next."

Faith sat down, Blue's head immediately resting in her lap.

Ah, irony. Back at the Buffalo-Niagara Airport, once again dumped. The tears wouldn't seem to stop leaking out of her eyes, but she gave her dog an ear-scratch nonetheless.

The first time she'd gone to San Francisco, she'd been fleeing in shock and heartbreak. This time, though, her heart was made of stronger stuff.

The trouble was, Levi Cooper had said heart in his fist. She loved him, the big dummy. No one—no one— could've done what he did the night he went out to the accident site and...oh, crap, just the image of him walking around in the middle of the freezing, dark night, measuring stuff, then doing an entire accident reconstruction, then knocking on her door at three o'clock in the *morning*...a little squeak escaped her throat, causing Blue to put his paws on her lap and lick away the tears.

Men. How could they do stuff like that, and then be completely unable to say, *Please come back soon,*

I'll miss you so much, I love you. Huh? Why? Any answers? Anyone? No?

Blue whined.

"You're right, you're right," she said to her dog. "We'll deal with him when we get back." He wagged his tail.

You know what? This trip back to California…this was her farewell to the city she loved. She'd design the common area and enjoy doing it, stick her chunky fee in the bank and say goodbye to all her pals and associates. She'd go to Golden Gate Park again with Liza and Wonderful Mike, eat butter-drenched sourdough toast, have sushi, go to Rafael and Fred's wedding, and pack up her apartment.

She wasn't going to waste her trip crying over Levi Cooper.

Well, okay, she'd give him ten more minutes of weep time. And then she really was going to stop.

Someone sat next to her. Faith looked up, ready to apologize for her tears and/or dog, and saw Jessica Does.

Jessica saw her at the same instant and gave a near comical twitch. "Holland. What are you doing here?" She glanced around, then frowned at Faith.

"I'm going to California for a few weeks," she said, wiping her eyes. Jess didn't ask why she was crying. That would be too human of her. "How about you?"

"Arizona."

"That's nice," Faith said. "Beautiful weather out there, huh?" For heaven's sake. Was she condemned for all eternity to trying to make Jessica like her? "So why are you going out there? You look really nice, by the way." Question answered.

Jessica didn't speak right away. If she ever would.

Then Blue put his paw on her foot, and she smiled a little at the beastie. "College," she muttered. "This low-residency program."

"Really? That's great." Faith opened another tissue pack. "What are you studying?"

"Marketing. Better late than never, right? I mean, we don't all have families who send us off to beautiful schools, do we?"

Sigh. "I guess not." Faith looked at her a second. She might be kind of a bitch, but the woman was beautiful. "Jess, why have you always hated me?"

"Why do you want to know?"

Faith ignored the hostile tone. "Because my plane doesn't leave for an hour?"

Jessica started to smile, then seemed to remember she was with Faith. After a second, she shrugged. "The usual reasons. Wearing your old clothes to school, that sort of thing."

"Which made it okay to bully me at recess and make fun of me behind my back?" What the hell. Time to be honest.

"No." Jessica paused, petting Blue with her foot, then looked at Faith and sighed. "You weren't the only one in love with Jeremy, Super-Cute."

Holy guacamole. "Oh."

Jess rolled her eyes. "Yeah. But you know…clearly he was gonna go for you and not someone like me."

"Because you're so mean?" Again, what the hell.

To her surprise, Jessica laughed. "Not exactly what I meant, but who knows?" Her cheeks grew pink, and she looked away. "I was jealous. Whatever."

Faith felt a pang of sympathy. Imagine being Jess, serving Jeremy and his super-cute girlfriend back in the day. Imagine seeing him adoring someone else, all that tender attention, that perfect teenage love. Having to wait tables at their rehearsal dinner, and then being a guest at the fairy-tale almost wedding. "I'm sorry, Jess. If I was ever a jerk, I'm sorry."

"You were actually always pretty damn nice, Holland." She glanced at Faith and shrugged.

"We should be friends," Faith said. "We've been in love with the same boys."

"Well, I was never in love with Levi," Jessica said.

"I don't see how you could avoid it," she said, and just the thought of him made her eyes fill.

Jessica gave her a condescending stare. "Wow. You've got it bad."

"I know." She gave a hiccupping sob.

Jessica started to laugh. "I always sit next to the crazies," she said. "Sure, Holland, let's be friends. What the hell."

"SARAH, I DON'T CARE! You have two weeks left! You're not coming home to study."

"I'd get better grades if I could study from home." His sister was at the whining phase of their daily conversation.

"No. I mean it."

"Levi! Don't you even care how I'll do on finals?"

"Of course I care!" he snapped. "But you can study there, Sarah! You're surrounded by entire buildings devoted to studying!"

"Fine! I'm so sorry to be such a huge pain in your ass."

He sighed. "Don't cry. You're not a pain."

"Of course I'm gonna cry. You're so mean to me, Levi."

"Sarah, come on." He paused. "I'll drive up tomorrow and take you out for dinner, okay?"

"I want to come home."

"Two weeks, Sarah. I'll see you tomorrow." He hung up from his sister, feeling worse than ever.

Faith had been gone for twenty-two days. Three weeks of one day after the next, three weeks of hardly sleeping, three weeks of every place in this damn town being about her.

The stupid phone rang again. *Jeremy,* the screen said. Levi let it go to voice mail. Despite the ridiculousness of the argument, he kind of hated Jeremy these days for being Faith's first and perfect love. He sighed.

"Enough with the sighing!" Emmaline barked. "Knock it off, or I'm gonna go work for Jeremy, and don't think he hasn't asked."

"Do it. I still don't know what you do here."

"You'll find out after I quit, won't you?"

He closed the case he was working on—all those petty burglaries had been courtesy of Josh Deiner, the kid who'd gotten Abby Vanderbeek drunk that day. Another rich kid who had to get his jollies by breaking the law. "I'm done for the day."

"Thank you, Baby Jesus."

"Everett, will you close up tonight?"

"Roger that, Chief! Thanks! Closing up, roger. Will call with a report at oh-eighteen hundred."

"No need, Ev."

"Will do anyway, Chief!"

Levi started to sigh, caught Emmaline's murderous look, and walked out instead. Went home, glancing automatically at Faith's door. Right. It wasn't her door anymore. Some middle-aged guy had moved in.

He went into his own apartment, which had once been very peaceful and relaxing and now seemed enormous and barren. Ignored those stupid thoughts, changed out of his work clothes. The refrigerator cycled on. From downstairs, he heard the theme song of *Game of Thrones,* which Eleanor Raines had recently discovered and was watching at extreme volumes to compensate for the fact that she refused to admit that she needed a hearing aid.

He didn't particularly want to go to O'Rourke's, but it beat staying home listening to all those beheadings and wolf attacks.

Which reminded him: he missed Blue.

Two minutes later, he walked into the bar. "Hey, Levi," Connor said.

"Connor."

"How about a beer?"

"Thanks."

"Hey, asshole," Colleen said to Levi, leaning down to make eye contact. "I'm not speaking to you, but if I was, that's what I'd say."

"Hi," Levi grunted.

"Coll, get the man a beer and leave him alone," Connor said, going into the kitchen.

The only good thing that had happened in the past three weeks was that Nina was gone. She'd knocked on Levi's door the day after his and Faith's ~~breakup idiocy~~ argument and told him that she'd be on her way, sorry for the inconvenience, best wishes.

"Why the change of heart?" he'd asked. "I mean, I'm relieved, but…" He'd shrugged.

Nina had looked at him a long minute. "You're in love with your little birdie," she'd said. "I saw you yesterday. Okay, fine, I was spying, but her windows are right there overlooking the green." She smiled. "Saw you fighting."

"And?"

"And you never fought with me." Much to his surprise, Nina's eyes had filled with tears. "We never had a fight, not once. What does that say?"

Levi would have guessed that said they'd been compatible, but then again, he was dealing with a female, and females didn't make sense.

"I'm sorry for what I put you through," Nina said. "I really am. I'm not proud of walking out on you. I just... I don't know. I couldn't stay."

"It's okay," he said. "I'm over it."

"I know, moron. That's why I'm going." She inhaled sharply, dashed a hand across her eyes, then smiled at him. Hugged him hard. "See you, big man," she'd said, had given him a noisy kiss on the cheek, and off she'd gone.

Life in a small town during the winter...there wasn't a lot going on after the long and busy tourism season. The ice harvest would be any day now; that meant a bunch of workers out in frigid temperatures, usually at night, gathering the frozen grapes to make the sweet wines the region was famous for. In a few weeks, the village would have its Christmas stroll, lit up like a movie set. And then...not much.

"Hey, buddy." Jeremy came over and took the stool next to him. "I just called you, not ten minutes ago."

"Hey."

"How are you?"

"Great." He took a sip of his beer.

"One-word answers," Jeremy said to Colleen as she set down a glass of red wine in front of him.

"I know. It's enough to make me spit in his beer," Colleen said, causing Levi to look up sharply. She smiled enigmatically and gave him the finger.

"Coll, have you heard from Faith?" Jeremy asked, for Levi's benefit, he was sure.

"We talk every day. You?"

"Almost every day. She sounds great, doesn't she?" He smiled.

"So great. So happy, now that she's not stuck with an idiot, don't you think?"

"Oh, I don't know," Jeremy said. "He's only an idiot maybe half the time. Sixty percent, tops. Hey, Carol! How's your bursitis? You're doing what I told you, right?"

"Jeremy, give me a hug," Mrs. Robinson said. "You're so handsome! Don't make that face, just do it. You can have Levi arrest me on sexual harassment later." She giggled like a twelve-year-old as Jeremy obliged.

At that moment, Levi's phone buzzed. Dispatch. "Chief Cooper," he said.

It was an MVA out on Route 154. A rollover, people inside, possible injuries. Not a job for Everett, in other words.

Within seconds, Levi was in the cruiser, lights and sirens on. No ice tonight; it was cold and dry. On his way out of town, he saw three volunteer firefighters heading to the station in their pickup trucks, blue lights flashing in the early dark of the November night. That meant Levi would be first on the scene.

Sure enough, he was. He parked across the road, aiming the headlights at the vehicle. "Car on its roof," he said into the radio. "Someone's trying to open the door. I'm investigating."

He ran up to the Toyota minivan, which was flipped, having slid to the side of the road. Minimal damage. A blonde woman was yanking on the door. "My kids are inside, and the door's stuck!" she yelled, hysteria edging her voice.

"Fire department and ambulance are on the way," he said. "Don't worry. I'm a cop and an EMT."

"Thank God," she said. "One minute we were fine, the next minute, a deer ran out, I jerked the wheel and we flipped. Should've hit the damn thing."

"Mommy! Get us out!"

The road was flat, so the chances of the van rolling farther were small. The side window was broken; Levi lay on the asphalt and worked his way in. His leather jacket would protect him from the shattered glass, and with little kids in the car, he wasn't going to wait for the fire department.

Both kids were strapped into booster seats, dangling upside down. No blood, though the older one was pretty pale. "Hey, guys," Levi said. "You okay?"

"Get us *out!*" the bigger kid said. He was maybe six or seven.

"My juice spilled," the younger one said.

"Oh, yeah?" Levi said. "You get it all over you?"

"Yes. It's yucky."

"That's okay," Levi said. No apparent injuries. "You'll get dry soon. Anything hurt? Neck, stomach, anything like that?"

"I'm fine," the little guy said.

"I'm scared," said the older one.

"Well, I'll stay with you till the fire department comes, how's that?"

"Thank you," the older boy whispered.

"It's gonna be okay. Just a couple minutes more." He glanced at the mother, who was squatting next to the car. "They're doing all right, ma'am. I need you to step back a little, though." She didn't move. He didn't blame her.

"Mommy's right here," she said to the boys. "Don't be scared."

"I'm not scared," the younger kid said. "I'm really brave."

"You're both doing great," Levi assured them. "Just hang tough."

"I told them not to unbuckle," the mom said.

"That was smart," Levi told her. "How about you? You feel okay?"

"I'm fine," she said. "A little banged up."

In the distance, he could hear the sirens of the ambulance and fire trucks. "Boys, the fire department's on the way. They're gonna put a special brace on your necks to make sure you don't get hurt, and then we'll get you out of here, okay?"

"Can't you get us out now?" the older kid said.

"It's safer if we wait. They're almost here. So, how old are you?" he asked, just to keep them talking and calm.

"I'm seven, and Stephen is four," the older one said.

"Four and a *half,*" Stephen corrected.

"Got it. And what's your name, big guy?" Levi asked. The siren was louder now.

"Cody."

"I'm Levi. Nice to meet you." Engine One pulled up, and Levi could hear Gerard Chartier on the radio.

"Levi, is that your ass hanging out of there?" a familiar voice called.

"Hey, Jess," he answered. "Good to have you back in town."

"Thanks, and why are you doing my job?"

"Guess who's here?" he said to the boys. "The fire-fighters. You'll be out in a few minutes."

"I like upside down," the younger kid said, and there was something familiar about him. Levi wondered if he'd seen them in town. Hard to tell from this angle.

"Hey, Chief," Gerard said. "You want to do the honors, since you're already in there?" He handed in a neck brace, and Levi fastened it around the younger kid's neck, then did the same to Cody. Gerard got the cutter and clipped the hinges off the door.

"Keep them in the car seats and we'll just carry them to the rig. I'll check them out there," Gerard said. He was a paramedic, the senior ranking member of the fire department.

Jess was talking to the mom, telling her about transporting them to the E.R., wouldn't hurt her to be checked out, too, because sometimes shock and adrenaline masked an injury, and was there someone she wanted to call, her husband or a friend, the usual.

Both kids seemed okay. The older one probably understood more and was therefore more shaken, but now that help was here, they were starting to realize they were the stars of the show. The ambulance had pulled up right after the engine, so Jess and Gerard took the bigger kid out and carried him to the ambulance, booster seat and all. Levi and Ned Vanderbeek did the same with the little guy, setting his car seat right on the gurney. Kelly Matthews was strapping the older boy's seat onto the bench in the back of the ambulance, chatting away with the kid, getting him to laugh.

The mom, who'd done such a good job of keeping it together, started to cry at the sight of her boys in an ambulance, then did that horribly sweet thing moms did—tried to smile instead.

Reminded Levi of his own mom the day he left for Basic.

"Be right back," Levi said, going to the cruiser. He kept some of those little beanbag animals in the glove compartment for just this type of call. Grabbed two and gave a pig to Cody, a lamb to the little guy. "Thanks for giving us something to do tonight," he said.

"You're welcome," the little brother said happily, holding the lamb up to study it more closely.

"You take care, kids," Levi said.

"Thank you for staying with us," the older boy said solemnly, and Levi felt his heart squeeze a little.

"You bet, pal," he said.

Then he turned to the other kid, Stephen, and did a double take. His gut told him before his brain caught on, tightening so fast it stole his breath.

He looked back at Cody, then back at Stephen.

"Bye!" said the little guy, turning the stuffed lamb over to investigate its belly. His forehead was…what was the word Faith used? *Crinkled.*

Stephen looked like…like him.

The boys were his father's other sons.

He realized he was staring. "Uh…you take care, boys. You were really brave."

The boys' mother was looking at him, her mouth slightly open. Crap.

At that moment, a car screeched up, and Rob Cooper burst out of the door, running up to the back of the ambulance. "Heather! Heather, baby, are you okay? Are the boys—oh, God, hey, boys! Cody, you okay, buddy? Stevie? You doing all right?"

His father kissed the little boys, wiped his eyes and held their hands. He asked Kelly something, looked back at the older kid, ruffled his hair.

Get moving. Levi walked to the cruiser, head down. His hands buzzed with adrenaline. Almost there.

God, he wished Faith was around. Wished he could go home and pull her into his arms and breathe in that smell and have her dopey dog jump up against them.

And maybe he'd tell her he'd met his brothers today.

"Excuse me."

Shit.

His father's wife had followed him the few yards to the cruiser. She looked at him steadily, then held out her hand. "I'm Heather Cooper."

She was maybe thirty-eight, forty; in other words, closer to his own age than his father's. Levi took a breath, then shook her hand. "Nice to meet you, ma'am."

"Thank you for helping my sons."

"No problem. I'm glad they're okay." He hesitated. "They seem like great kids."

"They are. I'm sorry, I didn't catch your name." Yeah. She knew.

He took a deep breath. "Levi Cooper."

"I thought so." Her eyes were wet. "And my sons… they're your half brothers, aren't they?"

He nodded.

She sucked in a breath. "I—I didn't know."

"Sorry."

"You're not the one who should be sorry." She tried to smile, but it faltered. "My God."

"Um…I should go. You take care, Mrs. Cooper," he said.

"Heather. Since I'm your stepmother and all." This time, the smile was a little more resolute. "This is quite a shock."

"Heather? Babe, the ambulance is almost ready to— oh. Oh."

Yeah. *Oh.* It was almost comical, the expressions running across his father's face—anxiety, then shock, then that realization that yep, the shit had hit the fan. "Uh…hey," he said. "How are you?"

"I guess you two have met before," Heather bit out. "This man just saved your sons' lives."

"That's slightly exaggerated," Levi said. He looked at his father. Rob Cooper was smaller than Levi remembered. Skinnier, too. In addition to looking guilty as sin, his father looked…weak.

Because he was. Somehow, Rob Cooper had made something of himself, had found a nice woman, had been given two more sons, and he must've been doing something right. But he'd never once had the guts to own up to walking out on his firstborn. He'd never even told his wife he had another child.

"You two need to take care of your sons. I'm glad everyone's okay." He turned to his cruiser.

Then he stopped and turned back to his sorry excuse of a father and suddenly had him by the front of his shirt, lifting him off the ground. His father's familiar eyes were suddenly wide with terror.

"Do better with them," Levi growled, giving his father a shake. "If you walk out on them the way you walked out on me, you'd better pray to God I don't find you."

He released Rob Cooper, who staggered a few steps back and turned and went to his other sons. Fast.

Levi looked at Heather. "If you ever need anything, let me know," he said. "I'm the police chief in Manningsport."

It had never felt better to say those words.

She gave a wobbly smile. "Levi…for whatever it's

worth, you'll always be welcome in my home. I'd be proud for the boys to know you."

The words went straight to his heart. He looked at her another minute, gave her a nod, not quite trusting himself to speak, then got in the cruiser and carefully drove away from the scene.

When he was a few miles off, he pulled over, and before he was aware of what he was doing, his sister's voice was on the line. "Calling to be a prick again?" she said, her voice slightly sullen.

"You can come home whenever you want," he said. "Tonight, tomorrow, Saturday, any time you need to, day or night."

There was a pause. "Who is this?" his sister asked, and Levi smiled.

"Look," he said. "I just want to help you get through this time, get you on your feet, whatever. If that means coming home twice a week, that's fine, Sarah. You're gonna turn out great no matter what."

There was silence on the other end, then a snuffle. "Thanks," she whispered.

"I love you, you know."

"I do know. I love you, too."

When he got back to the station, Everett was still there, playing Angry Birds. "Hey, Chief!" he said, bolting upright and falling out of the chair in the process.

"Is your mother home?" he asked.

"Um, I think so. Why?"

Levi punched in the mayor's phone number. "Marian, it's Levi. Listen. I need an actual cop to help me out here. Your son can go to the police academy, but I'm hiring someone else, too. Probably Emmaline. You have a week to find the money, or I quit. Have a great night.

Oh, I'm gonna be taking some vacation time. Starting now." With that, he hung up. "Good night, Ev," he said.

"Roger that, Chief," Everett said.

O'ROURKE'S WAS MUCH the same as he'd left it. Colleen hissed at him once more, Jeremy was feeling Carol Robinson's glands. Those two should get a room.

Prudence Vanderbeek sat alone at a booth, clicking away at her phone. "Hey, Chief," she said amicably. "I'm sexting my husband. Give me a minute." She muttered as she typed. "'I refuse to sign your contract, Mr. Grey, and furthermore, I've never even heard of that Japanese thingamajig you mentioned in your last email. And yes, I remain untouched, I have never even kissed a man before, yadda yadda.'" She looked at Levi. "I'm forty-seven years old, Levi, and the mother of Carl's children. Why I have to pretend to be an insipid virginal college student is beyond me."

"Because you enjoy it?" he suggested.

"Probably." She put her phone away. "So. How you doing?"

He sat down.

The thing was, he had no idea what to ask.

Prudence shoveled some popcorn into her mouth. "Let me guess. This is about Faith," she suggested.

"Yes."

"Go for it."

"I kissed her once. A long time ago."

"How thrilling."

"I wondered if she ever talked to you about it." This was…unexpected. He hoped like hell that no one could overhear them.

"Honor!" Pru bellowed. "Levi wants to talk about Faith!"

So that hope was dashed.

Honor Holland came over, a glass of wine in her hand. "Really?" she asked, almost kindly, making him a little wary.

"Yeah," Pru said. "He says he kissed her one time and wants to know if she got all swoony and some such shit."

Levi made a note never again to ask for help from evil sisters. "Thanks, ladies," he said, standing.

"Oh, man up," Prudence said.

"Sit down," Honor said at the same time.

Levi sighed and obeyed. "Okay, so, I screwed up."

"Of course you did. You're a guy," Prudence said. Her pocket buzzed, and she jumped. "God, that felt good," she said, almost to herself, taking her phone out to read the text. Laughed and began typing her response.

"I thought you dumped my sister," Honor said.

"I did."

"And what makes you think you deserve her?"

"I don't."

"That, Chief Cooper, is the correct answer." Honor smiled. She didn't say anything else. Pru was busy sexting Carl. Honor still said nothing, just looked at her nails.

Right. He waved to Colleen, who flipped him off. "Another round for these two on my tab," he said, standing up.

"Order me something expensive," Pru instructed her sister, not looking up from her phone.

He was halfway across the green when Honor called his name. She didn't have her coat on, and he shrugged out of his and handed it to her.

"Thanks," Honor said, putting it on. "Great jacket.

I'm keeping it, by the way. She called me when I was a senior at Cornell. So Faith would've been a senior in high school. Would the timing be right for your little dilemma?"

Levi nodded.

"Well, I remember it, because it was the one and only time she ever said anything weird about Jeremy, and also, I had finals and the last thing I wanted to talk about was her love life." Honor crossed her arms. "But it was strange, because from day one, Jeremy was Prince Charming and Dr. Wonderful all rolled into one. And she was asking me for advice, and that didn't happen too much. We weren't…" Honor cleared her throat. "We weren't that close back then."

"Do you remember what she said?" he asked.

"Yes, but I'm inclined to make you wait, just to watch you suffer."

"Give me back my coat."

"Fine. She asked me how to know if you were in love. She said she and Jeremy had taken a break, and something had happened and…I don't know. What did being in love feel like."

"What did you say?"

"I told her I had finals and she should read *Seventeen* magazine. I was kind of a bitch." She looked at the ground. "Sorry. I wish I had more."

"It's enough."

"Good. Then get your ass in gear. And thanks for the coat."

Levi went up to his apartment and booted up his computer. Called Sarah once again.

"What? I'm trying to study for my exams, Levi! Can you please leave me alone?"

"Hi," he said, clicking on a travel site. "I know I said

you could come home, but I'm going to San Francisco for a few days."

"Fine, whatever. Love you, gotta go." She paused. "I have a friend here to study."

"I thought you didn't have friends."

"Bite me. Call me when you land, and make sure you bring me a present."

CHAPTER THIRTY

THE PHONE RANG AT TWO o'clock in the morning, and it took Faith a minute to remember where she was. Her apartment in San Francisco? Nope. Opera House? Nope. Goggy's? No.

The phone shrilled again. "No!" came a sleepy wail from down the hall. Right. She was at Pru's, having gotten in from California a few hours ago. At the moment, she was so tired she felt dizzy, but if your last name was Holland, a phone call in the middle of a November night could only mean one thing—someone was dead, or it was time for the ice wine harvest.

Pru was already up. "Hey! Ice wine!" She banged on Abby's door, then Faith's. "Ice wine! Come on, Ned's already gone. You don't want to miss it, do you?"

"I so want to miss it," Abby muttered, stumbling into the hall, Blue leaping excitedly about, looking for somebody to love. "I hate my life."

"Oh, come on, now," Faith said. "It's fun."

"It's hell. A frozen, barren wasteland."

For weeks, Dad had watched the forecast like a hawk, sleeping in his truck some nights, waiting for his special alarm-thermometer to announce that magical second when the temperature hit seventeen. Then the phone calls went out, and every living Holland was expected to show up within minutes to cut down the frozen grapes, which would be pressed that night.

"Bet you wish you were in San Fran still, huh?" Abby asked as she, Pru and Faith drove up the hill to Blue Heron, bundled in their warmest gear.

"And miss this?" She smiled at her niece.

"I'd kill to miss this," Abby muttered.

"Well, Faith, your timing was perfect," Pru said.

Faith's project had finished early, everything going ahead of schedule, which was practically unheard of. She'd done the job she was hired to do and did it well, took her buddies out for ridiculously beautiful and expensive martinis, went to Rafael and Fred's wedding, hired movers to pack up her stuff from the apartment, formally turning her lease over to Wonderful Mike.

Then she'd taken a long walk in the cold, damp air, and said goodbye to the city that had welcomed her, where her heart had mended, and went back to the place she loved with every molecule in her body. And to the man she loved just as much. More, even.

Twice in her life, Faith had been in love. Once with a man so perfect she should've known there was something wrong. And now with a man who wasn't perfect at all, who was stubborn, occasionally irritable, and mildly to moderately constipated when it came to emotions, and maybe had some abandonment issues going on, too, not to mention the weight of the world on his shoulders.

He was also the best man she knew.

There was nothing he wouldn't do to help someone. Find a cat on a dark night, drive an hour to do his sister's laundry, wash a dog covered in chicken poop, let his ex-wife say her piece.

Go out in the middle of the night to reconstruct a twenty-year-old accident.

Stop his best friend's wedding when he knew it would only lead to misery...for Jeremy *and* for her.

But the thought of his expression when he broke up with her…that hurt like a splinter in her heart. Just so… decided. So damn resolute.

"Are you getting out of the truck or what?" Abby said.

Right. They were here.

"Ice wine!" Dad called, the veritable kid at Christmas. It was a genetic defect or something. Jack was talking to the grapes already. "Are you ready to get pressed, sweeties? Are you excited?" Ned rolled around with Blue on the thin film of snow that had fallen sometime when Faith was asleep. Even Abby accepted her grandfather's hug and said, yes, she, too, was so excited. Honor already had half a basket full of grapes, and Goggy was manning the forklift, shining the headlights down the row so they could all see what they were doing, snapping at Pops to take a step back or she'd run him over and enjoy her widowhood. Carl was here, too, and returned Faith's wave a little shyly, perhaps guessing (correctly) that Faith knew far too much about his sex life.

The faint smell of bacon was in the air; Mrs. J. would be making breakfast at the New House.

Faith got to work. The frozen clusters of grapes came off easily in her hand, firm, cold little bundles. The stars were brilliant overhead; no moon tonight, the brief snow squall finished. The night air was filled with the sounds of her family bickering, laughing, shouting insults and encouragement to each other. Lights shone over at the Lyons Den, too, as just about every vineyard around made ice wine.

Mom had always loved the ice harvest. She used to bring cocoa in Thermoses, and muffins hot from the oven. One year, there'd been enough snow to go sledding, and Faith could recall, in a bright flash of memory, the feeling of her mom's arms around her, the sound of her laugh, the thrill of flying down the hill, knowing her mom would keep her safe.

She glanced up to find Dad looking at her with a smile, as if he was thinking the same thought.

After a good hour, they heard another motor. "Ahoy, Hollands!" came Jeremy's voice. It was another tradition started when the Lyons had first moved to New York; the two families took turns bringing coffee to the other. Attached to Jeremy's tractor was a small trailer, and leave it to the gay guy, he had a bright red plaid blanket, a huge Thermos, thick ceramic mugs, matching sugar and creamer set, two trays of sugar cookies and a flask of good brandy to lace the coffee.

"Thank God," Abby said. "I'm freezing."

"If your eighty-four-year-old great-grandmother isn't complaining, should you be?" Pru said. "Jeremy, pour me a coffee, easy on the coffee, okay?"

"Will do, will do," he said. "And how's pretty Faith?" He gave her a warm hug, which she returned. He'd called her almost daily while she was in San Francisco, sent her funny emails, and she knew he was doing his best to make her feel better about Levi.

"What a great night!" he exclaimed, releasing her to serve as coffee host. "Beautiful skies, don't you think?"

"A great night," Honor quipped. "Easy for you to say, lord of the manor. You have people to do the work for you."

"Good point," he agreed, handing her dad a cup of coffee. "I should've done what you did, John, and just had a litter of children. Would've been cheaper that way."

"Better get adopting," Abby said. "I know I'm available."

Jeremy put his arm around Faith's shoulders, his dark eyes smiling. "You know, it's my biggest regret about our breakup. We would've made beautiful babies."

"That's a lovely sentiment, Jeremy dear," Goggy said, pouring a liberal amount of brandy into a mug and handing it to Pops.

"She's not making babies with anyone but me."

Faith jumped.

Levi stood just outside their little circle, jeans and a couple of layers of flannel, seemingly oblivious to the cold. His hair was rumpled, and he looked tired.

Faith felt that slow, golden heat starting in her heart. Her knees wobbled; her heart did, too. He looked so... good. Kind of grumpy, but good, too.

"You look tired," Jeremy said. "Getting enough B12?"

"Shut up, Jeremy," he said irritably. "I *am* tired. I've just spent nineteen hours flying back and forth across the country." He shot Honor a glare. "Couldn't have made a phone call, Honor? It would've been nice to hear she was on her way home."

"Oops," Honor said, unsuccessfully trying to hide her smile with a coffee mug.

"Faith, listen," Levi said. He stood in front of her, glanced at her family, then back at her. "Look."

"Look. Listen. He's so bossy," Pru said.

"Quiet," Faith said. "Not you, Levi. You go ahead."

He ran a hand through his hair. A big, masculine, capable hand that, in the fairly recent past, had elicited all sorts of interesting noises from her. *Down, girl,* Faith's brain murmured. *Let the man say what he came to say.*

Her heart was pretty sure it was going to be good.

"Faith," he said again. "I know that Jeremy is pretty damn near perfect—"

"Thank you, Levi, I appreciate that," Jeremy said solemnly. Faith shot him a look, and he smothered a smile.

Levi glanced again at her family.

"You know what? Ignore them," Faith said, taking him by the hand. She towed him away a few rows, farther from the little cabal. "Do *not* follow us," she said over her shoulder. She turned back to Levi, wanting so much to simply wrap herself around him, to kiss him until he smiled. "It's good to see you again," she whispered.

"Yeah, you, too." He scowled, most definitely *not* looking happy to see her. "I went to San Francisco to see you. But you'd left already."

"Right. So you said." She raised her eyebrows, hoping to encourage him. It didn't seem to work. He just stared. "Was there anything else, Levi?" she asked.

"Right. Yes. There is." He fished something out of his pocket and pressed it into her hand, then curled her fingers around it, holding her hand in both his own. Despite the temperature, he was warm. "I love you, Faith. I'm sorry for being an idiot. I hired someone to help at work, and I'll try to tell you more about…stuff. But I don't want to lose you, I love you, and…and that's all I've got."

As speeches went, it wasn't great. As *feelings* went… different story. Looked like the branch may have been removed.

She looked into those soft, green eyes, at the slight frown on his face. "It's more than enough," she whispered, feeling the sting of tears in her eyes.

"Oh. Good. That's good." He nodded. Looked over her shoulder. Back at her.

"You should kiss me now, Levi."

Before the words were fully out of her mouth, he was doing just that, her face cupped in his gentle hands, and his mouth on hers was…well, she hated to even think the word, but it was perfect. Most things in life weren't, but this was. He kissed her the way a man kisses the woman he loves, as if they were alone, or on an altar, as if they weren't standing in the freezing dark night with far too many relatives watching their every move.

"You need a ring and a date, young man," her father called. "This is my princess we're talking about. None of this living together nonsense."

"Again with the princess crap," Jack said.

"Why can't I be the princess once in a while?" Prudence added.

She felt Levi smile against her mouth. He kissed her forehead, held her close, then looked over at her father, who was doing his best impression of a stern parent. "Way ahead of you, sir," he said.

He uncurled her fingers—right, she'd almost forgotten—and there, in her palm, was an engagement ring.

"I'll need to think about it," she said.

"She said yes," he told her family, and a cheer rose from the ranks. Jeremy even wiped his eyes. Dad, too.

Then Levi kissed her again, and slid the ring onto her finger, and nothing had ever felt so right.

EPILOGUE

THE REHEARSAL DINNER was at Hugo's so Colleen and Connor wouldn't have to work, and where Jessica Dunn was a guest this time. Tomorrow, everyone would be dressed in their finery, but tonight was loud, casual and fun; Faith walked in on Pru and Carl in the coat-room; Goggy and Pops had danced half of one dance before the bickering became too intense; Mrs. Johnson scowled, criticized the food and drank piña coladas.

Ted and Elaine Lyon had come for the wedding, as well as Liza and Wonderful Mike. Freakishly enough, Lorena Creech was also there; Levi had invited Victor Iskin, and apparently Victor and Lorena had made a quickie trip to Vegas on Christmas Day and came back married. "I just want someone to take care of, Faith, you know what I'm saying?" she'd said, and yes, Faith did. The Bible Study Babes were knocking back the pinot grigio, and the fire department was playing cards at a table in the back.

Tomorrow, the cast would be much the same as Faith's first attempt at getting married, with a few minor changes: Colleen was still maid of honor, Faith's sisters bridesmaids, as well as Abby and Sarah Cooper.

Jeremy would be best man. Of course.

He'd also brought a date, which was rather wonderful—a good-looking guy named Patrick who was shy and sweet and a terrible dancer.

When the party was over, Levi led Faith across the icy town green to his apartment. They'd be living in the Opera House for a while, though Faith had her eye on a little house on Elm Street. It was in a nice mix of a neighborhood—outside the Village but close enough to walk, a peek of the Crooked Lake from the top floor window, a lovely porch. But for now, they'd live at Levi's place, which was looking much improved with a red-painted wall. Sarah would still live here when she was back from school, and Faith thought it was nice, finally having a little sister to boss around as Honor and Pru had bossed her all those years.

"You're not getting any action tonight, Chief Cooper," she said, her breath clouding the quiet air. "You're not even supposed to see me after midnight."

"Well, then," he said. "I've got half an hour to go." With that, he scooped her up over his shoulder and carried her, caveman style, up the stairs, making her laugh so hard she could hardly breathe.

"I have something for you," he said, setting her down to open the door. "Blue, you'll have to wait."

"You don't have to wait for me, buddy," Faith said, kneeling down to rub the dog's tummy. "You'll always be my first love. Right? Who's my best boy, hmm?" She took off her coat as Levi rustled around in his desk. "Whatever it is, it'd better be good," she added, sitting on the couch. Blue leaped up next to her.

"Here you go," he said, sitting across from her. He held a little package, but handed her a folded up piece of paper first.

"If this is a poem, I may faint," she said, smiling. Her smile stopped. He looked...tense.

"Just read it," he said.

She unfolded the paper—notebook paper, soft with age and filled with rather sloppy, youthful handwriting.

Dear Faith, it said.

I'm sorry your mom died. I wish could think of something better to say. I think you're a nice girl, and also pretty. That probably doesn't help any. But I mean it.
Sincerely, Levi Cooper.

"Oh, Levi," she said, feeling the hot burn of tears down her cheeks.

"You're not the only person who keeps stuff, I guess," he said, looking at the floor. "I should've given it to you back then. It just felt…inadequate at the time."

"It's not inadequate," she said. "It's beautiful."

He reached over and wiped her tears away. "I don't want you crying the night before we get married," he murmured.

"Then you should've thought of that before," she said, smoothing the paper. "I'm very mushy, in case you didn't notice."

"I noticed. Which is why I think you'll like this, too." He smiled and handed her the box.

The rose quartz heart had been set in silver with a tiny chain. "Where did you get this?" she exclaimed. "I thought this was in a box at my dad's."

"I stole it."

"Then you're finally admitting you gave it to me?" she said, a few more tears slipping down her cheeks as he fastened it around her neck.

"Actually, I think it was Asswipe Jones, but I'm gonna take the credit here."

She gave a watery smile. "Sorry, pal. It couldn't have been anyone but you."

He smiled, his green eyes softening. "You happen to be right, Holland."

Then he kissed her, and kissed her again. And then he pulled back and smiled. "All right, let me get you back to your dad's. I have a wedding to go to tomorrow."

On a beautiful day in January, in front of literally half the town, wearing a wedding dress that made her look like a 1940s film star and holding a bouquet of perfect red roses, Faith Elizabeth Holland married the man she was meant to have. The man, you might say, she was *fated* to have, if you believed in that stuff.

Which we absolutely do.

* * * * *

A remarkable true story about an unlikely hero

LISA J. EDWARDS

A Dog Named
BOO

*How One Dog and One
Woman Rescued Each Other—
and the Lives They Transformed
Along the Way*

One of *Publishers Weekly's* Top 10 Memoirs of 2012!

—

"A DOG NAMED BOO…touched my heart."
—Brett Witter, *New York Times* bestselling coauthor
of *Dewey* and *Until Tuesday*

How One Dog and One Woman Rescued Each Other—and the Lives They Transformed Along the Way

REQUEST YOUR FREE BOOKS!

2 FREE NOVELS
FROM THE ROMANCE COLLECTION
PLUS 2 FREE GIFTS!

YES! Please send me 2 FREE novels from the Romance Collection and my 2 FREE gifts (gifts are worth about $10). After receiving them, if I don't wish to receive any more books, I can return the shipping statement marked "cancel." If I don't cancel, I will receive 4 brand-new novels every month and be billed just $5.99 per book in the U.S. or $6.49 per book in Canada. That's a savings of at least 25% off the cover price. It's quite a bargain! Shipping and handling is just 50¢ per book in the U.S. and 75¢ per book in Canada.* I understand that accepting the 2 free books and gifts places me under no obligation to buy anything. I can always return a shipment and cancel at any time. Even if I never buy another book, the two free books and gifts are mine to keep forever.

194/394 MDN FVU7

Name (PLEASE PRINT)

Address   Apt. #

City   State/Prov.   Zip/Postal Code

Signature (if under 18, a parent or guardian must sign)

Mail to the Harlequin® Reader Service:
IN U.S.A.: P.O. Box 1867, Buffalo, NY 14240-1867
IN CANADA: P.O. Box 609, Fort Erie, Ontario L2A 5X3

Want to try two free books from another line?
Call 1-800-873-8635 or visit www.ReaderService.com.

* Terms and prices subject to change without notice. Prices do not include applicable taxes. Sales tax applicable in N.Y. Canadian residents will be charged applicable taxes. Offer not valid in Quebec. This offer is limited to one order per household. Not valid for current subscribers to the Romance Collection or the Romance/Suspense Collection. All orders subject to credit approval. Credit or debit balances in a customer's account(s) may be offset by any other outstanding balance owed by or to the customer. Please allow 4 to 6 weeks for delivery. Offer available while quantities last.

Your Privacy—The Harlequin® Reader Service is committed to protecting your privacy. Our Privacy Policy is available online at www.ReaderService.com or upon request from the Harlequin Reader Service.

We make a portion of our mailing list available to reputable third parties that offer products we believe may interest you. If you prefer that we not exchange your name with third parties, or if you wish to clarify or modify your communication preferences, please visit us at www.ReaderService.com/consumerschoice or write to us at Harlequin Reader Service Preference Service, P.O. Box 9062, Buffalo, NY 14269. Include your complete name and address.

ROM13

New York Times bestselling author

NORA ROBERTS

brings us two classic stories about the risks
we will take when love is on the line....

Available wherever books are sold!

Be sure to connect with us at:
Harlequin.com/Newsletters
Facebook.com/HarlequinBooks
Twitter.com/HarlequinBooks

KRISTAN
HIGGINS

77703	JUST ONE OF THE GUYS	___$7.99 U.S. ___$9.99 CAN.
77679	CATCH OF THE DAY	___$7.99 U.S. ___$9.99 CAN.
77675	FOOLS RUSH IN	___$7.99 U.S. ___$9.99 CAN.
77658	SOMEBODY TO LOVE	___$7.99 U.S. ___$9.99 CAN.
77611	UNTIL THERE WAS YOU	___$7.99 U.S. ___$9.99 CAN.
77557	MY ONE AND ONLY	___$7.99 U.S. ___$9.99 CAN.
77515	TOO GOOD TO BE TRUE	___$7.99 U.S. ___$9.99 CAN.
77458	ALL I EVER WANTED	___$7.99 U.S. ___$9.99 CAN.
77438	THE NEXT BEST THING	___$7.99 U.S. ___$9.99 CAN.

(limited quantities available)

TOTAL AMOUNT	$ _____
POSTAGE & HANDLING	$ _____
($1.00 FOR 1 BOOK, 50¢ for each additional)	
APPLICABLE TAXES*	$ _____
TOTAL PAYABLE	$ _____

(check or money order—please do not send cash)

To order, complete this form and send it, along with a check or money order for the total above, payable to Harlequin HQN, to: **In the U.S.:** 3010 Walden Avenue, P.O. Box 9077, Buffalo, NY 14269-9077; **In Canada:** P.O. Box 636, Fort Erie, Ontario, L2A 5X3.

Name: _____
Address: _____ City: _____
State/Prov.: _____ Zip/Postal Code: _____
Account Number (if applicable): _____

075 CSAS

*New York residents remit applicable sales taxes.
*Canadian residents remit applicable GST and provincial taxes.